STARS
COLLIDE

Books by Janice Thompson

WEDDINGS BY BELLA
Fools Rush In
Swinging on a Star
It Had to Be You

BACKSTAGE PASS
Stars Collide

BACKSTAGE PASS ★ BOOK 1

STARS COLLIDE

A NOVEL

Janice Thompson

Revell

a division of Baker Publishing Group
Grand Rapids, Michigan

Published by Revell
a division of Baker Publishing Group
P.O. Box 6287, Grand Rapids, MI 49516-6287
www.revellbooks.com

Printed in the United States of America

Library of Congress Cataloging-in-Publication Data
Thompson, Janice A.
    Stars collide : a novel / Janice Thompson.
       p.   cm. — (Backstage pass ; bk. 1)
    ISBN 978-0-8007-3345-2 (pbk.)
    1. Hollywood (Los Angeles, Calif.)—Fiction. I. Title.
PS3620.H6824S73 2011
813'.6—dc22   2010029524

Published in association with MacGregor Literary Agency.

11 12 13 14 15 16 17   7 6 5 4 3 2 1

In loving memory of my father, Billy Hanna, who moved our family from Houston, Texas, to Los Angeles, California, in the late '70s so that he could pursue his dream of co-writing and producing a Hollywood movie.

Thank you, Dad, for opening a whole new chapter in my life—that of a writer.

1

Whose Line Is It Anyway?

"You want me to kiss him . . . where?" I stared at my director, hoping I'd somehow misunderstood his last-minute change to the script.

A look of exasperation crossed his face. "On the lips, of course. This is a family show, Kat. Remember?"

"Of course." I nodded and fought to keep my breathing even as I rephrased my question. "I mean, where in the *scene*? Beginning, middle, or end? What's my cue?"

"Oh." A look of relief passed over Mark Wilson's face as he sank into his director's chair. "At the very end of the scene. Right after Jack says, 'This has been a long time coming, Angie.' At that point I want the two of you to kiss. On the lips. In a passionate but family-friendly way. PG, not PG-13."

"Ah." My gaze darted across the crowded studio to Scott Murphy, my love interest in the sitcom *Stars Collide*. He raked his fingers through that gorgeous, dark, wavy hair of his and flashed an encouraging smile. Apparently the idea of kissing me on camera hadn't startled him. Why should I let it make me nervous? We'd both known for months this moment would come. And now that it had arrived, there would be no turning back. Kissing him—whether it happened at the beginning, middle, or end of the scene—was something the viewers had anticipated for three seasons. Ironically, I'd spent almost as long waiting, hoping, and praying for it myself.

Over the past two seasons, my off-screen friendship with Scott had morphed into something more, and I knew he felt the same. Still, we'd danced around each other for months, neither of us willing to open up and share our hearts. And now that the opportunity had finally presented itself, I felt like slinking back to my dressing room and diving under the makeup table. Would anyone notice if the show's leading lady skipped out on the scene?

"Kiss him, Kat! Kiss him!" The voices of the youngest cast members rang out, and my cheeks grew warm as I realized the sitcom's children had a vested interest in this too. They'd worked for two full seasons to push the characters of Jack and Angie together, after all. A kiss seemed inevitable, even to them.

Only now, it just seemed impossible. How could I kiss Scott, passionately or otherwise, with my heart in my throat? And how—I gulped in air as I thought about it—how could I kiss him when my feelings offstage were as strong as those my character Angie faced when the cameras were rolling?

My heart did that crazy junior high flip-flop thing, and for a moment I thought I might faint. Squeezing my eyes shut, I invited the opportunity. If I hit the floor, we could probably avoid filming the scene altogether.

Nope. No such luck. After a few seconds of feigning dizziness, I realized I was as steady on my feet as ever. Opening my eyes, I contemplated my options. Now what?

From across the studio, Scott smiled again, offering me a glimmer of hope. Was that a "come hither" look in his eyes? *Mm-hmm.* A sense of peace flooded over me and I whispered a prayer of thanksgiving.

I can do this. I can do this. With the eyes of the masses watching, I took my place on the set, ready to begin filming.

Scott continued to tease me with a smile. Oh yes, this certainly made things easier. His baby blues stared deep down into my soul, giving me the courage I needed.

At this point, everything began to move in slow motion.

I heard the director yell, "Action!"

Managed to speak my opening lines, then listened for Scott's impassioned response.

Watched as the cameras overhead swung near for the big moment.

Felt my heart race when Scott—as the character of Jack—took a step in my direction.

Heard him whisper those magic words: "This has been a long time coming, Angie."

Sensed the studio audience members holding their breath.

Closed my eyes in anticipation.

Then, just as Scott swept me into his arms for that magical moment we'd all been waiting for . . . the power went out.

Studio B faded to black.

2

Saved by the Bell

A collective gasp went up from the studio audience as the filming of the infamous kissing scene came to an abrupt halt. Ironically, the filming was the only thing that ended. What no one saw under the blissful cover of darkness—I hoped, anyway—was the long-awaited moment being played out just between the two of us. Scott's lips, tender and sweet, found mine, and the kiss that followed squelched any lingering doubts I might have had about his feelings for me. Our private exchange lasted an extraordinary length of time—*extraordinary* being the key word.

Wowza! Was this guy worth the wait, or what?

Scott eventually loosened his embrace and brushed his fingers through my hair. His words, "It's about time, Kat," were whispered gently into my ear, sending tingles down my spine. All I could manage was a lame nod, which, of course, he could not see in the dark. *Brilliant, Kat.* Still, what did it matter? Our kissing scene was the stuff Emmy awards were made of. Didn't matter that we'd missed our opportunity to share it with the world. Some things were better left off camera. At least the first time around.

I half expected a laugh track to shatter the moment, or at least some piped-in music. A dramatic love song, perhaps. Most everything in my life was staged these days, right down to my dialogue.

Fortunately, the only music was the impromptu drum solo going on in my heart. I felt sure no one heard it except Scott. My arms instinctively slipped around his neck, and he drew me closer still, offering yet another sweet promise that his feelings for me were as strong as mine for him.

Off in the distance, a tremulous little voice rang out, and the words "I'm scared" now hovered over us. As the darkness lingered, the children grew more restless and one began to cry. I could hear the studio audience members stirring now.

"Rex, what happened to the backup generator?" Mark hollered to Rex Henderson, our new producer.

"No idea, Mark, but I'm working on it." I recognized that voice. Jason Harris, cameraman. If anyone could figure it out, he could. Jason was our resident geek.

The lights came on just as Scott and I each took a giant step backward, creating a respectable chasm between us. By the time my eyes adjusted to the glare of the generator-powered lights flickering overhead, I realized chaos had struck the studio audience. People tripped over each other and shouted obscenities as they struggled to exit the studio. Lovely. Did they not remember we had a room full of children? And tearful children at that.

Scott shifted gears at once, morphing into protector and guardian. Turning to the audience, he hollered, "Calm down, everyone. Take it easy!"

Ironically, no one paid a bit of attention except the kids, who rushed his way. He pulled them into a fatherly embrace and began to comfort the ones most shaken.

I should have been reacting in some way too, I suppose, but my eyes were fixed solely on Scott. *Be still my heart.* This guy really knew how to get to me. Kind to children and romantic too. What next? Would he leap tall buildings in a single bound?

"KK, are you all right?"

As my grandmother's voice rang out, I turned to face her, finding her long, silver hair in disarray. In the madness of the moment, I'd forgotten about her. Not that Lenora Worth was one to be easily forgotten. Oh no. She made her presence known at each day's filming, showing up in a variety of ensembles from Hollywood days gone by. She had become a mascot of sorts, and everyone loved her. Right now, though, she looked frazzled and a bit messy.

"Your combs must've come loose," I whispered as I pointed to her untidy updo.

"Oooh, thanks." She fussed with them in an attempt to make herself look presentable, then turned her attention to her sparkling black gown.

I helped straighten the sheer black scarf across her shoulders. "There. You look lovely."

"Thanks again, KK. I think I panicked when the lights went out. Scared me."

"Me too."

"Mm-hmm." She squinted her eyes with an "I'm not buying it" look.

"W-what?" That little-girl feeling swept over me. I was a seven-year-old once again, caught with my hand in the cookie jar.

Grandma continued to fuss with her dress, her gaze never

shifting. "Honey, my hearing's not what it used to be, but my eyesight is twenty-twenty."

"O-oh?"

"Yes. Funny thing about working in a studio for so long. These old eyes get accustomed to the dark. Sometimes they even play tricks on me. Make me think I'm seeing things."

I swallowed hard, pretty sure I knew where this was going.

My grandmother took my hand and gave it a gentle squeeze. With tears glistening in her eyes, she whispered, "I'm thrilled for both of you, sweet girl. You know what a romantic I am. Sometimes the things we wait the longest for are the things most worth the wait. I've known for some time that Jack was God's man for you."

Jack?

"I, well, I . . ." My mind reeled as I fought to come up with a response. Thankfully I didn't have to. Grandma Lenora's gaze darted to her left.

"Incoming battleship," she whispered. "Stage left."

I turned just as Mark approached with Rex Henderson at his side.

"We just got a call saying the whole building is down. Utility company is working on the lines in the area for the next three hours." Mark began to pace. "This is a nightmare. We can't afford to get behind."

Scott took a few steps in our direction. "I say it's probably for the best that we stop for the day, anyway. The kids are having a hard time adjusting to what just happened, and the studio audience is, well . . . ." He shrugged. "Nonexistent."

"We should release the kids." Rex gave them a sympathetic look. "Emotions are running high."

Mark gave me a pensive glance before shifting his gaze to Scott. "Can you two stick around? I'd like to call a meeting."

"Sure." Scott and I spoke in unison, our voices sounding almost rehearsed. I wanted to turn to him and grin but resisted the urge. Now that we'd broken the ice, I wanted to sing, to dance, to . . . Hmm. Better stay focused.

Mark dismissed the kids, but several of them stopped by to share a hug before leaving the set. I gazed down at little Toby, the youngest cast member. At five, he was quite a star. I'd never seen—or heard—a child so young with such talent. Perfect comedic timing. Nice singing voice. This kid would go far in the business.

And then there was Candy. The eight-year-old came complete with a stage mother. Sure, the little beauty queen could sing and act and certainly deserved her part in the show, but talk about a diva. I'd seen Hollywood megastars with less attitude. I hated to think about what she'd morph into if she stayed in the business.

Scott—being Scott—took his time with each of the children, offering uplifting and encouraging words before releasing them to their parents. The kids responded with smiles and laughter. Well, all but Candy, who complained that she had wasted two hours getting her hair curled for nothing. She stomped off of the set looking more devilish than pixielike.

Once the children had left the room, Mark gestured for Scott and me to meet him onstage. Rex joined us as we settled onto the sofa and wingback chairs that adorned the living room portion of the set. The welcoming decor made me feel right at home. I knew that Grandma would be along shortly, so I saved her a seat next to me.

"So, what's up?" Scott asked. "Other than the obvious, I mean."

Mark pursed his lips, saying nothing at first. "I'm rethinking the direction of this episode," he said at last. "We want to boost ratings, but I'm not sure this last-minute addition of a kiss is my best idea. Not yet, anyway."

What? I could hardly believe his abrupt change of direction. Why switch gears? Now that I'd jumped the hurdle of kissing Scott, I certainly wouldn't mind jumping it again. And again.

Mark shrugged. "I've called in Athena and some of the other writers to help us figure this out. We might want to go a completely different direction for the time being."

Rex didn't respond. I had a feeling we'd be hearing from him later.

A shuffling behind us alerted me to the fact that the writing team had arrived. I turned to Athena Pappas—my best friend and confidante—and shrugged. She and the other writers had done a fine job already. Why stress them out by making them rewrite the scene?

I could tell Scott wasn't happy with the way things were going. "I hope you're joking, Mark," he said. "It's been three years. If Jack and Angie don't move ahead with their relationship now, viewers are going to give up on them. We can only drag this out for so long."

Mark shook his head. "But part of what makes *Stars Collide* work is the ongoing romantic tension between the two of you. I'm afraid if we release that tension, the viewers will lose interest. They'll think it's too . . . predictable. Love stories are about the chase, not the catch."

Hmm. I wasn't sure I agreed with that one but didn't interject my opinion just yet.

"I disagree." Scott held his ground. "Viewers have watched Jack and Angie take two opposing talent agencies and merge them into one. They get the whole 'stars collide' symbolism. They know what's coming. *Everyone* knows what's coming. These characters don't just care about the kids they represent,

15

they care about each other." His gaze shifted momentarily to me, and I tried to push back the smile that threatened to erupt. Thankfully Scott turned back to Mark and continued sharing his thoughts. "And if we don't show that emotion to the audience, sooner or later . . ." He shook his head.

"What?" Mark asked. "The world's gonna blow up? C'mon, Scott. I'm just saying we should draw it out a bit longer. Play it for all it's worth."

Athena shook her head. "Mark, I thought we all agreed that the timing was perfect to reveal the couple's feelings. Right? The show has a loyal audience, you know." She gave him a "please play along" look.

Mark stood and began to pace. "I know, I know. It felt right at the time. But now I'm not so sure. Have you seen our ratings? We've slipped from the number three spot to number four. Could be we're on a downward spiral."

"That's a bunch of hooey," Grandma Lenora said, drawing near. The sequins on her black evening gown sparkled underneath the generator-driven stage lights above. "Face it, Mark. You're just scared of the unknown. You don't know what will happen if these two kids share their feelings openly, and it scares you." A wistful look came over her. "But life is always like that. You hold on to your feelings, scared to express them, not knowing what will happen on the other side of that emotion." Her eyes got misty, and for a moment I wasn't sure we were talking about the show anymore.

I could read the exasperation on Mark's face as he responded, "Lenora, I really don't think you're the one to be telling us how to run this show. Honestly, you're not even—"

I glared at him, hoping he wouldn't say anything to hurt her. Except for a handful of brief appearances on the sitcom playing the role of my grandmother, she couldn't be counted among the regulars. But she *was* Lenora Worth, onetime Hollywood star, and deserving of his utmost respect. Mark's mouth eventually closed, and the conversation was left hanging midsentence.

Rex gave her a sympathetic look and nodded. "I agree with Lenora."

I decided to add my thoughts in an attempt to steer this ship into a different port. "I know we're concerned about ratings, Mark. But we have a strong fan base. They love us. And I, for one, love the idea of shaking the audience up a little." Of course, I hadn't loved it an hour ago, but now that I'd overcome the obstacle of kissing Scott, nothing could hold me back. I'd released my feelings to him . . . now I might as well release them to the viewers.

"We've already written in just about every funny bit I can think of for the kids," Athena said. "They've pulled dozens of pranks to nudge Angie and Jack together."

"That crazy scene last spring where they kidnapped Jack and Angie and locked them in a closet together was priceless." Scott chuckled.

"And so was that scene where they convinced Jack and Angie to act out the balcony scene from Romeo and Juliet to raise funds for charity," I threw in. "So cute. And very romantic." I hadn't minded playing Juliet to Scott's Romeo . . . then or now.

"Honestly, I'm not sure how many more of those kid-driven scenes I can pull out of my hat." Athena sighed and turned to Mark. "And I don't think the audience will keep buying it. Seems like overkill if we keep counting on the kids to push the hero and heroine together. By now, everyone knows they have feelings for each other. It's time to share those feelings with the world."

I couldn't help but squirm at that last line. After such a sweet kiss, I had to wonder if Scott and I would be sharing our feelings with the world in due time.

"Ultimately, it's up to Rex, not me. He's the producer." I couldn't help but notice a hint of sarcasm in Mark's voice. We all knew Mark hadn't taken well to Rex's new role. Then again, who could blame him? The show had been through a multitude of changes over the past season. Just about the time we got used to someone, they were out and someone else was in. Left us all feeling pretty unstable.

I turned to Rex and noticed, for the first time, his gaze lingered on my grandmother. From the look on his face, he'd been concerned about Mark's words injuring her too. Good for him.

Startling to attention, Rex addressed us, putting on his best producer voice. "Yes, well, let's think about this from a different angle. As I said, I agree with Lenora. Jack and Angie need to express their feelings to each other. It's the only way to move the show forward. And I don't think we need to use the kids to accomplish that. Not anymore."

Mark rose and began to pace. "I'm still not convinced, but if you've got your mind made up, we might as well take full advantage of it. Get the media involved."

"What do you mean?" Rex asked.

Mark looked my way and then shifted his gaze to Scott. "If we go ahead and bring you two together as a couple on the show, the gossip columnists are sure to read into it and think you're a couple in real life. Maybe we can stage a couple of appearances with the two of you out on the town . . . maybe even get you guys on *Entertainment Tonight*."

"W-what?" My heart rate skipped to double time. Glancing at Scott, I marveled at his ability to keep his cool. How could Mark even suggest such a thing? I looked into our director's eyes, trying to figure out if he was kidding. Surely he didn't think we'd really go along with this.

"Mark, I'm not sure that's the best idea," Scott said. "The

paparazzi are already a problem for both of us. Even going to the grocery store is getting tough. I don't know that I want to invite more media attention, especially as it applies to my personal life."

I couldn't help but notice that his cheeks turned red as he spoke the words *personal life*.

Mark looked back and forth between us. "What do you expect? You're doing a show about two talent scouts who used to be archenemies. The public will eat it up if they think you're falling for each other in real life. And what would it hurt, anyway? Neither of you is involved with anyone at the moment, right?"

A few hours ago I might've answered with a no, but that kiss from Scott convinced me otherwise. Not enough to share my thoughts or feelings with Mark, however.

"This is a brilliant idea." Grandma Lenora gave an abrupt nod. "KK hasn't dated anyone for ages." She went on about how she'd prayed for years that the Lord would bring just the right person into my life, and how—until now—he had remained silent. "Let the public see you as a couple," she said. "It will do you—and them—good."

Good grief. Could things possibly get any more awkward?

Rex gave me a fatherly look, his eyes twinkling with unexpected merriment. "I'm not saying I agree about involving the paparazzi. But I suppose it's inevitable the public will wonder if you two are really enamored with each other." He turned to Scott. "Sometimes people have a hard time separating fiction from reality."

For whatever reason, this last line caused all of us to turn to Grandma, who rattled on again about my lack of a love life.

Rex nodded and then piggybacked on her enthusiasm. "People will talk, and I suppose we can't really control what they say. You certainly can't control what appears in the magazines and on TV."

I sighed at that one, thinking of how I'd made the attempt more than a few times. The paparazzi had already labeled me "Kat with Nine Lives" because I'd been linked to so many failed television pilots. I couldn't stand the idea that they would find yet another reason to comment on my already-too-public life.

For the first time I noticed the exhaustion in Rex's eyes. "I've been in this business a long, long time," he said. "I've outlived most of the folks who used to work for those newspapers and magazines."

"If that's what you want to call them," I muttered.

"True. I'm just saying that I've outlived them, but their tactics haven't changed. They're out to get a story. And when there isn't one . . ."

"They have to make up something."

Mark joined in, his enthusiasm growing. "Only, maybe this time we'll use the story to our advantage." He went off on a tangent about how we could do that, but he lost me after a few words. Getting the public involved in my personal life didn't feel right—at all.

Thankfully Athena and the other writers began to express their opinions, and before long we had all come to an agreement. Jack and Angie would kiss. The viewers would love it. Ratings would rise. And the paparazzi would have a field day with it.

I groaned inwardly at that last part but kept my mouth shut. Playing along might be for the best . . . for the sake of the show. I couldn't bear the idea of *Stars Collide* unraveling. Surely the publicists could step in and save the day.

Rex offered a hand to Grandma Lenora, who took it with a shy smile. She rose and did a bit of primping, showing off her shimmering black dress. "No one asked me who I am today," she said at last. A rehearsed pout followed.

"Who are you today, Lenora?" Scott asked with a twinkle in his eye.

She grinned. "Bette Davis. *The Little Foxes*. 1941."

"Nice choice." Rex gave her a tender smile, and her gaze lingered on him before darting to the floor. "Bette was always one of my favorites." He dove into a story about a Bing Crosby fund-raiser he'd once gone to at the Beverly Hills Hotel, where he'd met her in person, but my attention shifted to Scott. I could feel his eyes on me. Was he as worried about this paparazzi thing as I was?

Looking my way, he gave me a little wink. My heart sailed straight up into my throat.

Heavens! I'd fallen . . . and I wasn't sure I wanted to get up.

3

The Golden Girls

As we prepared to leave the studio, Grandma Lenora turned to me, her hands clasped together. "KK, I have the best idea!"

"What's that?"

Her eyes twinkled as she responded, "Let's go to the Brown Derby for dinner tonight. My treat!"

Oh, yikes. Not again. "I don't really think—"

"You know, I once went there with Lucille Ball and Desi Arnaz . . . when they were still married, I mean." Grandma gave me a knowing look. "I realize they're divorced now. Such a shocker. Don't you find it sad that so many couples are getting divorced these days?"

I drew in a deep breath and counted to three before responding. So many times of late she'd asked me to take her to places that no longer existed. And I certainly didn't have the heart to tell her that Lucy and Desi were currently dining in that great Brown Derby in the sky.

"I don't think that's the best idea," I said at last.

"Oh, well, let's stop at Pink's then," she said with a glimmer in her eyes. "They've got the best hot dogs ever."

I couldn't argue with her there, but with her cholesterol on the rise, hot dogs weren't the best option. "I think we're better off going home," I said at last. "You're on a special diet, remember?"

She groaned. "There's nothing wrong with this heart of mine. I have no idea why that doctor put me on a low-cholesterol diet. He just wants to spoil my fun."

"No, he just wants you to be around so that he can enjoy seeing you in more episodes of our show. And who knows . . . if you stay healthy, you might be asked to compete on *Dancing with the Stars* next season. I heard they're putting together the list now."

"Oooh! Do you think they might pick me?"

"Sure, why not?" I could see it now—Lenora Worth, dolled up in a dress from the 1940s, waltzing around the dance floor and winning the hearts of the viewers. Stranger things had happened.

We walked side by side to the studio door. Once outside, we were met with glorious blue skies and perfect weather.

"Wow, great day to let out early." I could hardly wait to get home and take a dip in the pool.

Grandma Lenora wrapped her hair in a beautiful scarf and handed me one in leopard print. "Put this on, KK. Don't want your hair to get messy on the way home."

"You want to drive or should I?" I asked as I tied the scarf in place.

She giggled. "Oh, honey, it's midday. Tourists are out in force. You drive so I can wave to my fans."

I stifled a grin and nodded. Lenora Worth could work a crowd, that much was certain.

"Would you mind fetching the Pink Lady and pulling her around to the front? My hips are really bothering me today and I don't think I'll make it to the parking lot."

My heart went out to her. Grandma had been having a lot of joint pain lately. That, coupled with her ever-increasing memory loss and rising cholesterol, really had me unnerved. I'd spent more than the usual amount of time ushering up prayers for her health over the past weeks.

I gave an upbeat answer. "I'll be happy to. You just wait right here." Pressing my sunglasses in place, I headed off to fetch the car. I didn't really mind walking alone, not with my mind still reeling from Scott's kiss. I thought again of our private exchange, how he had pulled me into his arms and whispered so tenderly in my ear. Goose bumps covered my arms as I relived the special moment.

In the parking lot, I located the car at once. The pink Cadillac Eldorado Biarritz glistened under a bright Los Angeles sun. I'd never questioned Grandma's car choices. In fact, I'd rather grown to love the eclectic old vehicles. This one happened to be my favorite, though guiding the oversized vehicle through L.A.'s traffic often proved to be a challenge. Thank goodness I'd finally talked her into having the top customized, and with the push of a button it lifted and tucked itself away, out of sight.

Now, to pick up the grand dame of Hollywood. Or, rather, the woman who still fancied herself as such. With sunglasses and scarf in place, I pulled the car around to the front of the studio. Once there, I caught a glimpse of my grandmother leaning against the column in front of the studio in a rehearsed pose. Probably something she'd memorized from a scene she'd once acted out.

From a distance, I pondered how Lenora Worth must appear to others . . . the '50s Hollywood star, still dressing in gowns from days gone by. I found it sentimental and sweet—encouraged it, actually. Of course, I had my reasons. Still, I was keenly aware of how she might be perceived by others. Likely they'd just think she'd lost her marbles.

Lost her marbles. Hmm.

A sinking feeling settled over me as I reflected on how many times Grandma's memory had slipped over the past few months. The medication had held her symptoms at bay for a season, but these days she often surprised me with her off-the-wall comments.

Thankfully I'd come up with a plan to keep her mind active and alert. I pulled the car up to the curb and gave her a little wave. She responded with a grin, then reached to open the door on the passenger side. Glancing over at her, I gave her a knowing look and said, "Of all the gin joints in all the towns in all the world, she walks into mine."

Grandma Lenora smiled, adjusted her scarf, and came back with, "Humphrey Bogart. *Casablanca*. 1942."

"You're the best!" I shifted the car into DRIVE and set off toward home.

Grandma chatted on and on about the power outage and the subsequent meeting, but my thoughts were elsewhere. With that glorious sunshine beaming down on me and a delightful afternoon breeze casting its spell, I truly felt like a star.

My grandmother adjusted the CD player, and seconds later Doris Day's girl-next-door voice filled the car. I hummed along to "A Guy Is a Guy," one of Grandma's favorites. Most people my age would find it crazy, me being so fascinated with Doris Day, but I couldn't deny my addiction. Who else had a voice like that and was such a classy lady to boot?

Turning onto Sunset, I wound my way along, passing the Beverly Hills Hotel. As we waited at the light, Grandma went into her usual spiel about the many nights she'd stayed at the hotel as a young starlet and all of the glamorous parties she'd attended over the years. The light turned green and I edged my way forward, apparently too soon to suit her.

"Slow down, KK! Slow down." Grandma waved her hand, her gaze never leaving the hotel.

I put my foot on the brake, preparing for the inevitable.

"I stayed in that bungalow right there!" Grandma pointed, for the millionth time, to the third bungalow.

Behind us, a cranky driver honked. Apparently he didn't care that Lenora Worth was reliving her earlier days in Hollywood. He just wanted to keep things moving. Who could blame him? Life moved really fast these days. People didn't take the time to slow down and reminisce. Not on Sunset Boulevard, anyway.

I stepped on the gas, but Grandma gestured for me to move slowly. Tears filled her eyes as she shared the story once again. I knew from having stayed in one of the bungalows myself that they were really set up like individual homes, each quite luxurious.

"Liz Taylor honeymooned in that one." Grandma pointed, but I couldn't really look, what with the driver behind me now riding my tail.

I picked up the pace and countered with my usual question: "Which honeymoon?"

"Six out of eight!" Grandma chortled. "Guess she liked the place." She dove into her usual speech about all of the others who'd frequented the bungalows—Marilyn Monroe, Marlene Dietrich, and several others. Thankfully she was so caught up in the story that she didn't seem to notice I'd moved on down the road. Unfortunately, I didn't make it very far. Just a few blocks down, she let out a cry. "KK, stop!"

"What? Why?" I hit the brakes.

Grandma pointed to a makeshift building on the side of the

road with the words MAPS TO THE STARS emblazoned across the top. "I need to speak with the proprietor." She pointed to the young man who waved at passersby, ushering them into his place of business to purchase maps.

I turned the car into the rough driveway, groaning all the way. This wasn't the first time we'd made this stop, and I knew it wouldn't be the last.

When I shifted to PARK, Grandma eased her way out of the car. I could see from her slow movement that her hips were really giving her trouble, but I knew they would not prevent her from fulfilling this mission. Nothing could stop her when she was in diva mode.

Grandma walked directly to the fellow at the booth and wiggled her finger in his face. He looked a bit startled, and all the more as he took in her outfit. Still, to his credit, he let her pitch a fit without responding. At first, anyway.

I turned off the car and joined her, arriving just as she hollered, "What do you mean my house *still* isn't on the map? Young man, do you know who I am?"

"Yeah, you're that old lady who keeps stopping by here to chew me out." He shifted his gum to the other side of his mouth. "That's all I know."

"Back in my day, women were treated with dignity." She crossed her arms at her chest. "Particularly Hollywood stars. And I'll have you know my house—Worth Manor—is a top spot in Beverly Hills. So explain to me if you will why my home is no longer featured on that map you sell."

"Look, lady, I'll tell you what I said the last two times you stopped. I just sell the maps. I don't print them. There's a company that—" He never got to finish.

Her blue eyes flashed as she interrupted him. "I remember exactly what you said the last two times I stopped by. My memory is in fine working order, young man."

I swallowed hard at that one. She apparently had no idea just how jumbled her thought processes had gotten over the past few months. Still, when it came to her beloved home, she apparently had no trouble remembering she'd somehow been overlooked on the most recent copy of the map.

"C'mon, lady. I just work here." The guy, whose nametag read Damian, shifted his weight, his jaw growing tight.

"Yes, and if you want to go on working here, you will tell the people who print this map to include Worth Manor, or I will file suit."

"File suit?" He looked at her, eyes wide. "You mean, like a lawsuit? Seriously?"

"Yes. I am Lenora Worth. I have the best attorneys in the city."

Another slight misstatement. Her personal attorney, Leroy Finkelstein, had passed away in the '80s, but I didn't have the heart to remind her of that. Not now, anyway. And most of the others from his firm—at least the ones she'd worked with—were approaching retirement or had already passed on to that great courtroom in the sky.

I looked at the young man and offered a half smile as I pulled off my sunglasses. "Thanks for your help, Damian. I'm sure you can see how important this is to my grandmother. She's very proud of her legacy and wants to make sure others see her lovely home when they're touring the area." I pulled out a business card and scribbled the studio's phone number on it. "I hope you can help us. Please call me if you can. Ask for Kat Jennings." I pulled off my scarf, allowing my long blonde hair to hang loose. Hopefully he would put two and two together.

"Kat Jennings?" He gave me a closer look. "Wait a minute . . ." A knowing look passed over his face. "I know you! You're on that TV show, that one about the two talent scouts who are secretly in love."

"*Stars Collide.*"

"Yes." He nodded. "My girlfriend loves that show. But she wants to know when Jack and Angie are going to get together. She's tired of waiting. She thinks all that stuff with the kids pushing them together is cute, but she's about to give up on them ever ending up a couple."

"See?" Grandma turned to me. "I *told* Mark the viewers wouldn't wait much longer. And that kid stuff might be cute, but it's getting old."

I leaned toward Damian to whisper, "Tell your girlfriend to keep watching," and had just started to add, "They'll be a couple before you know it," when Grandma added her two cents' worth.

"They're in love in real life too!"

"W-what?" He looked at me, and I felt the color drain out of my face. "You're in love with Scott Murphy? Are you serious?"

"Oh, I, uh . . ."

Thankfully a car with a couple of tourists pulled in. Grandma greeted them with an exuberant "Hello, fans!" through their open passenger-side window. "Glad you could stop by. Would you like to take a picture with me?"

The young woman inside turned to look at the driver, a guy who looked to be in his midtwenties. He shrugged in response.

"I don't know," she said finally.

"We can take photos later," Grandma responded with over-the-top flair. "In the meantime, welcome to Hollywood, kids! I'm Lenora Worth. Perhaps you remember me from some of my best-known films." She rattled off the names of a few of them, and the girl stared at her in silence, clearly perplexed.

"Who?" she asked. "I'm sorry, what did you say?"

"I'm a movie star!" Grandma explained. "From Hollywood's glamour days."

"Right. I guess that would explain the getup," the girl
responded. "Interesting."

Before Grandma could say anything, the young woman
looked my way and then bounded from the car, heading
straight for me.

"Oh my goodness! You're Kat Jennings!" She turned back
to her companion. "Joey, grab the camera. I don't believe it.
Kat Jennings!"

"Yes, I'm Kat Jennings." I played along, posing as Joey took
a couple of pictures. No one said a word as Grandma wea-
seled her way into the last one, standing front and center.

"I'm Courtney Ballinger from Topeka," the young woman
said, her smile brighter than ever. "This is my husband, Joey.
We just got married last week. We're on our honeymoon."

"Oh, wow," I managed.

"Speaking of honeymoons, did you know that Elizabeth
Taylor honeymooned at the Beverly Hills Hotel, just a few
blocks from here?" Grandma Lenora interjected. "Not just
once, but six times!"

"Elizabeth who?" Courtney's brow wrinkled. She quickly
turned back to me. "So, what's up with you and Jack?" Giggling, she said, "I mean, with *Angie* and Jack. Are you two
ever going to get together, or what?"

Damian took this as his cue to come closer. "Wait till you
hear!" he said. "Not only are they getting together on the
show—"

"How would you like tickets to be in our studio audience
for tomorrow's filming?" I interrupted. "Then you can see
for yourself."

Courtney let out a squeal. "I would love it! I can't believe
you're doing this for me, Kat. You don't even know me."

"I know you now. You're Courtney from Kansas and I'm Kat from L.A."

"Beverly Hills," Grandma threw in. "Kat from Beverly Hills."

"Hey, aren't you the one they call 'Kat with Nine Lives'?" Joey asked, now pointing at me.

Ugh.

I'd just started to answer when Courtney interrupted. "So, how do we get the tickets to the show?"

Perfect diversion.

"I'll have two waiting for you at the gate. Warner Brothers Studio. Studio B. Do you know where that is?"

"It's on the map," Damian said with a nod. "You'll find it, no problem."

"Ooh, speaking of the map . . ." Courtney reached to grab one. "Is your house on here, Kat? We want to drive by and see it, if so."

"It's funny you should ask." I directed her attention to Damian. "There appears to be an oversight of some sort. But Damian here assures me that the home my grandmother and I share will soon be listed." I gave him a smile. "Isn't that right, Damian?"

"Y-you live with your grandmother, Kat?" he stammered. "W-why didn't you just say so? Everyone will want to know where *you* live."

A quick glance Grandma's way revealed her displeasure at the way things were going, and I felt a quickening in my heart. "I have lived with my grandmother since I was seven. And her home—Worth Manor—was once the talk of the town."

"Still is," Grandma said with a nod. "Nothing has changed."

"That's right," I said. "Nothing has changed. The home

is beautiful and is very near the Barrymore estate, so if
you go by there, you'll find us just around the corner." Not
that I particularly wanted anyone to know where I lived.
I'd rather have my privacy, thank you very much. Still, I
knew how much this meant to Grandma Lenora. She wanted
her fans—what was left of them, anyway—to know where
to find her. With that in mind, I spouted off the address.
Courtney scribbled it on the back of the map, which she
quickly paid for.

"Ooh, I can't wait. Thank you so much." She gave me an
admiring look as I took a few steps toward the car.

"You're welcome!" I slipped the sunglasses back on, then
reached to tie the scarf over my hair. "See you both tomorrow."

Damian followed us to the Cadillac, opening the passenger
door for Grandma. Her smile put me at ease.

"Thank you, young man," she said. "I apologize for my
earlier outburst."

"Oh, please don't apologize," he said. "The whole thing
was a terrible misunderstanding. I'm glad we got it worked
out. Stop by in a couple of days. I'll make sure your house
is on the map."

"Thank you for that," I said. "We're grateful."

As we pulled away, we left Courtney, Joey, and Damian
staring at us, eyes wide, mouths open.

Grandma chuckled as she pressed the button on the CD
player. "Did you see how starstruck they were, KK? They
must've recognized me from my earlier films." She went off
on a tangent about one of her leading roles as Doris Day's
voice kicked in once again, this time singing another of my
grandmother's favorites, "Secret Love."

Unfortunately, my thoughts had already shifted. Had
Grandma Lenora really told a total stranger that Scott and I

32

were an item in real life? If so, how would I ever keep that story from spreading? Did I even want to keep it from spreading?

Grandma warbled out a few lines along with Doris, then leaned her head back against the seat with a dreamy-eyed expression on her face. I could tell she'd slipped away to that place she often visited, where I had a hard time reaching her.

As I drove the final few blocks to Beverly Hills, I thought about the kiss Scott and I had shared. By the time we pulled up in front of our house, I'd settled the issue in my mind. Scott and I needed to keep our relationship under wraps, at least for now. We'd only kissed once, after all. Okay, twice. Neither of us had expressed our undying love for the other. Why, he could just as easily walk away and forget all about me.

At the thought of that, my heart lurched. Just as quickly, I remembered the tenderness of his kiss, his soft words whispered in my ear. Nope. Scott Murphy wasn't going anywhere . . . and neither was I.

Grandma continued to hum the song as she fussed with the remote, trying to get the gate to open. "Goofy thing," she said at last. "Why is it so temperamental?"

"Here, let me try."

I pushed the button, smiling as the gate slowly moved back and allowed us entrance. My gaze shifted to the words WORTH MANOR on the gate. The metal letters had seen better days. In fact, the whole house had seen better days. As I pulled forward into the driveway, I took a look at the grand old home with its dilapidated shutters and faded front door.

Putting the car in PARK, I voiced my thoughts. "Grandma, don't you think it's time the house had an update?"

"Update?" Grandma looked aghast. "Whatever for?"

"Well, you know. The paint is peeling. The metal letters

are rusted out. And the inside of the house is really, well . . ." I wanted to say "dated" but didn't dare.

"It's a perfectly good house, just as lovely as the day I bought it in '57."

I sucked in a breath and willed myself not to say anything. Why my grandmother insisted on living in the past was beyond me. Driving a '57 pink Cadillac Biarritz convertible was fun. Quirky, even. And so was keeping a room or two in the house decorated from days gone by. But to let the whole place fall down around us to somehow preserve its integrity? It just didn't make sense. Unless her memory was really that far gone.

"Secret Love" ended and suddenly Grandma Lenora was herself once again. I looked over at her and, with a cheerful smile, said, "There's no place like home."

To which she responded, "Judy Garland. *The Wizard of Oz*. 1939."

4

Toast of the Town

Three days after my infamous kissing scene, I slept in. With such a crazy work schedule, I'd earned a leisurely Saturday morning in bed. And there was no better place to feel more like a Hollywood star than reclining against a satin pillowcase in one of the most famous houses in Beverly Hills. Well, once famous, anyway.

In my half-asleep, half-awake state, I found myself thinking of that moment . . . that awesome moment . . . in Scott's arms. Had I dreamed the whole thing, or had he really kissed me and whispered sweet nothings in my ear?

Ah yes, he had kissed me all right! And then, of course, there had been the actual filming of the kiss between Angie and Jack, which had taken place the following day. How fun that my Topeka fans were in the audience to witness it. Now, if I could just keep my heart in my chest between now and the airing of the episode three weeks from now,

I'd be just fine. In the meantime, my feelings for Scott could continue to blossom and grow. I couldn't be sure where things were headed, but we were certainly off to a great start, judging from his tenderness toward me over the past few days.

I drifted back off to sleep, thinking about the feel of his lips against mine.

Sometime around nine thirty, a rap on my bedroom door woke me up. "Good morning, sunshine!" Grandma Lenora's voice rang out.

I let out a groan and pulled the pillow over my head. Maybe if I didn't respond, she would give me a few more minutes in dreamland.

"Up and at 'em, girlie," Grandma hollered. "Company's on the way."

"Company?" I sat up in the bed, slowly coming awake. We always spent our Saturday mornings alone. It was our special time. From the time I'd arrived on Grandma Lenora's doorstep as a seven-year-old, she'd treated me to luxurious Saturday morning breakfasts. Just the two of us.

She poked her head in the door. "Hope you don't mind, but I've arranged a date this morning."

"A date?" None of this made sense. Since when did Grandma date? "Wait a minute . . ." I waggled my finger. "It's our new producer, isn't it? I've seen Rex making eyes at you ever since he took over last month. And you're nervous every time he comes around you."

Her cheeks flamed red and her gaze shifted downward. "Heavens, no. You know me better than that. I might be a silly flirt at times, but with a man like Rex Henderson . . ." Her voice faded away.

"Mm-hmm. Well, who is it, then?"

She stepped inside the room and for the first time I saw

what she was wearing. A flowing silver-gray dress with intricate beading.

I let out a whistle and gave my usual spiel. "Who are we today, Grandma?"

She primped, showing off the glittery gown. "Rita Hayworth. *Tales of Manhattan*. 1942."

"Wow. Gorgeous. Almost as nice as that dress you wore yesterday. The gold one with the high neckline."

"Thanks." She began to hum a haunting little melody, something familiar. Didn't take me long to recognize it: "Secret Love." Again. Doris had certainly left her mark.

Grandma Lenora pulled back the comforter, leaving me scrambling in my nightie. "You've got to get ready, KK. A man is on his way. For breakfast."

Yanking the covers back toward me, I said, "You're really not going to tell me who? C'mon, Grandma. No secrets. Ever. We promised, right?"

"Aw, it's just a breakfast date, that's all. But dress nice, okay? We want to make a good impression on him. Put our best foot forward and all that."

"Okay, okay."

"Help me with my hair first?" She pointed to the long silver strands, and I nodded. I gestured to my vanity—the same one my mother had used as a child—and my grandmother crossed the room to sit on the little round stool, facing the mirror.

I ran my brush through her gorgeous mane of silver hair, thinking back over the thousands of times she'd done the same for me. When she handed me her combs, I used them to fasten her hair up in an elegant style. As I worked, she continued to hum "Secret Love." What she lacked in pitch, she made up for in enthusiasm.

"What do you think?" I asked as I finished.

She stared in the mirror, a mesmerized look on her face. "Oh, KK, it's lovely. You could have been a hairdresser."

"Hardly." I laughed.

She scooted out of the room, still humming the same little melody. I spent the next half hour showering and doing my makeup. My mind reeled as I prepared myself for the day. Whom had she invited . . . and why?

By the time I came back into my room, I realized that my grandmother had laid out an outfit for me. I took in the soft chiffon blouse and flowing skirt with some degree of curiosity. Seemed a little much for a Saturday morning breakfast, but if this was what it took to make her happy, so be it.

I slipped on the comfy ensemble and gave myself another glance in the mirror. Not bad. I added a bit of jewelry and stood back, examining my appearance. My long blond hair was pretty enough, I supposed, and I'd received more than one compliment on my high cheekbones and tall, slender physique. Oh, if only I could change these green eyes to a lovely shade of blue and get rid of the smattering of freckles that still plagued me. Whose nose and cheeks were covered in freckles at twenty-seven?

Through my window, I heard the sound of laughter. Glancing down onto the front drive, I noticed Grandma talking to the yardman. He was an older fellow, one who had worked for us for years. Surely this wasn't our breakfast guest. Or was it? Squinting to get a closer look, I pondered the possibilities, then made my way down the arching staircase into the foyer below.

As I passed through the great room, I noticed the small round table decked out with breakfast goodies. Grandma came through the front door, all smiles, and met me there.

"Carolina slaved all morning over a hot stove, just for us. Wasn't that nice of her?"

"Very." We owed our housekeeper so much. She'd been nothing but good to us, and for nineteen years, no less. A vacation to the Caribbean wouldn't be enough to repay her, though I planned to offer it next month when things slowed down. Likely she would insist on taking Grandma along. And I would let her. If they included me.

The doorbell rang and my grandmother startled to attention. Her expression tightened slightly as she said, "I guess the cat's out of the bag now, isn't it?"

I still hadn't quite figured this out. If Grandma wasn't interested in Rex, then who? She'd gone to a lot of trouble with her hair and makeup this morning, so it must be someone pretty special.

I tagged along on her heels, my mind going a hundred different directions. When she swung the door open, my heart rushed to my throat. "S-Scott? You're Grandma's date?"

He looked nearly as startled as I felt. The tips of his ears turned red, and he raked his fingers through those unruly waves. "I . . . I am?"

"Oh, KK, you silly thing. Did you think I meant a date for *me*?" Grandma giggled. "Whatever gave you that idea? I meant a date for you. Jack gave me his cell number ages ago and was thrilled to come for a visit. Weren't you, Jack?"

A look of sheer relief passed over Scott's face, but he came back with just the right response. "Lenora, I'm thrilled, of course. But I must admit I'm a tad bit disappointed. Here I was, all set up to believe I was going to get to spend the morning on a date with the great Lenora Worth."

"Oh, I'll be here all right." She batted her fake eyelashes. "Wouldn't miss this for the world."

"Mm-hmm." I groaned but decided to play along. If it meant spending the morning with Scott, why would I fight it?

"Looks like we've been set up." Scott laughed as Grandma took him by the arm and led him into the house.

"You don't mind, do you?" I asked.

He shook his head, eyes widening. "Are you kidding? I get to have breakfast with not just one but two lovely ladies. In Beverly Hills, no less. This house makes my place in Bel-Air West look second-rate."

"Surely not." I had never been to his home but couldn't imagine it being too bad. He was, after all, Scott Murphy. I snuck another glance at him, overcome by his handsomeness. I liked his relaxed look too. The jeans and soft blue polo shirt were just right for a Saturday morning at Worth Manor. Besides, they brought out the color in his eyes. Yummy.

Scott chuckled. "Just wait till the paparazzi get a load of this. We'll be on the front page of *The Scoop* in nothing flat."

Grandma ushered him inside, all smiles. "It's been weeks since I made the cover of a magazine, honey. I wouldn't mind a bit."

Well, I might.

We entered the great room, and Scott made his way to the table Carolina had filled with goodies. "Wow. Quite a spread." His eyes shifted to the room and then to me. I felt my cheeks turn warm. Popping a grape in my mouth, I willed myself to stay silent.

"This room is unbelievable." Scott made his way to the east wall. Grandma tagged along on his heels every step of the way. "I've never seen so many autographed photos." He stared at a black-and-white picture of Richard Burton and let out a whistle. "You knew him, Lenora?"

"Knew him?" Grandma crossed her arms at her chest. "I dated him."

I almost choked on the grape at that one. "You did?"

"Sure. Dated a lot of those fellas back in my day." She let out a girlish giggle. "Kirk Douglas. Henry Fonda. Steve McQueen."

I did my best to absorb this news. "I knew you *worked* with them, Grandma, but, dated? Was this before you married Grandpa, or after he . . ." I didn't want to use the words "passed away," so I left the sentence hanging in midair. We rarely talked about my grandpa, but I could tell my grandmother still pined for him.

"Both." Grandma wiggled her penciled brows and a mischievous look settled on her face. "You don't know everything there is to know about me, KK. Trust me. Your grandmother was quite the looker, back in the day. Folks said I had star quality."

"I'll say." Scott let out a whistle as he paused in front of a beautifully framed black-and-white eleven-by-fifteen photograph of Grandma, taken in the early '60s. "You were . . . *are* gorgeous, Lenora." He turned to face her, showing off his pearly whites. She appeared to be dazzled by him.

Her soft, wrinkled cheeks turned pink as she shushed him. "Aw, go on with you." When he paused, she gave him a stern look and punched him in the arm. "No, I mean, go *on* with you. Keep going."

"Ah." He chuckled. "Well, as I was saying, you were quite a beauty back in the day and you've only gotten lovelier with age. Er, with time."

I stifled a laugh and gave him a thumbs-up from behind her back. This guy was definitely a keeper. Great with kids, a fine actor, and he cared about my grandmother's feelings. Who could top that?

Grandma Lenora paused in front of the photograph and sighed. "Those were the good ol' days. Back then, Hollywood was really something to behold. Not like now."

"What do you mean?" Scott glanced her way.

"Back then, the movies—and people—had substance. Women were beautiful, not . . ." Her cheeks reddened even further. "Not like these girls traipsing through Hollywood today. And back then you had to have talent—real talent. You couldn't just depend on making it big because your parents were famous." She looked my way and groaned. "Oops. Sorry, KK. Guess I walked right into that one."

"No harm done." I knew she hadn't meant to accuse me with her words, but they'd hit the mark. No one doubted that I'd been offered so many opportunities because I was the granddaughter of the much-loved Lenora Worth. But that didn't mean I was talentless. Right?

To his credit, Scott said nothing. Instead he continued to make his way around the perimeter of the room, gazing at every beautifully framed photograph. He paused in front of a picture of Rock Hudson and Doris Day. "I always loved their movies when I was a kid."

"Me too." I offered up a smile, reflecting on a couple of my favorites. *Pillow Talk* had always been a big hit at our house, and to this day I had half of the lines from *Send Me No Flowers* memorized.

Scott turned back and nodded. "They made such a great couple."

Grandma Lenora snorted. She quickly recovered with, "Coffee, anyone?" then headed over to the silver coffee server and lifted it with a trembling hand. Coffee sloshed every which way, but I didn't offer to help. I knew her pride wouldn't allow it.

"Here you go, young man." She gestured to one of the filled cups. "There's cream and sugar, if you like it."

"I do." He added a sugar cube and a bit of cream to his cup.

"I was born during the Great Depression." Grandma reached a trembling hand to grab the tiny sugar tongs. "So my parents never used sugar and cream. I guess they considered themselves fortunate just to have coffee, and they learned to like it black. I always drank mine black too. Until 1968, anyway." She dropped a couple of squares of sugar into her cup, then added an extra one for good measure.

"What happened in '68?" Scott asked, settling into one of the wingback chairs.

"Oh, that's the year I got my star on the Walk of Fame." She poured in several tablespoons of the flavored creamer and gently stirred it with a silver spoon.

Scott almost spewed his coffee at that news. "Y-you have a star on the Walk of Fame?"

"Well, sure. I can't believe you didn't know that. Anyway, the craziest thing happened that year. A revelation of sorts. The good Lord laid it on my heart that my depression years were behind me and I needed to start acting like it. I could afford the cream and sugar. Why not use them?" She grinned as she added another lump of sugar. "I've taken my coffee sweet ever since."

Very sweet.

"Nice story," Scott said with a smile.

It was a nice story, and I enjoyed hearing it again. Sometimes I forgot the rough patches my grandmother had gone through as a kid raised in the Midwest. I saw her only as a Hollywood legend, not the daughter of a Depression-era farmer.

Making my way to the sofa, I gave Grandma Lenora's chubby gray calico a nudge. "Move over, Fat Cat." He opened one eye just a slit, then closed it and dozed back off. Undeterred, I gave him a little push and he reluctantly yawned and stretched, then scooted over to the arm of the sofa.

"So, fat cat . . ." Scott gave me a funny look. "Does he have a real name?"

"That *is* his real name," Grandma said, now gazing at the ornery feline. "It's the only name he ever had." She muttered something about all of the Hollywood fat cats she'd known over the years, and Scott chuckled.

"I love your sense of humor, Lenora. You make me smile."

He made me smile. In fact, I felt like I was smiling from the inside out whenever Scott Murphy came around.

Carolina entered the room and swooned as she saw Scott. "As I live and breathe! It's you, Scott Murphy!"

Embarrassment crept into his face. "Yeah, it's me."

Carolina gave Grandma Lenora a stern look. "You should have warned me. I would have fixed my hair. Put on a little lipstick. Here I am in my stretchy pants and faded T-shirt."

"Oh, don't worry about it," Scott said. "To be honest, I much prefer a more natural look."

I took my napkin and wiped off as much of my lipstick as I could while his attention was focused elsewhere.

"So, are you hungry, Scott?" Carolina asked.

"Am I ever!" He rubbed his stomach and all three of us women laughed. It had been a long time since we'd had a man in the house. Felt good.

We spent the next half hour eating Carolina's delicious foods, which she served up with much chatter and enthusiasm. Between her stories and the ones Grandma told, I hardly got a word in edgewise. A couple of times I noticed Scott glance my way. I half expected to see a look of panic in his eyes, maybe a "get me out of here" expression . . . but no. He looked perfectly peaceful. Downright happy. And the happier he looked, the more comfortable I felt.

When we'd downed the last of the coffee, Grandma settled

onto the fainting couch, a peaceful look on her face. "There's something rather glorious about Saturday morning brunch in Beverly Hills," she said. "It has always been thus." A lingering sigh followed, which brought a smile to my face. Oh, the drama.

"I guess L.A. has changed a lot over the years," Scott said.

She nodded. "Oh yes, but inside Beverly Hills it feels as though nothing has changed at all. It's a world inside a world."

"Not quite like it appears on TV, though."

"Television shows these days don't do anyone—or anything—justice," she said. "But it wasn't always that way. You can't beat the old shows, not just for entertainment, but for wholesomeness too."

I wasn't sure what "old" television shows meant to her. To me, it meant reruns of *Beverly Hills 90210* or *The Fresh Prince of Bel-Air*.

"What are we talking here, Lenora?" Scott asked. "Which shows?"

Her eyes lit up as she explained, "Why, the classics, of course. *Father Knows Best. My Three Sons. Make Room for Daddy.*"

Interesting that the shows she mentioned had something to do with fathers.

"I had the privilege of working with Robert Young," Grandma said. "Such a gentleman. And you never met anyone nicer than Danny Thomas." She sighed. "Now, those were the men who paved the way. True actors in every sense of the word."

"What's your favorite television show of all time, Lenora?" Scott asked, leaning forward with his elbows on his knees. "Your very favorite."

"Hmm. This is a tough call." She thought about it for a few seconds. "If we're talking comedy, nothing beats *I Love Lucy*. Well, except maybe *The Honeymooners*. I was always a sucker for slapstick." She paused. "No, I'd still say Lucy beats 'em all for comedy."

"I agree," Scott said with a nod. "Great stuff."

"They just don't make 'em like that anymore," Grandma said. "Of course, that's just the sitcoms. But if we're talking variety shows, then I'd have to say *The Carol Burnett Show*. Or maybe those Bob Hope specials. Was there ever anyone more entertaining than Bob?" She snapped her fingers. "Oh, but I can't leave out Ed Sullivan. And Jack Benny. And Red Skelton." She laughed. "And I loved Burns and Allen. Great stuff with those two. So funny. I used to laugh till I cried."

We lost her at this point. She drifted off to television la-la land and we remained behind, simply observers as she relived some of her favorite moments. Not that I minded. Oh no. Not a bit. For through her eyes, I saw how Hollywood used to be, and I liked what I saw. These days, people were so focused on shock value, so riveted on money and ratings, that they didn't spend as much time on the things that really mattered—the wants and wishes of the viewing public. And good, wholesome shows that provided the real deal—entertainment.

Which was exactly why I loved *Stars Collide* so much. It was a show we could be proud of. One I didn't have to apologize for. One that deliberately—but gently—jarred the funny bone.

Grandma dismissed herself to the powder room, and Carolina headed back to the kitchen to do the dishes. Finally I had Scott to myself! I wanted to talk to him about what had happened between us. No sooner had I opened my mouth to begin the conversation than he rose and took a few steps my way.

"Can I sit with you?"

"O-of course." I pushed the cat aside once again, and Scott settled into the spot next to me on the sofa. He took my hand and gazed into my eyes. I could feel the trembling in his hand, and it somehow made me feel better knowing he was nervous too.

"Kat, I want to tell you something. I feel so stupid for waiting this long. For nearly two years now I've known that I . . ." His gaze shifted down to the floor, then back up to me. "That I've had feelings for you. I can't believe I waited this long to tell you. And that kiss was . . . it was unbelievable."

"Mm-hmm." I gave his hand a little squeeze. "I agree."

"I'm glad. And I'll do it again, if you'll let me."

"Oh, I'll let you."

He had leaned in to do just that when Grandma Lenora's singsong voice rang out. "Come on, you two lovebirds! Let's go outside and look at the cars!"

Scott released his hold on my hand at once, and we both turned to look as Grandma entered the room again, this time wearing a mink stole over her gown. Scott looked my way and grinned. I knew he didn't really mind. And besides, now that we were both wearing our hearts on our sleeves, there would be plenty of opportunities in the future for stolen kisses.

Grandma led the way outside to the driveway and began to show off her car collection, starting with the '67 Mustang, completely redone with silver paint and the shiniest chrome imaginable. From there, we oohed and aahed over the '77 Camaro and then finally made our way to the real prize.

"This is the Pink Lady," Grandma said, pointing to her '57 Cadillac Biarritz. "First car I ever bought with movie money, and I'll keep her till the day I die."

Should I add that she'd requested to be buried in it? Nah. That was a story for another day.

Scott let out a whistle. "I've seen it from a distance on the studio lot, but never up close and personal like this."

"Climb in, young man." She handed him the keys and he climbed inside, settling in behind the wheel.

I fought the urge to say, "You look pretty in pink."

Meanwhile Grandma seemed a bit preoccupied by something. Many times in our conversation she looked toward the gate, then glanced at her watch. What was it with her bizarre behavior lately? Scott continued to talk about the car's features, and before long—at Grandma's insistence—I was seated in the passenger seat beside him.

"You two look as pretty as a picture!" Grandma clasped her hands together and grinned like the Cheshire cat. A few seconds later, she let out a little gasp, and I looked up.

"What?"

"Oh, well, lookie there, will you. Paparazzi, downstage right." She pointed toward the open gate, and I saw a fellow with stringy black hair clutching a camera. He took a few steps toward us and flashed a media badge.

"I'm a reporter for the—"

"What in the world?" I interrupted. "You know better than to come onto private property uninvited." It was enough to be followed around the supermarket or to the beach, but for those knuckleheads to invade our privacy at home? No way. And who opened the gate? "You're trespassing!" I hollered, my hands raised in frustration.

The fellow looked perplexed. "Oh, weird. I thought she said to come at—"

"Never you mind all that!" Grandma Lenora gave me a warning look. "Let it go, Kat. Doesn't do any good to get angry. Besides, you want to be ready for a photo op at every occasion. You don't want them to catch you in an ugly pose. Remember that terrible shot they got of Zsa Zsa Gabor last spring, shouting at the police officer? She'll never live that down."

"Didn't that happen in the '80s?" Scott whispered.

I nodded before turning back to Grandma. "You're saying I should go out of my way to pose for them?"

"Well, why not?" My grandmother pulled her mink stole a bit closer and leaned against the pink Cadillac. She struck a Hollywood-esque pose, counting under her breath, "One, two, three, four . . ." Fascinating how she could do that without moving her lips.

"She's got this down to a science," Scott said. "You would think she'd summoned those reporters herself."

"I have always depended on the kindness of strangers," Grandma whispered, then gave me a wink.

I responded with the obvious. "Vivien Leigh. *A Streetcar Named Desire*. 1951."

Scott looked back and forth between us, clearly confused. I'd have to explain our little game later. For now, hopefully he would just join in.

"You two stay in that car, you hear me?" Grandma said. "It'll make a great shot for the magazines."

I groaned, realizing she'd obviously gone to great pains to set all of this up. But why? And how would Scott respond?

Ironically, he cooperated, gripping the wheel like we were headed off on an adventure down Route 66.

"What's with the ball gown, Lenora?" the reporter hollered, then started snapping photos.

"Rita Hayworth! *Tales of Manhattan*. 1942." She removed the mink stole and flung it over her shoulder, offering them a variety of poses to capture.

"Are you doing a remake or something?" he asked.

"Of course not. No one could top the original."

His camera continued to flash, then he paused to scribble

something into his notepad as Grandma rattled off one wacky comment after another.

"Kat and Scott, are you two an item?" the fellow called out as Grandma's chatter slowed. "Your viewers are dying to know if the on-screen chemistry is real or if it's just great acting on your part."

Okay, so he almost had me with the great acting line.

Still, my face warmed up as I contemplated my answer. Scott looped an arm over my shoulders, relaxed against the leather seat, and said, "Stay tuned to this station for further information."

For the life of me, I don't know why I did it. But for some reason—call me crazy—I leaned over and gave Scott a playful kiss on the cheek, which, naturally, made for a great photo op.

Never mind the clicking of the camera in the background. My heart had now fully sprung to life. I really *could* drive off into the sunset with this guy . . . if only the paparazzi weren't standing in the way.

5

Good Times

Bright and early Monday morning, Grandma and I headed back to the studio. As she climbed into the Pink Lady, I whistled at her powder blue dress with the tight cinched waist and full skirt. The chiffon sleeves blew me away. I couldn't remember seeing anything so pretty. Or delicate.

"Who are we today, Grandma Lenora?" I asked.

She eased herself down onto the seat and turned to me with a smile. "I'm surprised you didn't guess. We just watched the movie together last week, KK. Put on your thinking cap."

I racked my brain, trying to figure this one out. Finally it hit me. "Oh yes. Grace Kelly. *High Society.*"

"1956," Grandma threw in. "Have you ever seen anyone as pretty as Grace?"

"Never." I sighed.

"I know it's hard to believe, but she's even prettier in real life. Beautiful inside and out. And what an exquisite figure. Born for royalty, that one."

Now we both sighed. I did have to wonder, however, about my grandma speaking of Grace in the present tense. Odd. She dove into a story about a party she'd once attended with Grace. Then she fastened her seat belt and we set off for the studio. Of course, the morning wouldn't be complete without driving through our local Starbucks. I got the chai latte and Grandma ordered a caramel brulee frappuccino. Yummy.

As I steered the car toward the studio, Grandma coached me on my lines for this week's show. The longer ones stumped me. For whatever reason, I could usually remember shorter, snappier ones, but anything over, say, seven or eight words presented a problem.

After I pulled up to a red light, I shifted the hot cup from my right hand to my left. Time to get down to business. If I didn't memorize these lines, this episode would never see the light of day.

"What's that one line where I say something about the agency?" I took another sip of my latte, awaiting Grandma's response.

"You're supposed to say, 'We've already merged our agencies, Jack. Makes perfect sense to merge our hearts as well.'"

"Ah." I had to smile at that one. I ran the line a couple of times before asking for my next cue.

"Now you're supposed to say, 'The kids love you, the directors and producers love you . . . and I love you.'" Grandma gave me a knowing look and I grinned. No way could I say that line. Not yet, anyway. I'd have to work on that one back at the studio.

"Ooh, stop the car, KK!" Grandma pointed to a newsstand. "I want to pick up a copy of *The Scoop*. I just love

52

their stories. Did you see the one they did last week about Audrey Hepburn? She's just signed a contract with Warner Brothers to do a film version of *My Fair Lady*. I had no idea the girl could sing."

"Hmm." Better not comment.

"I always thought Julie Andrews was perfect as Eliza Doolittle," Grandma said. "I saw the stage play last week and Julie simply took my breath away."

Hmm. "Yes, I've always loved Julie Andrews too," I said. "But you must admit, Audrey looks the part."

"I suppose."

Grandma purchased a copy of *The Scoop* and got back in the car, clutching it like a prized possession. I groaned inwardly, knowing how cruel the stories buried within those pages could be. What had the reporter done with the photos he'd taken outside of Worth Manor? I had a feeling I was about to find out.

Grandma flipped through the pages of Hollywood's most notorious gossip rag with reckless abandon. Finally she found what she'd been looking for. "Here it is! He wrote an article about . . ." She paused, staring at the page. "Oh. It's just about you and Scott. Great picture of you kissing him, by the way."

Nothing could stop the groan from escaping. Why I'd kissed him in front of a reporter, I could not say. And the fact that he hadn't mentioned the great Lenora Worth in the article was sure to be a blow to her ego. I knew she'd hoped to lure in the paparazzi by telling him Scott and I would be at the impromptu photo shoot, but I also knew she'd secretly hoped for a bit of exposure herself. Who could blame her? She rarely got any recognition these days, at least not in the positive.

"Oh, look," she said at last. "They did mention me."

Thank goodness. "Read it out loud."

"Sure." She paused, trying to find her place. "'Lenora Worth, onetime Hollywood legend . . .'" She paused and looked my way. "What do they mean, 'onetime Hollywood legend'?"

I realized how the article must sound to her. Maybe I could put a positive spin on this. Ease her mind. "You know how they are. If you're not filming blockbuster movies in the moment, they treat you like a has-been. It's wrong, but that's just the way things are."

Another huff and her brow wrinkled further. "Back in my day, Hollywood stars were treated with respect, even those whose movie days were behind them. They were revered."

I stifled a chuckle. Grandma Lenora was revered, at least by those who knew her well. Still, I understood her plight. Aging Hollywood stars didn't get the same treatment these days. They were often overlooked. Well, maybe I could change that. I'd do my part. Starting today, I'd make sure everyone I came in contact with knew exactly who she was and who she used to be. In other words, I'd build her up. Maybe I could even talk that so-called reporter into doing a separate piece on Grandma. Something affirming.

She went back to reading. "'Lenora Worth seemed a bit off-kilter, wearing a mink stole and sequined dress on a warm Saturday morning in July. One has to wonder if she's been hitting the bottle again.'" Grandma made a grunting sound. She wadded up the magazine and tossed it over her shoulder into the backseat. I didn't blame her.

"Grandma, you . . . you okay?"

"How could I be?" she said. "They think I've been drinking? And why would they say 'again' as if it had happened before? You know I'm not a drinker, KK. Why would they think that?"

Looked like I had more to talk with the reporter about than I'd thought. How dare he say such a thing? And yet, as I thought about it, I realized she did appear pretty off-kilter to those who didn't know her. I could almost see how they would assume her erratic behavior came from hitting the bottle. Almost.

The most I could offer was a shrug. I knew this article had to hurt, but I didn't know what to do about it. Secretly, I was dying to know what the reporter had said about Scott and me but didn't dare ask Grandma to keep reading. I'd have to search through the magazine later on, when she wasn't looking.

She leaned her head back against the seat, tears now covering her lashes. It broke my heart.

"You know, KK, I've always hated my name," she said with a little sniffle.

"What?" This was news to me. "Lenora is a beautiful name."

"No, my last name," she said. "I hate the *Worth* part."

This intrigued me. She'd never let on that she didn't like the Worth name.

"I came to Hollywood as Doris Mayfield," she said. "The studio gave me the new name. At first I enjoyed it. When I heard the word 'Worth,' it made me think of dollars and cents. You know? Like I would finally be 'worth' something once I broke into the movie business. But now . . ." She shook her head.

"What, Grandma?"

"Let's just say it's been a haunting reminder of how worthless I've felt lately. How washed up. A has-been."

"Grandma!" I gave her a stern look. "I hope I never hear you say anything like that again. Besides, you know that your worth isn't in the things you've done . . . your accomplishments or your fame. It's always been who you are in him. In the Lord."

"I know that in theory," she said. "But feeling it—especially at my age—is tough. KK, you don't know how many older people feel like I do, like their days of being valuable to others are behind them."

"I'm sorry you've been feeling that way, but you're wrong about that," I said. "You have so much to teach up-and-coming actors and actresses. You're creative and imaginative, and you know what it takes to balance the spiritual life against any fame you might achieve in the limelight. Most of all, you're genuine. You're the real deal."

"No." She shook her head and tears filled her eyes. "That's just it. There's nothing real or authentic about me."

Now I knew her memory was slipping. Obviously she'd forgotten just how real she'd been to me over the years. And to Carolina. And her fans. How dare she think she had no worth? Why, the very idea offended me at the deepest level.

Thankfully Grandma shifted gears. She pulled a compact out of her purse and touched up her makeup. Interesting, since she already had on more than enough. The pancake base—in a creamy ivory—was lathered on pretty thick. And she certainly didn't need to add any more of the coral-colored blush to her cheeks. However, that's just what she did. Only when she reached for the liquid black eyeliner did I begin to get nervous.

"Um, Grandma, are you sure you want to do that in the car?"

"Drive slowly, KK. I just see a little spot here that needs touching up."

Unfortunately, driving slowly wasn't an option on the 405, which was where I now found myself. And I couldn't very well pull off, could I? How would I explain this to a police officer if he noticed my car on the side of the road? "Sorry, officer, but my grandmother's eyeliner took precedence."

"A lady always has to look her best in public," Grandma said, opening the container.

Hmm. Well, at least she wasn't driving. It could be worse.

Seconds later she gave a little yelp, and I glanced away from the road long enough to notice the thick black smudge under her left eye. She reached for a tissue and did her best to clean it up, but when we arrived at the studio, I noticed she still looked like she'd just climbed out of the boxing ring. Hopefully no one would pay much attention. They were all used to her eclectic look by now, anyway.

I pulled up to the door to let her out before parking the car. Grandma eased her way out. She turned back, showing off her gown and makeup. "Well? What do you think?"

"Very Grace Kelly–like," I said with a nod.

"You think so?" She grinned. "If only Fred Astaire would sweep me off my feet."

The Lord, with his wonderful sense of humor, provided just the right opportunity to play out this fantasy. Rex Henderson happened by, took one look at her, and let out a whistle. "As I live and breathe, it's . . . wait, let me guess." A few seconds later, he snapped his fingers. "Grace Kelly in the flesh. A vision of loveliness, as always."

Grandma's cheeks—already heavily blushed—turned crimson at his words.

"Aw, go on with you," she said. He offered up a shrug, and she punched him in the arm. "No, go *on* with you. You were saying?"

Rex chuckled. "I was saying that Fred would like to escort Grace inside the studio."

He offered his arm and she took it, then turned back to me

with a grin. "You know what I always say, KK. It's not the men in your life that counts, it's the life in your men."

I paused until it registered, then responded, "Mae West. *I'm No Angel*. 1934."

"1933," Grandma corrected me. "And you're right, KK. I'm no angel. But I did play one once in a movie." She disappeared into the studio on Rex's arm.

After parking the car, I joined them inside. Something about walking into Studio B put me at ease every time. I thought it weird that I often felt more at home on a television set than in my own house. Maybe it was because the house really belonged to my grandmother and carried her signature. Her mark. This place—albeit completely fabricated— was my home. The *Stars Collide* set was my favorite. With its childlike qualities, it really looked like a children's talent agency. I loved the kid-friendly colors and decor. I also loved the furniture they'd chosen for my living room set. That's where I'd been when Scott—er, Jack—had kissed me for the first time. Seeing it brought back lovely memories.

Hmm. Thinking of Scott made me wonder where he was. My heart fluttered in anticipation. I thought again of the words in the script. Angie had fallen in love with Jack and was ready to tell him so. How long would it be before I could honestly convey my feelings to Scott as well? Oh, if only I could find him.

I rapped on his dressing room door, then popped my head inside after a few seconds of silence. Nothing. I made my way to the round-table reading room to see if perhaps he'd already ventured inside. Nope. Not wanting to appear anxious, I headed back to the set, my thoughts shifting to other things.

Ironically, Scott wasn't the only one missing. I searched through the various crew members in search of our director, but Mark was noticeably absent. I needed to run a couple of things by him before we did the round-table reading. If only I could find him.

"Where's Mark?" I looked around, perplexed.

"Oh, he's gone today," Athena said as she passed by. "I think I heard someone say something about a meeting. Or a doctor's appointment or something. I'm not really sure."

"Gone?" I couldn't quite believe it. "In three years, Mark hasn't missed one day on the set. Remember? He even came when he had the flu. Wore a mask."

"That's right. We all ended up getting sick in spite of it." Athena laughed. "He's always been so good at sharing." She headed down the hallway, continuing to talk to herself.

My mind reeled as I thought about all of this. Had Mark given us any signs he was sick? If so, I hadn't picked up on them. I ushered up a silent prayer on his behalf, asking the Lord to heal him—quickly!

Fortunately—or unfortunately—I didn't have much time to think about Mark's disappearing act. Jana, a petite blonde from the wardrobe department, stopped by.

"Hey, Kat."

"Hey." I leaned in to ask, "How are we doing on our little project?"

"I've found quite a few more dresses in Lenora's size." Jana chuckled. "I think we can keep her stocked for a few more weeks. After that, I've got a friend I can call over at Paramount. She's got a huge stash of evening gowns from the '40s and '50s. Really nice things. They'd just be on loan, you understand, like the ones I've already passed your way."

"Of course." I laughed. "I still can't believe she hasn't noticed that the gowns are coming and going from her closet. Carolina has done a fine job of helping me shuffle things around. Thanks for sending a driver with the dresses each week."

"You're welcome. Anything I can do to help. As long as we get them back before they're needed elsewhere, it's no skin off my teeth. And it's not like the studio executives are going to argue about it. They love Lenora. And they love you too."

"This means so much to me." I felt tears well up. "The gowns really seem to be energizing her . . . and helping with her memory too. She always had a closetful of beautiful dresses from the old days, but I was getting a little tired of seeing the same ones over and over again, so this helps. Besides, some of her old gowns don't fit anymore. I don't know if you've noticed, but she's lost a little weight."

"Yes." Jana nodded. "She tells me she's a size seven, but a five swallows her alive. I've been disguising the size tags so she won't notice I'm giving her threes."

"Thank you."

"And get this . . ." Jana leaned closer to whisper, "She tells me nearly every day that she's still five foot eight."

"I'm sure she was . . . at one point," I said. "I'm guessing she's . . . what? Five six?"

"Five five. But she looks great in the gowns, and that's really all that matters. Keeping her happy is my priority."

"Mine too," I whispered. In fact, it was one of the top priorities in my life.

I was just wrapping up my conversation with Jana when Rex walked up. I couldn't quite read the expression on his face. Worry? Fear? Sternness? *Hmm.*

"Kat, do you have a minute?"

"Sure."

Jana excused herself and headed back to the wardrobe room.

I turned to Rex with a smile. "What's up?"

"I know we need to get through our round-table reading,

but I wanted to talk to you and Scott before meeting with the rest of the cast."

"Sounds interesting."

"It is. I've already asked Scott to meet me on the set. He should be here any moment. Will you join us?"

"Sure." As if I would dare turn my producer down.

Scott appeared moments later. He looked great in his UCLA T-shirt and jeans, and I couldn't help but notice he'd had a haircut.

"Sorry I'm late," he said. "Had to stop for a trim."

"I like it. Very nice." In fact, it was so nice that it made my heart flutter.

Scott responded with a grin and a "we'll talk about this later" look.

Rex led the way to Angie's living room set and took a seat in the wingback chair. We tagged along behind him. I had a feeling something was amiss.

"So, I have some news." Rex shifted in the chair.

"Oh?" Scott and I settled on the sofa across from him.

"Actually, I have two pieces of news." He drew in a deep breath and exhaled slowly. "First, Mark is gone."

"Oh, right, I know. He's got a doctor's appointment or something." I reached to brush a piece of lint off the arm of the sofa.

Rex shook his head. "No, I mean he's gone. I let him go. He won't be coming back . . . at all."

My breath caught in my throat. "R-really?"

"Are you serious?" Scott asked. From the look on his face, I could tell he didn't quite believe this.

Rex nodded. "Yes. I called him Saturday morning, so we've known for a couple of days now that he wouldn't be back."

I had to wonder who "we" was. Network executives, likely. But why?

My reaction to losing Mark as a director surprised me. We'd never been very close, and he certainly wasn't the type to make friends. In fact, he'd frustrated me on at least a dozen occasions with his on-again, off-again ideas. Still, there was something about the ornery fellow that I'd grown used to.

I pondered this for a moment before responding. "I . . . I don't know what to say, Rex. I really don't."

"No need to say anything, I guess," he said. "It's not like talking about it can bring him back. And I can assure you this is the right thing for the show. It's a step in the right direction."

Scott shook his head. "Rex, I know you and Mark didn't always agree on how things should proceed, but there's got to be more to it than that. What's really going on?"

Rex cleared his throat, and I could read the anxiety in his eyes. "If you really want to know, the advertisers are worried about the slip in the polls. One of them actually threatened to pull their ads."

"No way." Scott shook his head. "That's crazy."

"It's true," Rex said. "And I don't doubt for a minute they'll do it if we slip one more point. So it's critical to keep the show in the best possible slot."

"I just don't understand," I said. "It's not like we're truly dropping in the polls. We're just down from three to four. Big deal. The viewers are fickle. Next week we'll be back up again. And it will keep shifting over time. That's the way the game is played."

"The studio execs are under the impression that we need some fresh blood. Someone with a firm plan who isn't afraid of moving the show forward. So I, um . . . I've been looking."

"And?" Scott looked worried.

"I found a gal. She's young—just thirty—but she's got an impressive résumé. Very impressive."

"What's her name?" I asked. "Do we know her?"

He nodded. "Tia Morales."

I rolled the name around on my tongue. Sounded familiar, but I couldn't place it. Then again, there were so many directors and producers around these days, it was getting harder and harder to keep up.

"What has she directed?" I asked.

"*Give Me Liberty.*"

"Wow." Great nighttime drama about life in the military. I'd gotten addicted to it a couple of seasons back. The stories were incredibly powerful, and the actors weren't shabby either. "That show was up for an Emmy," I said.

"Yes, but when they didn't win, it fizzled out after just two seasons," Scott threw in.

"Not even two full seasons," I reminded him. Hollywood could be a tough town. You were in one day, out the next.

"I know all of that," Rex said. "Trust me when I say I've done my homework. I wouldn't bring someone aboard who wasn't qualified."

Scott did not look convinced. Not that I blamed him, exactly. The show had been through enough ups and downs over the years. Seemed every time we turned around, we encountered another change. Hadn't Rex just joined the team a month ago? And hadn't one of our secondary characters been dropped without warning? Seemed the more things shifted, the less stable we all felt. And unstable was never a good thing in Hollywood.

"So . . . this Tia Morales . . . she knows drama, but how is she with comedy?" I asked. "They're completely different animals."

"She'll do fine, Kat." Rex gave me a warning look, his green eyes peering directly into mine. "We just have to give her time to get adjusted. I've already filled her in on what's been filmed thus far. She's totally on board to see Jack and Angie cement their relationship with a proposal. And she won't be wishy-washy, I'll guarantee you that."

"Wait . . . a proposal?" Scott's eyes widened. "So soon?"

"There's nothing soon about it," Rex said. "This thing has dragged on for three years. I'm of the opinion that's why the ratings are down. Viewers have given up. And network executives agree, by the way. I'd think you two would as well."

"I'm anxious to get the ball rolling," I said. "But . . . a proposal? You don't think that's a bit much?"

"The kissing scene won't even air for a few weeks," Scott said. "Can we really expect the viewers to make the jump from just kissed to engaged? Most relationships don't move that fast in the real world."

"Don't worry. We're dropping hints that more is coming," Rex said. "Much more. If you took a look at this week's script, you'll notice the l-word."

"Saw that." The tips of Scott's ears turned red.

"And we'll have four or five episodes between the kiss and the proposal. So it will be fine." Rex grinned. "But if I have my way, you two—or rather, Jack and Angie—will be engaged quickly and married by the season's end."

"M-married?" For some reason, the word stuck in my throat. I felt like I'd somehow ended up on a roller coaster, one that sent me plummeting from the highest heights to the lowest lows. Thank goodness all of this was happening to Angie, not me. Personally, I found it all a bit overwhelming.

Apparently, so did Scott, who gave his watch a nervous glance.

Rex ran his hand over his balding scalp. "Maybe it's because I've lived longer, I don't know. I just don't see any point in dragging things out. If you're in love, you're in love. None of this modern-day living together or sleeping together even.

We're going to handle this the right way. And not just for the sake of the kids."

"And we're grateful for that," Scott said. "I wouldn't be doing this show if it wasn't family friendly."

"Same here," I added. I'd made up my mind early on that I wouldn't take any work that compromised my beliefs, and I'd already had a couple of opportunities to prove it. Take the audition for the nighttime melodrama *Soap Floats*, for instance. Supposedly I was physically perfect for the character of Bridget. I went through with the screen test, bubbling with excitement . . . until I found out Bridget the bombshell was known for her sexual promiscuity. Thumbing through the script for the pilot, I'd figured out it wasn't the role for me.

I thought again of Doris Day and her girl-next-door persona. She never compromised herself in any of her roles, and the fans adored her for it. If purity had worked for her, it would work for me too. Hollywood needed more people willing to stand up for what they believed. Too many had sold out.

Lost in my thoughts, I almost didn't hear Rex's next words.

"Scott, thanks for your time. I'd like to talk to Kat alone for a minute."

My heart plummeted as I pondered the whys and wherefores. He'd already fired one member of the team. Would I be next? I prayed that would not be the case.

Mustering up a bit of false bravado, I gave Scott a little wave. He returned it before disappearing from view. I sucked in a deep breath, gathered my courage, and turned my attention to Rex. Whatever he had to say, I could take it. I was a big girl. Besides, I could always get work filming commercials, right? Just last week I'd been offered one for a shampoo product I happened to love. A girl could go a long way on a shampoo commercial.

The expression on Rex's face softened with his opening words. "Kat, I hope you don't find me too nosy, but I'm curious about something. Something . . . well, of a more personal nature." He looked around, and I sensed he wanted to make sure we were really alone. This only served to make me more nervous. What was he leading up to here?

"What would you like to know?" I offered. "My life is an open book." I groaned internally as I remembered the article in *The Scoop*. Perhaps my life was more open than I'd hoped.

The oddest look passed over Rex's face, and his next words were a bit shaky. "Well, not that it's any of my business, but I've been trying to figure out your connection to Lenora."

"Lenora? Well, she's my grandmother, of course."

"I know that much," he said. "But I don't really know much beyond that. You two live together, right?" He looked up, suddenly appearing shy. Odd. When I nodded, Rex's brow wrinkled. "Have you always lived with her?"

"Since I was seven. That's when my mom . . ." I looked up, lips pursed, hoping he'd take the hint. Talking about my mother's death, even after all of these years, wasn't easy. She had been the most important person in my life . . . until that horrible day. And even though I'd lived through nearly three-quarters of my life without her, I still got that horrible lump in my throat when her name came up. Like now, for instance.

What would I tell Rex, anyway? That the room I slept in was next to the one that had been Mom's as a child? That my grandmother kept every item in her room as it had been all those years ago? That the haunting reminder of my mother's presence hovered over me every day, bittersweet and painful?

Something in my expression must've tipped Rex off to the fact that I wasn't comfortable with this. He reached over to pat me on the arm and gave me a sympathetic look. "I'm sorry, Kat. This is none of my business. I'm a nosy old man. I just wonder about Lenora sometimes. She's so . . ." He shook his head. "Different from the Lenora Worth I used to know when we were youngsters in this business. Completely changed, I'd have to say."

"Wait. You . . . you knew her?"

"Well, sure." He looked startled. "We worked together on several projects in the late '50s. She didn't tell you?"

"No. Not a word."

"Odd. I would've thought . . . Anyway, we worked together. She was quite the star back then. I was just a kid trying to break into show business, and not doing a very good job of it at that."

"Really? It took you a while to break in?" For whatever reason, this surprised me. I guess I'd always pictured Rex to be the hotshot Hollywood producer he was now.

"You have no idea how long," he said. "Decades. I tried a few acting roles but never garnered the acclaim Lenora did. Ended up working behind the scenes, which, ironically, suited me just fine. Who knew I'd be happiest offstage? Not me. I was sure I'd be the next Marlon Brando." A smile lit his face. "I was just a small-town kid with big dreams."

"So was my grandmother," I added.

His face lit into a smile, and I could read the excitement in his eyes. "Oh, but Lenora went on to do great things. Her film work was really something. She made quite a name for herself."

"Yes, I've seen the movies. She keeps them in a safe at the house. We've watched a couple of them over and over again. Grandma wants to keep the lines memorized."

"Of course she does." He laughed. "She's Lenora Worth, after all." He dove off into a story about a film they'd done in '57, sounding almost as nostalgic as she often did.

What was it with these two living in the past? Maybe someone needed to nudge them . . . right on into the present.

6

Who's the Boss?

The following day, Rex gathered the cast and crew together on the set for a meeting. I couldn't read the expression on his face. Only when he said, "Meet your new director," did it sink in. Tia Morales had arrived.

A petite woman about my age stepped up to the front of the group. Her gorgeous olive skin contrasted perfectly with that jet-black hair and those dark brown eyes. Yowza. Talk about pretty. I twisted a loose strand of hair around my finger and squinted to give her a closer look. I hadn't counted on our new director being such a knockout. Obviously, neither had the cast and crew. Several of the guys stood with wide eyes.

Rex introduced Tia, listing her credits. She did indeed have an amazing résumé. But I still had my doubts as to how that would transfer to our stage. And how would our crew take to working with a woman? Some of our cameramen were a little rough around the edges. I couldn't imagine them treating a female director with the same respect they'd given Mark.

To their credit, the guys in our crew gathered close and seemed ready to hang on her every word. After the somewhat elaborate introduction, Tia dove right in. "Thanks for that intro, Rex. Glad to be with you. I've been around the block and seen a few things, so I think I've got something to bring to the table."

For someone so petite, she had quite a booming voice. Must've taken acting lessons. The gal really knew how to project. And project she did. Her lyrical accent only made her more intriguing, and I could tell she'd cast a spell on the guys with her gorgeous physique. And with the build-up Rex had given her, who could blame the guys for being intrigued? This woman was part Wonder Woman, part technical guru, and part . . . Miss America.

She stared us down, her voice all business. "People, I'm here to take this show from the number four spot up to number one. That's why Rex called me and that's why I responded to the call. I'm a fun person, but not on the set. Once those cameras get rolling, it'll be all work and no play. You might as well get used to that now. I'm a go-getter. Like to see things done, and done right. My reputation is on the line and so is yours."

Several eyes widened, including those of a few guys in the crew. No doubt they'd pegged Tia as a pushover, based on her natural beauty and petite form. But she was clearly no pushover.

Okay. So this would be interesting.

Scott leaned over and whispered in my ear, "Does this stage have an escape hatch? If so, I'd like to utilize it."

"Me too," was about all I managed to squeak out.

On and on Tia went, talking about how she planned to

run a tight ship. How the only way to make a mark was to give 110 percent. How she planned to stay up nights figuring out the best camera angles, the best timing for our lines, and the best scene layouts.

I kept a watchful eye on the kids, who looked . . . well, terrified. I felt our family environment slipping away bit by bit with each word she spoke.

Thankfully Tia turned her attention to the guys in the crew, talking about technical things. While they looked a bit more reserved now, I could see a tremendous amount of respect in their eyes as she shared her vision for how the show would be filmed from now on. Jason Harris, our cameraman, was the only holdout. He shook his head and turned to one of the other guys, whispering something. Hmm. I sure hoped we could all just get along. There had been enough tension on the set already, and for the sake of the kids, we needed this to be a calm and safe place.

Speaking of children, they gathered around the edges of the stage, their little eyes wide as Tia talked. A couple of the youngest ones still looked frightened, but Candy rolled her eyes and leaned back against the stage, clearly bored. Lovely. Someone needed to teach that little diva some manners. Could she at least feign some respect? The kid was an actor, after all. She could certainly act respectful.

I couldn't help but think that Tia's arrival had ushered in a new season of sobriety for the cast and crew. No more pranks while the cameras were rolling. Yikes. How would we handle that? Our crew members made a sport of playing pranks on the actors, and vice versa.

There had been that time one of the boom mics whacked me in the back of the head midscene. I'd been told it was an accident but suspected foul play based on the laughter from the camera crew. And then there was the time I'd opened the onstage refrigerator to what was supposed to have been a stash of diet sodas, only to have thousands of walnuts roll out on top of me. From what I'd been told, it had taken the tech crew hours to get them in there and they had only one chance to film it. I challenged them to be more original next time, knowing they'd stolen the idea from an old Dick Van Dyke episode.

We always had fun at each other's expense. In a healthy way, of course. And all of these things made for great outtakes, or so I was told. But would all of that end now that Tia had arrived? Would she put an end to our merriment altogether? Only time would tell.

The meeting ended, and she seemed to soften a bit. A smile lit her face as Rex drew near. She extended her hand, obviously thinking he wanted to shake it. In usual Rex style, he swept her into his arms for a fatherly hug. She looked a bit taken aback at that but didn't say anything.

Grandma watched this transpire in silence but then took a few steps in my direction. "What do you think of her, KK?"

"She's, um, something else."

"Sure is. She reminds me of someone. What about you? Who does she put you in mind of?"

I was torn between Attila the Hun and Mommie Dearest, so I said nothing.

Thankfully Grandma Lenora did all of the talking for me. "I know! She reminds me of that lovely young woman who delivers the flowers, don't you agree?"

"Delivers flowers?" Frankly, it had been so long since I'd received any that I couldn't say.

"You know, honey," Grandma said, patting my arm like she would a small child, "when I was under contract to Paramount and used to get flowers weekly. Beautiful pink sweetheart roses. The same girl would deliver them. I'm pretty sure that's her."

"Ah." Should I tell her Tia wasn't born yet when she was under contract to Paramount? Nah. I'd let it go.

"I like her," my grandmother said with a nod. "She's just what this show needs. Business and spunk. A nice combination indeed." Leaning in, she whispered, "And I'll bet if you asked her, she would tell you she used to work for a florist." Grandma gave me a wink.

I paused to think about what she'd said, the florist comment aside. Mark had been all business too, though he had trouble sticking to a plan. But having someone in charge with a nice personality would be good. Hopefully Tia was just trying to make a strong first impression.

Grandma gave Tia a look of pure admiration. "You know, back in my day, a woman would never have become a director, so I think it's wonderful. She's made inroads into a man's world, and that's pretty impressive. I always said a woman could give a man a run for his money." Giggling, she added, "I know I've given a few men a run for their money, anyway."

I didn't even want to know what that meant.

Grandma ventured off to the dressing room to touch up her makeup, and I made up my mind to speak to Tia. After a deep breath, I headed her way, ready to break the ice. Might as well get this over with.

"Tia, I'm Kat. Kat Jennings."

She turned to me with a warm smile and took my extended hand. "Of course. I've seen you on-screen so many times. Good to meet you in person. Rex has told me so much about you, and I can't wait to get started working with you. I've loved this show since its inception and see such great things happening in the future." Releasing my hand, she gave me an inviting smile.

Okay, so maybe she wasn't Attila the Hun. Now I was confused, trying to figure out this mysterious director Rex had hired.

Her gaze darted to him. "He, um . . . well, he told me to come on strong so that everyone would take me seriously. I've always worried a little that people won't see me as a professional in my field, but he said making a vivid first impression would help. Do you think I went too far?"

Ah, so that explained it. She didn't have a heart of steel after all. She was just intimidated.

To my right, Jason messed with one of the cameras, swinging it a bit too close for my liking. A statement, perhaps? Nah, probably just a coincidence.

"I guess time will tell," I said. "But one thing's for sure—everyone will line up and walk straight. And I do think you'll take this show up a notch in the ratings. I feel sure of it."

"Good." A wide smile lit her face. "That's the goal. Oh, and Kat . . ." She leaned in, lowering her voice. "I didn't even know they were letting Mark go, so none of this was planned or anything. I want you and Scott to know that. I wasn't out to get his job. I would never do that."

"Oh, I didn't think you were," I assured her. "I just assumed this was . . . is . . . God's timing."

"Wait . . . you're a Christian?"

When I nodded, she said, "I'm so glad. And to go back to what I was saying a second ago, it's no fun to get ahead of God. His ways—and his timing—are perfect. If I've learned anything in my life, it's that. Well, that, and it's not wise to get ahead of him. I'm pretty bad about taking the reins myself. Just part of that type A personality, I guess."

"I'm more prone to hang back and wait too long," I said. "Sometimes I hesitate. Wish I knew what was coming next. That sort of thing."

"Sounds like we need to meet in the middle."

"Maybe. But I'm glad you're here, Tia. I think you'll be a breath of fresh air. We need a new vibe."

Jason coughed. Loudly. I looked his way and he turned his attention back to the camera. Hmm. Maybe he didn't care for the new vibe.

"Just hope people will accept me." She glanced at Jason then the other tech guys. "Might not make much sense to some of these people that I'm here and Mark's not. Women still have to fight for their place in the industry."

"Tell me about it." I paused. "But the way I look at it, things don't always make sense to us. They don't have to. That's part of the adventure. Some things in life defy explanation."

"Right. Like my crazy family, for instance."

I wasn't sure what she meant by that exactly, but I smiled anyway.

She dove into a conversation about how great it was going to be to work with a live studio audience again. Then she went off about something having to do with the multicamera setup, but she lost me when she got to the part where she started discussing camera angles. To be honest, my focus was on Grandma Lenora, who'd cozied up to us in her eye-popping red gown. Her eyeliner was a bit wobbly, as always, but she looked dazzling in every other respect. More than dazzling, actually. If someone turned a spotlight on her, she'd light up the city.

Tia, God bless her, managed just one word: "Wow." I'd have to explain later. If she wanted to be part of the *Stars Collide* family, she had to accept Lenora Worth as a substitute grandmother figure.

Athena passed by with scripts in hand—a welcome distraction. The dark-haired beauty gave me a little wave, then turned her attention to Grandma and let out a whistle. "Who are we today, Lenora?" she asked.

My grandmother grinned. "Ethel Merman. *There's No Business Like Show Business.* 1954."

"Ooh, love that one!" Athena said. "Watched it over and over with my mom when I was a kid." She continued to pass out scripts, handing one off to Scott, who watched all of this with a smile.

"So did I," Jana called out.

"Me too!" Tia added, now joining in.

"I auditioned for a role in that movie as a teenager, fresh off the farm," Grandma said with a wave of her hand. "I was always a little jealous that Ethel got the role and not me. But I was a nobody back then. Just a silly little Midwest girl with dreams of grandeur. Had to wait another four or five years before I got my big shot." Grandma giggled. "Those were the good old days, though. Back then the men were so suave and debonair. Why, they practically swept the women off their feet." A dreamy-eyed look came over her and for a minute I thought we'd lost her. For more than a minute, actually.

"Oh, but I must disagree," Scott said, dropping his script into a chair. He swept her into his arms and danced with her across the set. "*These* are the good old days." He began to sing "There's No Business Like Show Business" in an upbeat, rhythmic way, and before long she joined in.

Grandma gave an Ethel Merman–esque performance that made everyone on the set cheer. Scott played along every step of the way, even when she changed keys a couple of times. Man. This guy continued to amaze me. Who knew he could dance? And had such great pitch? Best of all, he'd made my grandmother's fondest memories a current reality. I had to give him credit for that. He really knew how to make a lady feel special. That much was obvious from the look of bliss on Grandma's face. And the rush of warmth that passed over me as I watched.

Something about seeing her in Scott's arms reminded me of that Scripture about God singing over us. If I closed my eyes, I could almost envision the Almighty—so loving, so sensitive to my needs—sweeping me into his arms at just the right moment for a waltz around the dance floor while he sang words of love over me. His timing was even more perfect than Scott's. And his pitch was certainly better than my grandmother's.

I looked over at Scott and happened to catch his eye. He gave me a boyish smile, and I felt that catch in my throat. Sure, I'd been taken in by his good looks and great acting. That's what had drawn me to him initially. But what held me steady now was his heart. I had no doubt it really was made of gold. Only a man with a heart after God could be so sensitive to the needs of others. If I'd learned one thing about Scott Murphy over the years, it was that he truly lived to serve—and love—others.

Right now, he kept my grandmother mesmerized with his singing and dancing. Who knew we had a Donald O'Connor in our midst? Round and round they went, Grandma's eyes closing as she allowed him to fully take the lead.

Tia watched all of this, clearly mesmerized. So much for being all business. So far we were anything but. Then again, we hadn't started filming yet. In fact, we hadn't even read this week's script.

A couple of the kids took Scott's actions as a cue and flew to the set to begin performances of their own. Candy burst into a rousing rendition of "Memories" from *Cats*, and little Joey began an interesting—albeit loud—tap routine. Maddy took Ethan by the hand and they began to dance in silly circles, soon growing dizzy. A few of the others began pounding along with makeshift drumsticks, and one boy even started a funny, nonsensical rap.

Before long, Scott and Grandma had incorporated the kids into their dance, and within minutes they all formed a conga line around the set.

Tia watched all of this with a look of—what was that, horror?—on her face. Well, until Scott extended a hand and asked her to join the line. She looked at me, eyes wide, and I shrugged.

"If you can't beat 'em, join 'em," I called out.

And with that, we both jumped in line.

7

Real People

On Saturday morning, Scott took me for a drive to Laguna Beach. As we headed south on the Pacific Coast Highway, I leaned my head back against the seat and listened to the worship music coming through his amazing stereo system. Nothing soothed the soul like great worship tunes.

A slight tilt of the head and I caught a glimpse of the Pacific to my right. Who could ask for more? God surely knew what he was doing when he created those fabulous waters, and merging them with songs of praise only made the whole experience more spectacular.

Scott interrupted my moment of reverie. "Want to stop for food first, then take it to the beach?"

"Sure." I turned to him with a smile, my heart still filled with thoughts of worship. "What did you have in mind?"

He grinned. "Johnny Rockets okay?"

"Are you kidding? It's one of my favorites. I love their chocolate shakes."

"So that's how you keep your slim, trim figure." He waggled his brows at me and I laughed.

"I won't be slim and trim much longer if I eat at Johnny Rockets, but a little won't hurt, right?" I gave him a wink and he reached to squeeze my hand.

"Right."

After locating a place to park—never easy near the PCH, especially in Laguna—we made our way to Johnny Rockets. The tiny room was crowded, as always, but I loved the ambience. The '50s decor really made you feel like you'd stepped back in time, and the individual jukeboxes at each table offered that extra oomph.

After ordering a couple of burgers and shakes to go, we walked across the traffic-heavy PCH to the most gorgeous stretch of white sand on the planet. Well, close. I'd loved this area of Laguna for as long as I could remember. And with the tourist season in full force, we were surrounded on every side. Usually I worried about being spotted or harassed in some way—and I knew Scott did too—but today we just ignored that possibility. Between the baseball caps and sunglasses we'd both donned, we could pass for ordinary beachgoers. Hoped so, anyway.

As soon as we reached the beach, I pulled off my sandals and carried them in my left hand. My right held the chocolate shake I'd ordered.

I caught a whiff of that familiar scent of coconut suntan oil. Mmm. A lingering breath escaped, and I paused to wriggle my feet deep into the white sand. "I love the feel of the sand between my toes."

"See, that's the difference between growing up in Arkansas and growing up in California," Scott said. "The only thing between my toes back home came courtesy of the critters we kept in the barn at night."

My laugh that erupted morphed into an ungirlish snort, and a couple of people glanced my way. I ducked my head and kept walking, trying to blend into the crowd. I took a sip of my chocolate shake, savoring its creamy goodness. Could this day possibly get any better?

"What about that spot right there?" He pointed to a space off to our left with more sand than people, and I readily agreed.

After settling down onto the warm sand, I breathed in the salty air. Closing my eyes briefly, I listened to the sound of the waves as they moved in ribbons over the sand, changing its texture. My thoughts sailed away once again as the majesty of the water meeting the shore held me in its grasp.

"Thank you for bringing me here," I said after a few moments of reflection. "It's been ages since I've been to the beach."

"You're welcome. I live to please." He grinned. "Next time we'll go to Dana Point. I've got a boat docked there."

"A boat?"

"Well, a yacht." He shrugged. "But don't be too impressed. It's a small one."

"Small or not, that's pretty impressive." I leaned back, wondering what it would be like to board his yacht. We would sail off into the sunset, just the two of us.

After a few moments of pondering, I closed my eyes, the waves now playing in my ears like an unexpected symphony. "There's nothing like the Pacific," I said at last.

Scott chuckled. "You've apparently never been to Mud Creek."

"Mud Creek?" My eyes popped open. "Where's that?"

"Half a mile from my parents' place in Alma, Arkansas. Just off of Little Frog Bayou."

I withheld any comments, thinking he might be teasing me.

"We've always called it Mud Creek because it's more mud than water," Scott explained. "But what it lacks in charm, it more than makes up for in mosquitoes. Oh, and the biting catfish. They're entertaining."

"Biting catfish?" Now he'd hooked me. Pun intended.

Scott gave me a knowing look. "Yeah. Don't let folks tell you a catfish's bark is worse than its bite. I happen to know the opposite is true. Don't ask for details."

I was dying to know more—about biting catfish, about his life before L.A.—but didn't ask. We'd have time for that later. As I turned my gaze back to the waters of the Pacific, I did think of one quick comeback. "At least it wasn't a shark."

"Try telling that to a nine-year-old boy in swim trunks." He reached in the bag and pulled out the cheeseburgers, passing one my way.

I opened it up and peeked at it, my nose wrinkling. "Ugh, no way. Ketchup."

"Wrong burger."

We swapped, and I opened the one with mustard and pickles and offered up a sigh. "Perfect. Just like I like it."

"Everything today is just like I like it," Scott said.

As he flashed a boyish grin, I realized we weren't talking about cheeseburgers anymore. It felt good to have him say such sweet things. A girl could get used to this.

"Everything is just like I like it too," I whispered in response.

We settled into an easy silence, chomping away on our burgers. Felt good to let the quietness cradle us. Well, quietness in theory. Just yards away, tempestuous waves crashed against the shoreline, children squealed in high-pitched voices, mothers called out marching orders, and vendors hawked their wares. Other than that, this place was sheer bliss. So was the burger, actually. It had been a while since I'd allowed myself the calories of a sloppy cheeseburger. Yum.

I'd nearly finished mine when Scott broke the silence. "There's something I've been wanting to talk to you about." He pushed the burger's wrapper back into the sack.

I squinted and put my hand up to block the burst of sunlight as I turned his way. "What's that?"

He reached for my wrapper and stuck it into the bag along with his, then wadded the whole thing up into a ball. "My brother and his fiancée work with a Christian organization in Ensenada, just a few hours south of Tijuana. They oversee an orphanage there."

"Wow. That's admirable."

"Yes, I'm very proud of him." Scott paused, and for a moment I read something else in his expression. I couldn't tell what, exactly.

I took another sip of my chocolate shake, wondering why he paused. "You okay?" I asked finally.

"Yeah." He snapped to attention. "Anyway, the home is in need of renovating and Bryan is trying to raise the money to do it. I've already pledged a certain amount but would like to get others interested too, so I thought maybe we could do a talent show, using some of the kids from the cast. Maybe people could pay to get in, or just make donations or something. What do you think?"

"I think you're amazing for thinking of this. It's brilliant. I'm sure the parents will be thrilled. They love watching their kids perform. Maybe they'll even invite their friends and family members."

"I'm counting on that."

"It's great that you want to help your brother," I said. "And it gives the rest of us a way to contribute too."

His expression shifted to one of concern. "Oh, trust me . . . if you saw the pictures of the children from that orphanage, you'd be even more excited."

To our right, a little boy let out a whoop, and seconds later a beach ball came flying through the air. It whacked Scott on the side of the head. Instead of getting upset, he laughed and tossed it back, hollering, "Here you go!"

The boy grabbed it and waved, then went back to playing.

As I observed all of this, I thought about what a good person Scott Murphy was, inside and out. What you saw was what you got with him. And I liked what I saw. A lot.

"I'd be glad to help with the fund-raiser," I said, coming back to the matter at hand. "Have you thought about a date? And a venue?"

"Yes, I've already talked to my pastor. Our church has a huge fellowship hall with a decent-sized stage at one end. They're going to let us use it at no cost. They'll even provide snacks."

"So we just have to come up with the various acts then get the word out?"

"Exactly. And as for the date, I think we'll need a few weeks to pull it off."

"True. Sounds like fun, though. Maybe we could act out a scene."

He laughed. "We do that every day, Kat. Aren't you tired of acting?"

"Maybe something completely different . . . like a parody of *Stars Collide*, or maybe . . ." I snapped my fingers. "Something totally random. Like Shakespeare. Or Jane Austen. We could do a *Saturday Night Live* take on it, though. Something really wacky."

He rolled his eyes and I laughed.

"Okay, okay," he said. "I'll give it some thought. And I'm

sure we'll come up with a ton of others who want to participate, including your grandmother. You know she'll want to get in on the act."

"Oh, no doubt." I nodded, thinking about how she would react to this news. "We'll have her reprise something from one of her old movies. I can see it now. She'll need a love interest, though. Someone her own age, preferably."

"Let's pair her up with Rex." Scott gave me a knowing look. "I've seen the way they look at each other."

I stared at him, dumbfounded. "It's so funny you should say that. I thought I was the only one who'd noticed the chemistry between the two of them."

He shook his head. "You're definitely not the only one. I think they're both smitten."

I paused, wondering who else might have caught on. "I think there's more to it than that," I said at last. "Rex told me that he actually knew Grandma back in the '50s."

"Interesting. Wonder what the story is there."

"Yeah. Me too." I paused, looking back over the ocean. There were so many mysteries in life. My grandmother was one of them. She was a treasure chest of stories, some obvious, some hidden. I'd made it my goal to read every one while I still had her with me.

Scott moved closer, putting his arm over my shoulders. I cradled close to him, still holding tight to my chocolate shake.

"Hollywood is filled with drama. Some of it on the set, some off." He grinned. "Your grandmother is quite a character."

"No kidding. You're not going to believe what she said to me the other day."

"What's that?"

"She said, 'Let's take a dip in the cement pond, Elly May.'"

A chuckle escaped. "I guess she'd been watching *The Beverly Hillbillies* on TV or something. Still, I do worry about her fading memory. She can remember things from years ago, but not what she saw five minutes ago. That alarms me."

"I don't blame you for being nervous," Scott said. "But maybe some of her eccentricities are just that—eccentricities. I mean, did you ever think about that? Maybe that Elly May line was supposed to be funny and you just read too much into it."

"Probably. She even had Elly May bathing suits for us to wear."

"Some people have a bizarre sense of humor. Your grandmother is a hoot." He paused. "So . . . speaking of fun-loving people, my parents are coming to town for a hardware convention."

"Hardware convention?" I couldn't help the chuckle that followed. "Should I bring my tool belt?"

"You own a tool belt?" He grinned. "Seriously, if you did go, you would be stunned at what a big deal it is. People are coming from all over the world to look at the latest, greatest inventions."

"You mean like power tools and stuff?"

"And stuff." A laugh followed. "And my dad's the king of power tools, so this is right up his alley. He'll probably get some great ideas for things to sell in his store. That's the idea, to generate interest in new products. To convince people they can't live without all of the tools they've lived without up till now. That sort of thing."

"He sounds great. And your mom's coming too?"

"Yep. They're making a real vacation out of it. Mom wants to spend as much time as she can with my brother and me. And I'd like to factor you into that mix, Kat." He gave me a serious look and my heart fluttered.

"O-oh?"

"Yes." He smiled. "I know we haven't been seeing each other very long, but my parents don't make it out to L.A. very often, and I was hoping . . ."

"Hoping . . . ?"

"I want you to meet them, Kat." His expression grew more serious. "They're going to love you, and vice versa. And just for the record, I hope you and I will go on seeing each other for a long time to come, so I want this to be the first of many family get-togethers."

Suddenly I could hardly wait to meet his parents. "I'd like that. Very much."

"Me too." He gave me a wink that set my thoughts twirling.

"And I want you to bring your grandmother too," he said. "I think my mother would love her. They're as different as oil and vinegar, but I have a feeling they'll get along great."

"Are you sure?" I asked. "You know how risky that is, right?"

"I know. But I'm willing to take the risk."

Wow. He really did care about me. After a pause, I posed a question that had been on my mind. "So, your brother is coming from Mexico?"

"He is. And he's bringing his fiancée, Julia, to meet my parents for the first time. Should be an exciting week." Scott paused and for a moment seemed to drift away in his thoughts.

I reeled him back in with, "Everything okay?"

"Just thinking about my brother."

"What about him?"

"For one thing, Bryan is younger than me. Only twenty-four. But he's got a great head on his shoulders. I'm so impressed with the life he's lived. And the work he's done. He's making a

87

real difference in the world. I'm just . . ." Scott raked his fingers through his hair, a look of disappointment on his face.

"You're doing great things, Scott," I said. "You love God. You're using the gifts he's given you. And the way you reach out to the kids on the set is so awesome. I think you've just started to scratch the surface of all the great things you're going to do."

"I guess." After a few quiet moments, he finally looked my way. "Here's the deal. My dad isn't keen on this acting thing. He thinks it's a phase I'm going through until I get a real job."

"A phase?"

"Yeah. He always hoped I'd become a doctor, then come back to Alma and start up a practice there. I still don't think it's registered that I'm planning to keep this as my career."

"Does he watch TV?" I asked. "Or read magazines? If he did, he would know you're already the greatest thing since sliced bread."

"The greatest thing since sliced bread, eh?" Scott chuckled. "Now there's a compliment I wouldn't want to trade."

"Maybe when your parents are out here, they'll see for themselves," I said. "They'll see you in your element and understand that God is using you here, just like he's using your brother in Mexico at that orphanage."

Scott shrugged. "Maybe." He paused and a funny expression crossed his face. "I used to think about moving my parents out here. Buying them a place of their own. But I can't blame them for wanting to live the ideal life in a small town. They don't really fit out here, and I sure don't fit in Alma anymore. Honestly, if it weren't for my relationship with the Lord, I'd have to wonder where I fit at all."

"Right here," I whispered, then shyly gave him a kiss on the cheek.

"You're right, Kat," he said tenderly. "And I'm grateful to God for arranging such a perfect fit."

My heart swelled with joy at his words.

"I can't really blame my parents for being stunned that I chose acting," Scott said after a few moments of silence. "I'd never done any acting in school or anything."

"No way."

"Yeah." He laughed. "I played sports like all of the boys in Alma. But acting? Um, no way."

I couldn't believe I was talking to the same Scott Murphy, the one with the impeccable acting skills. "So how did you get from point A to point B?"

"Actually, I got my first acting job by accident. Our church in Alma was putting on an Easter production and they needed guys. You know how that goes."

"Sure."

"So I offered. And the next thing you know, there's a talent scout in the congregation."

"No way." I laughed. "Do you still know him?"

"Sure. Bert Frasier. He's still my agent."

"And he knows you play a talent scout on TV?"

Scott chuckled. "Of course. He got me the audition. And we've joked about the whole talent-scout thing, trust me. I would never have ended up working in television at all if not for him and that Easter production. The whole thing has been quite a ride."

"I hear ya."

"I'll be honest. After my first couple acting gigs, I had a crisis of faith. I'd bought into the idea that I was supposed to be a doctor. Couldn't quite fathom that God would call me to act."

"Why not?" This one really stumped me. "God doesn't like actors?" I took the plastic top off my cup and swallowed down what was left of the chocolate shake.

Scott laughed. "That's not what I meant. I guess I just thought acting was . . . you know, menial. Small stuff. Anyone can act."

My chocolate shake practically came shooting out of my nose at that one. After all the years I'd spent studying the craft, and he thought anyone could act?

"I'm just saying I want to do great things with my life," Scott said. "Like Bryan."

"You *are*," I reminded him. "So don't ever let me hear you compare yourself to him . . . or anyone else, for that matter. You are who you are, and you're doing what you're called to do. Period."

"Okay, okay." He gave me a little salute and I laughed.

"So, back to your brother and his fiancée. When are they getting married?"

"Next summer." Scott paused. "Guess it makes sense that Bryan would marry first. He's on the mission field most of the time these days, so he really needs that other person to walk alongside him. He met Julia in Ensenada. She's the pastor's daughter at the church he attends down there."

"Oh, wow. Crazy how he had to go halfway around the country to find her."

"I feel the same way about meeting you, Kat." Scott's penetrating gaze cut straight to my heart. "I came all the way from Arkansas to California, which is practically another country, to meet you."

I gave him a shy smile. "Was I worth the trip?"

"Oh yeah." The gentle kiss that followed offered all the reassurance I needed. I nestled into his embrace, more content than ever. The two of us fit together perfectly, and not just physically. He was strong in so many areas where I struggled. And he had such a great heart for others. Maybe God really had brought him all the way from Mud Creek to the Pacific Ocean to meet me. Crazier things had happened.

"I'd like to think the Lord has us all exactly where he wants us," I said. "Your brother is in Mexico working with kids. You're here working with kids and using your talents. I'm with my grandmother, taking care of her—" I started to say, "in her final years," but stopped short. Every time I thought about losing her, my heart went straight to my throat.

"You know what makes me think the trek from Alma to L.A. was worth it?" Scott asked. "Other than the obvious acting stuff, I mean."

"What?"

"I've found someone who loves the Lord and isn't afraid to say so. I wasn't sure I'd find any girls in Hollywood with your convictions."

"Oh, we're here," I said. "There's a quiet undercurrent of Christians in Hollywood." I grinned and added, "And maybe a few not-so-quiet ones too. I'm just trying to say that for all of the wild living going on out here, there's a contingent of folks who still love God and want to make an impact in their own way."

"I think it's awesome. And I love that I can travel halfway across the country and still find people I can relate to." He paused. "My parents raised me in church," he said. "We were there every time the doors were open."

"Awesome. I'll be sure and tell them they did a fine job raising you." I gave him a playful wink.

"So what about you?" he asked. "You said that you went to church with your grandmother, but you haven't really talked about your faith."

"Ah." I chose my next words carefully. "I gave my heart to

Christ when I was little, but it hasn't always been easy to trust him. When I was seven . . ." I got the usual catch in my throat, and I couldn't seem to get the rest of the words out.

Scott reached to grip my hand.

I could barely speak above a whisper. "When I was seven, my mom was killed in a car accident. It happened off of Mulholland. She was on her way home from work."

Scott gave me a sympathetic look. "I'm so sorry, Kat. Did she work in the movies like your grandmother?"

"Oh no. She was never really into the whole movie thing. My mom was a legal secretary."

"Interesting. The daughter of Lenora Worth a secretary."

"Yeah, I know. Probably because she was the daughter of Lenora Worth, she'd seen too much of the whole Holly-wood lifestyle. She was much more down to earth and office work suited her. But as she was coming home from work that day . . ." The memories washed over me afresh and another lump rose in my throat, but I managed to speak above it. "She lost control of her car going around a curve. I guess she was going too fast."

"Kat, I'm so sorry."

"I loved my mom. She was my best friend. My dad was never really . . ." Now the tears really welled up. I pressed them back, though, just like I always did. No point in letting an MIA father rule my life. I'd done that long enough.

Scott gave me a kiss on the forehead and I sighed. "Let's just say I've always had a hard time picturing God as a father figure because the word *father* conjures up so many bad memories. My dad was never around much when they were married. And after they divorced, he just walked away and forgot he ever had a daughter. I think it's crazy that someone could do that."

"Wait. You're saying you haven't seen him since you were seven?"

"Right." I nodded. "Not that there's anything right about it. And if you want to get specific about it, he left the first time when I was five. Then after a few months he came back and they tried to put their marriage together again. It didn't take. I don't really remember the details. I just know that when I was seven, he was gone for good. I didn't find out till later that he'd been seeing someone else that whole time."

Scott shook his head but didn't say anything. I could tell he wanted to, though.

I pushed away the mist of tears that now covered my lashes. "My mom had been crying on the morning of her accident. A lot. I heard her in her room. I always wondered if she lost control of her car because she was so upset. So emotional. You know?"

"Kat, I'm so sorry." Scott reached to brush my cheek with his fingertip. "I had no idea."

"I'm not saying I blamed him, exactly. Just always wondered if things would've been different if he'd been a different sort of man. If he'd stuck around. It stinks that I'll never know. And what stinks even more is that he married that other woman and they had a daughter together. You can read all about him in the papers. And online. He's a prominent attorney in Newport Beach."

"Ouch." Scott shook his head. "Well, he'll never know what he missed by not being there for you. And with you." He gazed into my eyes with such tenderness that I calmed immediately. "And listen, Kat. You've learned from his poor example, so now you know what *not* to do. You'll be an awesome parent someday. There's still time to turn things around for the next generation."

"True. I hadn't thought about that." After drawing in a deep breath, I stared out at the vastness of the ocean. With the crashing of every wave, I felt the tension release. Funny how the water could do that. "Let's go back to planning the fund-raiser, okay?" I said at last. "We can talk about personal stuff later."

"Deal. But one thing I need to take care of first." Scott leaned over and gave me the sweetest kiss I'd ever received. After a few lingering moments, he ran the backs of his fingertips along the edge of my cheek and whispered, "Thank you for telling me your story. I know it was hard, but I feel like I know you better now."

I nodded, my heart working overtime. One of these days I'd have to finally deal with the remnants of the pain my dad's leaving had caused. But for today I would sit on the white sands of Laguna Beach and look out over the brilliant blue waters of the Pacific with a good man at my side. A really good man.

Scott's next words were tender. Soft. "The past is in the past, Kat. Hanging out there isn't really for the best, anyway. I know God has great things coming for both of us. After all, tomorrow is another day."

I brushed aside any remaining tears and, with the hint of a smile, said the only thing that made sense at the moment . . .

"Vivien Leigh. *Gone with the Wind.* 1939."

8

To Tell the Truth

On the morning of the proposal scene filming, I was filled with nervous energy. I sensed an unusual vibe in the cast members as well. Tia Morales's arrival had brought new life, new enthusiasm, to us all. Hopefully it would spill over to the viewers too. Of course, I had something else to be nervous about. Tonight I would meet Scott's parents for the first time. I'd been looking forward to this ever since our day at Laguna Beach.

As Nora worked on my hair and makeup, I looked over my lines one last time. I'd deliberately avoided asking Grandma to help me with them. They were too personal. Besides, she'd been acting odder than usual lately. I didn't know what to make of it. Many times the thought occurred to me that we needed another trip back to the doctor to see if her current medication regimen was working. Getting her there, however, was another thing altogether. Lenora Worth apparently had an allergy to doctors.

I found myself lost in thought, focusing on her latest memory lapses, as Nora continued to work on my hair, never missing a beat. The bright lights on the makeup mirror did a number on my eyes and I started to rub them, but Nora stopped me. "Don't you dare! I've got your eye makeup just like I want it."

"Ugh." I winced as she tugged on a section of hair, and then I glanced at her reflection in the mirror. It always struck me as odd that hair and makeup people were so bare-skinned themselves. Nora wore her hair in a messy ponytail, and I couldn't find a smattering of makeup on her freshly scrubbed face. In fact, I could hardly remember a time when I'd seen her in anything but the tiniest bit of lipstick and mascara. Interesting. And under the glow of the makeup lights, she seemed tan, but I knew the girl hadn't been out in the sun in ages.

"Sorry, Kat." She released her hold. "Guess I'm nervous today." She tried once again to get my hair to cooperate but still struggled, her hands trembling.

"How come?" I asked.

She grinned. "You and Jack are getting engaged." She paused and chuckled, then corrected herself. "I mean, you and Scott are getting engaged." Shaking her head, she tried again. "I mean, Angie and Jack are getting engaged. Good grief."

Now I joined her in laughing. "It is pretty confusing, isn't it? But that doesn't explain why you're nervous."

She crossed her arms at her chest and stared me down. "Are you kidding? A girl only gets proposed to once—in an ideal world, anyway—and I want you—er, Angie—to look great."

"Aw, that's sweet." I rested the script on my lap and stared at my reflection in the mirror. "It's going to be a lot of fun." *Even if it's not real.*

"Tell the truth, Kat . . ." Nora leaned down to whisper, "You like Scott in real life too."

"Oh, well, I . . ." We hadn't exactly shared our relationship with the cast and crew. Not yet, anyway.

"I saw that write-up in *The Scoop*." Nora gave me a knowing look. "Didn't look staged. You were kissing him on the cheek." She worked with my hair as she talked, finally getting it the way she wanted. In the meantime, the bright lights continued to blind me.

"Well, yes, but . . ." I stopped before saying something I'd regret. If only Nora knew that Lenora Worth had set the whole thing up with reporters in advance.

"He looks smitten too," Nora continued, still working to make me look beautiful. "I know acting. He's not acting. And neither are you. I've been watching. I know you think no one has noticed, but I'm good at reading the love signals."

"Love signals?" Now she had me. I'd never heard of love signals before. And if I'd been exhibiting them, someone should've told me before now.

"Oh, c'mon, Kat. You know. The shy glances. The shifting gaze. The rosy cheeks. A certain tone of voice. Love signals."

"Nora, you're nuts." I turned back to check out my reflection in the mirror, for the first time noticing my cheeks were pretty rosy. Then again, Nora had just applied blush, so that didn't really count. Or maybe they were just scorched from these makeup lights.

"I'm just saying, Kat . . ."

I put my finger to my lips, hoping to keep her quiet before Candy, who was being made up in the seat next to me, overheard. Nothing like letting the kids in on the secret.

"I'll talk to you later, I promise." My words came out as a hoarse whisper. Picking up the script, I studied my lines once again, though my thoughts kept shifting back to tonight's meeting with Scott's parents. Would they like me? And what about Grandma? Would throwing her into the mix confuse or delight them? Only time would tell.

After a few moments, Nora stepped back, examining my hair. She gave a whistle. "Girl, I've made you look like a real Hollywood star today."

I stared at my reflection, hardly able to believe the transformation. I had to give it to her. This was her finest work. Perfect for a proposal scene.

Proposal scene. My heart jumped to my throat. *Lord, help me!*

Rex tapped on the door and hollered out, "Five minutes!"

After one last glimpse in the mirror, I turned to Nora. "Well, this is it."

"Yes." She giggled. "Break a leg, Kat."

I laughed. "That's a theater expression, honey. Not very Hollywood. And if it's all the same to you, I'd like to keep my arms and legs intact."

Nora followed me to the stage, where she got her first glimpse of my grandmother for the day. She let out a whistle. "Wow, Lenora! You look like British royalty. Who are we today?"

Grandma turned in a circle, primping. "Katharine Hepburn. *The Lion in Winter.* 1968."

"1968, eh?" Rex said as he passed by. "Tragic year in American history. I'm surprised you went with that one."

"I never could resist Kate Hepburn." Grandma Lenora grinned at Rex. "Kat is named after her. Did you know that?"

"No." Rex gave me an admiring look. "Nice name to live up to."

"I do my best."

Grandma's eyes took on a faraway look. "Remember that time we all went down to the Villa Nova and Kate Hepburn accidentally ate my shrimp cocktail instead of her crab cakes? She was always such a hoot!"

"Well, of course," he said, looking quite matter-of-fact. "You were wearing a blue dress that afternoon. And if memory serves me correctly, Kate was dressed in blue also. I remember saying you looked like twins." Thank goodness he played along. Relief swept over me.

"Oh, go on with you." Grandma waved her hand. "I was never as pretty as Kate."

He shook his head, and for a second I thought I saw his eyes grow misty. "Yes you were, Lenora," he said with great tenderness. "And you've only improved with age." He reached out to take her hand and kissed the back of it. I'd never seen my grandmother's cheeks so red.

"Th-thank you, Rex."

He turned and walked away with gentlemanly flair. I would have to remember to thank him later. Talk about working overtime. The man could win an Academy Award for his performance today.

Still, as I pondered the scene the two of them had just played out, I had to wonder about my grandmother's random stories from the past. It was getting harder and harder to tell fiction from reality where she was concerned . . . and that worried me. Not that I needed to be worrying right now. Or ever, really.

Snap out of it, Kat. No time for sadness today. Not with so much work to be done.

Like getting proposed to would qualify as work. I chuckled as I thought about that. Why not just relax and enjoy the ride? See where it might take me?

After a couple of deep breaths and a quick, silent prayer, I got ready to take my place on the set. Nora stopped me long enough to touch up my lipstick. Great. Now I'd probably get lipstick all over Scott when we kissed. Not that kissing was first and foremost on my mind today. No, that faux diamond ring he was about to slip on my finger took precedence, even over great kissing.

"There." Nora nodded. "Go out there and knock 'em dead, Kat."

"Um, okay."

Butterflies took flight in my stomach as I pondered what was about to happen. Just as I took my first step onto the set, I heard Grandma Lenora's singsong voice ring out. "You're going out a youngster, but you've got to come back a star!"

Perfect distraction. I turned around and, with a grin, responded, "Warner Baxter. *42nd Street*. 1934."

"You're good," Grandma said. "Real good. But it was '33, not '34."

With a chuckle, I turned back to the matter at hand.

Scott glanced my way, smiling as he took in my hair and makeup. He mouthed the words, "You look great," then offered a shy smile. Good grief. We really were in junior high again.

"Quiet on the set," Tia called out. She took her place in the director's chair, glanced at Rex, and gave him a thumbs-up.

The lights in the studio audience went down, and the overhead lights on the stage sprang to life. I took my place, ready to begin. Scott joined me, standing so close I could smell his yummy cologne. As we waited for our cue, I realized just how ready I was . . . for anything that life with Scott had to offer, both on stage and off. What a lovely revelation.

After a few seconds, Tia was ready to roll. She took one last look at her notes, then hollered, "And . . . action!"

The scene board snapped and we were off and running.

Stay focused, Kat. Keep your mind on the matter at hand. Just think about the scene. Nothing else.

I went over it all in my head, bit by bit, thinking of it as the script had laid it out.

Location: Stars Collide Talent Agency, back room audition stage

Synopsis: Kimberly—played by Candy—auditions for a major role in a Broadway show.

Action: After Kimberly's song, Jack proposes to an unsuspecting Angie in front of all the children they represent.

Reaction from children: Shock, surprise, and glee—from all but Kimberly, who is angry that they've interrupted her big moment.

Reaction from Angie: Pure bliss as she accepts his ring and his proposal.

Reaction from the real-life characters of Kat and Scott: A mixture of delightful emotions, thoughts, and internal questions as they forge ahead with a relationship of their own.

Okay, so that last part wasn't in the script, but I knew we were both struggling with a mixture of emotions. Reality and fiction had blurred all right. And things were just getting more tense with this ring about to slide on my finger. Was Scott feeling the heat of the moment like I was? One glance his way—that smile, those soft eyes, that little wink—convinced me otherwise.

I took my stance as Angie, talent scout extraordinaire.

Piped-in music began for "Lullaby of Broadway," and Candy—playing the part of the young, yet-undiscovered star Kimberly—took the stage, her blonde curls bouncing and dimples showing. The little charmer almost convinced me. Almost.

She sang the familiar song with unbelievable strength and gusto. I had to give it to her, the kid was great. And who knew? Maybe she really would end up on Broadway someday. Funny, the places life took you.

When the song ended, I spoke my first line: "What do you think, Jack? Is she ready for her big day?"

Scott—as Jack—joined me on the stage, taking my hand in his. "She's ready, but the bigger question is . . . are you?"

"Am I what?" I quoted from memory.

"Ready."

"Ready for what?" I asked, gazing into his blue eyes.

"The big day."

"Jack, you're not making sense."

Scott gazed longingly into my eyes, and I almost forgot we were still on the script. His words, "Angie, there's something I need to ask you," caused me to catch my breath.

I noticed the look of expectation in his eyes. And in the eyes of the children, who hung breathlessly on his every word. You would have thought this was really happening . . . right here, right now.

I looked directly into Scott's eyes, not even having to act. My heart was fully in this, which made it not only exciting and romantic but also a little unnerving. When he dropped to one knee, one of the kids hollered out an impromptu, "Go, Jack!" Not in the script, but Tia didn't stop the filming, thank goodness. I wasn't sure I could go through this scene again. Hopefully we could get it in one take.

"Angie, I love you." He spoke the words, his hand clutching

mine. For the first time, I noticed he was trembling. Or was that me? I couldn't really tell.

"O-oh?" I responded.

"From the minute you walked through the door of my agency, I found you irresistible. Your smile. Your zeal for life. Your temper."

"Hey now."

"Seriously. I love everything about you. The way you play with your hair when you're nervous. The way you stutter when you're mad. The way you work to make our business the best it can be. You're the best business partner in the world. But I want a different kind of partnership now, Angie. Totally different."

I could hear some of the children giggling in the background. The camera overhead moved in closer, and Scott—er, Jack—reached into his pocket, coming out with a tiny box.

At this point, I slipped off into a self-induced fog. Thank goodness I'd memorized my lines. Otherwise I never would have made it through this next part without fainting.

Scott's next lines came out flawlessly, but I never heard them. In fact, the only thing I heard was the sound of my heartbeat inside my ears as I glanced at the beautiful ring he'd slipped on my left ring finger. I held it up for closer examination, my heart going crazy. Then, as Scott pulled me into his arms for a passionate kiss, the children began a rousing rendition of "The Hallelujah Chorus." Before long, the studio audience joined in, lending their support.

I would have joined them, but my lips were busy.

Coming up for air, I looked over the group of children, who now rushed my way and swept me into a group hug. I could tell they weren't acting. These little ones were really thrilled at the idea that Jack and Angie were getting married.

I caught a glimpse of Grandma Lenora off in the distance.

She stood next to Rex with tears streaming down her face. Wow. Never saw that coming. In fact, the whole studio audience seemed awash with emotions. Some folks sniffled. Others cheered. Even the crew members clapped and shouted. I'd never seen such a positive—and strong—reaction to a scene before.

Looked like everyone had waited for this one special moment. Now if only I could figure out where to take it from here.

After a couple more lines from Jack, the scene ended. Cameras pulled back, lights dimmed, and I felt beads of sweat pop up on the back of my neck. Tia yelled, "Cut!" and the audience went crazy. Everyone in the place started talking, voices layering on top of each other.

"Oh, praise the Lord and pass the wedding bouquets!" Grandma Lenora said, entering the set. "It's finally happened. My two favorite people in all the world are engaged!"

"Well, yes, but Grandma—"

"Oh, honey." She grabbed my left hand and gazed at the faux diamond ring. "It's exquisite. Jack did such a lovely job of picking it out." She gazed up at him with an admiring smile. "But who can tell with these tears in my eyes. I'm such an old softy, getting emotional over my granddaughter's engagement."

"But Grandma, I—"

"We'll have to start planning for your big day right away," she continued. "I know just what we'll do. We'll have the wedding at the church and then host the reception at the house. In the backyard. The gardens are beautiful this time of year, don't you think?" After a second's pause, she said, "Then again, you might not be thinking of getting married right away. Oh, but don't wait till the winter, honey. You want a lovely warm wedding so that your guests can be comfortable outdoors. I always say a warm wedding is better than a cold one any day."

"Lenora, I don't think you understand—" Scott tried to get a word in edgewise, but she was too busy chattering to notice.

On and on she went, telling us all of the reasons why we should have our wedding sooner rather than later. She ended with a doozy. "Besides, honey, we don't know how long I'm going to be here. And I know you'll want me to be in the wedding, right? Why, I plan to be your maid of honor!"

Okay, I loved that idea . . . and if I ever really did get married, she would be the obvious choice. But enough already! I put up my hand to stop her midsentence. Unfortunately, she headed over to Rex. I could hear her cheerful voice as she shared her joy.

"Rex, they're engaged! Can you believe it? After all this time, he finally popped the question!"

Rex looked at her, the creases in his brow deepening. "Of course, Lenora. I know that. It's all arranged."

"Yes, it is." She beamed ear to ear. "And now I'm going to see that my granddaughter has the one thing I never had—a wedding!"

Wow. Well, if that wasn't enough to stop us all in our tracks, I don't know what would be. Of course my grandmother had a wedding. The idea that she'd forgotten about it . . . and my grandfather . . . brought a lump to my throat the size of a baseball.

As tears filled my eyes, I reached for Scott's hand and gave it a squeeze, then whispered, "This is worse than we thought."

He nodded and I could read the concern in his eyes. She'd gone over the edge this time, but I didn't know how to bring her back.

Rex gave her a concerned look and took her by the arm. "Do you need to rest, Lenora?"

"Rest? Of course not. I'm fit as a fiddle. There's no time for napping right now. We've got a wedding to coordinate. Do you have any idea how hard it is to plan a wedding in Beverly Hills? Just finding the right caterer is going to be a nightmare. They're booked months in advance. And never mind about the flowers. Getting a florist this late in the season is going to be murder. Thank goodness I've got connections. I can pull a few strings." She paused, deep in thought. "I wonder if Liberace is busy. He's a shoe-in to play the piano. Have you ever heard his version of the 'Wedding March'? Nothing can even come close."

The "Wedding March" he's currently playing on that great white baby grand in the sky, you mean?

"Grandma, are you sure you don't need to sit down and rest?" I whispered. "Maybe get calmed down a little?"

"Heavens, no." Turning to me now, her words came faster. "KK, we've got to go shopping for a wedding dress. And shoes. You can't get married without the right pumps. You've got to make sure they're comfortable, though. There's nothing worse than uncomfortable shoes on your wedding day. Pretty but practical, that's what I always say. Of course, it doesn't really matter what I always say, does it? This is about you, honey. All about you. So pick uncomfortable shoes if you like. And the veil. I think a long veil is best, don't you? Though I have noticed that brides these days are often choosing shorter ones. Practicality, I suppose. But who needs to be practical? This is a wedding, after all! Toss caution to the wind and have it your way!"

On and on she went. By now, everyone on the set—and in the studio audience—hung on her every word. I could only pray the guy from *The Scoop* hadn't snuck into the building. He would go a long way on this act.

Act. Hmm. Maybe the people in the audience would think this bit with my grandmother was indeed part of the act. Perhaps this all looked scripted to them.

Sure. They would all think this was some sort of promotional gag. After all, she did play my grandmother in the show as well. Yes, surely they would find this funny. And staged.

Finally Grandma caught her breath. Before she could start up again, I took her by the arm and suggested we head to the dressing room. Along the way, I waved at the crowd, playing the whole thing up.

Once we reached my dressing room, I encouraged her to rest for a few minutes. She settled onto the sofa and I turned out the light, promising to return quickly. I went in search of Scott, who'd slipped off to his dressing room at the far end of the hall. Who could blame him?

I rapped on the door. "Safe to come in?"

"Yeah. C'mon."

I crossed the room to where he stood, almost afraid to face him after my grandmother's emotional outburst. This day had been crazy enough already without adding Lenora Worth to the mix.

For a moment I couldn't say a word. Then finally I managed, "Scott, what are we going to do? We're meeting your parents for dinner in a few hours, and Grandma . . ." I couldn't finish the sentence over the lump in my throat.

He gave me a sympathetic look and brushed a loose hair out of my eye. "For one thing, we're not going to panic, Kat. That won't help anything. So no abrupt change of plans."

"But did you hear her? Her memory is fading fast. She's losing pieces of her past and has no real connection with the present, except for me. If she thinks you and I are really engaged and then figures out that we're not, I don't know what it will do to her. She's on medication for her blood pressure and cholesterol, you know. And I don't know if I've mentioned it, but she's also on meds for—" I started to say the word but couldn't. I finally settled for "memory loss."

"It's going to be okay, Kat."

"I'm so worried about her, Scott." Biting my lip, I thought about how sad all of this was, really. "I mean, I've been concerned for ages, but now I know I have to do something."

"Like what? You've been doing something all along, Kat. You're her caregiver, and a really good one at that. You've taken every problem that's come up in stride, and you've managed to keep a good attitude. I say we do the same thing this time around."

"Th-thank you." I stopped talking for a moment to clear my head. "I'm making an appointment for her to see the doctor next week. I think he needs to increase her medication. Or maybe . . ." A lump rose in my throat, making it hard to speak. "M-maybe she's just going to continue to slip away from me, one awful bit at a time." I looked at him, tears starting. "What happens then, Scott?"

He wrapped an arm around me. With his fingertip, he brushed away a tear. "Kat, don't worry about tomorrow. Each day has enough trouble of its own."

"You can say that again. We're in trouble all right."

"It seems huge to you right now, but God is bigger."

I willed myself to take a few deep breaths before responding. The words finally came, barely more than a whisper. "I know. This is just scary. I don't know what to do for her."

"We're going to pray about it and ask for a revelation from on high. Until it arrives, we just keep moving forward without saying a word, one way or the other."

"You mean we're not going to tell her that her only granddaughter *isn't* engaged?"

"We're not going to say anything at all, either way. We'll

just act like none of this ever happened. And if she brings it up, we'll simply smile and change the subject. We won't lie, but we won't make a big deal out of it either. From everything I've read, it makes things worse to argue with a person who has memory-related issues. They can become belligerent."

"I know. You're right. I've experienced that firsthand." I plopped down on the sofa, completely overwhelmed. Suddenly I just wanted to go home and climb in bed. Pull the covers over my head. Did we really have plans to meet his parents for dinner tonight? How could I manage that . . . and all of this too?

Only one way. With the Lord's help. Squeezing my eyes shut, I appealed to him for mercy. And wisdom. And patience. "What are we going to tell the others?" I asked.

"The cast and crew, you mean?" Scott raked his fingers through his hair. When I nodded, he shared his thoughts on the matter. "I say we tell Rex what's going on with the two of us. He's probably already got it figured out, anyway. If he feels like we need to tell the others, we will. We all want to be on the same page with your grandmother, after all."

"You're right." I shrugged. "I guess it's time to let everyone else know that we're a couple." Somehow just saying those words made me feel better.

Scott joined me on the sofa and slipped his arm over my shoulders, pulling me into a comforting embrace.

Seconds later, Athena stuck her head in the door, her lips pursed. She looked back and forth between us, her eyes twinkling as she noticed our comfortable position. After a moment, she voiced her thoughts. "So, does your grandmother think that you and Scott are . . ." She pointed to her ring finger.

Scott nodded. "Yep."

"So she somehow thinks you're really getting married?"

"Yep." He offered up a woeful shrug.

"Well, there you go then." Athena shook her head, saying absolutely nothing for a few moments. As she turned to leave, I heard her mutter, "Houston, we have a problem."

At that very moment, a cheerful voice rang out from the hallway. "Tom Hanks. *Apollo 13*. 1995." Grandma Lenora popped her head in the door, gave me a wink, and then kept right on walking.

9

Who Wants to Be a Millionaire?

The trip home was made with Grandma Lenora chattering all the way. I'd never seen her so happy or so excited. As we rounded the turn on Sunset just past the Beverly Hills Hotel, she let out a squeal. "KK, stop the car!"

Not again.

"It's important. I want to see if they fixed the map. We need them to get it right, now more than ever."

I pulled the car off the road, and before I could even slip it into PARK, my grandmother scrambled out of her seat belt. Minutes later, I followed her to the stand where Damian stood waving.

Unfortunately, he looked right past Grandma to me. "Kat! You're back."

Mustering up as much enthusiasm as I could, I nodded. "Yes, I'm back." *Whether I want to be or not.*

"Might I see the new and updated version of the Hollywood map?" Grandma Lenora extended her hand in his direction.

"Certainly, madam," he said with flair, passing one her way.

My grandmother squealed with delight as she located Worth Manor on the map. She turned to Damian with a smile. "It's more important now than ever that people are able to find my home."

"Oh?" He looked confused. "Why is that?"

"Because . . . we're having a wedding!" Grandma's ripple of laughter followed.

I squeezed my eyes shut, preparing for the inevitable.

"Are you getting married, Lenora?" Damian asked, throwing his arm over her shoulders. "Who's the lucky guy?"

Grandma began to fan herself with the map. "Don't be silly. I'm not getting married. KK is. We're meeting her future in-laws for dinner tonight, in fact."

Oh, yikes.

Damian released his hold on Grandma and turned to me, his eyes huge. "Are you serious? You're getting married?"

"It's not really like that," I whispered. "See, this is what happened . . ." I started to explain, but with my grandmother standing so close, I couldn't.

Lord, help me out here!

Grandma's eyes twinkled with merriment. "Oh, Damian, you should have seen it. Jack got down on one knee and popped the question. In front of all the kids and everything. The look on KK's face was priceless. Oh, it was perfect. I couldn't have planned it any better myself."

"Jack?" Damian looked confused.

I whispered, "It's not what it sounds like."

He nodded. "I'm sure your house is the perfect place for a wedding."

"Oh, just the reception," Grandma said with a wave of her hand. "My granddaughter will get married in church. We're firm believers in going to church." Her gaze narrowed. "Do you go to church, Damian?"

"Uh, well, when I was a kid, I used to go with my mom. Haven't been in years, though. Not really my thing."

"You should get back in church, young man." She put a fingertip on his chest and he nodded. "Whether it's your thing or not. It'll do you some good."

"Guess I should." He appeared to be thinking about it.

Grandma Lenora's eyes took on a faraway look. "KK will be married in church. Her dress is going to be the most beautiful thing you ever saw. And the veil too, but we haven't really made a decision about all of that. Oh, I can't wait till the newspapers and magazines post their photos. Don't you think she will look beautiful coming down the aisle?"

"Of course." Damian nodded, then looked back and forth between Grandma and me.

I said nothing. Maybe Scott was right. Letting things ride would be for the best. To stop my grandmother now would create an avalanche effect. Then again, letting her ramble on wasn't doing much good either.

"The reception will be a wonderful affair at Worth Manor." Grandma began to pace. "I plan to renovate between now and then, but surely I can have the place ready for guests in a month or two."

"A month or two?" Damian and I spoke in unison.

Grandma nodded, clearly lost in her ponderings.

Damian snapped to attention. "Well, I've got the maps, if anyone needs to know how to get there."

"In that case, I'll take two hundred." My grandmother reached inside her purse and came out with a checkbook. "How much are they?"

I don't know who was more stunned, Damian or me. I could see the dollar signs where his eyeballs used to be. "T-two hundred?" he asked.

"Grandma, you really don't need to—"

She shushed me. "KK, I have the most glorious idea. We can fold the maps and put them inside the wedding invitations. Won't that be cute? Then everyone will know just where to come." As she made out the check, she continued to ramble on about the wedding. I did everything in my power to warn Damian that her story was fatally flawed by giving him frantic glances. Unfortunately, he was too busy snagging the check to pay any attention.

We left ten minutes later carrying two hundred maps of Hollywood. What we would ever do with them, I had no idea. Maybe, if I lived through all of this, I could throw a party and invite everyone I knew. Give each of them a map, just so Grandma's money wouldn't go to waste.

As we climbed back in the car, I glanced at the clock and gasped. Five thirty? We were supposed to meet Scott and his parents for dinner at seven. My heart gravitated to my throat as I contemplated the potential for disaster. Hopefully Grandma Lenora would forget all about my so-called engagement before seven or we would be in a world of trouble.

When we arrived home, I sprinted up the stairs to my room, then peeled out of my jeans and raced for my closet, anxious to find the perfect outfit. What was one supposed to wear when meeting the mother of her fiancé?

Oops. Just a slip.

What was one supposed to wear when meeting the mother of the man she was engaged to on a television sitcom?

I settled on a soft green blouse, a pair of black capris, and my favorite strappy sandals. I'd paid a pretty penny for them, but they were worth it. Nothing like impressing the future in-laws.

I giggled as I thought about it. Even though the whole thing was based on my grandmother's confused state of mind, I now knew what it would feel like if it ever really happened. Nerve-racking!

At six thirty, Scott called to say he would be arriving shortly to pick us up. While I had him to myself, I decided to fill him in on the latest events.

"Scott, I'm really worried about what happened today. Grandma is planning our wedding. You won't believe what she told the guy at the map place. And wait till you hear what she bought."

I conveyed the whole story—every gory detail—and Scott groaned. "Man. Do you think he'll try to sell that story to a reporter?"

"I don't know. He seems like a good kid and he's familiar with my grandmother now, so I hope not. I think we can trust him."

"Good."

"Do you still want to stick with the original plan?" I asked. "Do nothing, say nothing? Just let her go on with this? Even with your parents in town? Heaven only knows what she might say to them. You know?"

"Yeah." He paused. "I tried to call my dad's cell phone a few minutes ago, but he didn't answer. I wanted to bring him up to speed on her . . ." He stumbled over the word. "Condition."

I sighed. "He didn't answer?"

"No, but I'll try to figure out a way to tell him—or my mom. It's going to be okay." Scott paused. "I've prayed about this, Kat, and I just keep coming back to the fact that she's not well. I certainly don't want to lie to her, but neither do

I think we should make a big deal out of the fact that she's wrong. That will only lead to trouble and more confusion on her part. What's the harm in just not saying anything at all as long as all the people around her are aware of what's really going on?"

"For one thing, she's going to want to start planning a wedding. A real wedding. The kind with dresses and flowers and food and stuff. She's already talking about the guest list and has the invitation worded. You don't realize how females are. Once they hear there's a wedding coming, they slip into planning mode."

"I've been thinking about that too," he said. "And I've already talked to Athena about it. The writers are at work, planning the end-of-season finale, our wedding day. I mean Angie and Jack's wedding day." Scott's words came much faster now. "Anyway, Athena says it'll be fun to sit and plan out the wedding scene with the writers—you, me, and even Lenora. That way she feels included."

"You don't understand. She's got a big church wedding planned."

"So we'll create a church setting for the scene. The viewers will love that. And I'm sure Rex will like the idea, since it's a family show and all. A church wedding makes sense for Jack and Angie."

"And when we tie the knot on the show, then what?" I rose and began to pace. "Then she'll think we're married in real life, and that will create an even bigger mess. Don't you see? She'll probably try to send us on a honeymoon."

A nervous chuckle erupted from his end of the line. Then he grew more serious. "I don't know, Kat. I'm just trying to spare her feelings. We'll keep praying about this. But right now I have to let you go. I'm pulling up to your house."

"I'll open the gate."

A couple of minutes later, I met him at the door.

Scott whistled when he saw me in my new outfit. "You look great, Kat." A kiss on the cheek followed. Then he turned his attention to Grandma, who had appeared in a lovely cream-colored dress, slightly less elaborate than the one she'd worn earlier but still over-the-top. I'd never seen her in an off-the-shoulder gown before. Not bad.

"So, where are we going to dinner?" I asked as we walked together to his SUV.

Scott gave me an odd look, one I couldn't quite interpret. "Promise you'll play along?"

"Sure."

"They want to go to IHOP."

"IHOP?"

"The International House of Pancakes."

"Oh, sure. I know what it is. I've been there before." *Once. On a road trip with my parents. When I was four.* So much for the nice hairdo and makeup job. I'd had visions of taking them to Spago in Beverly Hills, really doing it up nice. Obviously they had other ideas. "Okay." I managed a shrug. "IHOP it is."

"It's my dad's favorite place and they don't have one in Alma, so he always looks for them elsewhere."

Scott's cell phone rang. As he talked to his agent, he also played the role of gentleman, opening the car doors for us. Grandma sat in the back and I joined Scott in the front. Though I tried not to be nosy, I couldn't help but overhear his conversation. Sounded like big plans were in the works. Very big.

"Everything okay?" I asked when he hung up.

"Yeah, that was weird."

"What?"

"He said that the Coen brothers have asked for me. For a movie, I mean."

"Wow. Really? What kind of movie?"

"I'm not sure yet. Bert's going to send me the script. I don't know, though. Doing movies is a big risk right now. I'm not sure this is the best timing. And I want to be really careful about the work I choose, so finding something family friendly is critical. You know?"

"I do."

Grandma clucked her tongue. From the backseat, she warbled out her thoughts on the matter. "You're getting married, honey. That's enough of a production, and plenty family friendly. You don't need a movie career right now. If they really want you, they will wait on you. That's what my agent always said, anyway. Patience is a virtue. And if those Coen brothers have any virtue at all, they'll wait."

Scott chuckled. "Great advice, Lenora. I might just have to follow it."

"I've been around," she responded. "I know a thing or two. Now, let's talk about your wedding. I'm ready to start planning your big day."

She continued to chatter all the way to the restaurant. Several times I looked over at Scott to make sure he hadn't slipped into panic mode. As always, his features were relaxed and friendly. I could tell he wasn't acting. This guy was the real deal, through and through.

Thank you, Lord. I'm not sure what I ever did to deserve him, but I'm so grateful.

For the first time all day, I paused to think about Scott as real husband material. He certainly had everything I was looking for, right down to a strong faith in the Lord. I let my thoughts slip off, my imagination running away with me. If we really got married, would we go on filming the show? Sure, why not. Maybe we'd even have a couple of kids and incorporate them into the plot.

"Kat, you okay?" Scott looked my way and grinned.

I tried not to let my embarrassment show as my gaze shifted to the window. "Mm-hmm."

"Where are we going?" Grandma piped up. "I've haven't been out this way for ages."

I had to agree with that. There were certain places in L.A. we rarely saw. These days, our whole world was the stretch between Beverly Hills and the studio. Strange, what a small world it had become. There really was life beyond it all.

"Where we're going is a surprise," Scott said.

My grandmother clapped her hands. "Ooh, I love surprises!"

The look on her face as Scott pulled his SUV up to the front of IHOP was priceless. To my knowledge, she'd never been inside a pancake house before. Not in this decade, anyway. This should be interesting. And her '60s cream-colored gown was more than a little out of place.

We'd no sooner arrived than a couple of teen girls ran our way. "You're Jack and Angie."

They began to squeal, and before long a crowd had gathered and we were signing autographs. One after another the fans came, each one louder than the one before. I'd been swarmed by fans in the past, but never with Scott at my side. Apparently he was quite a draw. The teen girls went gaga over him. He played along, but I could see the tension underneath his smile. Funny, this was the first time I'd ever seen his nervous side. Perhaps it had something to do with the impending arrival of his parents.

They showed up just as one of the teens pulled out her cell phone to snap our photo. I was introduced first to Scott's father, Charles. Sizing him up didn't take very long. He stood about five foot ten. Balding. A stern expression but kind eyes. Not terribly vocal, but that was okay. I wasn't sure I could keep a conversation going with him, anyway.

Next I turned my attention to his mother as Scott introduced us. "Nancy." I extended my hand. "It's so great to meet you."

"Nice to meet you too," she said. She stood about five three, slightly chubby, with a delicious sparkle in her eyes. Her slacks and blouse were plain but nice. She didn't seem the type for makeup, though I detected a hint of lipstick and some powder. Her salt-and-pepper hair was cut short, like many women her age.

I could hardly get past the look of shock on her face as she took in my grandmother's formal attire. Still, she responded with graciousness and greeted us like old friends.

The hostess seated us at a large table, and I found myself between Scott and his mother. Grandma Lenora sat across from us in all her glory. She pulled out her compact and touched up her lipstick. And her blush. And her eyeliner. Lovely. Thankfully she didn't say anything about our engagement. That would've been the icing on the cake. With all of the hoopla with the teen fans, Scott hadn't had a chance to warn his parents about Grandma's volatile state of mind. That would likely have to wait till after dinner. In the meantime, I would pray. Hard.

"Where are Bryan and Julia?" Scott asked, looking around. "Running late?"

"They should be here any minute," his mother said. "They were just getting into the Los Angeles area when they called about half an hour ago. It's been a long drive from Ensenada." She turned to me with a smile. "We've never had the privilege of meeting Julia in person before, and I'm a little nervous."

"Why nervous?" Grandma asked, sticking her lipstick back in her little purse.

"I don't know." Nancy's brow wrinkled. "I want to make a good impression, I guess."

Boy, could I ever relate to that.

Grandma gazed at Nancy and offered her two cents' worth. "Honey, she will love you just as you are. I've lived long enough now to come to the conclusion that if folks don't love you for you, well, there's no point in trying to impress them."

"I . . . I suppose." Nancy did not look convinced.

"So, are you staying with Scott?" I asked.

Scott's father looked up from his menu and shook his head. "No. At the Super 8 just a couple of blocks from here."

"I'm surprised they're not staying at your place." I gave Scott a curious look.

"That wouldn't have worked," his mother said. "We needed something within walking distance of the convention center."

"Super 8 suits us just fine," his father mumbled. "Don't need any of this Hollywood hype to make an old couple like us happy."

Well, if that didn't state it plain and simple, I didn't know what would.

"Oh, I know a lovely hotel you could have stayed at." Grandma lit into a story about the Beverly Hills Hotel, honing in, as usual, on how Elizabeth Taylor had honeymooned in the bungalows not once but six times. Nancy didn't really say anything, but I could read the curiosity—and humor—in her expression.

"We do hope to make it to Beverly Hills while we're in town," she said at last. "I've been telling Charles that I want to buy one of those maps so we can see where the stars live."

Talk about a Hollywood moment. Grandma pulled a map out of her purse, lifted it in the air, and gave me a triumphant look. "See, KK! I told you these would come in handy."

Nancy gave the map a curious look. "Why, thank you. Have you been sightseeing too?"

Grandma nodded. "Every day since 1957. That's the year my home was built. I was under contract with Paramount back in those days."

"My grandmother was a film star," I whispered in Nancy's ear.

Nancy looked flabbergasted. "Wait . . . Lenora Worth? You're *the* Lenora Worth? From that wonderful movie *It Had to Be You*?"

"That's me," Grandma said, now beaming with delight.

Nancy gasped. "Oh, that's one of my favorites. I can still remember where I was when I saw it the first time. Alma had a little theater called the Bijou, and movies were twenty-five cents. And for another quarter I could get a soda and popcorn."

"Boy, has that ever changed." Scott laughed. "These days you have to mortgage the house to go to the movies."

"True," his father said. "That's why I stay home and watch football on TV. It's cheaper."

"You have to pay for cable too, Charles." Nancy shook her head and laughed. "Men." She gave my grandmother an admiring look. "I'm sad to say they tore the Bijou down years ago, but I still have such fond memories of my years there as a child. And so many of the ones I loved were yours! Unbelievable. I'm actually sitting at the dinner table with Lenora Worth. *The* Lenora Worth. The ladies at my Bible study are never going to believe this. They're just not."

Grandma beamed from ear to ear. "Would you like me to sign something for you, honey?"

"Hmm." Nancy reached into her purse, coming out with a receipt from Target. "This hardly seems appropriate."

"What about this?" Grandma reached for an IHOP napkin and scribbled her name across it with a pen that Scott provided.

"Write 'To Your Biggest Fan,'" Nancy said. She turned to me and whispered, "I'm going to frame this when I get back to Alma. My friends will be green with envy."

All of this, of course, made my grandmother's day. With added flair, she finished the autograph, then looked up with a grin. "Oh, it feels good to be among lovers of great film again. This really takes me back."

"Me too." Nancy clutched the napkin to her chest with a look of sheer bliss on her face. "Are you still filming movies, Lenora?" she asked.

"No. I have made a few guest appearances on television, but that's about it. I prefer to watch from the background these days."

"But you enjoy wearing the dresses from the movies?" Nancy gestured to the cream dress Grandma had chosen to wear. "Is that it?"

"Oh yes. They really take me back to the good old days." She gestured to her gown. "This is a Debbie Reynolds number. She was always one of my favorites."

"Debbie Reynolds?" Nancy's face lit up again. "I used to love her when I was younger. Did you ever see the Tammy movies?"

"Did I?" Grandma chuckled. "Why, I was on the set when Debbie filmed the first Tammy movie. I helped her memorize the words to the theme song. We were very close."

"R-really?" Nancy did not look convinced, so I nodded. Not that I could confirm my grandmother's story, but it would keep the conversation flowing.

"Wasn't she fabulous in *Singin' in the Rain*?" Grandma asked.

When Nancy nodded, the two women lit into a conversation about Gene Kelly, which served as a lovely segue to a chat about the weather. After that, they went back to talking about Hollywood stars once again. Apparently Nancy was a quintessential tourist.

"So you plan to visit Hollywood while you're here?" Grandma asked, gesturing to the map in Nancy's hand. "If so, we would love for you to stop by our place in Beverly Hills."

Nancy suddenly looked very excited. "I told Charles that if we came all the way to Los Angeles, I'd better get to see at least one star. And not the kind in the sky," she added with a wink.

"Hey, what am I—chopped liver?" Scott asked, crossing his arms.

Out of the corner of my eye, I noticed Scott's father rolling his eyes. Thankfully he didn't comment. Still, it was clear he didn't like the direction this conversation was heading.

Nancy laughed and patted Scott on the arm. "We already know you're famous, son. And Kat too, of course. We think you're both brilliant on that show of yours. Don't we, Charles?"

He grunted something that almost sounded like, "Yeah."

"I watch it every week and even record it on that . . ." She looked at her husband. "What's it called again, honey?"

"DVR."

"Right." She nodded. "DVR. Don't know what we ever did without it. You can skip right through the commercials."

Scott and his father started talking about modern technology, and I found myself stuck in the middle between two completely different conversations. I tried to focus on the women, who spoke my language. For the most part, anyway.

Nancy gestured to me first and then to my grandmother. "Honestly, I can't wait to tell my friends back in Alma that I had dinner with Lenora Worth. Why, they'll just flip!" She opened the map, gave it a glance, and looked back up at us, her face lit with joy. "This is all so wonderful, isn't it? It's as if God arranged every last detail."

"He's in the detail business," Grandma said, her eyes sparkling. She dove off into a lengthy discussion about life in Hollywood, focusing on some of the people she'd met over the years.

From across the table, Scott's father shook his head and mumbled, "We're not in Kansas anymore, Toto."

Naturally, Grandma could not resist. She looked at him, serious as you please, and responded, "Judy Garland. *Wizard of Oz*. 1939."

"Yes, that's right." He looked her in the eye. "But my point is, things are different here. Very different."

"Oh yes, gloriously different." She giggled. "There's no business like show business, honey! And there's no place like Hollywood!" Grandma dove into a story about what her life had been like as a farmer's daughter, and before long she had everyone at the table laughing. God bless her. For all of her eccentricities, she sure knew how to turn things around.

To my great relief, we were soon distracted by Bryan and Julia's entrance. As Scott's brother made his way to the table, I couldn't help but notice the resemblance. Though Bryan was younger, the two could pass for twins. Julia, on the other hand, was petite and olive-skinned, Bryan's polar opposite. In many ways she reminded me of Tia. A bit younger, though.

Introductions were made as the two joined us. Julia settled into the spot between Grandma and Scott's mom. This should be interesting. Grandma went off on a tangent about Julia's beautiful smile and put everyone at ease, even speaking a few words to Julia in fluent Spanish. Yes, Lenora Worth certainly had that way about her.

From there, the conversation turned to the fund-raiser. Scott shared our ideas, which Bryan seemed to love. The more we talked about it, the more I realized this event would be a lot of fun. I turned to Scott, pleased with how things were going. Finally I could rest easy.

Just about the time I'd relaxed, Julia let out a squeal. I stared at her, wondering what had provoked it. She pointed to my left hand—in particular, my left ring finger. I gasped as I realized I'd somehow forgotten to take off the ring Scott had slipped on my finger during our earlier filming. Julia released a string of words in Spanish, none of which I recognized. Still, I got the gist of it. She thought we were engaged.

I quickly shoved my hand behind my back, but it was too late. The damage had already been done.

"Son . . . is there something you'd like to tell us?" Nancy asked, her face turning pale.

His father's fork froze in place just a couple of inches from his mouth as he stared over at the two of us.

Grandma clasped her hands together, a broad smile lighting her face. "Oh, happy day! Isn't it the best news ever? I can't believe you didn't know! Why, I thought everyone knew they were getting married. The angels have been singing songs of praise all day long. Isn't it divine!"

I slipped off into a catatonic state from which I planned never to return. Scott could handle this one without me. I hoped. He tried to offer a few words of explanation but then looked at my grandmother, who beamed ear to ear. Dead silence followed.

Nancy took over. "I just don't believe it," she said, her hands pressed to her heart. "Both of my boys are getting married. I . . . I . . . well, I'm so happy, I could cry."

And she did.

I would have joined her, but I figured if this dam broke, the river would overrun its banks. My tears would have to wait until I got home and crawled under the covers. Only there could I do them justice.

Scott looked my way, his eyes wide. I shifted my gaze to the table and fidgeted with my napkin. Ah, blissful avoidance!

We somehow made it through the rest of the meal. Thankfully the conversation shifted to more exciting stuff—like Charles's steak and eggs, which he claimed to be the best he'd ever eaten. Soaked in ketchup like that, they looked pretty gruesome. I did my best to focus on my salad, picking out the tomatoes.

By the time the meal ended, everyone seemed to have forgotten about our big news. Well, most everyone. Nancy occasionally glanced my way, offering a shy smile. Apparently she approved of me as daughter-in-law material. On some level that made me feel better, though I certainly planned to tell her the truth before the night ended. Surely she could see how fragile my grandmother's state was. She would understand.

When we wrapped up the meal, Scott's father insisted on paying for the group—made quite a production out of it, in fact. I couldn't help but think it might have injured his pride if Scott had objected.

As we walked out of IHOP, we were met at the door by a host of paparazzi, their cameras flashing nonstop. I put my hands up to cover my face. Could this night possibly get any more awkward?

Obviously so.

From my right, a reporter hollered, "Hey, Kat . . . is that an *engagement* ring?"

Cameras began snapping madly once again, and I shoved my left hand behind my back and groaned. Whether I'd meant to do it or not, I'd just given these guys the story of a lifetime.

Only one problem—it wasn't true. But what could I do about that now?

10

Cheers

The night after meeting Scott's parents, I had the strangest dream. Scott and I were in Ensenada, Mexico, at the orphanage, visiting with the children. For whatever reason, we'd decided to hold the fund-raiser there instead of in L.A.

Nancy was there. So was Charles. Grandma Lenora was up on some sort of makeshift stage, singing a funny song in her off-key voice, and the kids danced around her. Just about the time she reached the height of the song, the paparazzi appeared, cameras in hand. The flash of lights nearly blinded me, and I hollered out, "Leave us alone! Can't you see we're trying to do something good here?"

Grandma didn't mind, of course. She posed and counted to ten, encouraging them to add to the chaos. Off in the distance, Scott did a random tango number, spinning his mother around until she grew dizzy. They danced my way, where he got down on one knee and offered me not a ring but a plateful of steak and eggs covered in ketchup.

The dream morphed, and I saw myself as a little girl sitting in IHOP. My mother sat to my right, and my father, dour faced, sat directly across from her. They didn't speak. Not a word. I chattered on and on, trying to fill the quiet space, but things only got more awkward as I talked. As the dream twisted and turned, I grew up . . . right there in the chair at IHOP. Only, as I glanced at the chair next to me, I now found it empty. For that matter, so was the one across from it.

The tears flowed in abundance. While I had struggled through their pained silence, even silence was preferable to absence.

I awoke in a puddle, my heart heavy for my mother. And my father. Strange, how a dream could make me want to see a man who had deliberately disappeared out of my life. And stranger still that I'd actually dreamed about the uncomfortable silence between my two parents. The tears continued to flow until I managed to get them under control. My thoughts shifted to prayers, and I gave my hurts—as best I could, anyway—to my real Daddy. Surely he could handle this.

After spending a bit of time composing myself, I rose from the bed feeling queasy. My thoughts gravitated from my parents to the events of last night, particularly the paparazzi incident. How could I ever live this down? Would Scott decide I was more trouble than I was worth? I hadn't intended to keep the ring on. In fact, I'd completely forgotten about it. Or maybe—if I had to be honest with myself—maybe I'd liked the feel of the ring on my finger so much that I'd kept it on subconsciously.

I glanced at my bedside table, taking in the faux diamond ring with its silver-coated band. The marquis cut was nice. I might've preferred a princess cut, though. And this one was a little big for my taste. How brides managed such huge rings remained a mystery. I'd prefer something more practical. Pretty, of course. But practical.

Kat, what is your problem? Are you actually thinking about real engagement rings?

That realization both terrified and intrigued me. Did I really want to wear Scott's ring, or had I just slipped over the edge, never to return?

I thought about it all day Saturday as Grandma and I talked through her plans to renovate the house. And I pondered it all through the Sunday morning service at church, especially when Pastor Garrett stopped me after the service to congratulate me on my upcoming nuptials. Oy! Now what? I tried to explain what was really going on, but Grandma wouldn't let me get a word in edgewise. Why oh why did she have to tell him he would be performing the service?

On Monday morning, I arrived at the studio feeling a little discombobulated. And despite our many back-and-forth phone calls over the weekend, I had to wonder how Scott would act once he saw me—and Grandma—in person.

I didn't have long to think about it. Several people stopped me as I came in the door, offering random congratulations. Most had stunned looks on their faces, particularly the guys in the crew. I just shook my head and gave out several looks of warning, but no one seemed to catch on. They were too busy listening to Grandma share the details of my upcoming wedding ceremony to notice my rising blood pressure.

After a few minutes, I couldn't handle it anymore. I headed off to find Athena to pick up my copy of this week's script. Fear and trembling took hold as I tried to imagine what the writers had come up with this time around. Now that Jack and Angie were engaged, what would happen next?

I reached the writers' room—a crazy, chaotic-looking place

with papers strewn everywhere—and found Athena inside. Alone. Praise the Lord.

"Kat, get in here." She pulled me through the door. "Is it true?"

I stared at her, shock now oozing out of every pore. "Athena, you of all people should know it's a misunderstanding." Over the next couple minutes I offered an explanation of what had happened, right down to the part where I'd accidentally left the ring on.

"Oh." She frowned. "Okay. I guess I knew that, though it is a little weird that you forgot to take the ring off. But still, a girl can hope. You and Scott are perfect for each other." She leaned in to whisper, "Did you see that you guys are going to be the lead story on *Entertainment Tonight*?"

I groaned. "No. Tell me it ain't so."

"Oh yes. Some guy who runs a map business on Sunset Boulevard says he has some sort of proof that you're really engaged. They're going to interview him. I can't wait to see what he has to say."

Another groan escaped. Apparently I'd been wrong about Damian. Sounded like he'd ratted us out—the scoundrel. Any control I'd formerly had—or thought I had—over this situation had dribbled through my fingertips.

"What are you going to do?" Athena asked as she gestured for me to sit next to her.

"After I move to the remotest regions of the Amazon, or before?" I asked as I took a seat. "Because I feel pretty sure I won't have to deal with any of this when I'm living in the rain forest."

"You're moving to the jungle?" she asked, her brow now wrinkled in confusion.

I slapped my head. "No, goofy. I already live in the jungle. I'm moving to the Amazon, where the natives are friendly and the only headhunters are the kind that eat you for dinner. I'll be safe there. Safer than I am here, anyway."

She chuckled. "Okay, I get it. You're worked up. I'm not saying I blame you, exactly. I guess this is pretty embarrassing."

"You can say that again."

She'd just started to when Scott stuck his head in the door and smiled. "Hey."

"Hey." I forced a smile, but my heart wasn't really in it.

"So, I hear we're a pretty hot topic," he said, entering the room. "My mother called this morning to say she saw us in the paper and on television. Apparently we made *Good Morning America* and *The View*."

"Scott, I'm so sorry." I buried my face in my hands. "How are we going to fix this?"

"Let them talk, Kat. Let them all talk. I still say we just ride the wave. If nothing else, this will be great PR for the show, like Rex said." He shrugged. "It's not hurting my reputation any for people to think that a girl like you would even think about marrying a guy like me. It's pretty flattering, in fact."

Okay, maybe I could get used to this. My bundled nerves began to loosen as I observed the smile on Scott's face. How did he do it? Even with the storm waters raging around him, he still managed to be calm, cool, and collected. The guy was a walking advertisement for antiperspirant.

"She's thinking about moving to Africa," Athena said, gesturing to me. "You're not going to let that happen, are you, Scott?"

Before he could answer, I corrected her. "Not Africa, the *Amazon*." Turning to Scott, I sighed. "Do you ever just wish you could run away?"

"I already did that," he said. "It's how I ended up in L.A., remember? Small-town boy leaves small-town life to pursue opportunities in bigger places . . ."

"Touché."

"You're not going anywhere, Kat," he said, his eyes filled with empathy. "I don't think my heart could take it."

Athena looked back and forth between us, her eyes narrowing into slits. "I knew you were head over heels for each other! I can't believe I thought it was just great acting on your part."

"Hey now," I said, crossing my arms at my chest. "Are you saying my acting isn't great?"

"Not as great as this." She pointed to the two of us. "This is better than any script I could write, Kat. And trust me, God's lines are far better than mine, so I'm not arguing."

Scott slipped an arm over my shoulders. "We've already told Rex," he said. "And when the time is right, we'll let others know too. It's just been a little tricky."

"So you didn't want people to know you were dating, but you're perfectly okay with letting everyone think you're engaged?" she asked. "Because half of America has already gotten the memo, in case you haven't noticed."

"That's different."

"Okay." After a moment's pause, she asked, "But are you sure you two aren't really engaged?"

"We're not," I assured her. "If I'm ever engaged, you'll be one of the first to know. I promise."

"Okay then." She offered a satisfied smile.

"Oh, and speaking of people knowing, I called my parents on my way home from our dinner the other night," Scott said. "I explained everything."

"Thank goodness."

"Actually, my mom was really disappointed. She was hoping we were really engaged. My dad seemed a little confused by it all, but then again, everything about life in Hollywood confuses him."

I heard a commotion out in the hallway, so I stuck my head out of the door to see what I'd missed. Bianca Jacobs, Candy's mother, stood nose to nose with Tia Morales, letting her have it about something. Picture the mighty Goliath facing down little David. Tia's petite form seemed dwarfed by this stage mom's overwhelming presence. Bianca's voice grew shriller, and she waved her hands in Tia's face.

"Wow." I watched in amazement as Bianca continued to rant.

"This is better than the WWE," Scott whispered. "Who do you think is gonna come out on top?"

"Hmm." I paused to think about it. "Tia's got the power, but Bianca's got the guts. This is going to be a close call."

"My money's on Tia," Athena whispered. "She's got a lot to prove. Besides, she's one tough cookie."

"Maybe not as tough as Bianca, the ultimate stage mother," I added. I'd never known anyone as aggressive as that woman, except, perhaps, her daughter. Candy regularly pitched fits when things didn't go her way. Most of us had grown weary of the youngster's ongoing temper tantrums, but even she looked mild in comparison to mama.

I listened as Bianca ranted, trying to get a feel for what was going on.

"Is it really true that you've decided to cut over half of Candy's song from that last episode?" she asked.

"Well, the scene went a little long, and—" Tia never had a chance to finish because Bianca looked like a teakettle about to blow.

"What?" Bianca glared at her. "Do you know how many gigs we turned down so that we—I mean, she—could play the role of Kimberly? We had a deal. Mark promised to showcase Candy's talents in this stupid sitcom of his. This is completely ridiculous."

Ouch.

Silence fell over the cast and crew at this proclamation. Tia took a couple of steps back. For a second there, I thought she might take Bianca down. Instead she drew in a few slow, calculated breaths, then managed what had to be a rehearsed sentence. "There has been a change in plans, Ms. Jacobs. And let me remind you that Mark is no longer here. *I'm* here, and I've decided that Candy's song was too long to include all of it in the scene. We're trimming back a little, only using half the song. There will be plenty of opportunities to showcase her talent later. Right now, we need to focus on the proposal and the upcoming wedding."

Lovely.

Bianca opened her mouth but stopped herself from saying more when she realized everyone in the place was now watching her. Oh, if only her daughter could practice the same amount of restraint. I caught a glimpse of the eight-year-old with her perfect curls and frilly dress standing nearby. Nothing could match the child's beauty on the outside. But, on the inside?

Hmm. Looked like we were about to find out what she was made of.

Everyone watched with calculated breaths as Candy rose and took a few steps in Tia's direction. She maintained her composure for a moment, but I was pretty sure I saw steam erupt from her ears as the foot-stamping episode began. Then her high-pitched voice rang out.

"Mark *told* me I could sing my song! The whole song, every word! Why are you cutting it?" She had morphed from adorable child star to demon-possessed thriller material. She drew closer to Tia, waving her hands and shouting all sorts of obscenities. Even the prettiest of blonde curls couldn't mask this sort of ugliness. To her credit, Tia took a giant step backward and refused to join in the chaos.

Then Bianca dove in again, speaking more forcefully to Tia. "We've said all we have to say on the matter. And just so you know, Candy and I will be leaving at three fifteen today. Mark already approved it. She has an audition for a movie at four o'clock, and we're going to be there one way or another."

"Ms. Jacobs, you know perfectly well that won't happen," Tia countered. "We won't even get to her scene until three thirty at the earliest. You saw today's production schedule."

"Maybe I didn't make myself clear," Bianca huffed. "Candy has an audition and she can't miss it. This is the opportunity of a lifetime."

"She's only eight years old and she's already got a prominent role on one of the top-rated sitcoms in America. I would think that would be opportunity enough." Tia stared her down. "I won't be adjusting the schedule."

The tips of Bianca's ears turned bright red, and before long her clenched jaw became evident. Goodness. I had a feeling she might blow like a top. Thankfully she turned away from Tia and headed to the side of the room where Candy had settled, a pout on her face. Seconds later, the child's piercing wail filled the room.

"But I want to audition for the movie! It's not fair. She's such a—" A repulsive word escaped the child's lips, and everyone in the studio turned—in slow motion, no less—to see what might happen next. Candy stamped her foot, not just once, but twice. "I. Am. Going. To. The. Audition." She marched in Tia's direction again and began to scream bloody murder.

The rest of the cast members looked on, mortified.

I turned back to Scott but didn't see him. Ah. He'd already headed in Candy's direction. Within minutes, he had her calmed down. Amazing, the power he had over even the unruliest of people. If this acting thing didn't work out for him, maybe he could seek out work as an exorcist.

Rex walked up to Bianca, his voice unusually tremulous. "Ms. Jacobs, I would like a word with you in my office."

"Whatever you have to say can be said here," she said.

"Fine. Let it be understood that you will never again speak to Ms. Morales in the way I just witnessed. And if you have a problem with anything related to your daughter's role in this show, please come to me, not her."

"Now, why would I come to you?" Bianca looked down her nose at him. "No one even knows why you're here. Mark told me himself that you should have retired years ago." She rambled on, but I didn't hear another word. I was still trying to recover from the shock of what she'd just said. Talk about nervy.

Rex appeared to be handling himself better than I would have. "Ms. Jacobs, I don't believe my role here at *Stars Collide* is in any way hindered by my age. Most of these folks believe my years in the business lend credibility to my job as producer. Sure, I'm older than most. But you know what? With age comes wisdom. And understanding. And that, frankly, is the only reason I'm able to stand here and accept this sort of irrational attack at all."

She crossed her arms at her chest. "Well, I never—"

"No, I don't suppose you ever paused to think about how hurtful your words could be to others," he said, giving her a stern look. "Your daughter, even. But I can and will tell you that this has to stop. If you can't get these emotional outbursts under control, you will be in breach of contract."

"I . . . I beg your pardon?" She gave him an incredulous look. "That's ridiculous."

"Actually, it's not," he said. "Read your daughter's contract. You signed it yourself. There's a morality clause, and it covers not only the child but also the parent. These constant battles you wage are detrimental to the well-being of the other children. And frankly, they're embarrassing, not just for those of us who produce the show, but for you as well. It's a shame you don't see that."

She grew quiet, but I could see her hands shaking. Why in the world did she have to get so worked up? Didn't she realize how awkward this was?

Grandma Lenora chose this moment to enter the room, wearing a brilliant purple gown.

Rex took one look at her and let out a whistle. "Hello, gorgeous!" he said, extending his hand.

"Oh, Rex, you got it right!" She batted her eyelashes . . . so hard they almost came loose.

"Barbra Streisand. *Funny Girl.* 1968." He nodded. "Same year you got your star on the Walk of Fame."

Grandma's face turned crimson. "Your memory is incredible."

"My memories are . . ." He paused, his eyes taking on a faraway look, then ran his hand over his balding scalp. "Anyway, you look lovely."

Grandma looked around the room, clucking her tongue as she saw Bianca with a feisty expression on her face. "I don't know what all of the fussing and fighting is about anyway," she called out. "What's wrong with you people? This is a joyous day! My beautiful granddaughter is getting married . . . and you are all invited!" She dove into a lengthy description of the reception she planned to host in the gardens of Worth Manor, and before long even Bianca was completely silent.

One of the little boys came up to me and tugged on my sleeve. I looked down.

"Yes, Toby?"

"Kat, you and Mr. Scott are really getting married?"

I groaned. "It's a long story, honey. Just don't believe every-thing you hear, okay?"

"O-okay." Looking more confused, he sprinted off to join his friends.

I could sense the eyes of everyone on the set on me, so the time felt right to head to my dressing room. Scott caught up with me in the hallway.

"Kat, slow down."

"I can't."

"Sure you can."

"Nope. Can't."

"Kat, it's going to be okay."

I turned to face him, shaking my head. "I don't see how." Leaning back against the wall, I closed my eyes, deep in thought. A couple of minutes went by, and I said nothing.

"What are you thinking about?" Scott asked finally.

"How I'm going to decorate my hut." I opened one eye.

"Your hut?"

Both eyes popped open. "When I get to the Amazon, I'm going to have to figure out how to decorate my hut. I don't think I can transport my stuff from home. I'll never get half of it through customs. So I'll have to start from scratch. Do you think they have a Container Store down there? Maybe an IKEA?"

"Kat, you're not going anywhere."

"I have no choice. How can I stay here and face everyone? There's no way to fix this, Scott, and it's only going to get worse. Before you know it, Grandma will spend thousands of dollars fixing up the house for the reception. She'll buy roses for nonexistent flower girls and have invitations printed for a ceremony that's not real. And there's not a thing in the world I can do about it." I paused, my thoughts shifting. "Do you think I can get Wi-Fi in the rain forest?"

"Maybe you're not the one who needs a vacation," Scott said. "Did you ever think of that? Maybe your grandmother needs to get away for a while until all of this simmers down. We can send her on a vacation until the scene is filmed. When she comes back, all will be forgotten."

"That sounds good in theory," I said. "But she can't possibly travel alone. No telling where she would end up."

"True." He laughed. "Though it would be kind of funny to see her land someplace in the Sahara wearing one of those sparkling dresses. Might give a whole new meaning to the word *mirage*."

Finally I found something to laugh about.

"It's going to be okay, Kat," Scott whispered, leaning so close it sent delightful shivers down my spine. "Athena is right. God is a great scriptwriter, better than any we know. He's got this one figured out and he knows what's coming next, even if we don't."

I shrugged. "Wish I could see the upcoming scenes. My guess is they're going to be pretty unbelievable."

Athena stopped by at just that moment. "Oh, you're wanting to see the upcoming scenes? No problem. We're already working on your wedding scene. I know it's not going to be filmed for a few weeks yet, but Rex wanted us to get a running start on it."

I realized she'd misunderstood me, but I never got the chance to say so.

"Why are you working on it so soon?" Scott asked.

Athena lowered her voice. "Rex is nervous because there's talk of another writers' strike. Didn't you guys know about that?"

"No way." I shook my head. "Talk about lousy timing."

"No kidding. But if the writers go on strike, we'll have to join them." She released an exaggerated breath. "I'm not saying I agree with it, Kat. But that's how the cookie crumbles."

"Stop. You're making me hungry." I reached into my purse and came out with a Snickers bar, which I shoveled down in short order. Athena and Scott both watched me, clearly mesmerized with my speed. Only when I reached for a second did Athena stop me.

"Kat, don't. You're not going to fit into your wedding dress."

I groaned then pressed the still-wrapped candy bar back into my purse. "Who cares? I could gain a hundred pounds and it still wouldn't change a thing. Jack would just be marrying a chubbier version of Angie."

"Still. The people in wardrobe would kill you." Athena chuckled and grabbed my hand. "Want to see what we have so far? I think you'll be tickled by it."

"Sure. Why not." I gave Scott a woeful look as he headed off toward the men's dressing room, then I followed Athena to her office, where three of the other writers sat congregated in the middle of the room, brainstorming.

"It's going to be hysterical," Athena said, pointing to the storyboard. "Angie is going to be coming up the aisle and trip over something on her way to meet Jack."

"Of course she will."

"We haven't decided what she should trip over yet," she explained. "That's up for debate."

"Flower girl basket," one writer threw in.

"Her veil," another countered. "It can be one of those really long ones. Maybe it will get tangled in a candelabra or something. Your grandmother's been helping us come up with some of this stuff, by the way."

"Of course she has." *Only, she won't remember it to-morrow.*

Athena shook her head. "Anyway, Jack is going to catch Angie before she hits the floor. It will be so romantic."

"Of course it will."

"Great opportunity for a close-up," a writer named Bob said. "Maybe when the camera pans in close, one of your fake eyelashes could fall off and get stuck on your cheek."

"Lovely." I sighed. "Just the way I always dreamed my wedding would be."

"Oh, and your grandmother came up with a great line for when Jack catches Angie," one of the other writers threw in. "He's gonna say, 'Here's looking at you, kid.'"

"Humphrey Bogart. *Casablanca*. 1942." I paused. "But I suppose that's somewhat irrelevant at the moment."

Athena continued on as if she hadn't heard a word I'd said. "Anyway, Jack catches Angie and the ceremony goes forward and you both live happily ever after. I mean, Jack and Angie will live happily ever after." She clasped her hands together, as if that solved the whole thing.

"In a hut in the Amazon," I threw in for good measure. When everyone turned my way, I shrugged. "Now you see why I'm not a writer. That's the best I can come up with. Angie runs away from the wedding and lives in a makeshift hut in the rain forest. With Wi-Fi."

"That's not half bad," Athena said. "Maybe we can use that in the episode before the wedding. Angie and Jack can have a fight over something trivial. Angie can run away and he comes after her. Maybe we could do a boat scene, where he's traveling down the Amazon in search of you . . . in his imagination, anyway." She looked at me with a grin. "I like this rain forest idea, Kat. Let me see what I can do with it. It wouldn't be a real rain forest, of course. Just something that

142

represents running away from your troubles. How would that be? Might be a nice break from the comedy to have Angie deal with some internal turmoil before the wedding. I'll run that idea by Rex, anyway."

I groaned, my brain now in a fog. Dealing with inner turmoil was exactly what I'd be doing. "Great," I said, turning toward the door. "Just leave me to wallow in the swamp till then."

They all had a good laugh at that one.

"Great line. Angie can say that as she's leaving the room," Athena added. "You know what I always say—everything's funnier on the out."

"Huh?" I gave her a curious look.

"You know, Kat. Everything is funnier as the character is leaving the room . . . or leaving the scene. That's standard in comedy writing. It's a great technique to leave 'em laughing."

I decided to test that theory. After taking a few final steps toward the door, I turned back and delivered my closing line: "If anyone needs me, I'll be in my hammock, swatting mosquitoes."

"Good try, Kat," Athena called out. "But to be honest, that wasn't really very funny."

"Oh, I don't know," said Paul, one of the other writers. "We might be able to use it." He dove into a detailed explanation of the scene they now planned to write about my visit to the Amazon, but I didn't really hear all of it. No, my mind was coiled around the obvious dilemma I now faced. Angie and Jack would live happily ever after, sure, but what about Kat and Scott? Would we survive this maddening turn of events, or would the paparazzi ruin any chance we had for a true romance?

Only one way to know for sure. I'd have to walk this road one day at a time. One prayer at a time. And I'd start . . . right now.

11

Dancing with the Stars

Later that evening, about an hour after Grandma and I arrived home from the studio, Rex called to say he was stopping by the house with an updated copy of this week's script, one that included an inserted scene—a tiff between Jack and Angie. His willingness to bring it by the house felt a little suspicious to me. For one thing, Athena could have emailed it. For another, Rex had been acting more than a little odd lately.

From the minute Grandma Lenora found out Rex was on his way, she went into frantic mode. I'd never seen this side of her before, and it threw me. She went up to her room not just once but three times to change dresses, finally settling on a soft pink calf-length number I'd never seen before. Unlike most of her other ensembles, this one didn't have a lot of glitz or glam to it. In fact, its simplicity startled me. Man. Was the plot ever thickening, or what?

Scott called a short time before Rex's expected arrival and I filled him in on the latest.

"I think I've got this figured out," he said after hearing the details. "They didn't just know each other back then. They didn't just have a little fling either. They were an item. And my gut tells me they still have strong feelings for each other. I see it all over Rex's face when he looks at her."

"I think you're right. Might do a little snooping tonight on the internet to see if I can locate some clues. Maybe an old newspaper article about the two of them . . . or something. Want to help me?"

"Sure." He laughed. "Don't you find this funny, Kat? Here we are, hoping we'll find some newsworthy gossip about your grandmother and Rex at the very same time we're trying to avoid the paparazzi. Sort of ironic. We're leaning on the very media we're trying to avoid. I guess that would make us hypocrites."

"Wow. Never really thought about that."

"Maybe someday someone will be looking on the inter-net—or whatever form of communication they have in the future—for clues about us."

"What would they discover?" I asked.

"Hmm." His pause was followed by a laugh. "They would assume we liked to eat at IHOP and that I was too cheap to buy you a real ring."

The laughter that followed felt really good. We ended the call on a high note and then I flew into gear, ready to do a little sleuthing. After all, Rex would arrive shortly.

Five minutes later, I pushed the button to let him in the gate. Grandma entered the great room looking pale and a little shaky as she heard the buzzer. "Is that . . . is that him?"

"Yes." I paused to take in her expression. "Gran, are you ill?"

"Hmm? Oh, well, no." She shook her head. "Maybe a bit headachy. I'll go lie down. Please give Rex my apologies. I'll see him tomorrow at the studio." She turned to head toward the hallway, but I caught her by the arm and gently led her back to the front door.

"Oh no you don't. You're coming with me. No running."

The mist of tears that covered her lashes caught me off guard. Yes, I was truly seeing a completely different side of my grandmother today. *Pull out the magnifying glass, Sherlock. There are clues all over the manor.*

When the bell rang, Grandma gave herself another quick glance in the hallway mirror, mumbling something about how that was the best she could do under the circumstances. I encouraged her to be the one to open the door, which she did, albeit hesitantly. Standing back in the shadows, I prepared myself to watch the scene progress, wondering just how the Lord would write it.

Rex entered with something behind his back. As he pulled out a bouquet of tiny pink sweetheart roses, my breath caught in my throat. For a moment no one said a word. I looked back and forth between the man with the bouquet and the woman whose trembling hands he eventually placed it into.

"A rose for a rose," he whispered.

Okay, so the line was a little hokey. And positively outdated. But I still found it incredibly sweet. And who knew Rex could be such a charmer?

Grandma clutched the bundle of pink roses to her chest, her eyes filling with tears. "Oh." She glanced his way, then back down at the flowers. "Oh my." She took them and disappeared into another room, saying they needed to go in water right away. For whatever reason, she never reappeared. I offered Rex a spot on the sofa, wondering if she'd ditched us for good.

146

"Sorry about that," I said. "I'm not sure what to say in her defense."

"You don't need to say anything, Kat." A wistful look came over him. It pricked my heart and raised a multitude of questions.

"Rex, can I talk to you about . . . well, about something of a personal nature?"

"Sure." He looked toward the door where Grandma had disappeared, and I realized he probably wouldn't hear a word I said. No, his thoughts were elsewhere, from the look of things.

I fumbled around for a few seconds, trying to figure out the best way to begin. Just diving in seemed the best option. "I know you said you knew my grandmother when you were young, and that you worked together."

"Yes." He shifted positions a bit and looked my way.

"It's obvious you care about her, either as a friend or . . ." I let my words hang in the air. As Rex's gaze shifted to the sofa, I knew I had him. If the moisture in his eyes didn't convince me, nothing would. "Anyway, something else is going on here, and I have a feeling it's relevant to her current situation. Can you help me sort this out?"

He gave me a pensive look. "Kat, why are you asking me all of these questions? Has Lenora said something to you?"

"No." But my antennae went straight up in the air at his question. "I'm just running with a hunch here, Rex. Lately she seems to be stuck in the past, and I don't just mean the evening gowns and the cars. I'm concerned. There's got to be some reason she's so fixated on her life as a young star."

He reached for a hankie and began to dab at the back of his neck. "Is it warm in here?"

"Not at all." But it *had* warmed up in here, hadn't it? Yes, from the look on the man's face, he was now sitting directly in the hot seat. Only, he wasn't sitting for long. Rex rose and began to pace the room, pausing to look at one of the photos on the wall. Ironically, it happened to be a photo of Grandma as a young woman, posing in front of her car. Wearing . . . Hmm. I'd never noticed it before, but she was wearing a soft pink dress. And holding a bouquet of sweetheart roses.

"She still drives that '57 Cadillac." I spoke over the catch in my throat. "And her favorite song is 'Secret Love' by Doris Day."

His gaze remained fixed on the wall. "Right."

I rose and joined him. Looking toward the door, I made sure Grandma hadn't returned before voicing my thoughts. "Rex, this is more than just me trying to figure out if my grandmother has a crush on you. Or vice versa. Whatever happened—or didn't happen—between the two of you back then isn't really what I'm trying to get at."

His quirked brow clued me in to the fact that he didn't quite believe me.

"Well, maybe I am, but there's more too. I'm genuinely worried about her mental stability. She's not herself lately. Her memory isn't what it used to be. Sometimes she's Grandma Lenora, and other times . . ." A lump rose in my throat, making it impossible to continue.

"I know." Rex faced me and, for the first time, looked me directly in the eye. "I've been watching. And I've been worried too."

I lowered my voice. "Can you answer the question about why she seems so stuck in the past?"

His eyes filled with tears. "A lot of people with impaired memory issues gravitate back to the past. I've seen it many times. They can't remember what they had for lunch, but every vivid detail from an event fifty years prior is right there within their grasp."

"Yes, but there's more to it. I can sense it. Here." I pointed to my heart.

Rex flinched and his jaw grew tight. When he did speak, his words were strained. "Kat, it really might be better if you talked to Lenora about this yourself. I don't want to say too much. It's not my place."

I looked him straight in the eye. "But I've got to believe there are some clues from her past to help me figure out her present. And her future."

"We were friends." He sat on the edge of the desk. "Not that her agent wanted me hanging around. I was just a kid with aspirations of making it big in the movies. She was already a star. We worked together on a couple of shows. I worked as a key grip mostly, or played bit parts when they needed someone to fill in. Lenora was . . ." His face took on a wistful look. "Well, she was a true star in every sense of the word. Some of those dresses she wears were the same ones she wore back then. Only, back then all of the women dressed like that."

"Did you have a crush on her, Rex?" I hoped to tease the information out of him with my question, but he didn't want to play along.

He looked at the door. "I appreciate your concern for your grandmother, Kat, but I really think you need to talk to her. If there's anything to be told, she needs to be the one to tell it, not me. Okay?"

"O-okay." Confusion overwhelmed me, but I did my best to stay calm. "But promise me this, Rex. If she ever needs you, you'll be there for her?"

He paused before whispering, "I always have been. Whether she wanted me there or not." He headed to the sofa, where he sat with a dazed expression.

Well, if those words didn't convince me we had a real-life drama unraveling before my very eyes, nothing would.

At that moment the grandfather clock in the front hall-way let out several loud gongs. Grandma made her entrance on the seventh and final gong, holding a tray of sandwiches and tea. She looked at Rex with a winsome smile, suddenly her old self again. "Only seven gongs! At least I'm not going to turn into a pumpkin. No point in leaving the ball early!"

Maybe not. But I had a feeling Lenora Worth had slipped away from him once before at the midnight hour. In the '50s, perhaps? And whether either of them realized it, Rex Henderson still held her glass slipper firmly in his grasp.

Grandma put the tray of sandwiches down and settled onto the sofa beside Rex, as calm as a kitten. Even a little flirtatious. He seemed to spring to life too as she jabbered on and on about a movie she'd filmed years ago. The two of them dove into an easy conversation, and before long my questions about Grandma's past were, well, a thing of the past.

Before long, Grandma was telling Rex about the upcoming fund-raiser. "I just love events like the one the kids are planning," she said. "They remind me of the variety shows from days gone by."

"Like *The Carol Burnett Show*?" Rex quipped. "Or Flip Wilson?"

"Oh, and *The Dean Martin Variety Show*." She grinned. "I was a guest in the early '70s."

"You were?" I looked at her, more than a little surprised. "How did I not know that?"

"It's true," Rex said. "I remember watching it. You did a great dance number with him, Lenora."

"It started out as a funny little comedy routine. He pretended to be in love with me." Her face lit up. "Hey, maybe I could revive that bit for the fund-raiser. But I'd need someone to play Dino's part."

150

"I might know someone who would be willing to do that." Rex smiled. "If you would allow me the privilege."

"Oh my." Grandma's face flushed. "Would you really?"

"I would be honored." He reached for her hand and gave it a squeeze. "For you, I would even shuffle off to Buffalo."

"Ruby Keeler shuffled off to Buffalo in *42nd Street*." Grandma grinned. "But don't worry. I don't expect you to dance, Rex. That would mean I'd have to do the same, and my dancing days are behind me."

"Oh no they're not." He sprang to his feet and swept her into his arms, and the two began to trip the light fantastic . . . all the way across the great room and out into the foyer, where I heard my grandmother's giggles.

Heavens. Could things get any more bizarre?

Rex stayed longer than I'd anticipated. When he finally left at ten thirty, I'd already excused myself to my room. Giving them some privacy felt right. I did peek out of the window as his BMW pulled out of the driveway, and I listened for Grandma to come up the stairs. She passed by my room, pausing in the door with a girlish grin on her face.

"He's a handsome boy, isn't he, KK?"

I couldn't think of a proper response, so I just nodded.

"And talk about talented," she added with a doe-eyed look. "That Rex is really going places." Creases now formed between her brows, and she crossed her arms at her chest. "They'll see. One day. They'll all see." A lone tear slipped down her cheek, and she whispered the words, "A heart can be broken, but it will keep beating just the same."

I knew the source, for sure. Jessica Tandy had spoken that line in *Fried Green Tomatoes*. But I wouldn't dare mention it now. No, my grandmother meant those words with every fiber of her being. Her heart had been broken, and yet she'd somehow kept going. Life had moved forward in spite of her pain. If only I could figure out what had happened. Then this would all make sense.

Her mood shifted abruptly. With a broad smile, she said, "You know, sweet girl, our conversation about working with Dean Martin reminded me just how much I miss him."

I managed one word. "Aw."

"Let's invite Dino for dinner one night soon, KK." She chuckled. "That sounds funny. Dino for dinner. Sounds like he's on the menu."

Finally. Something I could laugh at to release this tension.

"Do you think he's free?" she asked. "I know he's got such a busy schedule, recording and all. And you know, he's doing movies now too. I heard he's got a great one coming out with Jerry Lewis."

I paused, unsure of how to respond. Dino was, after all, currently crooning "That's Amore" from a distant star. Finally an idea occurred to me. "Tell you what. I'll call Scott and see if his parents can come too. How would that be?"

"Scott? Who's Scott?"

I swallowed hard and tried to think of the best response to avoid further confusion. Thankfully I didn't have to. Grandma blew me a kiss and headed off to her bedroom.

I reached for my laptop, determined to get to the bottom of this. Typing in her name alongside Rex's, I came up with three or four sites. Unfortunately, they were just movie credits from a film they'd worked on together. In 1957.

Hmm. I stared at the title, realizing this was a movie I knew quite well. One she watched regularly. *It Had to Be You*. Lenora Worth's first starring role. And apparently Rex had worked as a key grip. Interesting.

A *ding* alerted me to the fact that an instant message had come through. I smiled as I read Scott's words: "Find anything yet?"

"Yes. They worked together on a movie in '57," I typed.

"Saw that. Great reviews, by the way. And she was nominated for a couple of awards for her performance."

"They were in love," I typed.

"Yes, they were," he responded. "And they still are."

"Very in love. Makes me wonder if she's sorry . . ." I started to type, "that she married my grandfather," but stopped short. My heart twisted as thoughts of him flooded over me. How did he fit into this picture? Had my grandmother broken Rex's heart by falling for my grandfather, perhaps? Or did she—my heart jumped to my throat as I thought about this—did she marry one man, secretly loving another?

The thought caused almost physical pain. Surely not. Lenora Worth was not the type to hurt people. That much I knew to be true. And no amount of memory loss could change it.

Another *ding* told me Scott had continued instant messaging without me.

"You know what they say, Kat," he typed. "Love means never having to say you're sorry."

I couldn't help myself. I really couldn't. I punched in the words, "Ali MacGraw. *Love Story*. 1970."

"Actually, Ryan O'Neal's character said it too," Scott responded. "At the end of the movie. But I'm not sure I agree, regardless."

"Oh?" I typed.

"Admitting you're sorry—and that you've made mistakes—is critical to the survival of a relationship, especially when you're in love."

I realized just how right he was.

"And by the way," he typed, "there is one little thing I'm sorry for."

"Oh, what's that?" I asked.

"Pick up your phone and I'll tell you."

Seconds later, my cell phone rang. I grabbed it with a quick "Hello?"

"I'm sorry that I waited so long to tell you this, Kat."

His words caught me off guard and my heart rate skipped to double time. "Tell me what?"

I could hear the smile in his voice as he whispered, "I love you."

Now my breath caught in my throat. He'd delivered the line I'd only dreamed of hearing. Talk about great timing. Athena and the other writers would have given their stamp of approval, no doubt.

I wanted to respond in some way, but my tongue appeared to be stuck to the roof of my mouth. I half expected him to deliver the rest of Jack's lines, listing all of the reasons why he loved Angie, but quickly put that thought out of my mind. This was very real. Not scripted.

"I couldn't tell you over an instant message," he said. "And I knew I couldn't sleep until I said the words. I love you, Kat. I've loved you for a long time now. And I'm not sorry about it."

"Me either," I whispered. "Because . . . love means never having to say you're sorry."

He laughed. "Okay, you got me. But now that I've told you how I feel, I'm just wondering if you, well . . ." His words drifted off.

I decided to put the boy out of his misery. "Scott, I've loved you for over two years. I've been upside-down, inside-out, crazy-for-you, gonna-lose-my-mind-if-I-can't-say-it in love." A giggle threatened to erupt but I squelched it. No nerves here. Not with so much left to say. "And I'm not sorry. I'm not sorry God brought you to me. I'm not sorry our paths crossed the way they did. And I'm not sorry that you told me this tonight of all nights. I really needed to hear it."

"Well, I'm a little sorry that I gave you this information over the phone," he said. "Because you have no idea how much I want to kiss you right now."

"Me too." Now the nervous chuckle escaped. "You'll just have to wait till tomorrow."

"When?" he asked. "And how? We'll be in front of all of those people at the studio."

"They already think we're engaged, anyway," I said. "Why not let them know we're in love?"

"This whole relationship is happening backward, isn't it?" he asked. "That's not a complaint, by the way. I'm intrigued by what the Lord is doing here. Not sure I would've written the script this way, but I totally trust him."

"Me too."

A delicious silence grew up between us, and I leaned back against the pillows, looking once again at the ring on my bedside table. Though I'd admitted it to no one else—even Scott—I'd carried that ring with me every day since the proposal scene. I reached for it now and slipped it on, giving it a closer look. The goofy thing might be fake, but there was nothing fake about the way it made me feel when I wore it.

Immediately a verse ran through my head. *I am my beloved's, and my beloved is mine.* Clearly the Lord was at work here, moving us into a deeper relationship, both with each other and with him.

"I guess I'd better let you go," Scott said at last. "I'll be praying about the situation with your grandmother and Rex. We can trust God with that too, by the way."

"Yeah, I know."

Another tender "I love you" came my way before Scott ended the call. I rolled over on the bed and plunked the phone on the bedside table, feeling as giddy as a girl who'd just been asked to the prom. Sweet thoughts of "I love you" rolled through my brain over and over. I found myself in a dream-like state, a place of sweet imaginings. Before long, my eyes grew heavy, and I dozed off.

Some time later, I awakened, my brain in a fog. Had I really fallen asleep without turning out the light? I heard the television from down the hallway but couldn't quite make out the words.

Rising from the bed, I made my way to Grandma Lenora's room. I found her curled up in her gorgeous four-poster bed, still fully dressed in her soft pink gown, the bouquet of sweet-heart roses clutched in her fist. In the distance, the DVD player rolled the credits for *It Had to Be You*. I watched, transfixed, as her name crossed the screen, and several seconds later Rex's name rolled by as well. Somehow, seeing their names in print solidified my suspicions about their relationship years ago.

Yes, they had certainly loved each other at some point in the past.

And yes, sometimes love really *did* mean having to say you were sorry.

12

Nip/Tuck

The next morning, I awoke to my grandmother's frantic words. "KK, wake up." She tugged on the covers, and I scrambled to come out of my sleepy fog.

"W-what?" I glanced her way, stunned to find her still wearing the pink dress from the night before. It took a second for my thoughts to gather. Was it morning? A glance in the direction of my bedroom window answered that question. Sunlight peeked in through the tiny split between the two curtains. Had I overslept or something?

"You need to get up, KK." She sat on my bed and patted my leg through the covers. "I've made a list and checked it twice. We've got a very full day ahead of us and we need to get to work. Up and at 'em."

A yawn erupted and I stretched. "We don't have to be at the studio till ten this morning, Grandma. Remember? The tech guys are setting the lights for the new set."

"I know, I know. But I've made plans for us, so we've got to get going. We're shopping for the wedding."

"What?" Propping myself up in the bed, I tried not to let my frustration show.

"We'll start at the bridal boutique and then we'll head to the print shop to look at invitations. From there I want to stop at Dr. Rey's office to ask him some questions."

"Wait. Dr. Rey? The plastic surgeon?"

"Yes. I'm thinking of having a little work done before your wedding."

Surely she jested. "Oh, please don't do that, Grandma."

"Why not? A little Botox never hurt anyone. When they put me in the coffin I'll be loaded with preservatives anyway. So what does it matter if I add a few more?"

"It matters to me." How could I explain? I wanted her to look like, well, like her. So many well-known people had gone under the knife only to come out looking like their own evil twin. Sweet Lenora Worth needed to stay just as she was. Beautiful. Soft. Lovely. Elegant. And if I had anything to do with it, she would.

Grandma rose from the edge of my bed and went to the window, where she pulled back the curtains. I squinted at the full burst of sunlight now streaming through.

"Take a good look at this wrinkled old face of mine in the sunlight, honey," she said. "Then you'll know why I've got my heart set on this. We'll be paying good money for your wedding photographer and we need the best possible shots—of you, Jack, me . . . everyone. How is that possible when I'm so wrinkled? Every picture of me will look like . . . me."

"Well, I happen to love you. Every single wrinkle. And it will break my heart if you get rid of them. They're a part of you."

She groaned. "That's easy to say when you're young and

have great skin. Just wait till you're in your midseventies and the skin that used to be on your face is now around your ankles."

"Grandma, stop. That's just silly."

"Still, there are parts of me that are not where they used to be." She sighed. "I've always talked about traveling south, but I wasn't referring to my body parts."

I suppressed a chuckle.

"I saw this new surgery on the Discovery Health Channel the other night," she said. "It's called a whole body lift."

I nodded. "Yeah, I think I've seen that. It's for people who've lost a significant amount of weight, right?"

"Well, yes, but I've been thinking it will work on elderly people too. We have a lot of excess skin."

"Yes, but it sounds painful." I gave her as stern a look as I could muster. "Surely you're not thinking about it. Seriously?"

Grandma gave me a knowing look. "Try me."

"Too extreme." I yawned and stretched again. "And it's just plain silly. I mean, I could understand if you wanted a day at the spa, or maybe a facial. But a whole body lift? No way."

"I've given this a lot of thought, KK. I figure Dr. Rey can start at the top of my head and pull up all of my skin at once. Just one big nip/tuck under the hairline at the tippy-top of my head, and suddenly my hips and breasts are in the same place they used to be when I was young."

I couldn't help the laughter that erupted. "Grandma, you're a hoot."

"I'm just saying. This soft, supple skin is nice and all, but I'm carrying far too much of it. I could easily do without a bit. Plastic surgery is a good option."

"I'm not sure I agree. Promise me you'll pray about it."

"Okay." She shook her head. "I suppose I should. Though

I'm sure even the Lord himself would agree that wearing your chin around your kneecaps is cumbersome at times."

Good grief. "One more thing, Grandma. Promise me you won't let them inject collagen in your lips. That's just gross."

"Collagen? In my lips?" She looked stunned. "Why would I do that?"

"To make them look pouty. It's the trend."

"Heavens, no." She began to fan herself. "If I want to look pouty, I'll just think about the amount of money I have to pay my agent every year!" She let out a laugh. "Harvey Klink is one rich man, thanks to the commissions he's making off of me."

I sucked in a deep breath and counted to three. No point in reminding her that Harvey Klink was now agenting from cloud number nine. So many of the people Grandma remembered with such fondness had already transitioned from this life to the next. But how could I relay that information without depressing her or creating some sort of upset?

"I have an idea, Grandma," I said, ready to offer a distraction. "Let's put on our Elly May bathing suits and swim in the cement pond instead of shopping. Doesn't that sound like fun? We can shop for the wedding another day."

"Shop for the wedding?" A look of complete confusion registered on her face. "Who's going shopping for a wedding?"

More counting under my breath helped bring my emotions under control.

Before I could reply, Grandma looked at me with tears in her eyes. "Oh, KK, I'm so worried."

"Worried?" About what?

"Yes. I think I've lost the key to my trunk."

"Your steamer trunk?"

"Yes, the one at the foot of my bed. I've searched everywhere, but the little key is gone."

"No, Grandma," I said. "It's in the buffet downstairs. You asked me to put it there for safekeeping, remember?"

"Oh, yes." A smile lit her face. "That's right. What a relief. There's a lovely shawl in the steamer trunk that I'd like to wear to your wedding. We were talking about weddings, weren't we? I'm pretty sure we were." A look of concern seemed to pass over her in a wave.

"Y-yes."

After a brief pause, she was back to her usual cheerful self. "You know, KK, I haven't been swimming in a month of Sundays. Maybe it wouldn't hurt. I could use the exercise. Oh, and guess what? I've been thinking about having plastic surgery." Her wrinkles grew even more pronounced as she whispered, "Have I told you that already?"

Instead of responding, I somehow managed to divert her. Before long we were swimming in the cement pond, talking about Granny, Jed, Jethro Bodine, and the rest of the *Beverly Hillbillies* cast. Poor Grandma really couldn't seem to remember that she'd started the morning asking me to go shopping, so I didn't remind her of that fact. How many times had she said something only to forget it seconds later? I silently thanked the Lord that we already had a doctor visit planned for later this week . . . and not to a plastic surgeon. Though, hey, maybe it wouldn't hurt to play it up as such.

We finished our swim, then dressed to head to the studio. Though the day was getting off to a late start, I knew we had much to do. Tuesday was always our run-through day. I was also more than a little curious about the new set. A chapel for the upcoming wedding scene. If Grandma wasn't confused enough already, this new chapel should be just the thing to get her going.

As I pulled up to the studio, I noticed an unfamiliar car. Candy and her mother stood alongside it, glaring at the person inside. Interesting. By the time I'd dropped Grandma off and parked, they were in a full-out squabble. I knew it wasn't my place to listen in, but how could I help it?

I passed by, glancing at them out of the corner of my eye. The man in the car was ranting about something. Something to do with money, it sounded like. His words turned vile, and for a moment I almost joined in the conversation just long enough to take him down a notch or two. How dare he use language like that in front of a child? Who was this jerk, and what was he doing here, anyway?

My answer to that question came from the most unlikely source.

"Daddy, stop!" Candy called out. "Stop calling Mommy that name."

I turned to face her, realization setting in. Daddy? This was her father?

The man—handsome enough on the outside, but clearly ugly within—turned to her with a condescending look and said a few more words, none of them positive or kind, then turned back to his wife. Er, ex-wife. The words that followed were anything but pretty.

"You're raising her to be just like you, Bianca. Mouthy."

Okay, I couldn't really argue that point, but now I saw where some of the mother-daughter angst came from. Papa Bear apparently ate his young. And his ex.

Before long, this foul-mouthed man and Bianca were doing some serious name-calling and using Candy as a buffer between them. I made busy, standing near the studio door with my script in my hand. Surely they would think I was waiting on someone. In truth, I was. Candy. I wanted to stick around for her just in case, and that meant not budging. Ironic that I suddenly had such empathy for her.

At some point Candy had obviously had enough. She turned and ran into the building, tears streaming down her face. The weirdest sensation came over me as she bolted past me. For whatever reason, I was reminded of that stupid dream where my parents sat across from each other in silence. Even their lack of communication was less painful than this.

On the other hand, both were awful, if you were the kid stuck in the middle.

My thoughts shifted and I realized I had to do something. I needed to get to Candy—right away. I entered the studio, looking around the set. No sign of her. The next logical place to look was the children's classroom. I glanced inside and saw the kids gathered around their teacher. The perky twentysomething nodded in my direction and I offered a little wave. Toby looked my way with his toothless grin. Something about his sweet face always did my heart good. Still, no sign of Candy. Only one other place seemed logical.

I found the youngster in the bathroom, sobbing. Well, I heard her, anyway. And saw her little shoes under the door of one of the stalls.

"Honey, this is Kat. Are you okay?"

She didn't answer, but I could hear her sniffles.

"Candy, you don't have to talk to me about this if you don't want to. But I'm here if you do want to talk, okay?"

"O-okay." More crying followed, but not the dramatic, over-the-top kind I'd witnessed from her in the past. No, this was the real deal. Heartfelt tears from a brokenhearted little girl. As I listened in, I was transported back in time to my own childhood.

My introspection was interrupted by Candy's voice. "I . . . I hate him."

I didn't respond. I could tell she wasn't quite through yet. Better let her get it all out.

After a minute, she whispered, "My dad is so stupid. I hate him. And I hate my mom too."

Okay, this wasn't getting any better. I wasn't sure how to go about salvaging things, though. Candy's crying turned to full-out sobs now.

Before long Bianca came in the restroom hunting for her daughter. I could tell from the smeared mascara that she'd been crying too. Only, now she was in full-out mama mode, and not in a loving, protective way. She spoke to her daughter through the closed stall door. "Candy, come out of there right now."

"No."

"Stop acting like this. We had a deal, you and me. We're not going to let him get to us anymore. Right?"

More sobs erupted. So much for that deal.

Bianca turned to me with a sigh. "It's always like this. He doesn't come around for months at a time and then shows up at the worst possible time. And it's always the same. He needs money. Can you believe the nerve of a man who would let his eight-year-old daughter support him?"

A rhetorical question, I hope.

"Why they've even let him on the set is beyond me. I've asked them not to allow it, but who listens to me?"

Obviously not Candy, who still remained in the stall, crying.

"They say he's her father and he has a legal right to be here. Well, no one asked my opinion on that. Some father he's been. A deadbeat one, if anything."

Bianca rambled on, her anger growing in miles, not inches.

As she progressed in emotion, so did Candy, who now wailed unceasingly.

"Mom. Please. Go. Away!"

Bianca leaned down and looked at her daughter's shoes, then shook her head. "I'm giving you five minutes to get your act together and come out of there, Candace Renee. We've talked about this a thousand times. Hold your head up high and keep going. No pain, no gain."

No pain, no gain? What were we talking about here, a Jane Fonda workout video or a child's life?

As Bianca stormed out of the restroom, I drew in a couple of deep breaths, trying to stay calm. For a minute there, I couldn't figure out who made me madder—the deadbeat dad or the irrational mother. One thing was glaringly obvious, though. Candy was a victim. A little girl who had somehow ended up stuck in the middle between two parents who couldn't seem to see past themselves. And though her situation was completely different from my own, I could relate.

A rush of emotions flooded over me as images of my father crept in. The few times I'd thought about contacting him, I worried he might react like Candy's dad did today. Would I come to him only to be rejected? Ugh. A sick feeling took root as I pondered the unknown.

I will never leave you nor forsake you.

The Scripture washed over me like a flood, and I drew in a deep breath, whispering, "Thank you, Lord, for that reminder." I brushed my tears aside, remembering my mission. Candy. She needed me.

From the other side of the bathroom door, she called my name. "Kat?"

"I'm here, honey," I whispered in response. "I'm not going anywhere."

"I hate them, Kat," she whispered back. "I really do."

I wanted to say, "I don't blame you," but stopped short. No point in adding fuel to the fire.

"Why doesn't my daddy love me?" she whispered. "Is it my fault?"

Pushing back the lump in my throat, I tried to respond. However, I never got the chance. The dam broke and the flood hit. Candy began to pour out her story, one ugly detail after another. As I listened, my heart began to beat in sync with hers. I got it. All of her angst. The temper. The spoiled nature. All of it pointed directly to a lack of relationship with her father and a strained relationship with her mother.

"Mom says he only wants to see me because I'm famous and I make a lot of money. She's scared he wants to take it."

"He can't do that." Could he? I wasn't quite sure. I knew there were laws to protect children in the industry, but I wasn't up on them.

"This is so stupid," Candy whispered.

Ugh. How awful to be eight years old and this depressed. What this child needed, more than anything else, was for someone to point her to the love of her real Father, the one who would never abandon her on any level. And I would do just that.

Ashamed that I'd never seen her as anything other than a spoiled child, I began to restrategize, to think of ways I could pour into her life. And I might just have to confront a few demons of my own. This deadbeat dad thing was a tough one, even for us big girls.

After a few minutes, her cries dissipated and she began to blow her nose. I remained silent and still. If she wanted to talk, I would talk. If not, I would be here for her when she came out of that stall.

Minutes later, the door eased open. Her poor, swollen eyes broke my heart. Instead of the usual brusque demeanor, she looked like a wilted flower. Like someone had drained every ounce of energy out of her.

I reached to grab a couple of paper towels and dampened them with water from the sink. Then I knelt down in front of her and began to wipe her little face. Funny, I'd never noticed the freckles before. For a second I thought I was looking at a picture of myself from elementary school.

In that moment I was transported to a time years ago in my grandmother's bedroom. I'd been crying. She'd reached for a cloth hankie and dried my tears, then reached into her trunk—the one at the foot of her bed—and came out with a wonderful, soft hairbrush, which she began to run through my hair. Her motions had calmed me.

I continued to wipe Candy's face until all of the tears were gone. She looked stunned at my gesture but didn't stop me. In fact, she didn't do much of anything. Just stood there sniffling.

After wiping her eyes, I decided more therapy was in order. Drawing a deep breath, I reached for my purse and came out with my hairbrush. I began to run it through her hair, using careful, gentle strokes. The movements were steady, repetitive. Hopefully she would find them reassuring as well. Closing my eyes, I saw myself in her place once again, my grandmother seated on the edge of that trunk, me standing directly in front of her. Oh, how the Lord had used her that day. Her actions had spoken far louder than any words ever could.

"You know, you have the prettiest hair, Candy," I said at last.

"I—I do?"

"Well, sure." I dove into a soothing conversation about her many attributes, careful not to go too far. Flattery wasn't the goal. Making her feel better was. And letting her know that I was here, willing to touch, willing to soothe, seemed critical to the equation.

After a few moments, I grew silent. The two of us now stood side by side, staring in the mirror. The double image caused my heart to twist. We were one and the same, Candy and me. Only, I'd never really realized it until today.

The beautiful little girl spoke to my reflection. "Did he leave because of me?"

Her words caught me off guard, and the catch in my throat nearly prevented me from responding. Oh, how many times I'd asked the same question as a little girl. How many times I'd wished someone had just said, "Honey, this has nothing to do with you. Grown-ups sometimes do stupid things and it's not your fault."

And so I said those very words to her now.

She looked stunned but didn't respond. Neither did she turn around to face me. Instead she continued to stare at our double reflection in the mirror.

"Do . . . do you think I'm pretty, Kat?" she asked finally.

Some people might not make the connection between her father leaving and her perceived ugliness, but I got it. In a strange and twisted way, I got it. Those of us who saw ourselves as fatally flawed often wondered if we could change things by working on our outward appearance. Maybe in doing so, we could salvage the relationship. Or maybe if we'd just been prettier, that person wouldn't have left in the first place.

"Candy, you're a beautiful little girl," I said. "But can I tell you a secret?"

Curiosity was etched on her face. "A secret?"

"Yes." I nodded and continued to look at her reflection. "You're a beautiful girl, but even if you weren't, God would still love you. He would still think you were gorgeous because he created you."

She turned and looked at me. "Really?"

"Yes, really." I forged ahead, telling her that she was created in the image of God and that he didn't make mistakes. "He won't ever leave you, honey," I whispered.

She turned to me, tears tumbling. "Really?"

"Really."

Turning back, she nodded, and continued to stare at her reflection.

I could certainly relate to her tears. After all, it had taken me years to believe that God wouldn't abandon me like my father had.

As I continued to share my heart, I gently ran the brush through her hair, hoping she would see it as a sign of tenderness and caring. Before long, she calmed down and we both fell into a peaceful silence. My prayers, though silent, were some of the strongest of my life.

A few seconds later, Bianca appeared again, this time with Athena and Grandma trailing her.

"We were getting worried about you two," Athena said, looking back and forth between Candy and me. "Everything okay?"

"Better." I nodded and gave them what I hoped would be a reassuring look.

Candy looked at her mother and shrugged.

"Let's get you into the dressing room, Candace," Bianca said. She took her daughter by the arm and pulled her out into the hallway. I couldn't help but notice the youngster glance back at me with a wistful look on her face. I gave her a smile and she nodded.

As soon as they disappeared from view, Athena turned to me, her brow knotted. "What was all of that about?"

"It's pretty complicated. Let's just say I saw a side of Candy that I've never seen before."

"Wow. I'm assuming you don't mean worse than usual."

"No. I actually feel sorry for her."

"Poor kid." Grandma sighed. "It always upsets me to see children caught between the parents. And that mother . . ." She shook her head.

"I know." I gazed into the mirror at my reflection, noticing how tired I suddenly looked. All of this emotion was draining me. Grandma stepped beside me, and we were now two peas in a pod.

"See what I mean, KK?" She pointed to the wrinkles around her face. "Time to have a little work done."

"But Gran . . ." I thought again of how those of us who'd faced rejection or pain often saw ourselves as physically flawed. If Grandma wanted to go on believing plastic surgery would fix whatever was really bothering her, I would not argue. Not this time, anyway. I would back away and let the Lord do his work.

To my surprise, she chose to go a different direction. Instead of complaining about her looks, she threw her hand up in dramatic fashion and said, "All right, Mr. DeMille, I'm ready for my close-up!"

I cracked up, more relieved than anything.

"Ooh, I know that one!" Athena clasped her hands together and attempted to look glamorous. Not easy in the ladies' room. "Gloria Swanson . . . *Sunset Boulevard?*"

"Yes, that's right," Grandma Lenora said as she turned away from the mirror. "1950."

"1950?" Athena frowned. "Wow. My mom wasn't even born then."

Grandma swatted her on the backside before responding. "Sassy girl. And I'll bet your mama isn't wrinkled either." She sashayed out of the bathroom, talking about the call she needed to make to the plastic surgeon. Athena followed along behind her, giving me a second glance to make sure I was coming too.

"I'll be right there," I said.

Turning away from my reflection, I was struck by something rather odd. I'd seen three faces in the mirror today—mine, Candy's, and Grandma's. And though the conversation had drifted to plastic surgery, I couldn't help but think there was a different type of surgery needed here . . . for each of us. We all needed a little nip/tuck of the heart.

But which of the three faces in the mirror needed it most? Candy, with her shattered dreams? Grandma, with her fading memories? Me, with any unresolved issues I had concerning my MIA father?

The idea that the Lord still had work to do in my heart caused a moment of reflection. We'd come so far already, he and I.

Turning back to the mirror, I stared at my freckled face. As I did, one lingering question remained: could I really lay down my insecurities and move forward in a relationship with Scott, unscathed by the pain in my own past?

Man. If only I had a copy of tomorrow's script.

13

Hart to Hart

On Saturday morning I called Scott and asked him to come by the house, offering the promise of Carolina's sweet rolls and hot coffee. He arrived in record time. I greeted him at the door with a kiss, which brought an immediate smile to his face.

"That was worth the drive."

I gave him another kiss then whispered, "That's to make up for the fact that you'll have a long drive home later. And then the drive back again to bring your parents over for dinner tonight."

Scott chuckled. "Thanks. I needed that." Then he gave me a curious look. "So what's up? Just a breakfast invitation, or do you have something up your sleeve? You sounded a little suspicious on the phone."

"Yeah, I guess I am up to something. A covert operation, if you will." I narrowed my eyes in an attempt to make myself look mysterious. Not that I really needed to pretend. I did have something up my sleeve.

He quirked a brow. "Covert operation? Intriguing. Have you been watching *CSI* again, by any chance?"

I laughed. "No. But I do need your help with something while Grandma's shopping with Carolina."

"And what would that be?"

"I want to do a little snooping while they're gone. They'll be back in less than an hour, so we've got to hurry."

"Okay, but what do you mean by snooping?" He shrugged. "Your grandmother's life is an open book. Just look at the walls and you'll find out everything you need to know about Lenora Worth." He gestured to the many photos. "And what you can't find on the walls, you'll find on the web. When you're in the public eye, it's all out there for everyone to see."

"Not always." I shook my head. "There's something else going on here, Scott. I've known for days there's more to her story, and I've got a suspicion she's hiding something."

"Hiding something?" He leaned down and whispered, "Like . . . in a safe? In the wall? Are we going to blow something up?"

"Hope not." I laughed. "But something my grandmother said triggered a memory. She keeps this trunk in her bedroom. It's one of those old steamer trunks. Probably came over from Europe in the 1700s."

"Wow. She really does hang on to things from the past."

"Well, don't be too impressed. I think she bought it at an auction when she was my age. Anyway, it sits at the foot of her bed. I tried to open it once as a kid and she came unglued."

"Probably just stuff she didn't want you to break."

"No, it's got to be more than that. A few days ago, I heard her say something about the key."

"The key?"

"Yes, she keeps it locked. But I know where the key is."
I walked over to the buffet and opened the smallest drawer.
Reaching inside, I came out with a tiny skeleton key. "Right
here."

"Ah." He pursed his lips. "And you've got your mind made
up to do a little breaking and entering?"

For a moment I paused to think about how this must look
to him. Just as quickly I released my concerns. My actions
would be taken out of love for her. Nothing more and nothing less.

"Scott, I'm worried about her. Something's not right. She's
not herself lately. It's not just the memory loss. She's actually
saying and doing things to raise red flags. It's like she can't
tell fiction from reality anymore. And I can't help but think
the answer is hidden away in that trunk. Otherwise she would
never have brought it up the other morning."

"Makes sense, I guess."

"I've been dying to open it ever since she mentioned it, but
I didn't feel like it was my place."

"And now you do?"

How could I explain this in a way that made sense? "I'm her
caregiver, Scott. And it's obvious she's struggling to maintain
her memory and possibly her sanity. If I can find any clues
whatsoever, it will be worth the embarrassment of getting
caught going through her things. I honestly think this is for
her own good."

"I understand."

In my heart, I knew he really did. He cared a great deal
about my grandmother. So did I. And together we would
figure this out.

We made our way into her room, and Scott whistled when
he saw the large four-poster canopy bed. "Wow. Looks like

something out of the Civil War era. What is that? Mosquito netting?"

"Well, I suppose you could call it that. It's really just for decoration. She said the bed came from a movie she did in the '50s."

"There was a bed scene?" Scott looked more than a little surprised.

"Not the kind you're thinking," I said. "It was just a scene of her as a young widow, grieving the loss of her husband. Very dramatic stuff. I've always said it was one of her most realistic scenes. Anyway, the doctor came to her room to give her something for the pain. Or the grief. Or whatever you call it."

"I see." He gazed at the bed. "Hey, speaking of doctors, how did her doctor visit go?"

I pursed my lips, unsure of how to respond. "I guess it went okay. He visited with Grandma then took me in another room to chat. They've upped her meds. He seems to think it will slow down the progression of the memory loss." Shaking my head, I added, "I hope he's right. She didn't even realize we were in a regular doctor's office. She thought he was a plastic surgeon."

"Funny."

"I don't know. It's getting to the point where none of this is funny anymore. I'm having trouble making light of it, though that's certainly a better option than getting depressed."

Scott pulled me close and placed a tender kiss on my forehead. "It's going to be okay, Kat," he whispered. "You don't have to walk through this by yourself. I'm here."

"Thank you." I smiled at him, feeling the weight lift. "It feels good to have someone to talk to about all of this. My grandmother is like a puzzle to me, one I have to solve while she's still with me." I stepped away from him and walked to the foot of the bed, scooting Fat Cat off of the large trunk. I removed the afghan that always sat on top, tossing it onto the bed, then stuck the key in the lock. "You ready?"

"Yes." He gazed into my eyes with such tenderness that my tears arose. "The question is, are you?"

"I think so." Turning the key in the lock, I eased the lid up. It creaked its displeasure at being moved.

"Sounds like it hasn't been opened in years," Scott observed.

"Right." With the lid fully upright, I peered inside. Most of the items on top were things I'd expected to see. A couple of movie posters rolled up. A stash of old movie contracts. A pair of lace gloves. Some dried flowers.

"Wow. This is cool." I lifted one of the contracts, startled when I felt how heavy the pages were. "It was done on a typewriter."

He glanced at it. "These belong in a museum somewhere, Kat. They're antiques."

"No kidding." I sneezed as I pulled out a couple of hankies. Dust particles floated in the air. Digging a little further, I came out with Grandma's old hairbrush and mirror set. My thoughts immediately sailed to Candy, and I wondered how she was doing today.

Scott knelt next to me, looking over a newspaper clipping.

"What is that?" I asked.

He read the headline. " 'Lenora Worth, Hollywood's Hottest Ticket, on Hiatus between Movies.' " He looked up at me and shrugged.

"Interesting."

"I guess if I filmed a movie, I'd want to take a break afterward. I'm sure she was exhausted."

"True." I nodded. "But look at this," I said, pressing the paper into Scott's hands. "It's dated 1957. According to this article, Grandma disappeared off the Hollywood radar for several months near the end of that year."

"Maybe she was just worn out. Needed a break. Stranger things have happened."

"Maybe." Though I couldn't help but feel that he was wrong this time. "Maybe she had a breakdown of some sort." Suddenly I realized what must have happened. "Oh, silly me. My mom was born in '57. Grandma was on hiatus because she was a new mother."

"Well, that explains that." He held up another newspaper, turning it so I could see. "Look, this is a picture of your mom as a newborn. This is dated November of '57."

I clutched the paper, thrilled. "I've never seen this picture before, Scott. Look how cute she was. And look how gorgeous Grandma was!"

"Wow. She was pretty done up for a new mom."

"She's always been into the glitz and glam."

I reached for another paper, scanning the society page. "Oh, Scott, look. This one's about my grandfather." Sad thoughts came through my mind as I thought about him. Grandma might have forgotten about him, but my memories—at least the things I'd been told—were still fresh. "From what I hear, he was a wonderful man. He died at a young age."

"Oh, wow." Scott's eyes widened. "Think about that. Your grandmother has lost two of the people nearest to her—a husband and a daughter. She's been through the ultimate pain a wife or parent can withstand."

A lump rose in my throat as I pondered how sad that must feel. Still, I didn't want to turn this into a grief counseling session. I'd been through enough emotions this week already.

Scott read the opening of the article aloud. "'Jonathan Billings, husband of the elusive Lenora Worth, was killed in action today in South Korea.'" Scott looked up, wrinkles forming in his brow. "Korea. Odd. I knew we had military presence in South Korea for years after the war, but I never thought about anyone being over there in the late '50s."

I nodded. "Must've been. I always heard that he died in South Korea."

"Interesting."

I reached for the newspaper, reading the rest of the obituary. "Billings leaves behind his wife and three-month-old daughter. Funeral services will be closed to the public."

"I was hoping to see a picture of him," Scott said. "I want to see if you look like him."

"I'm sure we'll find one in here." I scrambled through the trunk, looking for something, anything, that might give me more information about him. "Maybe she has a wedding album or something buried in here. I always figured she was so grief stricken after losing him that she buried all of that stuff in here. Out of sight, out of mind."

Scott nodded. "Probably."

I didn't come up with a photo album, but I felt a stack of envelopes near the bottom of the trunk. "What is this?" Pulling them out, I frowned.

"Letters." Scott nodded. "Maybe from your grandfather?"

"Likely." I stared at the return address, a bit confused. "They were mailed from Los Angeles, though. Weird. Must've been written when he was on leave from the military." I opened the first letter and marveled at the beautiful stationery and excellent penmanship. The note was dated August 15, 1958. "Oh, Scott, it's a love letter." My eyes skimmed the note. "Really sweet. Oh, I'm so glad to see these." My heart swelled with joy at this find. Finally I might learn something of the man I'd only heard about from others. I could read his words. Share his thoughts through these letters.

I skimmed a couple of the letters, tears coming to my eyes. The depth of his feelings for my grandmother completely blew me away. A feeling of wholeness flooded over me as I realized how deeply in love they must have been.

A puzzled look crossed Scott's face. He turned over one of the envelopes, giving it a closer look. "Wait. What was that date again?"

"August 15."

He held up the newspaper. "This story about your grandfather's death was dated February of that year. The love letters came after that."

"W-what?" I rose and began to pace the room, reading the love letter again. "No, that's got to be a mistake. These are from him. They have to be."

"Hmm." Scott released a breath.

Any feelings of joy I'd felt washed away as I read the words in the letter. Deep, passionate words. Intimate words. Signed only with the phrase "Your Sweetheart." I knew in my gut who had written them . . . but how could Grandma Lenora turn to another man for comfort so soon after losing her husband? It just didn't seem right. And if she and Rex were willing to share their feelings so openly in these letters, why had they remained apart all these years? Something was definitely amiss here. Probably a misprint in the paper. Wrong year, likely.

At that moment a car's horn sounded, and I nearly came out of my skin. I glanced out of the window. "Oh, man. They're home. Help me get this stuff back in here, Scott."

We quickly pressed most of the items back into the trunk and Scott turned the key in the lock. I held on to a couple of the letters, unwilling to let go of the feelings that now gripped me. Yes, Grandma certainly had a lot of explaining to do. But would her memories allow it? Did I even want to go there?

I pressed the letters and the key into my pocket, then raced down the stairs with Scott on my heels. Just as we arrived in the great room, Grandma Lenora entered, her arms full of packages.

"There's a sale at Saks!" she proclaimed. "It's my lucky day! Wait till you see the beautiful blue dress I bought for your wedding, KK!" She paused and gave me a funny look. "You okay, honey?"

"S-sure."

"Okay. You look a little pale. Maybe you need to eat."

"Oh, we ate some of the sweet rolls Carolina left for us. Besides, I'm trying not to overeat today. Scott's parents are coming for dinner tonight, remember?"

"Scott?" Grandma looked confused, then seemed to shake it off, her face lighting up with a smile. "We invited Dino too, right?"

"Well, I'm afraid he won't be able to make it, Grandma. He has a, um . . . another engagement."

She looked disappointed. "Such a shame. I guess we'll just have to play one of his records. I have *The Best of Dean Martin* on an LP."

I wasn't sure what an LP was but took her word for it.

"So, tell me about your shopping day." I directed my attention to Carolina, who rolled her eyes.

"Don't ask," she muttered.

"Oh, I had the time of my life," Grandma interjected. "We went to Saks, like I said. Then on to several other stores. On the way home we stopped at Whole Foods to pick up some goodies for tonight. Jack's parents are coming, you know."

Didn't I just say that?

Scott nodded but didn't say a word, God bless him.

"I could spend hours in their bread department," Grandma raved. "I've never smelled or tasted such divine bread products."

180

I smiled. "Glad you had fun. What else did you do?"

"She took me to every bridal store in town," Carolina said, flashing me a warning look. "I tried to talk her out of it, Kat, but she bought all sorts of things."

"Oh, just a few little trinkets," Grandma said with a grin.

"Trinkets?" Carolina crossed her arms at her chest. "Tell the truth, Lenora. You bought the girl her wedding china."

"W-wedding china?" Surely I'd misunderstood.

Scott looked at me, stunned. "We have wedding china?"

"You do now!" Grandma Lenora laughed. "Oh, I hope you like it, KK. I picked it out myself. It's very much like the pattern I loved back when . . . well, a long time ago. Don't be mad, honey. I only bought two place settings. Your guests can buy the rest."

My mind reeled at the idea that she'd actually picked out and purchased wedding china. What else had she done?

"I can't wait to call Athena and tell her." Grandma looked through one of the bags.

"Athena?"

"Well, sure. She's your wedding planner, right? The one putting together all the details? She and the others at the studio, I mean. I'm so glad they asked for my input."

Ah. The writers. I guess they would look like wedding planners to Grandma.

"I've had such a nice time working with them," she said. "Oh, it's lovely to be included."

Carolina muttered something indistinguishable then began to carry bags of stuff up the stairs. Shaking her head, she turned to me. "Kat, listen. I did everything in my power to convince her not to buy all of this stuff, but she wouldn't listen. She never listens."

"Oh, pooh." Grandma waved a hand, dismissing her.

"What's the harm in having a little fun? At my age, I figured I've earned it."

"A little fun? You spent a fortune, Lenora."

"Have a fortune, spend a fortune . . . what's the difference? It's there for a reason. I might as well use it. Can't take it with me. There won't be any bank accounts in heaven, you know!"

"Yes, but you don't need to be spending your hard-earned money on me," I argued.

At this, my grandmother turned, disappointment etched on her face. "Oh, but I love spending money on you, KK." She faced Scott. "And you too, Jack. It's the least I can do, after all you two have done for me. So I did a little shopping. So what?"

From the stairs, Carolina let out a grunt. "See what I'm up against?" she said. "I talk, she doesn't listen. What we've got here is failure to communicate."

"Oooh, let me take this one." Scott looked at Grandma, his eyes bright. "*Cool Hand Luke* . . . Can't remember the name of the guy who said it."

Grandma, Carolina, and I all spoke in unison: "Strother Martin. 1967."

"Thanks. I needed that." Scott flashed a boyish grin, which made my heart flutter.

Carolina disappeared up the stairs and Grandma walked to the little table to grab a sweet roll. After taking a nibble, she turned our way. "So, what did you two kids do while I was gone?" she asked. "KK, did you show Jack around the gardens to make sure he likes the setup for the reception?"

I drew in a deep breath and silently counted to ten. If I didn't overreact, maybe she would walk away and forget she'd even brought up the wedding at all. This was getting tougher every day.

Thankfully Scott was quick on his feet. He turned to me. "Kat, let's do that now. A walk in the gardens sounds great."

"I agree." I took his arm and he led me outside. As we strolled down the cobblestone pathway gazing at the beautiful flowers, I became distracted by the obvious. I reached into my pocket, coming out with one of the letters.

Scott gestured to one of the concrete benches and we sat together, reading the beautifully scripted words of the first letter. I couldn't help but marvel at the handwriting.

"The letters aren't signed with a name, so we don't know for sure who wrote them," he said.

I pursed my lips and gave him a knowing look. "Scott. Read this one. Do you see the reference to the pink sweet-heart roses?"

He sighed.

"Rex wrote them all right. And those dried roses in the steamer trunk? They've got to be from him too. I'm going to get to the bottom of this if it kills me."

Scott took my hand. "That's what I'm worried about, Kat. You're the most persistent person I know. And you like to keep at things until you figure them out. But this is much bigger than us. Maybe it's not meant to be figured out."

"That sounds like a line from a movie." I folded the letter and put it back in its envelope.

"Maybe it is. I don't know. I just know that you've got to be careful how you handle this. People could get hurt."

A little sigh escaped, followed by a whispered, "I know."

"Playing with real lives is a whole lot different from coming up with a great script for a show. We can't push these players around on the stage. And besides, God's the director here, not you. Not me. He's got this under control."

I closed my eyes and drew in a breath. "Thanks. I needed that."

Scott slipped an arm over my shoulders and whispered, "You're welcome. I love you, Kat."

Ah, those magic words! They not only lifted my spirits, they reminded me that love really did conquer all, even in tough situations like this.

After a little more conversation, we walked back in the house to find Grandma easing her way down the stairs. She moved slowly, favoring her hip, which appeared to be bothering her more today than usual.

She looked our way and frowned. "Did you see what that naughty kitty did in my room while I was gone?"

My heart gravitated to my throat. "N-no. What did he do?"

She clucked her tongue. "Pulled the afghan off of my trunk. Don't know how he did it, but he managed to get it onto the bed. Pretty talented cat, that one! Maybe he should be in commercials." She went on to talk about a cat she'd seen in a Meow Mix commercial.

"Ah." I shook my head and looked at Scott, who shifted his gaze to a photo on the wall. I didn't want to be deceptive, but neither did I feel led to tell my grandmother I'd been snooping in her things.

"Oh well. Fiddle-dee-dee!" Grandma paused on the steps, a smile lighting her face. She stood there, waiting for my inevitable response to the line she'd just delivered. Only one problem—I didn't want to play along today. I really didn't.

On the other hand, if I refused to join in, we'd be standing here until the sun came down. I'd just opened my mouth to give the answer when Carolina's agitated voice rang out from one of the rooms upstairs: "Vivien Leigh. *Gone with the Wind*. 1939. And if this little guessing game doesn't stop soon, I'm going to snap like a twig."

Yep. I couldn't have put it any better myself.

184

14

Keeping Up Appearances

Though I tried to squelch my roller-coaster-like emotions, much of Saturday was spent fuming. Even Carolina noticed my sour mood. She watched from the door of my room as I slammed dresser drawers in search of something to wear when Scott brought his parents over for dinner. I sensed her gaze but did my best to ignore it. Until I turned and faced her head-on.

"Something wrong, Kat?" The look of concern on her face clued me in to the fact that my behavior surprised her. It surprised me too. I couldn't remember the last time I'd felt this knotted up. The information Scott and I had gleaned this morning left my head reeling.

I plopped down onto the bed, feeling a little overwhelmed. "Did you ever think you knew someone, only to find out you really didn't?"

Carolina grunted. "My ex-husband. Enough said?"

As she settled onto the bed next to me, I reached to touch her hand. "I'm sorry about your ex-husband, Carolina. I'd forgotten you were divorced."

"Twenty years now. Seems like just yesterday we were dukin' it out in divorce court."

Sounded gruesome. "Well then, maybe you're the best candidate to answer this question. How did you live with him for so long, not really knowing him?"

She rolled her eyes. "Oh, that's easy," she said. "He was a phony."

"A phony?"

"Yes. The great pretender. Living two lives. Acting like he was perfectly happy with me, but spending time with someone else too." She shook her head. "Trust me, honey. We were ideal candidates for the Jerry Springer show. Lots of drama."

"Ugh." I thought of my father. From what I'd gathered, he'd pretty much been the same as Carolina's ex. How long had my mother known he was involved with another woman? Did he go on pretending that he wanted to be part of our lives, only to secretly want someone else?

This thought led me right back to my grandmother and her carefully hidden relationship with Rex. I wanted to pick up the phone and call him, to ask for details. With those letters as ammunition, I could surely drag the truth out of him.

Or not.

A couple of deep breaths later, I was reminded of Scott's calming words. This battle wasn't mine. Only the Lord could handle something this big. Still, I felt the need to get to the bottom of all this. Surely the Almighty wouldn't be put off by my need to know. Right?

Carolina's troubling words interrupted my thoughts. "Something kind of sad happened this morning."

"Oh?" I glanced her way.

"Lenora called me the wrong name."

"Really? What did she call you?"

"Hazel." Carolina's eyes filled with tears. "Doesn't that just break your heart?"

"Wait. Who's Hazel?"

"She was a housekeeper on a television show in the '60s," Carolina explained. "Played by Shirley Booth, one of the funniest ladies in television history."

"I'm sorry, Carolina." I reached to give her a hug. "I know that must've been hard."

"Harder than you think," Carolina said. "Hazel was always getting in trouble, causing all sorts of mischief. You don't think I'm like that, do you, Kat?"

"Heavens, no. You're the glue that holds this house together," I said.

"No." She shook her head and pointed up. "*He's* the glue that holds this house together. I just do the mopping."

"And the cooking and the shopping and the counseling. So don't put yourself down. We couldn't make it without you. I wouldn't trust tonight's dinner to anyone but you, by the way. You're the best cook this side of Hollywood, and we're blessed to have you."

Carolina glanced at her watch and startled to attention. "Oh no. Three o'clock? Scott's parents are coming at six, right?"

"Right."

"I'd better get busy. Your grandmother's been working on this menu for days. She's pulling out all the stops."

"Oh?" Anything would be better than steak and eggs with ketchup.

"She wants to start with a cheese platter, like she always does. She spent ages in Whole Foods choosing different ones."

"Yum. Hope she got the Havarti."

"Yep." Carolina nodded. "I'm making shrimp ceviche—

minus the tequila, of course. Baby arugula salad, blackened salmon, haricot verts, and bananas Foster."

"Wow." My mouth started watering. "That sounds amazing." It also sounded a bit over the top for the fine folks from Alma, Arkansas. Still, I couldn't fault my grandmother for trying. She wanted to make a good impression, after all.

Carolina started talking about the recipe for the ceviche, and I smiled as I listened to her exuberant presentation.

I paused to touch her arm when she finished. "Carolina, I don't say this often enough, but thank you for your hard work. You didn't have to spend your Saturday with Grandma, but you chose to. And now you're cooking on your day off. How can I thank you for that?"

"Thank me?" Carolina shook her head. "Girl, did you hear my story a few minutes ago about my ex-husband?"

"Sure."

"Well, listen closely. Twenty years ago when I tossed him out on his ear, I was working part-time at the same studio where your grandmother happened to be filming one of her later movies. She was reaching the end of her career by then."

"Wait. You worked at a studio?"

"Housekeeping, honey. But here's my point—when Lenora found out my husband was gone and he'd taken the checking account with him, she flew into action. Told me she had a little house behind Worth Manor where I could stay. Offered me the housekeeping position without any references or background check."

"Sounds like Grandma."

"When I moved into that little house back there, it became my home. And I'm keenly aware of the fact that it's a home I don't have to pay a penny for. All of my debts are covered by your grandmother."

"Sounds like a spiritual message of sorts."

"It is." Carolina nodded. "And trust me, the Lord has used it to remind me that my past is truly behind me."

"A lesson for us all," I whispered.

"I live in Beverly Hills," Carolina said. "And I have access to anything my heart could ever want. I'm fully aware that Lenora Worth has made all of this possible for me. With the Lord's help, mind you. So I don't mind a bit working on Saturdays, as long as I get to go on hanging out with you two lovely ladies."

"Thank you." I gave her a hug and quickly apologized for my earlier behavior. With a wave of her hand, she dismissed it.

Carolina headed to the kitchen and I spent a little more time on the internet, searching for clues about my grandfather. I had his name, of course: Jonathan Billings. And the date of his obituary. Surely I could find something.

An hour of searching for information left me frustrated. Looked like I'd have to do a little more digging later. Right now I had to get ready for company.

At exactly six o'clock, Scott pulled up to the gate with his parents in the car. I raced down the stairs, wearing my favorite white peasant blouse and summery skirt. I'd decided to forego the sandals, leaving my feet bare.

The tantalizing smells coming from the kitchen nearly stopped me. When I got to the bottom of the stairs, I was met by my grandmother, fully decked out in a black evening gown. She took one look at my bare feet and clucked her tongue.

"What?" I asked, feigning innocence. "Can't a girl be comfortable in her own home?"

"Well, sure." She shrugged. "You know what I always say: 'Take your shoes off.'" A knowing look followed. I picked up on the hidden clues and joined her for the rest of the line: "Y'all come back now, ya hear?"

We both chuckled and spoke in unison: "*The Beverly Hillbillies!* Closing credits."

"You're good, girl." Grandma patted me on the back. "Very good. And if Jack doesn't love you in your bare feet, then he's not the man for you."

"Amen to that."

"Well, c'mon, tiger. Let's go get 'im."

The laughter that followed lifted my spirits. For a moment I saw my grandmother as a younger woman, waiting at the door for her beau to enter.

Hmm. Her beau. Would that be my grandfather . . . or Rex Henderson?

I didn't have time to ponder the question, thank goodness. Grandma threw back the door and walked out to the driveway, chattering a mile a minute. She rushed Nancy's way with arms extended, gathering her in a warm embrace. Nothing like kicking back and making people feel welcome. I tagged along behind, giving everyone a shy wave. Scott took in my appearance, apparently liking my off-the-shoulder blouse. I tried not to blush.

"Wow." His eyes grew wide. "You look . . . wow."

"Thanks," I whispered, then gave him a little kiss on the cheek.

Nancy stared at the house, her eyes wide. "Oh my. This is certainly bigger than I thought it would be. In fact, all of the houses out here are, well, they're just huge."

"Our place back home is 1,400 square feet. That's plenty of room for the two of us," Scott's father quipped.

"Dad did a lot of renovations on the house in Alma," Scott added. "He's quite a handyman. Even updated the kitchen last year for my mom."

"Yes, he's great with construction," Nancy said, a look of pride in her eyes.

I turned to Scott's father. "How was the hardware convention?" I asked.

"Oh, it was fabulous," Nancy interjected. "You wouldn't believe all of the new inventions they've got out this year. I've never seen anything quite like it." She began to talk about all sorts of things I'd never heard of, and I enjoyed the sparkle in her eyes. Apparently the woman knew her hardware.

"Find any good things for your store?" I asked.

Charles's gaze shifted. "Not really. I guess we're doing okay without all that fancy stuff, anyway. This trip was really more about seeing the kids than investing in new products."

"We did see some pretty remarkable things, though," Nancy said. "I spent nearly an hour just looking at kitchen faucets. Can you imagine? Why, they've got faucets so fancy it would make your head spin."

"Oh, speaking of faucets, I can't wait to show you the kitchen. Carolina's been cooking all afternoon." Grandma took Nancy by the hand and began to pull her toward the house.

Scott pulled me close and whispered in my ear, "Think you can handle this, Kat?"

"Of course," I whispered back, then giggled. "Might give us some great material for a future episode of *Stars Collide*."

"No doubt." He winked.

Nancy kept chattering the whole way. "I'm a little disappointed that we didn't get to go to the wax museum," she said. "And I had my heart set on seeing the Hollywood sign up close and personal. And a trip to Grauman's Chinese Theatre would have been nice."

"Guess that means you'll just have to come back," Grandma said. "In the meantime, come into the kitchen. We'll pretend we're looking at that faucet. But we'll really be sneaking a few nibbles of Carolina's food while we're in there."

"I'm starved." Charles rubbed his belly.

"Me too," Scott said with a nod.

"Carolina's got some great things prepared," I said. "Just wait till you see."

Grandma led the procession through the front door. "I just love having guests. It's been so long since we've had a party here, but back in the day this used to be the place where the most spectacular events in the Hills were held." She smiled. "Oh, the fun we used to have. I remember one time when Marlon Brando came. Oh, that boy was in a mood. But I cheered him right up by tossing him in the cement pond!" Grandma had a good laugh at that one.

Nancy drew near. "Kat," she whispered, "sometimes I can't tell if your grandmother's stories are real or imagined."

"Same here." I sighed. "But just about the time you think she's making something up, you'll stumble across a picture to prove it."

"I guess we'll have to assume Marlon Brando really got tossed into your pool then," Nancy said with a shrug.

"Stranger things have happened," I said.

We tagged along on Grandma's heels into the foyer.

"Great hardware on this door." Charles paused, giving it a closer look. "I haven't seen latches like this since I was a kid. My pop used to have some of these in a box in the barn."

"Really?" I smiled. "My grandmother likes to keep things the way they were."

"Nothing wrong with that," Scott said.

"The latches are made really well," Charles said. "That's a plus. The reason these things are still around is because they're still working. So many of the products out today are cheap. They fall apart. I wouldn't mind going back to days gone by myself, if it meant putting out decent products."

"Actually, this latch is coming loose," Grandma said. "I've been thinking of replacing it. I've been telling Kat we should renovate the house for the wedding. What with so many people coming for the reception and all, I might give some thought to changing out a few things." She looped her arm through his. "What would you recommend, Charles?"

Praise the Lord and pass the hardware. She had him from that point on. As for her wedding comment, I noticed the "I won't say a word" look from Nancy and breathed a sigh of relief. Looked like she would play along, for my grandmother's sake.

The look on Nancy's face as she walked through the great room was unlike anything I'd ever seen before. Always gracious, she complimented Grandma right and left. But what struck me as sweet were the many times she paused in front of photos to reflect on all of the movies she'd seen starring this person or that person.

"I saw Richard Burton and Elizabeth Taylor in *The Taming of the Shrew* at the Bijou," she said, standing in front of a photograph of the two stars with Grandma between them. "I'll never forget it. I was just a little thing, but my mama let me stay up late to go." She turned to us with a frown. "I can't even imagine meeting that duo in person."

"Well, they were quite a pair, let me tell you." Grandma's eyes took on that faraway look I'd noticed so much lately. "And talk about popular. Why, they were the cat's meow . . . for a season, anyway."

Charles grunted. "Movie stars put their pants on one leg at a time, just like us."

"Well, all but Liz," Grandma said. "She was never one for wearing pants. If you noticed, she was usually in a dress. And what a brilliant collection of gowns she had. Unequaled in her day, to be sure."

"Don't know why everyone out here has to work so hard to become someone they're not," Charles said. "I am what I am, and that's all that I am." His words were spoken with a familiar cartoonish accent.

Scott smiled, but I thought I noticed a hint of a sigh. Had his father's words struck a nerve?

"Alma is the spinach capital of the world," Nancy explained. "We even have a statue of Popeye on Main Street. So trust me when I say we all have the show memorized."

"Impressive," I said. And the fact that Alma was known for its spinach certainly explained Scott's muscular physique.

As if reading my thoughts, he flexed his arm and grinned. "I ate more spinach when I was growing up than any kid should be allowed to by law."

"That explains it then." I winked and his cheeks turned red.

We were just about to head to the kitchen to sneak a peek at Carolina's yummy foods when she called us in to dinner. We made our way to the formal dining room—a place that rarely saw any action these days—and gathered around the huge mahogany table, where I glanced down at the beautiful cheese tray in the center. Scott reached down and grabbed a piece. His dad quickly followed suit.

We clustered around one end of the large table to make things more comfortable, everyone now nibbling on cheese. I could see Charles scoping out the room, and I couldn't help but notice that his nose wrinkled when he glanced down at the little plates of salad.

Carolina must've noticed too. "Baby arugula salad with artichokes," she explained.

We all took our seats and Scott offered to pray. As I listened to his voice lifted in prayer, my heart felt like bursting into a worship song. I still couldn't get over the fact that the Lord had brought him all the way from Alma, Arkansas, the spinach capital of the world. Even the boy's prayers were powerful.

When the prayer ended, we dove into the salad. I noticed Charles ate every bite and had a satisfied look on his face at the end, though he never said a word. Nancy more than made up for it, however. She couldn't seem to say enough. Thankfully Carolina heard every word as she entered the room with the next course in hand. I could see her cheeks turn pink and wondered if this sort of flattery was embarrassing to her. She placed the glasses of ceviche down in front of each of us, ending with Scott's dad.

He pushed the martini glass away. "I'm not a drinker, thanks."

I stifled a laugh. "It's shrimp ceviche."

"Shrimp what?" He picked up the glass and examined it more closely, even giving it a sniff. "Never heard of such a thing."

"Oh, I saw this one on the Food Network," Nancy said. She took a little nibble and her eyes grew wide. "That's really good."

"It's kind of like salsa, only with shrimp in it," Carolina said. "And I promise, no tequila. I used orange juice instead."

"What do I do with it?" He stared down at the glass, clearly perplexed.

I pointed to the triangular tortilla chips Carolina had pressed into the side of the yummy mixture. "Scoop it up with the chip."

"Hmm." He took a bite, his eyes widening.

Nancy used her chip to scoop up a generous portion. "I want to have this for dinner every night!" she said between bites.

"Well, I wouldn't go that far," Charles said. "But it is good." He finished his up in a hurry.

Next came the main course. Carolina obviously felt an explanation was in order as she plopped the plate down in front of Scott's dad.

"Blackened salmon and haricot verts," she said.

Nancy's brow wrinkled as she looked down. "They look like green beans to me."

Grandma chuckled. "They are. *Haricot verts* is French for 'green beans.'"

"Well, why didn't you just say so?" Charles asked. He gave the blackened salmon a curious look. "This stuff looks scorched. I'm a fried catfish man myself."

"It's a shame you're not staying longer then," I said. "There's a great place in Dana Point that specializes in fried fish. I think you'd like it."

"I love catfish too," Grandma said. "But I think you'll like the salmon if you give it a chance, Charles."

To my surprise, the tension in his face released after he took a cautious bite. "Spicy. I think I like it."

And with those words, my fate was sealed. Scott's father liked the blackened salmon. That meant Scott's father would learn to like me as well. At least, I hoped so. He certainly loved the bananas Foster that followed, even though Carolina set off the smoke alarm when she lit the luscious dessert on fire. He didn't even argue about the rum that she poured on top to use as fuel.

By the end of the meal, the Beverly Hills crowd and the Arkansas crowd had come to an understanding. We were a perfect fit. They were a little bit Southern. We were a little bit West Coast. No problem! Any lingering issues had been settled over a martini glass of shrimp ceviche and a plateful of blackened salmon. Next time we'd have the fried catfish and a big helping of spinach. But this time it was L.A. all the way.

15

L.A. Heat

As we ate our dessert, the conversation shifted a thousand different directions. I learned that the city of Alma, Arkansas, got its water supply from Lake Alma, and that the city hosted a spinach festival every year.

"You'll have to come and check it out," Nancy said to my grandmother. "We have such a wonderful time. And if you come, you'll get to see our water towers." She practically beamed with pride at this announcement.

"Water towers?" Grandma looked perplexed at that one.

"Oh yes. They're famous," Nancy said. "They're painted green, and one of them has the Popeye-brand spinach label painted on it."

"They're known for miles as the largest cans of spinach in the world!" Charles laughed then slapped his knee.

"I've never been a big spinach fan," I confessed.

Everyone at the table turned to me, totally aghast.

"I like it in quiche," I quickly added. "But that's about it."

"Oh, honey, you've got to come to Alma and let me cook up a pot of spinach that you won't soon forget." Nancy fanned herself. "It will change your mind in a hurry."

"She is the best spinach cook in town," Scott said with a nod. "No one cooks it like my mama."

"Oh yes. I do a spinach soufflé, creamed spinach, and a spinach dip that's out of this world, if I do say so myself."

Hmm. Now that would be something to compete with. If I married Scott, would I have to learn to cook spinach like his mama? He might have to toss me aside based on that technicality alone.

The conversation shifted gears again, and I happened to glance out of the window, catching the reflection of the setting sun off of the swimming pool. Must still be early. I glanced at the clock, stunned to see we'd been sitting here for two hours. Eight o'clock? Really? Funny how easy, comfortable conversation caused the time to fly. Seemed like we'd all just taken our seats a few minutes ago.

I wondered if that's how life would be, should my relationship with Scott deepen over time. Would we become so comfortable that time would slip away from us? Would we one day be as old as his parents—or even my grandmother—and not even realize the passage of time because we'd been so busy enjoying each other?

Sounded like a great way to spend a life. I glanced his way, embarrassed at the depth of my ponderings. If he could see into my mind right now, what would he think? Would he want to sweep me away to Alma and bake me a lovely spinach pie? I grinned just thinking about it.

"You okay, Kat?" Scott asked, giving me a funny look.

I nodded, heat rising to my cheeks. "I'm great. But all this talk about food is really painful." Rubbing my stomach, I added, "I'm already full to the brim."

"We need to ask Carolina to do the catering at our fund-raiser," Scott said. "She's the best."

"I'd be happy to," Carolina said, entering the room with a tray in hand. "Just let me know what you'd like. I've catered many an event over the years."

This led to a conversation about the fund-raiser.

"I want you to come back as my guests," Scott said to his parents. "You can stay at my place this time."

"But it's only a couple of weeks from now, right?" his father asked.

"Two trips to L.A. in such a short period of time!" his mom said. "What a blessing."

"If you come, you'll get to meet someone really famous," Scott said.

"Who's that?" She leaned forward in anticipation.

"I've been thinking of asking Brock Benson to emcee."

"Brock Benson?" Every woman in the room suddenly came to life, especially Carolina.

I could hardly believe it myself. "Do you think he'll do it?" I asked.

"I think so." Scott shrugged. "I've worked with him before. He's a great guy."

"And the hottest actor in Hollywood," Carolina whispered. Scott threw her a look and she laughed. "Sorry, Scott. But this is Brock Benson we're talking about. Have you seen his movies?" She went off into a lengthy discussion about his latest pirate film, and before long all of the women were swooning.

Scott laughed. "I know he's very popular. He's also a believer, and he's been involved in inner-city outreach for the past couple of years. So I think he would be a great choice to emcee our fund-raiser. I met him a few months ago when I helped out at an after-school program he sponsors."

"Still, I can hardly believe it." Carolina fanned herself. "I'd better start shopping now. I want to look my best when I meet him."

"And we will definitely come back in town for that," Scott's mother said. "Wouldn't miss it for the world."

We convened to the great room, where Scott's dad joined his wife in looking over every photograph on every wall. Around nine, Grandma began to yawn and I knew the time had come to wrap up this party. Besides, I still wanted to look over those letters I'd found. Couldn't do that with a houseful of guests, now could I?

Scott must've noticed my grandmother's weariness. He turned to her with a smile. "Well, Lenora, thank you so much for a wonderful evening. We've got quite a drive ahead of us to get my parents back to the hotel, and I know they've got an early morning."

"I should get a little shut-eye," my grandmother said. "I have a big audition in the morning."

"You do?" Scott and I both turned to look at her. *On Sunday?*

"Yes, my agent called this morning. I'll be reading for the starring role in a new movie . . . something about disco dancing."

"Disco dancing?" We all spoke in unison.

"Yes." Her brow furrowed. "Can't remember the name of the kid they said would be playing the lead opposite me, though. John something. I think his last name started with a T."

"Travolta?" Scott asked, his eyes widening.

"That's it!" She snapped her finger. "A disco movie with John Travolta."

"Would you by any chance be referring to *Saturday Night Fever*?" Scott's father asked. "Because that movie—"

"Is destined to be a top seller," Scott interjected. "I've heard a lot of good things about that Travolta kid."

"Yes, he's great on the dance floor, from what I understand." Grandma yawned. "But if I don't get some shut-eye, I'll never feel like dancing in the morning." She gave Scott's parents a winsome look. "I am going to miss you both so much, though. Do you really have to leave?"

Charles nodded. "Yep. Gotta get back to the store."

Nancy frowned. "I can't believe the week is over. I've loved my time in L.A."

Charles slipped his arm over her shoulders and nodded. "Guess I have to rethink my former position on Hollywood. It's a great place. Why, everyone is just as normal as they are back home." He glanced at an autographed photo of Charo on the wall and said, "Well, almost everyone."

I laughed, and Scott gathered me into an embrace and pressed a light kiss onto my forehead.

"There are a lot of wacky people out here, to be sure," Grandma said. "But I think you would be surprised at how many believers we know."

Charles nodded. "Oh, I'm sure. The church is everywhere. Sometimes I lose sight of that, but the Lord is happy to remind me."

"Hollywood is filled with praying people," I echoed.

"Oh yes." Grandma nodded. "There have always been prayer warriors in Hollywood. Why, the great Cecil B. DeMille once said, 'I have found the greatest power in the world is the power of prayer.'"

"Wow." Scott and his father both nodded.

"You memorized that quote, Lenora?" Scott asked.

"Memorized that quote?" She looked perplexed. "He

shared that with a group of us over dinner one night. I'll never forget it. We had just prayed for the meal and he looked me squarely in the eye and said it."

Nancy glanced my way, a questioning look in her eye. I could read her thoughts: *Is she serious, Kat?*

This was a new one. Then again, the audition for *Saturday Night Fever* was a new one too. But who knew? Maybe Travolta was doing a remake and had asked for my grandmother to play an aging dance instructor. Stranger things had happened.

"Walk us out?" Scott asked.

I nodded. "Of course."

Grandma took Scott's father by the arm. "Do you like cars, Charles? I'd love to show you my babies on the way out. I've got a lovely Cadillac. And I'm sure you'll appreciate my '67 Mustang and the '77 Camaro. Any of those sound interesting to you?"

"Do they!"

Everyone headed for the front door. I tagged along behind the others, lingering as I heard the house phone ring. After the third ring, I realized Carolina probably didn't hear it, so I offered my apologies to Scott and his parents, then headed back to the great room.

When I reached the phone, I glanced down at the caller ID. I didn't recognize the number but picked it up anyway, thinking it might be Athena, calling from her house phone to ask how the evening had gone.

"Lenora Worth, please," the voice on the other end said.

"She's stepped out for a few minutes," I said. "Could I ask who's calling?"

"Is this Kat?" the male voice asked.

Something told me not to respond.

"James Stevens here from *The Scoop*."

Ugh. The *Scoop*? I chided myself for picking up the phone. Now what?

"Listen, I talked to Lenora earlier today and she told me everything. Congrats to you and Scott." He paused. Not a minute too soon. I needed a second to pick my heart up off the floor. Surely I'd misunderstood. Grandma had not given *The Scoop* a private interview.

"I . . . I'm sorry. What did you say your name was again?"

"James Stevens." He paused. "It's the weirdest thing, though. Lenora called Scott *Jack*. Thought that was humorous. Anyway, I know you've got a couple of busy months ahead of you. Just hoping for some details on the wedding. Local, right? That's what Lenora said."

"Well, actually, I—"

"Just placed a call to the registry department at Macy's. I understand you and Scott have chosen the Fantasia pattern for your china. I looked it up online. Great-looking plates. A little girly, but who cares when they're covered in food, right? I wouldn't mind eating off of them myself. I understand you and your grandmother have a great cook. What was her name again? Caroline? No, Carolina. Well, maybe you could invite me over to dinner sometime so I could get a sample firsthand. Sounds like fun, right?"

"W-what?" Surely I was hearing things.

"We'll have a little bubbly in your new stemware to celebrate. I saw a picture of it too. Nice stuff. Showed it to my wife and she got plenty jealous. Two hundred and fifty dollars a stem? You'll share more than a few toasts with those, I suspect. Hope to be there when it happens."

Ugh. Could this pit get any deeper?

"I understand you guys had quite a feast planned for tonight. Scott's parents are in town, right? Something about ceviche and salmon. Your grandmother even gave me a recipe for the ceviche." He laughed. "I passed it on to my wife. She's not much of a cook, my wife. A night at Spago suits her just fine, thank you very much."

"Well, that's nice, but—"

"Hey, speaking of Lenora, she's quite a pistol. Wouldn't give me any information until I named three of her most famous movies. Thank goodness I had my iPod with me. I googled her in a hurry. Not a bad résumé, really. She used to be quite the rage."

"Still is," I managed. *In more ways than one. And before the night is over, I'm going to be in one.*

"Funny thing. When she called us, she asked to speak to Ted Holliday. Holliday hasn't worked here since 1972. From what I hear, he was pretty good with a story, though." After a final pause to catch his breath, James added, "Anyway, enough about all of that. I'm hoping you can share more details with me before I stay up all night putting together this story. I'll handle whatever you give me with care."

Sure you will.

An awkward pause grew between us. I wanted to hang up on him but didn't dare. No telling what he would do.

"Hey, there is one more thing you could do for me while I've got you, Kat. We want to add some tidbits about Scott's family. Lenora says they're not from Hollywood."

"Well, yes, but—"

"Yeah, I know. They're from some small town in Arkansas. Al-ma." He dragged out the word with a thick Southern drawl. "Guess you know all that." Another pause and my heart gravitated to my throat as I anticipated what he might say or do next. "Crazy thing about that father of his."

"O-oh?" I managed.

"Vacationing in Hollywood when his hardware store

back home is about to be foreclosed on. Don't you find that odd?"

"What? I had no idea they—" My words stopped right there. I would say nothing else, one way or the other. Well, maybe one thing. "Mr. Stevens, I appreciate the fact that you want to do a story on us, but I would like to ask you to give us the privacy we need."

"Privacy?" He laughed. "Kat, you and your fiancé are public figures. Public figures don't have the luxury of a private life."

"Well, Mr. Murphy's father is not a public figure and I know he values his privacy very much."

"Which is why he hasn't told his future daughter-in-law that his store is about to be foreclosed on, no doubt. But he's got a couple of folks back in Alma-ville who aren't very fond of him, and they're happy to talk, so just keep that in mind."

Ouch.

"Oh, one more question before I forget. Lenora said something about Elly May and a cement pond. I'm assuming she was making a reference to Scott's family being outsiders in L.A. Guess she thinks small-town folks don't get out much, huh?"

"What? She compared Scott's parents to the Beverly Hillbillies?"

"Hope you don't mind if I quote you on that. Well, listen, Kat. Invite me over for dinner sometime soon. Can't wait to see those dishes. We'll talk some more. I'll go ahead and cover the story, but I'd sure like some input from you. Anything you want to add?"

"No comment." I bit back the other words that threatened to erupt. I wanted to give this guy a piece of my mind, but didn't dare.

"Okay, I get it. Next time we'll do it your way, so we won't have to lean on those folks back home in Arkansas. They sounded a little . . . bitter."

Ugh.

"If I don't hear from you by late tonight, though, you might force my hand. I've got to get a story out by tomorrow morning, one way or the other. Either we have your input or we don't. That part's up to you. Here's my number."

I didn't copy it down, of course. Instead I ended the call as politely as I could, then counted to ten in an attempt to regain my composure. Grandma had done a lot of crazy things over the years, but to contact *The Scoop*? Why would she go that far? And why that particular tabloid, of all places? They were notorious for hurting people and for getting the story wrong.

I gathered my emotions, rolled them into a ball, and stuffed them into my pocket. Keeping this information hidden for long wasn't an option, but I wasn't about to spoil a perfectly wonderful evening by telling anyone what had just happened. I would call Scott first thing in the morning and spill the beans. Hopefully he would find it in his heart to forgive my grandmother . . . again.

16

Friends

There are times in everyone's life where running away feels like the only logical solution. On the morning after I spoke to James Stevens at *The Scoop*, I had an overwhelming urge to pack my bags and catch a plane. Destination . . . unknown. Didn't really matter where I went, anyway, as long as the paparazzi didn't follow me.

My fascination with running did not date back to my childhood. I was never one of those kids who wanted to run away and join the circus. For one thing, clowns scared me. For another, there was enough tightrope walking in life already. And that whole thing about traveling with so many stinky, smelly animals held little appeal. I could barely tolerate Fat Cat. How could I share a train car with his distant cousin the lion? No, joining the circus wasn't an option. Besides, my life had already become a circus, hadn't it?

After reading the online version of *The Scoop*'s article on

Scott's family—which had apparently been posted at 5:52 a.m., according to the website—I revisited my rain forest option. An undecorated hut somewhere along the banks of the Amazon sounded pretty appealing right about now. I could buy some insect repellent. Maybe swipe the mosquito netting from around Grandma Lenora's bed to take with me. I'd also swipe the rest of those letters from the steamer trunk and take them along for the ride. Once I reached my hut, I'd have plenty of time to read them carefully and ponder the reality that my grandmother was not who she had presented herself to be.

Or maybe she was and I'd just never dug beneath the surface to really, truly know her. Were any of us who we presented ourselves to be, or were we just out there on the set, hair and makeup done, speaking the lines we'd been given by those around us?

I thought about Scott's parents, who were probably halfway to Alma by now. Hopefully the paparazzi would leave them alone. Surely those scoundrels at *The Scoop* wouldn't send any of their people to Arkansas . . . right?

A crash of thunder startled me. I walked across the bedroom and stared out of the window, watching as the rain showered down. I'd never been a fan of thunder and lightning, so as I stood observing the downpour, I reluctantly gave up on my idea of living in the rain forest. If I couldn't handle an occasional Southern California shower, how could I live in a rain forest?

My mind continued to whirl as the storm clouds grew overhead. As I showered for church, I replayed every minute of yesterday's events. The trunk. The letters. Scott's parents. That guy from *The Scoop*. Grandma's erratic behavior. The yummy ceviche. Popeye the Sailor Man. These things all ran together as the hot water poured down on my head.

208

I somehow kept my cool through church, not letting Grandma know of my inner turmoil. Talk about a great acting job. Thank goodness no one seemed to be aware of the story. If so, they weren't talking. Or maybe they were just taking it in stride. That's what most of the regular folks in L.A. did when a gossip-type story hit the papers, after all.

After church, we swung through KFC to pick up some chicken. Grandma chose the original. I chose the extra crispy. I made small talk during lunch, praying all the while that Scott would discover the voice mail and text messages I'd left on his phone in the wee hours of the morning.

Since he hadn't responded, I found myself in need of someone to talk to . . . preferably someone who could calm my nerves. After Grandma made her way up the stairs to take a nap, I decided to do just that. I picked up the phone and punched in Athena's number. When she answered, the many voices in the background clued me in to the fact that she was with her family. I heard the clattering of silverware and realized the whole Pappas clan must be gathered around the dinner table. From what Athena had told me, meals were of utmost importance in their household.

"Athena, do you have a minute?" I asked.

"Kat, I'm so glad it's you. Have you, um . . . have you seen the papers?"

"Yeah." I groaned. "I really need to talk to someone."

"No doubt. Well, come on out to our place," she said. "My cousins are here today, so it's going to be pretty chaotic, but we can sneak back to my room and have some girl time. You'll be safe here."

"You sure?"

"Of course."

She disappeared for a few seconds then came back. "Sorry

about that. Had two of my nieces sitting on my lap. Too hard to talk with toddlers chattering in your ear."

I didn't have any idea what that would feel like but found the idea intriguing.

"I'll be there in an hour," I said. "If that's okay."

"Sure. C'mon over."

Exactly fifty-eight minutes later, I pulled my car into the driveway at Athena's family home. Apparently folks in the valley had avoided the storm. The sun shone brightly overhead and I couldn't find a drop of rain anywhere, or any sign that storm clouds had passed by.

Several children played on the beautifully manicured lawn with parents looking on. As I shifted the car into PARK, I thought about what it would be like to live with so many siblings, cousins, aunts, and uncles. Chaos, likely. Still, it might be fun. I'd never had the opportunity to find out. No, Grandma and I had pretty much settled into our quiet, comfortable routine.

Until lately.

Athena met me at the door of my car with a toddler on each hip. I laughed when I saw her. "Practicing for motherhood?"

She snorted. "I'd have to find a husband first, and so far that scene hasn't been written."

"It will be," I said as I climbed out of the car. "But you won't have the privilege of writing it yourself."

"Well, I hope the Lord pencils in a great-looking guy with an amazing sense of humor," she said. "Otherwise I might just stay single. I get enough family activity in this house as it is."

Looking around at the crowd, I realized that being single in this environment was a far cry from being single at Worth Manor. Athena's world was as far removed from mine as I could imagine, and yet we had so much in common, especially when it came to matters of the heart.

We paused long enough for me to meet everyone. This process took quite some time. At Athena's house, you didn't just stop to shake hands. You heard about Aunt Melina's liver condition and cousin Leandro's overnight stay in the county jail. You were given the details of the wrestling match her brother Niko had just won, and you always walked away with at least one recipe from Athena's mother, Thera. When all of that was said and done, you were given something to eat. Then and only then could you sneak away for a few moments of privacy.

We eventually ended up in Athena's bedroom, where she shooed a couple of youngsters off of the bed, then closed the door so we could talk.

"Tell me everything," she said.

So I did. My stories ran together, none of them making much sense, even to my own ears. And I could tell from her wrinkled brow that Athena wasn't getting much of this either. At the end, she stared at me, shaking her head.

"How do you do it, Kat?"

"Do what?"

"Your off-screen life is even more dramatic than your on-screen one . . . and that's really saying something. I work hard to make your on-screen life pretty wacky."

I groaned. "Don't ask me. Just help me fix this. If you had written that phone call scene, how would you go about resolving it so the hero and heroine could live happily ever after?"

She paused, shaking her head. "I'm not sure. Give me a minute." She rose from her bed and paced the room. "Maybe you could . . . no, that would never work."

"What?"

"Well, have his parents read the article yet? For that matter, has Scott?"

"I don't know." A shiver ran down my spine. "I only know that it broke this morning and he's not responding to my texts or voice mail. I'm thinking about leaving town."

"Still building that hut in the Amazon?"

I sighed. "Rethinking that one after the storm this morning. Mosquitoes aren't really my bag. Neither is thunder. Do you think it storms at the North Pole? Can you write a scene where I visit Santa and the elves?"

A look of concern passed over Athena's face. "Kat, I don't really write the upcoming scenes of your life. You . . . you do realize that, don't you?"

"Well, yes. But sometimes I wish you could. That way I'd know what was coming. I'd know whether or not Scott would freak out and leave me because of this . . . this stupid Beverly Hillbillies story."

"Why are you so afraid he's going to leave? Don't you think your fears are a little . . . irrational?"

I was unable to speak over the tightening sensation in my throat. "Isn't that what guys do?" I finally managed, my voice barely a whisper. I felt the sting of tears. Frustrated, I brushed them away. No point in getting teary-eyed over this. Not again.

"Ah." She sat back on the bed, her eyes narrowed into slits. "You're afraid because your dad left that Scott's going to do the same thing. And you think that if you don't line up and walk straight, it will give him reason to take off."

"Maybe." A sense of relief passed over me as I realized she understood where I was coming from.

"Scott isn't your dad, Kat," she said. "And just so you know, men don't always leave. Sometimes they stay put and raise happy families. And for the record, I won't have to write that script for Scott. He's got sticking power."

"You think?" I gazed over at her, still not sure. "Because

once he hears what my grandmother has done, he's liable to think I'm not worth the trouble."

"Well, you are a piece of work, that's for sure." Athena laughed. "But you're worth it, Kat. You're so worth it. And Scott, of all people, knows that your grandmother isn't well. He's going to forgive her for this."

"I doubt his father ever will."

"He will, if he realizes this was all a mistake. You'll have to be really careful from now on, though, Kat."

"Careful?"

"About the paparazzi." Her brow knotted. "I have a feeling they're going to have a heyday with this one. And they're not going to play by the rules. You know how tricky they are. They use their cell phones or hidden cameras to snag photos of you, then sell them to the gossip rags. So be careful, okay?"

"If I wasn't paranoid before, I sure am now."

"Sorry." She shrugged. "I'm not trying to get you all worked up. Just want you to be safe. And I'm sure Rex wouldn't be thrilled if pictures from inside the studio hit the internet or something. You know? He's really a private sort of guy."

"Humph." I thought again of the letters he'd written my grandmother. She'd kept them buried for over fifty years. For whatever reason, she had kept their relationship private. I thought about the way they'd been signed: "Your Sweetheart." Pretty vague, even back then.

I stayed at Athena's well past dinnertime, reluctantly agreeing to have a meal with them before leaving. As always, her mother stuffed me full of all sorts of goodies, most of which I ate only at their home. In fact, half of it I couldn't even pronounce.

When I got into my car to head home, I checked my cell phone, curious to see if Scott had responded. He had not. And I was surprised to see I'd somehow missed a call from my grandmother. I called back as quickly as I could.

She picked up on the third ring. "KK, I've been worried about you. Carolina said you would be back by five, and it's nearly eight o'clock. Is everything okay?"

"Yes, I spent the afternoon with Athena. We had a nice visit."

"Oh, I love nice visits," she said. "I've had so many over the years. Burt Reynolds came for a visit while you were gone, and he brought that pretty young actress Sally Field with him."

I pushed back the groan that attempted to rise. "Well, I'm sure you had a lovely time."

"We did. He tells me they're making a movie together. Something with the word *Bandit* in it. I can't remember right now what he said exactly. I'm still a little tired from my nap."

I didn't have the heart to tell her that *Smokey and the Bandit* had been released in the late '70s. It would only confuse her more. Still, there was something I needed to talk with her about, and the sooner the better.

"Grandma, when I get home, can we have a talk?"

"Oh, I'd like that, KK. Should I make some tea?"

"Sure. That sounds great."

"You can tell me everything that you and Athena decided about the wedding. I'm sure you came up with some lovely ideas."

I spent the drive in prayer. Whatever I said needed to be carefully thought out, and there was really only one way to accomplish that. I had to ask the Lord for his words over this situation. In spite of her medication, my grandmother's condition was undeniably shaky. And yet she seemed blissfully happy. Would sharing the truth injure her in any way? I decided that was a chance I was just going to have to take. I couldn't risk any more conversations with the paparazzi.

When I arrived at the house, I found her dressed in a fabulous robe. She had apparently been waiting for me. The silver tea service glistened under the glow of the lamp above the small table in the great room.

"Hope you're thirsty!" she said. Grandma poured tiny glasses of tea, adding lumps of sugar and an abundance of cream.

We settled onto the sofa next to each other, and I racked my brain to figure out a way to transition into the conversation I planned to have with her.

"I do love high tea," she said after taking a little sip. "Makes one feel like royalty. Of course, being a royal does have its downside." Her smile immediately faded. "So sad, what happened to Grace Kelly. Did you read about it in the paper, honey? I understand there's been an accident. Every tabloid in town is carrying the story."

I decided to dovetail into the necessary conversation using this as a segue. "The paparazzi can be vicious, can't they?"

"I'll say." She took a sip of her tea. "They've had me for lunch a time or two, and I don't mean at the Wilshire." She giggled, and I drew in a deep breath, prepared to forge ahead.

"That's what I want to talk to you about, Grandma," I said. "About staying away from the paparazzi, not giving them any personal information."

"O-oh?" She suddenly looked nervous. The teacup in her hand began to shake. "Have I done something to upset you, KK?"

"Grandma, did you by any chance talk to a man at *The Scoop*?"

A look of relief passed over her. "Oh, is that all. Yes, honey. They called and I answered. It's the polite thing to do, to pick up the phone when it rings."

"Yes, but we've talked about this before. Sometimes the person on the other end of the line isn't a friend. Sometimes he's just a reporter out to get a story."

She grinned. "But that's the delightful part. We *have* a story. You're getting married."

"No, Grandma."

"W-what?" She looked at me, confusion registering in her eyes.

"No, it's a big misunderstanding. I'm not getting married . . . at all."

"Of course you are, sweet girl," she said. "I was there when Jack proposed. Lots of other people were too. Why, the whole room was filled with witnesses." A concerned look came over her. "Is he trying to weasel out of it now that he's made his offer of marriage? Has that father of his talked him out of it or something?" The creases between her brows deepened and her eyes filled with tears. "Don't you dare let anyone talk you out of marrying the man you love, KK. You hear me? You will regret it for the rest of your life."

Alrighty then.

I nodded, unsure of how to get this train back on track. "Grandma, you're not understanding," I said at last. "I'm trying to say that it's all a part of the show. That's all."

I could read the relief in her eyes. "Well, of *course* it's part of the show, honey." She chuckled. "The show's the thing, remember? If I don't know that after living in Hollywood for so long, then I've learned nothing at all." She turned to me, confusion registering in her eyes. "Where is Jack, anyway? He said he was going to fix the latch on my front door."

"No, that was his—" I started to say "dad" but stopped short. Arguing with her wasn't going to make things any better.

"Such a nice boy. And great muscles. He really eats his spinach, doesn't he?"

"Yes, but Grandma, I need to talk to you about something else. Something important."

"Oh?"

"I need to know what you told that man at *The Scoop*."

"Oh, *The Scoop* is such a lovely magazine. Such interesting pictures too. My old friend Ted Holliday works there. Great guy. Why, back in my day, he came around pretty often to take pictures of me."

"And he's the one you talked to about my wedding?"

"Yes, KK. He's the best reporter they have on staff."

"What did you tell him?"

"I think I told him . . ." She paused. "Oh yes. I told him that you and Jack are going to have a beautiful reception in the gardens, and that we're going to renovate the house in preparation. Told him the house is going to be even prettier than the last time he saw it, back in '68."

"And did you mention Jack's parents?"

"Hmm." She paused and appeared to be thinking. "I recall saying something about the small town they're from. You know, I really like them, KK. I can see now why Jack turned out as he did. Such a godly young man. It's the influence of his mother. Don't you think she's a peach?"

"Yes." I counted to three under my breath then forged ahead. "Grandma, did you by any chance say something to the reporter about our swimming pool?"

"Our swimming pool?" The creases between her brows deepened. "Well, yes. I told him that you and I made a little joke about the Clampetts coming to town when we put on our Elly May bathing suits and swam in the cement pond." Her cheeks flushed pink. "Oh, is that why you're upset with me? Was that information too personal? Are you afraid Ted will ask for a picture of you in a bathing suit or something?"

"No." I shook my head. "Did you lead him to believe that Scott's parents are in any way like the Beverly Hillbillies?"

"Scott?" Her brow wrinkled. "Who's Scott?"

I counted to three once again and whispered, "Jack. Did you tell him that Jack's parents are the Clampetts?"

She pressed a hand to her chest, a shocked look registering. "For heaven's sake. Jack's last name is Clampett? I could have sworn his parents were named Murphy or something like that." She chortled. "There I go, getting all mixed up again. I'll tell you what, KK. When you're my age, sometimes things get a little fuzzy."

At *my* age, sometimes things got a little fuzzy too. Like right now, for instance. And in this Lenora Worth–induced fog, I could barely see beyond the next bend. She rambled on and on about how my married name would be Clampett after I married Jack, but I refused to listen. Enough was enough already. I had to figure out a way to wind her down.

With that in mind, I suggested we watch a movie together. She opted for *Two Mules for Sister Sara*, going on and on about how much she loved Shirley MacLaine in this role. I didn't mind, really. My thoughts were elsewhere.

Thankfully Grandma dozed off about halfway into the movie. I found my eyes growing heavy as well. After helping her into bed, I moved to my room, exhaustion leading the way. As I pulled back the covers on my bed, I thought about Scott, wondering why he hadn't responded to my voice mail or text messages. Surely he'd read the story. Maybe he was so mad he couldn't make himself call me. Maybe he would never call again. Then what would I do? How would the show go on if the leading lady and leading man weren't speaking?

If I'd been writing the questions to end this particularly melodramatic scene in my life, they would have gone something like this:

"Will Scott forgive Kat and her grandmother for ruining his life?"

"Will his parents hightail it out of Beverly Hills permanently, never to speak to Kat again?"

"Will the media take this story and run with it, creating trouble for the Murphy family back home in Alma?"

And finally, "Will Kat ever figure out how to face the storms of life head-on, without wanting to curl up in a ball in the corner?"

I couldn't answer the first three questions, of course. But I had the final one down pat. I curled up on the bed in a fetal position . . . and cried myself to sleep.

17

Step by Step

Monday morning dawned bright and sunny. I squinted at the ribbons of light slipping through my curtains, wishing I could sleep in. On the other hand, the sooner I got to the studio, the sooner I could find out if Scott was upset. I just needed to get this over with . . . for both of our sakes.

I found my grandmother dressed in a gown I'd never seen before. The white glittery dress took my breath away. She looked lovely.

"Who are we today, Grandma?" I asked as we climbed into the Pink Lady.

"Barbara Stanwyck. *Christmas in Connecticut*. 1945." She fussed with her combs, and I noticed for the first time they were Christmas-themed. In fact, so was her jewelry. I'd never seen snowflake earrings before. I had to give it to her, though. They looked great with the winter-white dress. And I especially loved the fur trimming around the wrists and neckline.

A little odd in the middle of summer, though, especially with the temps soaring higher than usual.

"Let's stop and pick up a copy of *The Scoop* on the way, KK," Grandma said. "I want to see if the police ever figured out what caused Grace Kelly's accident. She died in Monte Carlo, you know. Did I tell you that already?"

I released a breath. "You told me that she had passed away, but you didn't mention the details. I'm so sorry, Grandma. I know what a great person she was and how much you loved her."

"Oh, everyone loved Grace. What a tragic end to such a beautiful life." My grandmother dabbed at her eyes. "Heartbreaking."

"Definitely."

"*The Scoop* will carry the story. Ted is always the first to report the news. He's so good at what he does."

"Yes, those folks at *The Scoop* are definitely good at what they do." Still, the last thing on the planet I wanted to do was to pick up a copy of any magazine today, but I couldn't figure out how to avoid it. Once Grandma made up her mind to do something, she did it.

Ironically, the lead story that morning in nearly every newspaper was the impending writers' strike. I glanced over a couple of the articles, more than a little worried about how this would affect *Stars Collide*. How could we finish out the season if the writers abandoned us?

Apparently I wasn't the only one in a dither over this. By the time we arrived at the studio, terror had struck every heart. Well, maybe not terror, but a healthy fear. We depended on the writers to give us a sense of direction. And as much as I hated to admit it, I depended on the writers to point me in the right direction, both on the show and off.

Strange, how scripted my life had become.

Rex called all of us together on the set at 10:00. I looked around for Scott, wondering why he wasn't there.

"I know you've heard the news," Rex said. "Looks like we've only got a day or two till we lose our writing team. That means we've got to get that script for the wedding pounded out today." He crossed his arms and looked at Athena, Bob, and Paul. "Do you think you can do it?"

"It's mostly done," Athena responded. "Lenora has been very helpful."

"Oh yes," Grandma said, her eyes now sparkling with pure delight. "I love planning weddings. This one's going to be a doozy."

I'll bet.

Rex gave her a wistful look, and I wondered if anyone else in the room noticed it. Before long, these two wouldn't be able to hide their feelings from the masses. What had been buried for years was sure to come tumbling out for all to see, if they weren't careful.

"Well, I for one don't mind admitting I'm nervous," Tia said. "The timing couldn't be worse."

"Our writers are a loyal bunch," Rex said. "They'll give us their best while we have them."

"I promise," Athena said. "It's going to be great."

Rex turned to the rest of us. "Still, we need to be prepared for how this is all going to play out. We'll go ahead and film this week's show, then probably take a few days off to watch and see what happens with this strike."

"This isn't going to be like last time," Athena said. "I doubt it will affect the show for more than a couple of days, at most. Just long enough for all of us to take a much-needed break."

Not that we needed to be breaking at this particular juncture in the show's history, but I wasn't about to say that.

Out of the corner of my eye, I caught a glimpse of Scott. He approached from behind my grandmother, who turned and gave him a little wave. He nodded in her direction, but I didn't see his usual cheerful countenance. Yep, he'd read the story. And from the looks of things, he wasn't happy. Who could blame him?

Rex continued to talk about how we were going to handle the writers' strike, but he lost me after just a few sentences. I tried to catch Scott's eye, tried to see if he would respond to me in any way, but his gaze remained fixed to the floor. This was not looking good.

"Tell me what you have so far," Rex said, his gaze falling on Athena and the other writers. "I want every detail of that wedding."

She proceeded to fill him in, giving every last snippet of information. The wedding scene sounded both sweet and funny. I particularly liked the part where my grandmother and the children did a little song-and-dance number at the reception. That would go over well with her. Still, there were a few details left undone. Hopefully the writers would get those parts written today, while they still had time.

When the meeting ended, I glanced Scott's way. When our eyes met, the color seemed to drain from his face.

The others left, and we found ourselves alone on the talent agency set. Ironic. This is where it had all begun. Angie, the fledgling talent scout, up against the best in the business— Jack, the determined businessman, savvy but set in his ways. They'd started out as mortal enemies. Would they end up that way too?

Hmm. There I go again, jumping back into the script.

The lines of fiction and reality really were blurring in my life. Maybe Grandma wasn't the only one having trouble distinguishing between the two.

Scott approached with a pensive look on his face. His words were soft but firm. "We need to talk."

I swallowed hard and nodded. "You, um . . . you got my messages?"

"Yes." He released a sigh. "The battery on my cell phone had died, but I didn't realize it till late last night."

"Ah." I paused. "So, um, I guess you've seen the paper?"

"I have."

Tears slipped over the edges of my lashes. I brushed them away. "Scott, I don't know what to say except I'm sorry. She meant well. And that whole Beverly Hillbillies thing was a complete misunderstanding. No one ever, at any time, compared your parents to the Clampetts. I promise."

He released a slow breath, then began to pace the set, finally coming to stop in front of the *Stars Collide* sign. "I'm only worried that they're going to get wind of this and be hurt," he admitted, his voice now so low I had to strain to hear. "But more than that, I'm upset that my dad's business is in trouble and he didn't come to me about it."

I waited for him to continue, not wanting to interrupt his train of thought. I could tell Scott had a lot on his mind.

"My dad is a proud man. Too proud sometimes. But he should know I would be there for him." Scott's jaw tightened.

"You had no idea?" I asked.

Scott shook his head. "None. Every time I ask him about the store, he always says the same thing: 'We're hanging in there.'"

"I'm surprised your mom didn't tell you."

"You want the truth?" He paused, gazing intently into my eyes. "I'd be willing to bet she doesn't know either. He's a very private man." Scott ran his fingers through his hair. "Only, now his privacy has been invaded on every conceivable level."

"I'm so sorry," I whispered.

"I know." He shook his head. "This is all my fault. I don't really know my dad. Maybe I never did. If I knew him, I would be aware of the problems he's going through. But he's never been the sort to 'be known,' if that makes any sense."

"You're talking to a girl whose father took off when she was seven," I said. "So trust me. I understand."

"I'm sorry, Kat." Scott reached to grab my hand, the first visible sign that he wasn't angry at me. "It's crazy to be nearly thirty years old and still so wrapped up in trying to please my father."

"Maybe he won't see the paper," I said. "Maybe this will blow over."

"Even if he doesn't, someone is sure to tell him. I have to let him know. He needs to hear it from me."

"Well, when you call, please remind him that my grandmother isn't well and that her comment about the Beverly Hillbillies had nothing to do with them. It was taken completely out of context."

"I will." Scott offered a faint smile then shook his head. "I'm trying to envision my mother swimming in the cement pond. Crazy, the image that brings."

I chuckled, relieved to have the hardest part of this conversation behind us. Surely God could work this out. In time. In his own way.

"Hey, Kat!" I looked around as I heard my name and saw Jana. "We need you in wardrobe as soon as you can get there. Time to have that wedding dress altered."

"Wedding dress." Hmm. I wondered what Scott must be thinking. My gaze shifted back to him and I noticed the sadness in his eyes. Whispering "I'm sorry" didn't really suffice, but what else could I do, really?

He nodded and slipped his arm around me for a quick hug

before I headed back to wardrobe. But somehow that hug didn't feel the same as the ones we'd shared before. Though I hated to admit it, our relationship had changed . . . and not for the better.

So many troubling thoughts rolled through my mind as I walked to the wardrobe area. IHOP. Steak and eggs. The map of Beverly Hills. Liz Taylor's honeymoon suite. Doris Day's soothing voice. My first stolen kiss with Scott. The sound of Candy's pitiful cries inside the bathroom stall. The letters Rex had written my grandmother. The dream I'd had about my parents. The call from that so-called reporter. Carolina's ceviche. All of these things ran together in my head, creating a jumbled mess.

One thing stood out above all others, though, and it could not be denied. My grandmother was clearly in the beginning stages of Alzheimer's. I hadn't voiced the word till now, but that's what it was. Her wackiness and fun-loving ways were always offbeat and unusual. But her erratic behavior, which I'd once considered quirky and humorous, could no longer be ignored. It genuinely concerned me, in fact. Everything in our world was changing, and I needed to figure out a way to get used to my "new normal."

When I arrived at the wardrobe department, I found Jana unzipping the plastic bag that held my wedding dress. Er, Angie's wedding dress. Sure, I'd picked it out. And yes, I would wear it. But ultimately it belonged to Angie, the fictional character who didn't really have a heart or soul and would never even know she was having a wedding.

Jana chattered with great abandon as she helped me into the gown. Fastening up the buttons in the back, I held my breath, anxious to see if it still fit after all of the salmon and ceviche I'd consumed the other night. Thankfully it fit like a dream.

I looked at my reflection in the full-length, tri-fold mirror and gasped. In that moment—that magical, ethereal moment—I felt like a bride. A real, honest-to-goodness, gonna-walk-down-the-aisle-into-the-arms-of-my-lovin'-man bride.

It terrified me.

And exhilarated me.

A rap at the door interrupted my reverie. Jana looked at me with straight pins in her mouth, gesturing for me to answer it.

I opened the door, stunned to see Rex Henderson on the other side.

He took one look at me in the white dress and his eyes grew wide. "Oh my. That's . . . you're beautiful. Radiant."

"Thanks." I swished to the right and then the left, showing off the dress's amazing skirt. "They gave me several to choose from, and this is the one I picked. I like the fitted waist and the full skirt."

"You're like a picture from a magazine," he said. "Oh, and speaking of magazines . . ."

"I know." I groaned. "You saw the article?"

"Well, Tia did. She brought me a copy. Thought I needed to know what was going on."

"Rex, I didn't set that up. I need you to know that."

"Lenora?" Just one word, but it spoke volumes.

"Yes."

"Say no more." He grinned. "She always did have a way with reporters. The woman knew how to get the papers to cover just about anything."

"She still does."

"Could I come in so we can talk?" he asked, a look of concern registering in his eyes.

Jana continued fussing with the hem of the dress then

looked up, pulling the pins out of her mouth. "Should I leave you two alone?"

"Do you mind?"

"Not at all. Do you want to get out of this dress first?"

"Are you done pinning it?"

She shook her head, so I agreed to keep it on until after she returned.

When she left the room, Rex took a seat on the sofa and gestured for me to join him. I wasn't sure how to go about sitting in the cumbersome dress, so I opted to stand. I caught a glimpse of my profile in the full-length mirror. Except for the messy hair and unhemmed dress, I almost felt ready to walk down the aisle. And Rex could very well be the father figure, heart swelling with pride as he escorted me to meet my groom. What would that feel like?

I shook off my daydreams, ready to deal with reality. For a change.

"Kat, I just talked to Scott," Rex said. "I know he's really trying to sort through all of this."

"Me too."

"I hope you two don't let this little situation keep you apart. That would be awful."

"Keep us apart?" I feigned innocence.

"Kat, you're a brilliant actor."

"Th-thank you." His words threw me a little. "I've spent years studying the craft and—"

"You're good," he repeated. "But not that good."

"Excuse me?"

"I can tell when you're acting and when you're not. The day you told me about your relationship with Scott, I knew it was the real deal. And because of that, I've been praying. For both of you."

"You have?"

"Yes. Relationships in Hollywood are tough. Tougher than any other place I know. So you've got to work extra hard to hang on to what you've got."

"Ah." I paused. "What did you mean with the brilliant actor line?"

"I've got you figured out," he said. "You'll forge ahead and act like everything's okay when it's not. You're the kind to just keep going, to make sure everyone else is okay, even when you're not."

Ouch.

"It's clear you and Scott are in love," he added, giving me a tender glance. "I'd have to be a fool not to see it."

I plopped down on the sofa next to Rex, not even caring about the dress now. Well, until a straight pin jabbed me in the side. I shifted positions and sucked in a breath. For whatever reason, I could only manage four words: "You're right. About everything."

He nodded and offered a sympathetic smile. "Don't let any walls rise up between you, Kat. That would be tragic, especially over something like this."

I looked at him and sighed. "I guess I thought you'd get a kick out of all of this publicity. This is going to be great PR for the show, right? Lots of drama."

"I like to keep my drama on the set, thanks," he said. "And to answer your question about publicity, no show—not even *Stars Collide*—is important enough to pull two people apart. Are you hearing me, Kat?"

Loud and clear. His words jumped straight out of those letters from 1958 into my heart. Though I didn't have the details, I knew the man spoke from experience.

"Do you mind if I share something with you?" he asked.

"Of course not."

"This is just between us, Kat." He paused and I nodded.

"One of the reasons we let Mark go was because of a difference in philosophy. Do you remember hearing him say that the show was as much about the chase as it was the catch?"

"Sure. He said that all the time. He wanted to drag the story out as long as he could to keep the viewers chomping at the bit."

"Right. Well, the chase is good, up to a point. We all love that feeling of being pursued." For a moment I thought I'd lost him—his eyes took on a faraway look. Then he snapped back to attention. "But we can't live there, can we?"

"I . . . I guess not." Though I wasn't sure what this had to do with anything.

"Relationships are tough, like I said. They take work. It's never as easy as it looks in books or on TV."

"I'm figuring that out."

"Scripted romances are formulaic," he added. "And sometimes I think we do our viewers a disservice by sticking to the formula."

"What do you mean?"

"In a typical romance, the hero and heroine don't even kiss or express their feelings until near the end of the story. It never ceases to amaze me that women will spend two hundred eighty pages reading a book, waiting on one kiss."

I shrugged. "Nothing new there. That's how the great Jane Austen stories were. People love that sort of thing. They always have. I guess that's why our viewers have been willing to watch for three full seasons, waiting on Jack and Angie to share their feelings."

"Yes, but this is what bothers me about it." Rex shook his head and gave me a fatherly look. "It's like people think the only love story is the 'falling in love' part. The part that produces romantic feelings. They forget that the story is really just beginning at that first kiss. The true love story—in real life, anyway—is the part that comes after. Walking with each other through thick and thin. Staying with that person when he does something stupid and you feel like killing him. Marrying him and having his babies and dealing with dirty dishes and laundry. Walking someone you love through a health crisis. The ravages of Alzheimer's, even."

I hardly knew what to say in response. The impassioned look on Rex's face told me he wasn't quite done yet.

"*That's* real love, Kat. It's 'I'm going to stick with you whether you have a job or not.' And 'I'm going to walk with you through the deepest valleys, overcoming every obstacle, even the worst health crisis.' That's real, God-breathed love."

"Wow." I stared at him, dumbfounded. Where was all of this coming from?

"We think that the only sellable love stories are the ones based on feelings," he continued. "But I'd challenge you to think about the fact that real love is the stuff that takes place after the feelings have been exposed. The day-in, day-out stuff."

"I guess that's true," I said. My mind shifted to the situation with Scott. If he and I really loved each other, that love would sustain us through the ups and downs we faced. Realizing this suddenly gave me hope that our relationship could continue to blossom and grow no matter what.

"That's where the story is," Rex said. "And that's why shows like *Everybody Loves Raymond* and *I Love Lucy* worked so well. We got to follow the couple beyond the point of expressing their feelings to the working out of their relationship. Maybe those shows didn't give us goose bumps, but they certainly made us laugh. And they taught us that love overcomes obstacles. They were wacky, but they were real. On some level, anyway. As real as we're able to handle."

Double wow. Was this guy on a roll, or what? I stared at him, still unsure of my response.

He reached to take my hand. "Kat, listen to me. Don't let life rob you of the real love story. Do you hear me? I'm trying to share my heart here."

"Y-yes." I heard him all right. Loud and clear.

"I've been in this business too long. And the scripts don't always play out the way you think they will. It's not always 'Boy meets girl, boy loses girl, boy gets girl.' Sometimes we lose each other and the pieces never get put back together again."

Perfect opportunity to transition into a conversation with him about Grandma.

"Now it's my turn, Rex. There's something I need to talk to you about."

I rose and made my way to my purse, pulling out the letters. As I clutched them in my trembling hand, I whispered up a prayer that God would guide this conversation. I didn't want to accuse. Didn't want to hurt anyone. But I had to have some answers or I could never move forward . . . in my relationship with my grandmother or my relationship with Scott.

I turned back to Rex and placed the letters into his hands. He thumbed through them, and for a moment he looked . . . confused. And then startled. And then the tears came. They filled his soft green eyes and nearly broke my heart in the process.

"W-where . . . where did you get these?" He looked up at me.

"She's kept them in a trunk in her room. There are lots more."

He nodded. "Probably at least ten or twelve more, in fact."

"Rex, I know you wrote these letters. And I know you loved my grandmother very much."

He shook his head. "Stop speaking in the past tense," he whispered. "I could just as easily have written these letters this morning, Kat. Nothing has changed. Nothing."

My heart began to race at his honest revelation. "Rex, everything has changed. Maybe not the way you feel about her, but the circumstances aren't what they used to be. And to be honest, I'm not even sure what the circumstances were back then. She loved you . . . but she married someone else?"

"Yes. She married someone else." His jaw became tight. "I don't know, Kat. I thought she loved me. But then . . ." He shook his head. "It didn't work out. She fell in love with another man. Married him. Had his child. And I . . ." He paused, his gaze shifting down. "I was never the same after that."

"Rex, these letters were sent after my grandfather died. You only waited six months to pursue her after his death. That's . . ." I fought to find the right words. "That's not very . . . honorable."

"I . . . I know." He rose and paced the room, coming to stop directly in front of me. "It was wrong of me, and I've lived to regret it. She never responded to any of those letters, Kat. Not one. I'm stunned she kept them. I always figured she tossed them as they came in. Any hopes I had as a naive young man slipped through my fingers all those years ago. So when I came to work here several weeks ago . . . when I had to face her every day and could see with my own eyes the condition she's in . . . it broke my heart."

"But it also gave you hope?" I asked. "That you could go back to the past, where things left off?"

He released a breath. "Maybe. When I see her . . ." His eyes lit up. "When I see her, it's like no time has passed at all. She's still that ravishing young starlet with her head in the clouds."

"And when she sees you, she can hardly speak or think clearly," I said. Shaking my head, I shared my heart. "Rex, I have to admit this is hard. I never knew my grandfather, but I . . . well, I almost feel sorry for him. I have to wonder if all of this would break his heart."

"I understand, Kat. And if it makes you feel any better, I never knew him either. We never met. Your grandmother was very private about her relationship with your grandfather, and about your mother's birth as well. She even stopped filming movies during that season." He smiled. "I guess that being a wife and mother made her happier than being a movie star. I can certainly understand that."

"Did you marry, Rex?" I asked. "Have a family?"

He nodded. "Married in my thirties to a fabulous woman named Emily. We had two daughters—Jeannie and Jackie. They're twins."

"Wow. I didn't know."

He laughed. "They're definitely not into the whole movie business thing. And Emily . . ." His eyes filled with tears. "She developed a rare brain cancer when she was only fifty-two. She didn't linger, but it was horrible to see her in such pain."

"Oh, Rex, I'm sorry. You've been through so much." I paused, deep in thought. "We all have."

He exhaled. "Kat, I've lived a wonderful life. I'm blessed with two daughters and several grandbabies. On top of that, I had several years with a fabulous woman. But a number of years have gone by, and I still haven't forgotten about your grandmother. She was my first love. And now she has no one. I have no one." He offered a shy smile.

"So I guess there's really just one question remaining."

He looked at me, hope in his expression. "What's that?"

"What are you going to do about it?" I asked.

A hint of a smile crossed his face. "You wouldn't think

it was out of line?" When I shook my head, he grabbed my hand and squeezed it. "Kat, I know her health isn't what it used to be. But I still see potential there. I want to take care of her. I want to be there for her. We've already missed out on so many years together."

"I . . . I think I would like that too."

He nodded and his eyes brimmed over with tears. "That's all I need to hear. Moving forward without your blessing would be impossible. But with you on my team . . ." He grinned. "Well, with you on my team, I think I stand a solid chance of winning her over."

"Winning her over?" I snorted. "I don't think you'll have to work very hard at that, Rex. The only question is how you'll go about it."

"Now that's something to pray about," he said. "But trust me, I'll figure it out."

"I'm sure you will." I reached to give him a hug and happened to catch a glimpse of the two of us in the full-length mirror. My heart caught in my throat. What a lovely picture. The blushing bride. The grandfatherly figure. Wow. How my life would change if Rex moved forward in a relationship with my grandmother.

At that moment the door flew open and Grandma scurried inside. She looked back and forth between Rex and me, a dazed expression on her face.

"What are you two up to?" she asked.

"Oh, just planning for the future," I said.

"Planning for the future, eh?" She reached to take my hand, her gaze shifting to my dress. "This is the best way to start! Oh, KK, it's perfect. Absolutely perfect. You're going to be the prettiest bride who ever walked the aisle."

"Thank you." I couldn't think of anything else to say in response, so I stopped right there. Turning again to face the mirror, I stared at the reflection of the three of us—Grandma, Rex, and me. With my grandmother in her glitzy gown, Rex in a suit, and me in my wedding dress, this looked for all the world like a family portrait.

I couldn't help but think it really would be. If the writers would just finish that script.

18

The Love Boat

On the day after Athena and the others finished writing the wedding scene, every writer in the city of Los Angeles went on strike. And while we weren't completely confident this would end soon, we did take it as a sign that we needed to get out of the studio and live life unscripted.

Scott came up with the idea of taking several cast and crew members out on his yacht for the day. I'd never been one for traveling the high seas. To be honest, the water rides at Six Flags made me nauseous. Still, I didn't want to look like a party pooper. Besides, with the paparazzi hot on our trail, getting out of town did hold some appeal. And it would also give me time to spend with Scott, away from cameras and nosy reporters. For that reason alone, I would endure any potential seasickness.

We arrived at the harbor in Dana Point, and I looked out over the collection of yachts and other sailing vessels. What an awesome display. And with the first hints of sunlight peeking through the early morning sky, it looked like something out of a painting. I could hardly wait to get on that boat. To sail away and forget about my troubles.

I glanced over at my grandmother, who wore a sailor getup complete with cap. She looked like something out of that old Frank Sinatra and Gene Kelly movie *Anchors Aweigh*.

"Grandma, are you sure you're up for this?" I asked as we stepped onto the pier.

"I love the sea, KK," she said. "Always have." She dove into a story about Humphrey Bogart and Lauren Bacall—something about sailing with them on his boat—but I wasn't really listening. Instead I watched as Scott drew near. The expression on his face when he saw me—and Grandma—was one of introspection. He greeted me with a kiss on the forehead and a polite hello to my grandmother. Things clearly weren't back to normal yet, but after today they would be—I prayed.

Rex arrived a few minutes later. He took one look at Grandma and beamed. "If I didn't know any better, I would think I was looking at Bernadette Peters in *Dames at Sea*."

"Oh, I've always loved her, so I'll take that as a compliment," Grandma said with a hint of flirtatiousness in her smile. She began to hum a little tune and before long was singing a little ditty called "The Sailor of My Dreams" in her funny, off-key way.

Rex didn't look like he minded a bit. In fact, he seemed completely enamored with the sailor girl standing in front of him. I had a feeling they would be having a serious chat before the day ended. Maybe our experience at sea would free them up to express their true feelings after all these years. In the meantime, he took her by the hand and they made their way aboard.

Tia arrived wearing heels and a frilly blouse over designer

jeans. I had to laugh. She would be sorry later on. Jason, our cameraman, looked pretty hunky in his tight-fitting T-shirt and swim trunks. Funny. On the set we occasionally chatted, but I couldn't say that I really knew much about him. Other than the fact that he operated a camera, anyway. And had once given the boom mic operator the okay to whack me in the head midscene. Just for fun, of course.

Still, Tia managed to get on his bad side right off the bat. The fact that both would be spending the day together in such cramped quarters made me wonder what sort of chaos might ensue. It looked like we had some interesting hours ahead. What would happen if they started bickering again? Likely we would have to toss one—or both—overboard. What a headline that would make. I could just see it now: STARS COLLIDE AS DIRECTOR AND CAMERAMAN TOPPLE OVERBOARD DURING FIGHT ON THE HIGH SEAS. I chuckled, thinking about the paparazzi's take on that.

I waved to Athena, Paul, and Bob, who approached in casual summer clothes. Our writing trio might be on strike, but that wouldn't stop them from sailing the high seas with our cast and crew. I had a feeling—knowing them—that the experience would produce future episodes for the sitcom. No doubt about it.

We boarded the yacht, and I found myself mesmerized as I took in the beautiful boat. Scott introduced her as *Little Star*, explaining that he'd named her after the kids on the show. That only made me love him all the more.

Everyone did a fair share of oohing and aahing as Scott prepared the ship to sail. When we pulled away from the dock, I felt an uncanny sense of peace. The yacht moved slowly, steadily, through the rows of other yachts and boats.

"This is great, Scott," I called out above the sound of the water lapping the sides of the yacht. "Not bumpy at all."

He nodded from behind the wheel, and I couldn't help but think he looked very much like a ship's captain, manly and confident. I'd seen him in a variety of roles before, but never one like this. I would have to work hard at not swooning.

Hmm. As we rounded the first turn, the boat swayed and my swooning began to feel more like nausea.

Deep breaths, Kat. Deep breaths.

After a few minutes, Athena and the other writers slipped into their usual creative mode. They were a clever bunch, always talking about the next story idea. But beyond that, they all seemed to get along. I'd never seen such a tight-knit group. All of them on the same page.

On the same page. Funny.

How exciting would it be to write scenes like they did? To push players around on the stage, tell them where to go and what to say? Must be pretty heady business.

The life of an actress was exactly the opposite. We just did what we were told. Most of us, anyway. Of course, today I was on my own, away from the studio. Away from the control of writers. Whatever the Lord wanted to do . . . wherever he wanted to take me, I would go.

Breathing in the salty air, I thanked him for this glorious opportunity to get away, to sneak a peek over the horizon. A few deep, cleansing breaths and my feelings of nausea passed. However, about fifteen minutes later as we headed out into rougher waters, my stomach began to do some serious gymnastics.

Uh-oh. I drew in a deep breath, hoping to hold steady. No such luck. Counting to ten sounded like a viable option, so I tried that.

By the time I hit three, I was barreling down the stairs to the restroom. Thank goodness I found it empty.

Minutes later, feeling somewhat slimmer and slightly less nauseous, I headed up to the deck once again. Popping a piece of gum in my mouth, I looked around. The sunrise was fully upon us now. Others were snapping photographs and talking about the various colors in the sky. Grandma and Rex seemed to be enjoying each other's company more than the scenery, but that didn't surprise me. Still, I found the sunrise captivating. Awe inspiring.

Funny thing, though. Whenever I looked out at the purple-orange sky hovering over the rough waters, my stomach revolted once again. And why did I feel so dizzy?

Easing my way down the stairs, I prayed for a reprieve. How would I ever kiss and make up with Scott if this didn't change? I was hoping to get our relationship back on track today. That wouldn't happen if I spent the entire day in a three-by-four bathroom.

Another wave of nausea hit. This time I made my way into the tiny bedroom and lay down on the bed, eyes squeezed shut. I gave myself over to the bobbing of the boat. Up and down. Back and forth. Up and down. Back and forth.

Ugh.

Thankfully, after a short period of time, the constant rocking slowed a bit and I felt like I might be able to stand. Minutes later I was topside, chatting with the crew and acting like nothing had happened. Talk about a great acting job. Grandma chatted with Athena and the others—probably about my wedding—and I approached our captain, who stood firm at his post, keeping a watchful eye on things.

Scott gave me a sympathetic look. "Kat, are you okay?"

I eased my way down onto the seat, my head beginning to swim. "Um, not exactly."

"I'm sorry you're sick."

The boat continued to rock. Off in the distance, Athena and her crew were laughing, as always. Tia and Jason appeared to be debating something . . . again. Nothing new there.

"I think this was a great idea, Scott," I said, gesturing to the water. "Getting away is just the ticket. And . . . well, I think it will do us some good too."

"We're fine, Kat. Really." He extended a hand and I took it. He placed my hands on the wheel and then stepped behind me, cocooning me while resting both of his hands on the wheel. In that instant, all of my fears sailed out to sea. I nestled against him, my heart completely happy. And relieved. I noticed Tia and Jason look our way. They both looked a little surprised, but I didn't care. It was about time we let people know the truth.

"I talked to my dad today," Scott said after a few moments of quiet.

"Oh?" I released my hold on the wheel and turned to face him.

"He didn't know anything about the story, but it's just a matter of time, so I filled him in. He seemed to take it all in stride."

"Thank goodness."

"He and my mom really like you, Kat. And Lenora too." He nodded in my grandmother's direction. "Hey, speaking of Lenora . . ."

"I know. Remind me to tell you later about my talk with Rex. But not now. I want to hear about your parents."

"Well, I was just saying that they were bound to find out about the article sooner or later, but I think I've distracted that guy at the magazine. I called him on my way down here and gave him a better story than the one he ran."

"Oh?" My mind reeled. "And what's that?"

"Well, let me start by telling you that I sent the money to help my dad get caught up on the mortgage. And I suggested he renovate. I really think that will help bring in customers and ensure he never gets behind on the mortgage again. I'll cover those costs too. I know he doesn't have the funds to do it."

"Oh, Scott. That's great."

"I also asked him for his wish list of all the items he'd like to carry—from the things he saw at the convention."

"Oh, wow. What did he say to all of that?" I asked.

"He refused . . . at first. But after I finally talked him through the process, he was fine. The store has been struggling since a new Home Depot came to town."

"And you think a renovation and update in product will help?"

"Well, sure," he said. "People need to know that Murphy's Hardware is going to be there no matter what other stores come and go." Scott paused. "And they've got to be competitive. That's a given. But I didn't tell the reporter any of that. I told him that my dad is going to run a campaign selling T-shirts with our faces on them."

"What?"

"Yep. Remember all of those pictures my mom took of us that last night at your house? Standing in front of the cement pond?"

"Sure."

"Apparently a couple of those photos look really great on a white T-shirt. Who knew? We're quite the rage in Alma, you and me."

"Well, of course we are. Big fish in a small pond and all that."

"Big fish in Mud Creek is more like it. But anyway, all proceeds from the T-shirts will go to the orphanage in Ensenada. And I promised to match the proceeds dollar for dollar. So *that's* the story *The Scoop* will run online. The other one—about my dad's store facing foreclosure—has already been removed from the website."

"Oh, Scott, that's awesome. I feel so much better. And just so you know, my grandmother didn't do any of that to be malicious."

"I know." He turned the wheel a bit to the right, then leaned over and kissed the tip of my nose. "And you've been working hard to protect her."

"Just like you've been trying to protect your parents." I sighed. "When did it become the job of the kids to protect the parents and grandparents, anyway?"

He shrugged. "I don't mind, Kat. I think it's biblical, anyway. We need to care for our own household, and my parents are my household. Even though, technically, they live on the other side of the country. But you get the idea."

"I think you're pretty amazing, Scott Murphy." I leaned over and kissed him on the cheek.

I heard Athena holler out, "Would you two cut that out? You're making us nauseous over here."

I laughed and hollered back, "Don't blame your seasickness on us." I looked at Scott and smiled. "So, you're okay with people knowing we're a couple?"

"More than okay." He kissed me on the forehead. "I plan to shout it to the whole world."

"Hope you've got good lungs."

"Won't need 'em. Not with the paparazzi hovering around us at every turn."

"True. What are we going to do about that?"

"Play along?" After a moment he grew more serious. "Kat, I've spent a lot of time thinking about this. I don't want to lose you. Next to the Lord, you're the best thing that's ever happened to me. I don't care what kind of stories run in the gossip magazines . . . I'll still love you. And I plan to go on loving you . . . well, for the rest of my life."

The kiss that followed almost sent the yacht sailing off

244

into uncharted waters. Fortunately Scott managed to get us back on course in record time. I felt invigorated by his words, yet a couple of lingering doubts remained. I couldn't seem to shake them.

I happened to glance over at Tia and Jason, who stared at each other in stony silence. For just a second I had a flashback to that dream, the one where I was sitting at IHOP with my parents. Their cold, hard stares left an indelible impression on my mind, searing my memory of them.

I looked at Scott. "Can I ask you a question?"

"Sure." His eyes remained fixed on the water. Probably a good thing, since the waves had grown up around us, tossing the boat to and fro.

"You know how sometimes in restaurants you'll be sitting near a couple you don't know?"

"Sure." He glanced my way and shrugged.

"Sometimes you feel like you're invading their space because it's just the two of them sitting there. And they don't look like they're having a very good time."

"Ah."

"I always wonder why some couples don't talk to each other at the dinner table. They just sit there. Silent."

"O-okay." He looked confused.

"What if that's us?" I whispered. "What if we run out of things to say?"

The laughter that erupted from him nearly rocked the boat. "Kat, you're hysterical. First of all, I can't ever imagine you running out of things to say."

"Hey now."

"Second, if I have the privilege of spending my life with you, I'll sit across the table from you and tell you how gorgeous you are . . . every day of your life."

"See, you say that now," I told him. "But it doesn't always

last. I'm sure my dad . . ." I paused, unable to speak over the lump in my throat.

"Ah." Scott reached for my hand and gave it a squeeze. "Is that what this is about? Your dad?"

As I nodded, a golf-ball-sized lump rose in my throat. For a minute I didn't say anything. "I know he cared about my mom once. I've seen their wedding pictures. No one forced him to marry her or anything. I know they used to travel and do all sorts of fun things together. They had a great relationship . . . until I came along."

"Kat, wait a minute. Are you trying to say you think you're somehow to blame for your father's stupidity?"

"Not me personally. I just have to wonder if I was an interruption to his plan or something."

"If so, you're the best interruption I've ever met." A mischievous look crossed his face.

I started breathing easier. Scott's words were just the medicine to soothe my soul. I drew in a deep breath and whispered, "Thank you. I needed to hear that."

"I know. And you need to hear something else too. You need to know that your father didn't leave because of you. Parents don't leave because of the kids. Rarely, anyway."

"I know that. In my mind. It just hasn't reached my heart yet."

"It will in time," he said. "But in the meantime, there's one more thing on my mind."

"What's that?"

"You're assuming that silence is a bad thing. I might argue that point. Sometimes people just need their space. If I ever sit across the table from you and don't speak, please don't assume it's because I don't love you. Maybe I'm just distracted, or maybe I'm plotting the next great vacation I'm going to take you on."

"Mmm." I quirked a brow. "To South America?"

"What is it with you and the Amazon?" he asked, then chuckled.

"I have no idea. I think it just started as a joke and went from there. But I have always had a fascination with the rain forest. Ever since I saw that movie *Medicine Man* with Sean Connery."

"Sean Connery." Scott smiled. "I haven't thought about him in ages."

"He used to date my grandmother." I shrugged. "Well, at least that's what she says. But she says a lot of things, doesn't she?"

"Yep." He nodded. "And some of them are even true."

At that, we had a good, long laugh. And as our laughter rolled across the waves, I felt my burdens lift. In that moment I realized that I could actually let go of the pain I'd been holding on to where my father was concerned. Whether he ever knew me or not, I was known—and loved—by the Creator of the universe, and by the Pacific's most fearless sea captain. What more could a girl ask for?

19

Days of Our Lives

Less than an hour into our trip, just about the time my queasiness lifted for good, Scott received a report from the coast guard.

"What's up?" I asked when I saw the concerned look in his eyes.

"There's a storm off Catalina. Came up suddenly, they said." He paused. "Whatever happened to that 'It never rains in Southern California' thing? We've had two storms in a row."

"Crazy. Something must be going on in the stratosphere," Bob said.

"Oooh, that would make a great scene for the show," Paul interjected. "Maybe a hot-air-balloon sequence. Angie and Jack could go sailing off into the stratosphere and float for days. There would have to be a bad guy, someone who set the whole thing up. Maybe someone out to destroy the talent agency. A Snidely Whiplash sort."

"Maybe he plans to steal the agency," Athena added. "But the only way is to get rid of Angie and Jack first."

"Gee, thanks," I said. "Are we going to drift off into the stratosphere, never to be seen again?"

Jason shook his head. "I don't think stratosphere is the right word," he said. "Technically, the stratosphere is above the troposphere, but below the mesosphere. I don't know if a hot air balloon would actually get that high."

Athena looked at him and groaned. "You're such a geek."

"Did everyone miss the point?" Scott asked. "I said there's a storm coming in. That changes everything . . . in the stratosphere and on this yacht. We're going to have to head back to shore. The trip is off."

"We don't get to go to Catalina?" Grandma asked.

"No, sorry." Scott shrugged. "Maybe another time."

"Oh, pooh." She pursed her lips. "I was hoping you two would end up like Doris Day and Chuck Connors in *Move Over, Darling*."

"Don't think I saw that one," Scott said.

"Two strangers stranded alone on a desert island," she said, then wiggled her thinly plucked brows. "I'm a firm believer in getting alone and working things out. Don't let anyone else keep you apart. Promise me that, KK."

I reached to give her a hug, noticing for the first time that she was trembling. "I promise, Grandma. And besides, we've already worked things out."

"Wonderful!" She looked back and forth between Scott and me. "Oh, Jack, I'm so happy! I'm still making plans for the most beautiful wedding ever!"

I looked at Scott, wondering how to respond. He slipped

his arm around my waist and nodded. "The wedding's back on. So get busy planning, Lenora. We want it to be spectacular, something the paparazzi will talk about for years to come."

"I'll go chat with Athena now. There are some loose ends we need to tie up." After taking a couple of steps, she turned back and looked at me with tears in her eyes. "Oh, KK, you're going to have everything I only dreamed of having. I promise. It will be spectacular."

I wanted to respond but was too overcome by the look of sheer joy on her face. She gestured to Athena, and the two of them disappeared into the hull of the ship. Moments later, raindrops began to fall. After I spent a few minutes of alone time with Scott above deck, he encouraged me to go down below to join the others. I did just that.

"So what's going on up there?" Athena asked as I took the seat next to her.

"We're racing back to shore, hoping to beat the storm," I explained. "It's getting worse."

"If I were writing this scene, it would be a hurricane," Paul added. "Can you imagine the tension we could add with a real hurricane blowing in?"

"We don't get a lot of hurricanes off the coast of California, though," Bob said. "It's got to be believable."

"Since when does comedy have to be believable?" Athena asked. "Viewers are willing to use their imagination. Did people really believe that Lucille Ball was that goofy? And did they really believe that the gal on *I Dream of Jeannie* could fit into that bottle?"

"Barbara Eden," I threw in.

"Right. Barbara Eden." Athena threw her hands up in the air. "I mean, she was petite, but not small enough to fit into a genie bottle. C'mon, guys. We're always asking viewers to allow their imaginations to take them places they've never gone before."

"I still don't think they'll buy a hurricane in Southern California," Bob said.

"The point is, we need something to get the viewer's stomach in knots," Paul said. "Something big. We've got to keep the tension building. Otherwise, what's the point?"

"True." Athena nodded. "Maybe an earthquake?"

"Nah, that's overdone." Paul shrugged. "I say we just stick with a storm. A plain, ordinary, generic storm."

Scott hollered down an update. "Just heard from the coast guard again. The storm is bearing down on us. We're racing it back, but I wanted to prepare you in case the waters get rocky."

"See what I mean?" Paul said. "Scott just upped the tension of the story. Now we get to factor in the element of time."

"Will they make it back to shore before the storm hits . . . or won't they?" Athena's eyes shimmered with excitement.

"You guys are enjoying this way too much," Scott called out.

"That's our job," Paul said, looking far too excited about the possibilities.

"Not when you're on strike," I reminded them. "You can rest easy now."

The boat lifted several feet and slammed back down, sending us all tumbling into each other. Even with Scott at the wheel, I still felt nervous.

"Fasten your seat belts," Bob hollered. "It's going to be a bumpy night!"

Grandma's face lit into a smile. "Oh, I know that one! Bette Davis. *All About Eve*. 1950."

"How does she do that?" Athena asked, still rocking back and forth. "It's absolutely amazing."

"It's a gift," Rex said. "No one can match it."

My grandmother's eyelashes fluttered. Talk about flirtatious.

Tia shook her head. "This is getting scary, if you ask me. To think we just went out for a little boat ride to Catalina, and now we're stranded in a storm."

Bob started whistling the theme song from *Gilligan's Island*, and we all laughed. Well, at first. About ten minutes later, only a handful of those on board—namely the writers—still found this exciting. The rest of us were looking a little green.

Athena, Bob, and Paul didn't look a bit fazed, even when Rex dismissed himself to the bathroom due to seasickness. The overly ambitious writers huddled together, laptop open on the tiny coffee table, plotting a great scene for the show. One that would, of course, involve a storm off the coast, which Jack and Angie would brave. On their honeymoon, no less.

"Just wait. It's going to be great, Kat," Athena said. "Angie will be seasick and Jack will be chasing the storm to shore."

"Will they live or will they die?" Bob spoke with excitement, using his best announcer's voice.

"Only the coast guard knows for sure." Athena chuckled. "Write that down. We'll use it in the promo material."

Bob continued to whistle the *Gilligan's Island* theme song, and my thoughts shifted to the show.

"Just promise me one thing," I said, giving Athena the most serious look I could muster.

"What's that?"

"If this boat we're on—the real one, not the one in the scene you're writing—ends up crashing on a desert island, I get to be Mary Ann. You can be Ginger."

"Aw, *I* wanted to be Ginger," Grandma said. "I always loved her dresses."

"Weird that she packed so many for a three-hour tour, though," Paul said. "That part always bothered me. The writers of that show sure expected viewers to suspend their disbelief in a lot of areas."

"Who cares?" Athena slapped him on the arm. "I'm willing to suspend my disbelief if I can be the glamorous movie star. Ginger's always been my favorite."

"Well, who does that leave for me?" Grandma asked with a pout.

"Mrs. Howell, of course," Athena said. She turned to Rex as he exited the restroom looking a little green. Calm as you please, she said, "We're playing *Gilligan's Island*. You're going to be Thurston Howell the Third."

"That figures." He laughed and a bit of color returned to his cheeks. "Fine with me, if I can have the bank account to go with it."

"Naturally." Athena nodded.

Bob looked thoughtful. "I guess I'll be Gilligan, since I'm pretty goofy. What about Scott and Paul? Which one will be the professor and which one's the skipper?"

"That's a given," Athena said. "Scott is the captain of this ship. He has to be the skipper."

"Scott?" Grandma's brow wrinkled and her eyes took on a faraway look. "Who's Scott?"

Thankfully Rex intervened. "That means you'll have to be the professor, Paul. Hope you're okay with that."

Paul nodded. "Whatever. I'm pretty geeky."

"What about me?" Tia and Jason spoke in unison. They looked at each other, then at us.

"Hmm." Athena pondered their question a moment. "I know. Tia, you'll be the Hollywood director whose plane crash-lands on the island. When you figure out that Ginger is one of the castaways, you'll try to kidnap her to star in your latest film. But Jason, your pilot, will fix the plane and deliberately sabotage your plan, causing the two of you to leave the island without Ginger."

Grandma looked at Rex, aghast. "The way these writers come up with stories is nothing short of miraculous."

Athena smiled. "It's a gift."

Suddenly the boat hit a huge wave and sent us tumbling all over each other again. As soon as we settled down, Athena went off on a tangent about the *Gilligan's Island*–like episode they would write as soon as we made it back to shore, and Rex turned her way with a grin.

"You know, Athena, it's good to know that even though you're on strike, you're still coming up with story ideas for the show. You're a real trouper."

With a wave of her hand, she dismissed any concerns we might have had. "Trust me, this strike is temporary, just to make a point. It'll be over in a few days and we'll be back on task."

"Or, if this storm catches up with us, we'll all be living on a desert island," I said. "Permanently."

"Isn't that what you wanted all along, Kat?" Athena asked. "To live in the rain forest? In a hut?"

"By myself," I said, crossing my arms. "What's the point in running away if everyone goes with you?"

"You're running away?" Grandma Lenora's words were quiet yet laced with fear.

Oh, man. Now what? I looked her way, trying to think of something to say that wouldn't add fuel to the fire.

Athena jumped in. "Well, you know how it is, Lenora," she said. "We all say we want to run away sometimes. Didn't you ever want to?"

For several seconds, my grandmother said nothing. Then, finally, a lone tear trickled down her cheek, and she shifted her gaze to the floor. You could've heard a pin drop. From a distance, Rex kept a watchful eye on her, his brow wrinkled. When her tears began to flow, we all sat, stunned, not knowing what to do. Rex moved to her side and took hold of her hand.

"I think I'll check on Scott," Bob said. "Er, the skipper. I'm his first mate, after all." He shot up the stairs, clearly anxious to leave this tearful scene behind.

"And I'm the professor, so I'll think of something to get us out of this jam," Paul added. He too headed for the steps.

"I'll entertain them with a scene from one of my movies," Athena said, then scooted up the stairs behind the guys.

What was it with these writers? They could write dramatic scenes but had trouble sitting through them when they played out firsthand. Not that I minded their leaving. In fact, I was happy to have the time alone with my grandmother, who had curled into Rex's embrace.

For a while no one said anything. Tia and Jason, who observed all of this in silence, finally decided to join the others topside.

Grandma's tears eventually slowed. Outside, thunder shook the little boat and we rocked back and forth. I gripped the railing next to the seat, and Rex pulled Grandma closer.

"What is it, Lenora?" he asked. "What has you so troubled? The storm?"

She looked at him and shook her head. "I . . . I'm sorry, Rex, but I have to talk to my granddaughter alone. Would you . . . would you mind?"

I could tell from the look in his eyes that he didn't like the idea—and probably all the more as another round of thunder shook the boat. He glanced up the stairs, then directed his attention to the little bedroom. "Why don't you two go in there and I'll be out here if you need me."

"Good idea." I rose, feeling nauseous all over again as the boat swayed this way and that. I reached for my grandmother's hand, helped her to a standing position, and led the way into the little bedroom.

She sat and reached for a tissue from a box on the bedside table. After a few moments of silence, she finally spoke in a tremulous whisper. "Kat, I need to tell you something, but I'm so scared you're going to hate me."

"I could never hate you." And since when did she call me Kat?

She leaned over, her head in her hands. Through her tears, I heard the words, "I'm a foolish old woman. And I've hurt so many people."

I gripped myself, the storm inside my belly now far exceeding the one causing flashes of lightning outside the porthole to my right.

"Grandma, just start from the beginning. Tell me everything. We promised . . . no secrets."

For a moment she didn't say anything. Then finally the dam broke.

"Your mama was born in 1957." Grandma dabbed at her eyes. "She was the prettiest little thing. Such a doll. The spitting image of her daddy. How could I not love her? She represented everything I loved." Her jaw tightened and anger flashed in her eyes. "Why couldn't people just leave us alone and let us be? I know I had a bright career ahead of me, but to tell me that I had to give up the person I loved because of a foolish mistake? Lots of people make mistakes." She began to cry in earnest now. "Oh, honey, not that I think she was a mistake. Not at all. I've never loved anyone like I loved that baby."

My heart began to race and suddenly I felt nauseous again. Only, this time it had little to do with the boat. "Wait, Grandma. What are you saying?"

She looked at me with a tearstained face. "I didn't know the Lord at the time. If I'd understood his grace back then, all of this would have been so much easier. Maybe. I don't know. It's hard to say. I just know that I did what they told me . . . and it ruined my life."

"You did what *who* told you? Let's go back to that part."

"Harvey Klink, my agent. He told me the baby would ruin my career, that studios would blackball me for having a baby before getting married. I was so scared, so young and foolish back then. And vulnerable. So I believed what they said. And I went along with their plan." A look of anger took over now, and I could read the pain in her eyes. "I always went along with what they said. I was such a scared little thing."

"Grandma, none of this is making sense. Were you . . ." I hated to ask but couldn't avoid it. "Were you pregnant with my mom before you and Grandpa got married or something?"

She nodded and my heart flew to my throat. Suddenly it all made sense. I could see the shame written all over her face. It was mixed with several other emotions, none of which I could clearly make out.

"So you married him because you felt you had to? Is that it?"

She shook her head. "No, Kat. You don't understand. I never married your grandpa . . . at all. And I've regretted it every day of my life since 1957." She completely dissolved in tears, throwing her body across the bed. Her combs came loose and that gorgeous silver hair tumbled down, burying her in its wake.

Okay, none of this made sense. Of course she was married to my grandfather. He'd died in South Korea. I'd seen the article in the paper. His name was Jonathan Billings. He was a military hero. My mother had shared countless stories of his valor.

I placed my hand on Grandma's back. The sobs intensified. After a few minutes, she took some gasping breaths and seemed to calm a bit. I took the opportunity to ask the inevitable question.

"Grandma, are you saying that you got pregnant but your agent made you marry someone else?"

"No." She looked up at me, her black mascara creating ribbons across the soft wrinkles in her face. "I mean yes."

"Which is it?" The lump in my throat made asking anything else impossible. My thoughts reeled at the possibilities here. If she was saying what I thought she was saying, my entire world was about to be rocked . . . more than this crazy yacht I was on.

"They wouldn't let me marry your grandfather, Kat. They thought he was out to ruin my career." She gazed into my eyes, and my heart suddenly felt like it had been invited to play a game of Twister. "Oh, but he wasn't, honey. It wasn't like that. He was my one true love. I adored him. And I went on adoring him for the rest of my life."

My heart broke. Okay, so that answered my question. She'd definitely been torn from the love of her life and forced to marry someone else.

"What about your husband?" I asked. "Did you learn to love him too?"

She gripped my hand. "You're not understanding, Kat. I never married at all."

"W-what?" I lost my grip on her hand, completely overwhelmed by this news. "Of course you did."

"No." Her voice lowered to a whisper. "Harvey and some

stupid publicist made up the story about Jonathan Billings. It was several years after the Korean War, but the US still had a military presence there, so no one was the wiser. All the public ever knew was that I had married and was expecting a child, and my husband was killed while protecting other soldiers overseas. A hero. All of this contrived to salvage my career. As if I ever cared more about my career than I did about your grandpa." Her tears came with such abandon that they broke my heart.

I wanted to respond, but the lump in my throat wouldn't allow it. As my grandmother continued grieving the loss of the man she had loved, her heartbreak became my own. No wonder she wanted to see me happily married to Scott. She had hit the nail on the head that day in the studio when she'd said she wanted for me what she'd never had for herself. A wedding.

My mind reeled, thoughts now tumbling madly. A missing page from my life's script had just been uncovered. Rex Henderson . . . was my grandfather.

"Grandma," I whispered, stroking her back. "Grandma, sit up. I have to ask you a question."

It took her a moment, but she finally rose and gazed into my eyes, her expression reflecting her complete and utter exhaustion.

"Grandma, have you told him? Does he know?"

She shook her head and dissolved into tears again. "No, KK. He's never known. I mean, of course he knows I broke his heart. I left him high and dry. But he never knew why. And he really thought I married someone else. They wouldn't let me tell him, even after . . . well, even after everything. So I never said a word. Not a word . . . and it's been ripping me to shreds for fifty years."

The sobbing that followed caused my heart to ache. Rising

from the bed, I began to pace the tiny room, rolling back and forth as the waves sent the boat this way and that. Moments later, a plan began to formulate. There would be no turning back. Swinging wide the bedroom door, I called Rex's name.

Turning back to my grandmother, I whispered, "It's high time we told my real grandfather that he has a family. And if my guess is right, this is one storm he won't mind weathering."

For a moment she looked at me with sheer terror in her eyes. Then, just as quickly, a peaceful look settled over her, and she nodded. By the time Rex entered the room, I knew God was on the move.

Come to think of it, he'd been on the move all along.

20

Shower of Stars

For the next hour, dark clouds swirled above us, and the ensuing winds caused the waves to toss the *Little Star* to and fro. From the hull of the ship, I dealt with not just one but two storms. Thankfully the one inside appeared to be dissipating. I listened with my heart breaking as my grandmother came clean with her story.

"Rex, I . . . I don't know how to tell you this." Tears poured as she choked out the words. "I . . . I've been living a lie."

"Living a lie?" He reached for her hand and gave it a tender squeeze. "Impossible. You've played many roles but never lived a lie."

"No, it's true." She shook her head, her cheeks still damp. "And I wouldn't blame you if you never forgave me. How could you, after what I've done to you?" She dissolved into tears once more.

He wrapped her in his arms. "Sweetheart, what is it? Tell me."

And so she did. Every gut-wrenching word spilled out, one on top of the other. Emotion got the best of her at several points along the way, but she forged ahead, telling him every last detail. He sat in what had to be shocked silence, not uttering a sound.

Still, I saw occasional flickers of joy in his eyes. Several times I caught him looking my way, as if to say, "Is it true, or is this another one of her stories?"

I knew in my gut this one was true. Every word. And it would change all of our lives . . . forever. In one afternoon, I'd learned that the grandfather I thought I'd lost wasn't lost at all. He'd been with me all the time. In some ways it felt like Christmas, with Rex being the unexpected gift under the tree. I could hardly imagine what must be going through his mind, but as he gazed at me, one thing was clear. He realized that he now had another granddaughter.

In that same breath, he had to realize that he'd lost a daughter—my mother. A thousand times, at least, Grandma begged his forgiveness for not telling him that she had given birth to his little girl. His tears were heartfelt, but when all was said and done, whispers of forgiveness ruled the day. If I'd never known the Lord before that conversation, I would have seen him clearly for the first time in how Rex responded to the news.

When she finished, Grandma glanced his way, a desperate look in her eyes. "I need you to know how sorry I am. There were so many times I wanted to tell you . . . started to tell you. But I couldn't. Oh, I should have. I know that. But . . . I couldn't." Her eyes welled over again.

"Lenora, look at me." His words were tender. Sweet.

"I . . . I can't." She kept her gaze downward, tears streaming.

Rex paused. "You've given me a lot to swallow. This is going to take some time to process."

Her sobs broke my heart. "H-how can you ever f-forgive me after what I've done to you?"

He lifted her chin with his index finger until they were eye to eye. "Lenora, I've loved you since I was a boy. And I love you today as much as I did then."

"That's impossible," she whispered. "How . . . how could you?"

"I love you because God loves through me. And I forgive you because he requires no less of me. I'm going to need some time to think this through, but it doesn't change the fact that I love you. I always will."

Rex's father-heart blew me away. And his love for my grandmother, despite any deception on her part, appeared unconditional. I knew it wasn't, of course. Only God could love unconditionally. But as I watched Rex sweep her into his arms and kiss away her tears, I knew what it must feel like to be that person in need of grace. How many times had I been there?

I stepped out of the room, making my way up the stairs. The others looked at me with some degree of curiosity. Surely my red-rimmed eyes tipped them off to the fact that something huge had happened, but I said nothing. Instead I mouthed the words, "Call me later," to Athena. She nodded. Then I slipped over to Scott's side and nuzzled up against him.

"Everything okay?" He gave me a curious look.

At first I shook my head. Then I nodded. "Yes. I mean no." I offered up a weak smile. "I mean, it's going to be okay. But sometimes the storms have to come before the sun breaks through. You know?"

"Um, yeah." He pointed to the sky and then gave me a tender look. "You can tell me all about it once we're safely on shore again. Shouldn't take more than a few minutes."

I nodded, then settled into the seat next to him, my mind reeling.

When we got back to the pier, the paparazzi were waiting for us—at least a dozen. I suppose I couldn't blame them. They apparently thought Jack and Angie were missing at sea just a week before they tied the knot, after all. I had a feeling network execs would be thanking us for this publicity. And I wondered if the public would think we'd drummed up the idea to garner attention. Crazier things had happened. Not that we controlled the weather, of course.

Because we'd beaten the storm back to shore—Scott being such an able-bodied captain and all—the folks on land were all high and dry. However, hovering clouds threatened to ruin their opportunity for a story.

My mind was focused not on the storm overhead but on the chaos we'd just braved below. No one else on board had any idea what had transpired, not even Scott. Our crew had to wonder why my grandmother's mascara had dried in rivers down her cheeks and why Rex's eyes were so red. But if they did, no one said a word. I had a feeling Athena would call me as soon as we got off the boat.

If we could just avoid these goofy reporters.

"Kat!" I turned as I heard a familiar voice and saw a fellow—maybe in his forties—with a camera. "James Stevens from *The Scoop*."

Of course.

He took one look at Grandma and pointed to his photographer, who started snapping photos.

"That's enough of that." Rex reached out, and for a moment I thought he might knock the camera to the ground.

"You'll get your story," I said. "But you will leave her alone. Understood?" I flashed a warning look. A couple more cameras clicked, and Grandma disappeared with Rex to the parking lot. I stepped into place and Scott joined me.

"Over here, Kat," one of the female reporters hollered. "Jenny Collins from *Tinsel Talk*. What was it like to face death and live to tell about it?"

"Face death?" Should I tell her that facing the paparazzi was scarier than any storm we could possibly face at sea? Maybe not.

"I knew we would make it all along," Scott said. "We had Kat with Nine Lives aboard, after all."

They all chuckled at that one.

"Hey, you two didn't elope out there, did you?" James asked. He scribbled down something before either of us could even respond.

"Of course not. If anyone deserves a real wedding, Kat does." Scott pulled me close and planted a tender kiss on my forehead. All around me, I heard the clicking of cameras but for once didn't care. I enjoyed the comfort of his embrace, not worrying a lick about the reporters. Let them have a field day with this. The truth would come out in the wash.

Scott shared the story of what had happened to us out on the water, and the reporters seemed happy with it. Athena stepped up and shared the funny bit about *Gilligan's Island*, and one of the reporters quipped, "Hey, aren't you supposed to be on strike?" which caused her to slink away from the cameras in search of her car. Bob and Paul followed her, doing their best to avoid being filmed.

A few minutes into the interview, the storm came ashore. Thankfully it chased the paparazzi away. I'd never seen so many people scramble so fast. With that much equipment to protect, they scooted to their vehicles in a hurry.

As they sprinted toward the parking lot, James and a couple of the other reporters looked back at Scott and me. We gave them a little wave, then ducked under his umbrella and headed back on board the yacht to secure her and do some cleaning downstairs.

Safely away from the rain, Scott turned to me. "What in the world happened with Lenora and Rex? She looked . . . awful. And you looked pretty teary-eyed yourself. What kind of storm were you talking about?"

Shaking my head, I said, "You're never going to believe it. In a thousand years, you won't believe it."

"Try me."

"I'm telling you, Scott, if the writers worked for weeks, they couldn't come up with a story like this. Only, this one's true. Every word."

"You're killing me, Kat. Out with it."

I faced him head-on and whispered the words, still not quite believing them myself. "Rex Henderson . . . is my grand-father."

I wish the paparazzi had hung around just long enough to capture the look on Scott's face. If a picture could paint a thousand words, his face at that very moment would have filled the pages of a book.

"What?" He shook his head. "Kat, are you sure?"

"Oh yes. Very sure. Grandma told me everything. She was never married to Jonathan Billings. There never was a Jonathan Billings. Her agent and some publicity guy made him up."

"Because . . . ?"

"Because she was pregnant with my mom."

"Ah." He dropped down onto the seat, shaking his head. "Well, I can honestly say I never saw this one coming. I'd pegged Lenora and Rex as a couple, but not this." After a brief pause, he asked the obvious question. "Rex . . . didn't know she was pregnant?"

"No, he was told that she fell in love with someone else and got married. By the time my mom came along—and who knows, they probably fudged the date of her birth—he had backed away. Until he got the news that Jonathan died. You saw the letters, so you know he still had feelings for her after that."

"Man." Scott shook his head. "I think I saw something like this once on a soap opera, but I'm pretty sure one of the characters had amnesia or something."

"Yes, it's definitely not your usual story," I said. "Only, it's true. And Rex Henderson is my grandfather."

Scott pulled me close. "Kat, I know this is shocking, but in some strange way I see it as an answer to prayer. You've struggled with father issues for years, and God has just dropped the best possible father figure in your lap. Whatever issues Rex has had are clearly in the past. When I look at him, I see an amazing man of God."

I thought his words through before responding. "True. And I'm grateful, trust me. I've never had a male role model of any kind in my life, so this is long overdue. Rex is just the ticket." My thoughts flashed back to that moment in the dressing room where I'd caught a glimpse of Grandma, Rex, and me in the mirror. We'd felt like family, even then. Crazy to think we had been all along.

"Yes, he is. He's going to be great . . . for both of you." Scott gave me a curious look. "So, what happens next?"

"I think the two of them just need time to recover from all of this," I said. "They're in Grandma's car right now, talking. I thought they could use some alone time. Rex will be riding home with us. He called his driver and told him not to come."

"Good plan. This is amazing, Kat." He kissed me, and I found myself lost in the sweetness of the moment as I lingered in his arms.

"It's crazy how nearly every area of my life has changed in such a short amount of time," I said. "When God moves . . . he moves fast."

"Tell me about it. Sometimes he blows in like a storm. Other times he waits offshore and you wonder if he's ever going to show up."

"Well, he showed up today. And trust me when I say that he caught me by surprise with an unexpected scene."

"Don't tell Athena just yet," Scott said. "She'll be jealous that she didn't write it."

I giggled, then a couple more kisses followed. As the thunder and lightning dissipated, we finished cleaning up the inner sanctum of the yacht and returned to the pier. I turned to give the *Little Star* one last glance. "My whole life changed on that boat," I whispered. "This is a day I don't ever want to forget."

Another sweet kiss swept me away to a far-off place. Landing on shore once again, I found myself in a swoony state. Seasickness, perhaps?

"You have a way about you, Mr. Murphy."

"So do you, Ms. Jennings."

He walked me to the car, where we found Grandma and Rex in the front seat, talking. Rex sat behind the wheel and my grandmother had scooted next to him on the bench seat, resting her head on his shoulder. I opened the door to climb in and Grandma looked my way.

"KK, there you are. We were wondering if you and Jack decided to go back out for a ride on the yacht."

"No, we were tidying up," I explained. "Are you guys . . . okay?"

Rex nodded and Grandma grinned. "Oh, KK, you're not going to believe it. Rex called my agent, and he said it's okay for us to date now. Isn't that wonderful?"

"It's the best news ever." I offered a smile. "And it's about time, if you ask me."

"Amen to that," Rex said.

Scott gave me one final kiss then I climbed into the backseat of the Pink Lady. With storm clouds hovering overhead, we couldn't very well put the top down. But that didn't matter. Some moments were better handled in private.

From the back, I watched as Rex reached over and took my grandmother's hand. She turned and gave him a tender look, clearly taken with his kindness.

On the drive home, God performed the miraculous. The Red Sea parted. Grandma and Rex were unleashed to openly share their hearts with one another. After a while, I realized they'd obviously forgotten they had a passenger in the backseat. I tried not to breathe too loudly for fear I would interrupt the sacredness of the moment.

Of course, the rapid-fire text messages coming through from Athena didn't help. She wanted news . . . and she wanted it now. I promised to call her the minute I got home.

We arrived at Worth Manor and Rex led the way inside, explaining that his driver would be coming to pick him up momentarily.

A few feet from the car, I could stand it no more. I had to ask Rex one lingering question. My grandmother had moved on a few steps ahead of us, rambling on about how much better the garden would soon look once the storm passed over.

I turned to Rex, speaking softly. "Rex?"

He smiled and slipped his arm over my shoulders. "Yes, Kat?"

"The sweetheart roses . . ."

His embarrassment was evident. "Yes?"

"Grandma once told me that a florist who looked like Tia

delivered sweetheart roses to her every week when she was under contract with Paramount."

He nodded and released a breath. "And let me tell you, that was quite an expense for a young kid trying to break into the business. There were weeks when I chose roses over food."

Somehow, knowing that only made me love him more.

"Why sweetheart roses?" I asked. "Some special significance?"

He chuckled. "She was my sweetheart, honey. Just made sense." Giving me a pensive look, he added, "You know, Kat, life was much simpler back then. We were much simpler back then."

I nodded, wondering what "simpler" would look like these days.

Grandma stood in the doorway, shivering. Only then did I realize her gown was still damp from the rain. "C'mon, you two," she called. "Let's get inside."

We met her at the door, where Rex pulled off his jacket and put it over her arms. She smiled up at him and whispered, "Winter must be cold for those with no warm memories."

I could have interjected, of course, but knew better. Rex could take this one. It seemed appropriate, after all.

"Deborah Kerr," he whispered. *An Affair to Remember.*"

"1957." They spoke the year in unison, and my heart shot up into my throat. Interesting coincidence.

Not that I would be pointing it out. No, I'd pretty much decided the past was better off left in the past. And from everything I could tell . . . the future looked bright and sunny.

21

The Biggest Loser

The next few days whirled by at breakneck speed. Nearly every evening, Rex came over for dinner. On Saturday night, much to our delight, he brought his daughters, Jeannie and Jackie. My aunts. With them came a host of kids and grand-kids. Turned out Athena and I had more in common than I knew. We both had large families—I just never knew it till now. Crazy how the unveiling of my grandmother's secret changed absolutely everything.

Thankfully everyone took the news relatively well. Jeannie seemed a bit more reticent than Jackie, but who could blame her? This must have been quite a shock. She approached me—and Grandma—with a stiff arm as we welcomed her into our home. For a moment I thought she might ask for a DNA test. Then we pulled out the baby books and began to show off pictures. Turned out I was a dead ringer for about half of the babies in the family. This revelation brought more than a few tears from all in attendance.

"No doubt about it, Kat," Jackie said as she closed my baby book. "You're a Henderson through and through."

"A Henderson through and through." I could still hardly believe it. It felt amazing—and somewhat surreal—to belong to something bigger than the tiny family unit I'd always known.

Another revelation brought more than a few tears. As I pulled out old photographs of my mother, I saw the resemblance between her and the twins. They saw it too.

"I wouldn't have believed it if I hadn't seen it with my own eyes," Jeannie said, dabbing at her eyes.

"I wish we'd known her," Jackie whispered.

Oh, how I wished that too. But we couldn't go back, none of us. We had to forge ahead, learning from the past and applying what we'd learned to the present.

When our meeting ended, we made plans to go to Jeannie's house next time. Then Jackie's the time after that. Turned out there were more people to meet—Rex's siblings, for instance. And their kids and grandkids. Wowza.

"Looks like our dance card is filling up, KK," Grandma said as we stood in the doorway, waving goodbye to our guests. "We're going to be busy girls."

"Yes, we are." I put my arm over her shoulders, noticing for the first time how bony they felt. "Times are changing, aren't they?"

"Mm-hmm." She yawned. "And to think, you and Jack will be married in less than a week! I hope those gardeners will kick into high gear and get the work done outside. The rest of the house is really shaping up, don't you think?"

"I do." I rather enjoyed the changes, actually. The new lettering on the gate. A fancy, updated mailbox. A lovely paint job on the outside of the house. Yes, things were really coming together. Embracing change was easier than I'd predicted. And to think, it only took a wedding to accomplish it.

Wedding. Hmm.

Scott and I still had to figure out what to do about all of that. We'd tossed around a couple of ideas, one in particular, but my stomach ended up in my throat every time. Looked like we still had some planning to do. Thank goodness we had one free day before heading back to the studio.

On Sunday morning, Scott arrived at our house bright and early to escort Grandma and me to his church. We decided that would be the appropriate place to worship, since we needed to meet with his pastor afterward to talk about the fund-raiser.

Rex met us at the church. For the first time, the four of us sat together in one pew—one big, happy family. I noticed the smiles of those seated around us, but no one asked any questions. If they had, I'm not sure how I would have responded. We weren't quite ready to share Rex and Grandma's story with the masses.

Afterward, the four of us headed off to Pink's for hot dogs. Nothing like a great Sunday dinner. As we ate, Scott and I continued to whisper our plans back and forth to each other. Slowly but surely, things were coming into place. Maybe we would survive this wedding week after all.

On Sunday afternoon, Athena came over for a swim. Though we'd spoken by phone several times over the past few days, I hadn't seen her in person till now. And what a relief to hear that the writers' strike had come to an end.

While we floated in the pool, Athena and I talked through the events of the past few days.

"I feel like my life is complete now," I said. "I have a family, Athena. A real family."

She laughed. "You say that now. Just wait till they're invading your space and keeping you up all night playing video games or having a slumber party in your living room."

"I won't mind. And I don't think Grandma will either."

"What do you think will happen with her and Rex?" Athena asked. "'Cause if I was writing this script, they'd already be married by now. They would have gone to a justice of the peace the same day she came clean with her story."

"That's exactly why you're *not* writing it." I laughed. "They need time to absorb the shock of all this. And Rex has some big decisions ahead of him. My grandmother's health isn't what it once was."

"All the more reason to marry quickly," Athena said. "They've missed out on a lot of years already. Why spend any more time thinking about it? Their time is already limited. Just go for it."

I nodded, but I wasn't sure. Rex had a lot on his plate, especially with the filming of the wedding scene coming up. No point in rushing him to the altar. They would make it there . . . in God's time. And besides, he probably still had some heart issues to deal with. Grandma's actions all those years ago had surely caused some pain that he would need to work through. With the Lord's help.

Thinking about the issues he needed to work through reminded me of the one area in my life that still needed healing. A little relationship remodeling.

"You okay over there?" Athena dog-paddled by me.

"Yes. Just thinking of my"—I hated to use the word—"father."

"Ah."

"Finding my grandfather has got me thinking more about my dad."

"Are you giving some thought to contacting him?" Athena asked. She leaned her arms against the edge of the pool.

I nodded. "Maybe. What do you think of that idea?"

"It's about time. One of you needs to make a move. It's a shame it has to be the child and not the parent, but that's often the case."

"Yeah." I shrugged. "I've been talking to Scott about it."

"And he says . . . ?"

"He says he'll support me, whatever I decide. But he knows it's really my decision. I just feel . . ."

"Scared?"

"Yes." A sigh escaped. "I don't have any idea what he'll say if he answers the phone."

She ran her fingers through her wet hair. "Let's talk it through then. Because I, as a writer, can tell you that there are three different directions this scene could go. You need to be prepared."

I groaned. "Athena, not everything goes according to the script."

"That's why I'm giving you three options," she said. "I can almost guarantee you it will go one of these three ways."

"Okay, fine. Give them to me straight, then."

She nodded. "Option A: he wants nothing to do with you. That will be a tough one to take, but you need to be prepared, just in case."

"Trust me, I'm prepared. That's probably how it's going to go, if he even picks up the phone."

"Maybe. Okay, here's Option B: he's curious about your call and willing to talk for a few minutes, but you won't be able to tell if he's interested in a long-term relationship. That would be hard too, but workable."

"Are there any good options floating around in that brain of yours?" I asked.

"Option C: he's been wanting to get in touch with you all of these years, and your phone call will trigger a conversation that will lead to an eventual relationship. God steps in, and voilà! All is forgiven. You start fresh."

"Sounds so easy," I said.

"Well, that's just the synopsis. Acting it out—er, living it out—will be more complicated."

"Naturally. It always is." I looked at her, boggled by her suggestions. "How do you do it, Athena?"

"Do what?"

"Come up with all of these ideas? Where do they come from?"

"Easy." She pushed away from the edge and floated toward the center of the pool. "From real life. I just observe people, places, and things. Then I add as much tension as I can. Tension is what drives a story, by the way. Never forget that. So your life thus far has a great plotline."

"Lovely. That's good to know."

"It's all about mountains and valleys, my friend. A good story has both." She dipped her head under the water, coming up with her curly dark hair slicked back.

"Huh?"

She grinned. "You don't want your story to be a flat line. How boring would that be? No, you need your life to have some low lows and some high highs. It keeps things interesting and ups the tension."

"Ah. I see. Well, I've had some low lows, that's for sure."

"And some high highs too," she said. "And it's easier to see the good times for what they are because you've had the low points. All I'm saying is this . . . if the Lord chooses to mend the relationship with your dad, that will add a nice high point to the upcoming scenes of your life. And if he doesn't, you'll surely have more mountaintop experiences ahead, so don't sweat the valleys."

I shook my head. "Athena, did you ever consider work as a psychologist? This is pretty deep stuff."

"I have, actually." She grinned. "But I have a better deal as a writer. When I tell my characters to line up and walk straight, they do it. When a psychologist or psychiatrist tells her patients to line up and walk straight, well, they don't always obey."

"Brilliant deduction," I observed.

"Thanks. I really said all of that to mean that it's easy to write upcoming scenes in books and televisions shows. Trusting God to write them in real life is a lot harder. But it's worth it. And you have to admit, it's an adventure."

"That it is," I agreed.

I thought about Athena's words all afternoon, long after she'd headed back home to her family. If I called my father on the phone, how would the next scene of my life play out? Would I soar to the top of the mountain or plummet deep into the valley?

Athena had made a good point. God would see me through this either way. And everyone needed a little tension to keep things interesting. Right?

Praying seemed like a good idea, but I wasn't sure what to ask the Lord for specifically. Healing in my heart? A restored relationship with my dad? Somehow that second one just seemed a bit like shooting for the moon. And the first—being healed—would be my decision, whether my father accepted me or not.

Still, I'd never know if he wanted to talk unless I picked up the phone and called him, so that's exactly what I did. At 6:47 p.m. Pacific time, I punched in the number I'd located on the internet years ago.

I called him.

For years I'd dreamed about this moment. Lived in fear of how it would turn out. But no longer. Today I would confront those fears . . . and confront the man who had disappeared out of my life at age seven, never to return. Maybe I would find answers, maybe I wouldn't. But at least I would take a step in the right direction.

A whirlwind of emotions greeted me as the phone began to ring on his end. The "hello" took me by surprise. He sounded older than I'd expected.

"Hello," I managed. *Deep breath, Kat.* "Is this David Jennings?"

"It is." His voice had an abrupt tone, as if I'd interrupted him. "And who is this?"

"This . . . this is Kat. Kat Jennings."

I was met with an uncomfortable silence from the other side. After a moment, he spoke, his voice now wavering. "Kat with Nine Lives."

Just four words, but they were like ointment on my soul.

"Is this an okay time to talk?" I asked.

"As good as any." He hesitated, but I didn't let the awkward spaces get me down. Surely the man had a pretty big pill to swallow right about now. I'd shocked him, after all. It would take a few minutes to register that the past had caught up with him.

I made light conversation, filling him in on my life. At a couple of different points, I found myself rambling, my words laced with nervous energy. I asked a couple of questions about his family, which he answered with some hesitation. I wondered if he picked up on my anxiety. If so, he didn't say. Instead he remained fairly quiet, only interjecting an occasional thought.

"I record your show every week," he said at last. "You've done really well for yourself, Kat."

No thanks to you.

The words slipped through my brain and I shook them off. No pointing fingers today. That's not what this call was about. No, this was just about opening the door. Giving the Lord an opportunity to work. What happened next was up to him, not me.

My father's next words startled me. "I read in the paper that you're getting married. Is that right?"

A sigh escaped and I quickly explained the situation with Grandma.

"Sorry to hear that about Lenora," he said when I finished. "Sounds like she's as feisty as ever, though. She's always been something else."

"She's been more than something else to me," I explained, my words calculated but not cold. "She's been a saving grace in my life."

His silence was eventually followed by, "I know, Kat. I . . . well, I know she's been there for you."

This would have been a perfect segue for him to tell me how sorry he was for leaving me in the lurch. For hurting my mom. For causing so many unanswered questions in my mind. Instead he used it as an opportunity to tell me he had another call coming in. Go figure.

We ended with a quick goodbye. Nothing personal or intimate about it. I glanced at the clock, surprised to see the whole call had lasted only eight minutes. Strange, after we'd been apart so many years.

If I had to choose from the options Athena had given me earlier, I'd say it was an option B conversation. He was clearly curious about my call and had been willing to talk for a few minutes. But just like she said, I wasn't able to tell if he was interested in a long-term relationship. Only time would tell. Still, I'd opened the door. And I'd somehow managed to do so without accusing him in any way. The Lord had stopped me from doing so on a couple of different occasions during the call.

After a few minutes replaying the conversation in my mind, I finally cratered. The tears flowed, eventually morphing into full-fledged sobs. All of those pent-up emotions I'd stuffed inside were finally free to come out and play.

I'd talked to my dad. Really, truly talked to him. I'd picked up the phone and called him. After years of wondering what that would be like, now I knew. Had it created world peace? No. Had it started a new chapter in my heart? Maybe. Regardless, I'd finally come to grips with the fact that my past was really behind me. Moving forward, though difficult, would be possible. And I could see so clearly that this man I'd thought about for so long was really just a shell of a person. Not the sort of person I'd be drawn to, anyway.

And yet . . . I also sensed that God saw him as his child, someone worthy of dying for. That put everything in perspective. Though I might never have a genuine relationship with my dad, I'd opened the door for the Lord to work in both of our lives. What happened next was up to him.

I wanted to tell someone. Grandma, maybe? No, she and Rex were downstairs, watching a movie. Really, it only made sense to tell Scott.

I punched in his number on my cell phone, thinking about how different this call felt from the one I'd just made. Thank goodness for real, genuine relationships. No awkwardness here. This was the real deal.

Scott answered on the second ring. Through my tears, I explained what I'd done.

"Kat, I'm so proud of you," he said when I finished. "How did it go?"

I managed to get my breathing under control before responding. "Well, I delivered a few lines. He delivered a few lines. There were some awkward spaces. Our scriptwriters could've come up with a better speech for him to deliver, but it was an attempt on his part." After a shrug, I added, "At least he didn't reject me."

"You took a step in the right direction, Kat," Scott said. "The rest is up to God. Of course, he's not going to mess with your father's free will, but he's pretty good at tugging on hearts."

"So I've noticed. Mine's been tugged a few times in recent days."

"Mine too."

"Hey, guess what?" I said. "When I asked my dad about his wife, he told me that he's divorced."

"That's sad. What about his other daughter?"

"I didn't ask. But it sounded like he was off doing his own thing, not really communicating with anyone from his past. Do you think he walked away from her too?"

"Maybe that's just his MO, Kat," Scott said. "Maybe he's a coward. He walks away because it's the easy way out."

"Maybe. But I'm not giving him the easy way out this time. I'm his daughter and he's going to know me. He's going to know you too."

"You sure about that?"

"Maybe not 'know' in an 'I love you, you're my daddy' sort of way. But I think we need to make an attempt now that I've found him."

"God knew where he was all along."

"True. And I guess God knows where he is spiritually too."

"Maybe that's why you're supposed to be reconnecting, Kat. Did you ever think of that? Maybe the Lord is going to use you in some way to bring your father to him."

"Could be." I paused to think about that. "But you know what? That's up to God, not me. I'm pretty sure I've done what I was supposed to do. The rest is up to the Lord."

"Amen." Scott paused, then came back with a slightly more exciting question. "So, do you have a few minutes? We've still got some planning to do, you know."

"Boy, do we ever." I leaned back against the pillows, ready to plot the next scene in my life. Between the Lord, Scott, and me, this one was sure to be a doozy.

22

Whose Wedding Is It Anyway?

On Friday morning, the 4th of August, I prepared myself to take the stage for the wedding scene of the century. For days, I'd thought of little else besides this event. Scott and I had schemed, plotted, talked things through with Rex, and tied up loose ends. All in preparation for Jack and Angie's big day. What fun this was going to be.

I smiled as I thought about the way the shooting would unfold. I could hardly wait to deliver my lines. With all that had happened between Scott and me, I honestly felt we were meant to go through this scene together. And why not add a final touch of drama before the season ended? The viewers would eat this up. So would Grandma.

About three hours before the shooting, Nora worked on my makeup. Her hands trembled more than usual. "I'm so sorry, Kat," she said. "I've never done hair and makeup for a wedding before." She paused to run a brush through my hair. "You want it up, right?"

"Right." I gave her a picture from a bride magazine. "That's what I want. And I'm pretty sure Angie would agree."

"I'll do my best."

Half an hour later, I had the prettiest updo in town. Staring at my reflection in the mirror, I gasped. "Nora, you did it. It's gorgeous."

She grinned, still chattering nervously as she finished my makeup. In the end, I looked like the real deal—a bride. Now, to get into that dress.

Jana appeared in the doorway, letting out a whistle. "Man. Can't wait to get you to wardrobe."

"Me either."

As I followed her down the hall, Scott's dressing room door opened. He popped his head out and almost caught a glimpse of me.

"Oh no you don't!" Jana stopped in her tracks. "The bride and groom aren't supposed to see each other on their wedding day."

"But—" He managed to get out one word before she shooed him back into his room. She turned to me with a smile. "I can pretend this is the real deal, right?"

"Right." I smiled. "Jack and Angie should not see each other before the ceremony. We want to stick with tradition."

"Of course."

We entered the dressing room, and I stared at the gorgeous white gown, which Jana had hung from a hook at the top of the door. It simply took my breath away. She helped me into the undergarments first. I'd never realized how much work went into the foundational garments for a wedding. A giddy feeling came over me as she fastened the corset and handed me the petticoat.

I happened to glance up as Grandma Lenora entered the room wearing the craziest peach dress I'd ever seen. It sported large, puffy sleeves and a huge flower at the waist. Frankly, I couldn't remember ever seeing anything so awful.

"Um, Grandma, I'm almost afraid to ask, but who are we today?"

She giggled. "This one's just for fun, KK. Jane Fonda wore this very same dress in *Monster-in-Law*, remember? It's that hideous bridesmaid dress."

"Is that what you're planning to wear in the scene?" I asked, dumbfounded. She had purchased a beautiful blue number at Saks, after all.

"Nah. I put this on just to get a rise out of everyone."

"Well, it worked," Jana said. "Now please change before I have to put on dark glasses to protect my eyes."

We all laughed at that one.

"I'm so thrilled I get to be in the wedding, KK," Grandma said. "It's going to be so exciting."

"Yes, it is."

And if we didn't hurry, we'd very likely be late on the set for the most important day of my—er, Angie's—life.

Within minutes, Jana had me properly suited up in the wedding dress. We stood together, staring at my reflection in the mirror.

"I don't think you could find a better dress if you searched for the rest of your life."

"I know." Swishing side to side, I couldn't help but smile. "It's divine."

"What do you think your groom will say when he sees you in it?" she whispered.

"Her groom will say she's the prettiest bride to ever walk the aisle," Grandma threw in. "And he will be right."

I gave her a kiss on the cheek then touched up my makeup

as Jana helped Grandma into her real bridesmaid dress. Sure enough, it made her look like a beauty queen. Of all the gowns I'd seen her in, this one topped them all. Perfect.

The bell rang out through the PA system, giving the signal that we would be ready to shoot the scene in fifteen minutes. We'd better get out to the set to meet the others.

"You ready, Grandma?" I asked as I took her by the hand.

"You betcha." She stared at her reflection for another moment, drawing close to the mirror. "I'm glad I decided not to have the plastic surgery, KK."

"Oh?"

"I think I like my wrinkles, after all. They make me look soft and cuddly."

"You are soft and cuddly." I slipped my arms around her waist. "And in case I haven't told you in a while, I love you so much. None of this would be possible if not for you."

"Aw, go on with you."

When I shrugged, she gave me a little pop on the backside and said, "Go *on* with you. I love the flattery."

"Of course you do."

As we walked to the set, I continued to sing her praises. She beamed ear to ear. We arrived to find the cast and crew in fine spirits. Everyone took one look at my dress and gathered around, offering all sorts of accolades about my appearance. I had to admit, it felt pretty good.

Crew members buzzed around in anticipation. Jason Harris and the other guys readied the cameras. All of this excitement seemed to spill over to the audience members, who looked on, chattering and laughing.

I took a look at the chapel backdrop and grinned. The designers had outdone themselves, creating a church with pews and a real aisle.

"Scott's still in his dressing room getting ready," Athena said as she passed by. "We thought it would be fun to leave him there until the last minute so he wouldn't see you."

"Sounds good to me."

Athena laughed. "Can you imagine how funny it'll be if you two end up really getting married someday? We'll get to do this all over again."

"Yep." And what a day that would be.

Athena came closer. "Kat, I just wanted to say something to you. You're a terrific actress, and I'm so glad I get to work with you."

"Well, thank you." Her words caught me off guard.

"We've worked so hard on this scene, and I'm grateful you're the one who gets to act it out. Some of these funny bits might seem a little over the top, but if anyone can pull it off and still make it look sentimental, you can."

"Ah. Well, I'll give it my best shot."

"You know, I've never told you this before," she said. "But we talk about it all the time between the writers. A television show is only as good as its weakest link. When we writers sit in that room and come up with the script, we're completely dependent on the actors and directors taking the ball and running with it the way we envision. Doesn't always happen that way. Everyone has his or her idea of what makes a scene good. And hey," she shrugged, "I have to admit, sometimes other people have better ideas. We lay the foundation, but others add the spice."

At that moment my grandmother approached. "Mmm, spice." She grinned. "Sounds yummy."

"I think you will be happy with my performance today, Athena," I said. "My lines are memorized. The scene is going to be perfect. Just wait and see."

"I'm counting on it." She gave me a hug. "We've got a lot

riding on this one. Now, go out there and knock 'em dead, Kat."

I saw Rex leaning in close to Tia, giving her some last-minute instructions. He looked stunning in his black suit and white dress shirt. Grandma sashayed his way as he and Tia wrapped up their conversation. A few moments later, Tia approached, worry creased into her brow. "Rex just told me the actor who's supposed to play the part of the pastor is out sick."

"Oh?" I gave her a curious look.

"Rex has a backup. Some guy with a bad toupee. But I guess that's okay, as long as he can deliver the lines."

"Thanks for the heads-up," I said. "I'm sure he'll do fine. Rex wouldn't bring someone on board without checking him out first."

"Right. Well, he suggested we film the wedding scene twice, just so you know. We want to get it from several different angles. And that way if this guy botches it the first time around, we'll have a second option."

"Sounds good to me." I was willing to go along with whatever Rex said.

"I just hope nothing goes wrong with the shoot. Like I said, this is a big one." Tia looked toward the studio audience. "I understand you have a lot of friends in the studio audience today."

"Family members too," I said. Looking out at the crowd, I located Jeannie and Jackie with their kids. They gave me a little wave, which I returned. Jeannie pointed to my dress and gave me a thumbs-up. I couldn't help but blush. To Jackie's right sat Carolina. In front of her, Athena's whole family sat clustered together.

A man in the front row stood and waved, and I grinned.

"Isn't that Scott's dad?" Athena asked, drawing near.

"Yes, they're back in town for the fund-raiser on Sunday. Scott thought it would be fun to invite them today. It will add to their trip."

"Okay, well, I can understand why they're here, but what's up with that reporter?" She pointed to James Stevens from *The Scoop*, who sat in the front row with Scott's parents. "Since when do we let the media into the studio?"

"You can blame my grandmother for that," I explained. "He's been so nosy about our personal lives, we thought this might calm him down a bit."

"Strange." Athena shrugged. "And what's up with that kid?" She pointed to Damian, who settled into the seat next to James. "Isn't he the one who ratted you out to the tabloids? I remember seeing his picture in the paper."

"Yeah." I sighed. "You know Grandma, though. She wanted to include everyone."

"Whatever it takes to pull off a great scene." Tia looked at her watch. "Speaking of which, we'd better get this show on the road if we're going through this thing twice."

She called the others to their places, and I happened to catch a glimpse of Scott out of the corner of my eye as Rex ushered him onto the set. Jana seemed to be doing a fine job of keeping him from looking my way. I'd have to thank her later. Even though we were filming a scene, I still wanted to have the surprise factor.

Tia took her place in the director's chair, and the audience members were given their cue to remain silent.

We all took our places. Looking over at Candy, I gave a little wave. She looked at me with wide eyes and whispered, "You look so pretty."

I winked, taking in her flower girl dress, and whispered back, "So do you."

Her gaze shifted down in embarrassment.

Though my heartbeat now pounded in my ears, I heard Tia call, "Action!"

The scene began. I watched as Scott took the stage, dressed in a tuxedo with tails. He looked yummy. More than yummy, really. Standing there decked out from head to toe, he looked very much the hero from an old movie. One where the boy got the girl . . . and they both lived happily ever after. He glanced my way, his eyes growing wide as he saw me for the first time. Oh yes. Just the reaction I'd been hoping for.

I smiled as the children took their places nearby. They were an integral part of the story, after all. Off in the distance Pastor Garrett stood next to Scott. I wondered if anyone recognized him as the actual pastor of Grace Chapel. Hopefully not. Funny, I'd never noticed he wore a toupee before. Leave it to Tia to catch that.

Overhead, *Pachelbel's Canon* began to play.

Candy flashed a smile then headed up the aisle, dropping rose petals from her basket. Toby followed, playing the role of ring bearer. The other children entered behind him, one after the other. I couldn't have asked for more than to include the kids who'd worked so hard to bring the happy couple together.

Grandma followed the kids up the aisle, beaming all the way. From her slow, determined walk, one might have thought she was the one headed to the altar. Oh, but not today. Today was my day.

Grandma took her place at the front of the room, turning to face the audience. The tears on her cheeks caused a catch in my throat.

Deep breath, Kat.

The wedding march began, and I looked over at Rex, who extended his arm. "You ready to go through with this?" he whispered.

"Oh yes." I whispered, "I love you, Grandpa," and gave him a quick hug.

Others on the set looked startled and even confused as Rex and I made our way to the appropriate place at the back of the aisle. Likely they were wondering when he had decided to take on the role of father figure in Angie's life.

Rex held my arm in his, walking me up the aisle as the wedding march continued to play. While the script called for a few antics—me tripping over the flower girl basket, for one—we'd decided to forego all of that. No, today called for something a bit more traditional. Athena would forgive me later. I hoped.

I could still see tears in Grandma's eyes as we drew near. To her right, front and center, Pastor Garrett offered me a warm, comforting smile. I returned it, feeling the joy of the moment from the inside out.

Scott stepped into place and took my arm. In that moment, the last three years flashed before my eyes. Everything we'd gone through up till now—the characters we'd played, the emotions they'd faced—had led us here. To this precious, holy moment.

"Who gives this woman to be married to this man?" Pastor Garrett asked.

"Her grandmother and I do." Rex's words were laced with emotion. He lifted my veil and gave me a kiss on the cheek.

Out of the corner of my eye, I saw Athena thumbing through her script with a perplexed look on her face. Thankfully Tia didn't yell, "Cut." I half expected her to, since we were so far off the script.

The pastor nodded. "Ladies and gentlemen, we are gathered here today to witness the union of Kat Jennings and Scott Murphy."

A gasp went up from the audience and crew as most finally figured out what was happening. It was exactly the sort of reaction we'd been hoping for. From beside me, I heard Grandma whisper the words, "Who's Scott?" Thankfully she didn't say anything else.

I caught a glimpse of Tia just offstage to my left. It was likely Rex had clued her in at the last minute, assuring her the second filming would follow the script verbatim. Jack and Angie would have their scene . . . right after Scott and Kat had theirs.

Rex took a seat in the front pew, his eyes filled with tears. From here on out, it was just Scott and me. Well, Scott, me, and Grandma, who stood just behind me, sniffling all the way. I knew they were tears of joy. Who could blame her? She'd pegged this one, hadn't she? Her granddaughter was getting married. Really and truly getting married.

When the pastor got to the vows, my heart started racing. He looked at me intently. "Do you, Kat Jennings, take Scott Murphy to be your lawful wedded husband?"

"Hey, he said the wrong names again," little Toby whispered to Scott's right. Fortunately, Pastor Garrett didn't stop. No, he kept right on going, leading us through the exchanging of the vows, and then the rings.

Candy moved to the front of the church to sing the song she'd rehearsed. As the words to "You Made Me Love You" rang out across the studio, her eyes met mine and I gave her a smile. She'd won me over, this little darling. I had a feeling there would be many conversations ahead of us. Right now, however, I needed to stay focused on the one person who'd stolen my heart.

As her song came to an end, the pastor ended with those beautiful, scripted words: "And now, by the power vested in me by the state of California, and in the name of our Lord Jesus Christ, I now pronounce you man and wife." He added,

"You may now kiss the bride," and the crowd began to cheer, many rising to their feet in spontaneous shouts. No canned applause necessary here.

I looked at Scott, my heart overflowing. The mist in his eyes only made me love him more. As he swept me into his arms, my mind went back in time to that day—that wonderful, glorious day—when we'd shared our first kiss under the cover of darkness.

As fabulous as that secret kiss had been, it couldn't hold a candle to the one sealing the deal today.

23

Happy Days

At the end of our very real wedding scene, Tia yelled "Cut!" and the studio audience went crazy. Laughter and cheers permeated the building. I heard several of the tech crew giving joyous shouts. They were joined by Scott's parents and my new aunties.

Grandma turned to face me, tears streaming down her face. "Oh, KK! It was prettier than I pictured it in my imagination. Perfect!"

She was right, as always.

Rex rose from the pew and headed toward me, wrapping me in his arms. "I'm so happy for you, baby girl," he whispered. "You've made this old man very, very happy."

"No, I'm the one who's happy," I whispered in response. "I've always dreamed of being walked down the aisle by someone who genuinely cared about me, and you made that dream come true."

He gave me a kiss on my forehead and nodded. "It was my pleasure." He turned to Scott—my husband—and shook his hand.

"How do I thank you?" Scott asked. "You made this possible."

"No, *he* made this possible." My grandfather gestured to the heavens—well, the ceiling of the studio, anyway—and nodded.

Tia approached, shaking her head. "Not your ordinary day in Studio B, that's for sure."

"No kidding." Nora and Jana spoke in unison as they approached.

"I can't believe you pulled this off," Jana said as she dabbed at her eyes. "No wonder you went with that dress, Kat. It was perfect."

"And it's mine," I added. "Paid in full as of just a few days ago."

"No way." She shook her head. "How did you manage that? It's a couture gown."

"I know. It cost a pretty penny. But my grandmother insisted. It was her gift to me."

"That's right," Grandma said, slipping her arm around my waist. "And did you ever see a lovelier bride?" Before anyone could answer, she said, "Of course not!"

"What I want to know is, how in the world did you do all of this without anyone knowing?" Nora stared at me with a dumbfounded look on her face. "It's remarkable."

I laughed. "Trust me, a lot of work went into making sure no one knew. Well, no one but the pastor and Rex. And Tia at the last minute."

"Last minute is right," Tia said. "Nothing like giving the director a heart attack sixty seconds before shooting a scene."

"I didn't figure you'd mind," Rex said. "It'll be something we can talk about for years to come."

"Besides, we'll use the footage," Scott said. "It'll be great to show our kids and grandkids."

Athena stood off in the distance with the other writers, still looking shell shocked. I had a feeling I'd be getting an earful. Soon. Before she could get to me, however, Scott's mom raced to the stage and swept us both into her arms.

"You did it," she whispered. "You really did it."

"Of course." Scott placed a kiss on her cheek. "We promised you a wedding scene, didn't we, Mom? When we deliver, we deliver!"

"So true." She laughed. "Only, I had no idea. Is that why you told us to wear our Sunday finest?"

"Yes." I nodded. "After we film Jack and Angie's scene, we're all heading back to the house to have the reception. In the gardens." My eyes filled with tears. "It's going to be beautiful, and you should see all of the foods that Carolina has prepared."

"Oh my, yes." Grandma's eyes lit up. "It's going to be grand." She looked out over the audience. "I'd better get busy handing out the maps. I think we must have overlooked the invitations." She headed off to fetch her purse, then made her way through the crowd, inviting one and all to the festivities.

"Now you see why I was so insistent you come back for the fund-raiser?" Scott said, flashing a smile in his mother's direction.

"You should tell a person." She slugged him.

I laughed. "We didn't want anyone to know . . . except Rex, of course. And Grandma. But she thought it was real all along, so it just made sense." I caught a glimpse of my grandmother forging her way through the throng of people, dressed in that gorgeous soft blue dress. She looked like an angel. Oh, and the joy I saw in her eyes. I'd never seen her in such a blissful state.

Athena drew closer. "Kat?"

"Yes?" I tried not to smile.

"Did you neglect to tell me something?"

"I'm . . . I'm married?"

"Got that." She paused. "So, let me get this straight. You replaced the actor with your real pastor."

"Yep."

"And he gave you real vows to repeat."

"Yep."

"You skipped everything we wrote for you, walked up the aisle, and got married. Just like that."

"Just like that." I grinned. "Are you mad at me, Athena? We didn't exactly follow your script."

"Follow my script?" She looked at it then tossed it into the air, and it landed on the edge of the stage. "Are you serious? You got me, Kat. You really, truly got me. And I'm not easy to get. Oh, but I'm mad at you." She began to fume. "I always counted on being a bridesmaid at your wedding."

I shrugged. "Sorry about that. But when you find Mr. Right, I'll definitely stand up for you."

"Like I would ever find Mr. Right in this crazy world I exist in."

I gave her a knowing smile. "Don't be so quick to ignore the possibilities. Someone very wise once told me that the next scene of my life could very well be a mountaintop instead of a valley. Remember all of that?"

"Yeah."

"Maybe you should have been preaching to yourself."

She groaned. "Whatever. But in the meantime, what happens next?"

"Hey, you're the scriptwriter. You tell me."

"Are you kidding?" She laughed. "I can't keep up with you."

"I'll tell you what's next," Scott said with a twinkle in his eyes. "We film the scene again, this time as Jack and Angie. And when we wrap up, you're all coming to the reception."

"Dressed like this?" She gestured to her jeans and T-shirt.

"See Jana in wardrobe. She'll find something great for you." I gave her a wink. "I told her to have several things ready, just in case."

"Ooh, that sounds like fun." She paused then gave me an inquisitive look. "Just one more question."

"What?"

"Do you two actually have a marriage license? I mean, is this marriage legit, or was it just some random thing you did for fun?"

"Got it," Pastor Garrett said, approaching with the paper in his hand. "Signed, sealed, and delivered." He gave it to Scott, who raised it into the air with a triumphant shout.

"We went to the courthouse several days ago," I added.

"How you kept the paparazzi from finding out is a miracle." Athena shook her head.

"Speaking of paparazzi . . ." I looked over at James Stevens, who had managed to sneak in a camera. "We knew he was coming, right?"

"Sure." Scott laughed. "But hey, we didn't get to hire a wedding photographer, so Rex gave him permission to take several shots during the filming. At least we'll have his photos to remind us of our big day."

"I don't think I'll forget it anytime soon," I said, giving Scott a peck on the cheek. "This was truly the best day of my life. So far, anyway."

"Okay, one other question," Athena asked. "Why did you film the real wedding first? I would think you'd do it the other way around."

"Because, goofy girl, you wrote in all sorts of antics for

me. I've got to trip up the aisle and generally make a mess of things. I might ruin my dress. Didn't want the real wedding to be ruined, so it had to come first."

"Good point." She grinned. "Now, get back out there and do as you're told, young lady. Stick to the script this time."

"Yes, ma'am." I saluted her then took my place, ready to film the scene once again, this time for our television viewing audience.

Tia gave the signal for the studio audience members to take their seats, and we were off and running . . . all over again. I sensed a new excitement in the crowd. Surely they wondered if the second ceremony would be as delightful as the first. We wouldn't disappoint.

This time I stumble-bumbled my way down the aisle, tripping over the flower girl basket and filling the scene with goofy, Angie-like antics. Perfect comedic timing, if I did say so myself. As I approached the front of the church, I tumbled squarely into Scott's—er, Jack's—arms.

He looked down and, with a Bogart-esque accent, said, "Here's looking at you, kid."

The audience members laughed, of course. And all the more as the camera panned in on my face, showing the missing eyelash stuck to my cheek. Jack plucked it off and stuck it on his upper lip as a mustache, which caused the children to roar with laughter.

Yep. Jack and Angie couldn't even get married without chaos attached.

Thank goodness they were fictional characters.

Still, I knew when to stick with the script and when to venture off on my own. This time I'd do things Athena's way. But outside the studio, it was God's script all the way. No doubt about it. For something as big as real life, only the ultimate writer would do.

24

Your Show of Shows

According to the script Athena planned to write to kick off season four, Jack and Angie would fly off to a thatched hut in the Amazon for their honeymoon. Wonder where she got that idea?

Scott and I actually flew to Acapulco for two glorious nights, returning just in time for the fund-raiser on Sunday afternoon. Our time together in the tropics was short but oh so sweet. Waiting for my real-life hero had been worth it in every sense of the word. Needless to say, we didn't see much of the beach. With only forty-eight hours to honeymoon, it hardly seemed logical. However, we heard the weather outside was lovely. Perhaps when we revisited in a few months, we could find out firsthand.

With the wedding happening so quickly, we'd left many unanswered questions back in L.A. Like where we planned to live, for instance. Every time I thought about leaving Grandma alone in that big, rambling house, a shiver went up my spine. Sure, Carolina would be there, but if the house lost its usual rhythm and flow, would it affect my grandmother's memory even more? Scott and I had discussed the issue at length but still hadn't settled on a plan.

On Sunday afternoon, we arrived at the church at 1:30, just an hour before the fund-raiser was set to begin. Grandma met me in the fellowship hall. She wanted details about my honeymoon, but they were slow in coming. Some things were just better left unspoken. I gave her a girlish grin and told her we'd had a grand time, emphasis on *grand*. She giggled in response.

"Come with me, honey," Grandma said when I finished. "I want to show you all of the items people have donated for the silent auction. I think we're going to make a lot of money for the orphanage."

She pointed out a few things that took me by surprise. A basketball signed by Kobe Bryant. A playbill signed by Angela Lansbury. A pair of Fermani boots with a handwritten note from the designers. These and several other things caught my eye. Looked like many of the people Scott had approached had actually come through for him. What a blessing.

Finally we arrived at a dress that looked oddly familiar. Soft pink. Simple. I remembered it from the picture hanging in the great room. Still, I couldn't believe Grandma would let it go.

"This was mine," she whispered. "I wore it in *It Had to Be You.*"

"Grandma, you're auctioning it off?"

She nodded. "The past is in the past, KK. I've lingered there too long."

Rex drew near. "You know what the great John Wayne said, don't you?"

"What's that?' I asked.

"He said, 'Tomorrow is the most important thing in life. Comes into us at midnight very clean. It's perfect when it arrives and it puts itself in our hands. It hopes we've learned something from yesterday.' "

"Wow. When did you become so philosophical?" I asked.

He smiled. "These last couple of weeks have turned me into a poet."

"Me too," Grandma said with a wistful look in her eye. "And you know what I've decided?"

"What?" I asked.

"Memories are lovely things. They can sweep us away to a happier time." She turned to look at Rex, who pulled her close. "But you know what? I think it's about time I make some new memories. What do you think of that idea, Rex? Would you like to make a proper lady out of me?"

"Lenora, are you saying what I think you're saying?" Rex whispered.

She nodded, and he gave her a kiss so tempestuous that I had to turn away. Thank goodness we were alone. Well, except for the woman working on a table on the far side of the room. Even she looked a bit taken aback.

Rex released his hold on her and turned to me with a smile. "What you don't know, Kat, is that I proposed to your grandmother while you were away. She wouldn't give me a firm answer."

"Hard for such a saggy old lady to give such a handsome fellow a firm answer," she responded, still sounding a little breathless.

We all laughed at that one.

"So I'll take that as a yes," Rex said.

When Grandma nodded, he tipped her backward and gave her another dramatic kiss. It rivaled any I'd seen in the old movies. I was pretty sure I heard the angels singing overhead. I, for one, offered up a triumphant shout of praise. Finally!

"I let you get away once, Rex Henderson," Grandma whispered as he lifted her up. "I'm not going to let that happen again. If . . . if you'll have me, I mean."

"If I'll have you?" His face lit into a smile. "I've waited over fifty years for you, Lenora Worth."

"You two were meant to be," I whispered. "Oh, this is the perfect ending."

"No, it's just the beginning." Rex kissed Grandma on the forehead. "Remember what I told you before, Kat. What some would call the end of the story is really just the beginning of the adventure."

"Amen to that," Scott said, slipping in beside me. He looked back and forth between my grandparents. The joy in his voice resonated as he said, "I never saw two people better suited."

"Yes, some couples are made to be together," I said, snuggling against my honey.

"Oh, yes," my grandmother said. "Take Bob Newhart and Suzanne Pleshette, for instance. They make the loveliest couple, don't they? I was just telling her that over lunch the other day."

Should I tell Grandma that they were married only on television and that their show had ended decades ago? Nah, better not.

"Talk about a great team," Rex said. "One that almost didn't happen."

"Sounds like us," Grandma said.

He turned to me. "Do you know the story of how Bob and Suzanne came to play a husband and wife on that show?"

"No idea."

"They were both guests on *The Tonight Show* with Johnny Carson, and TV producers noticed chemistry between the two." He looked back at my grandmother and smiled. "There's no denying chemistry when it's there."

"Amen to that," I said.

"I was always a little jealous of Suzanne Pleshette," Grandma said. "That beautiful dark hair. Those gorgeous eyes. And that perfect figure. Did you ever see anyone so beautiful?"

"Actually, yes." Rex took hold of her hand and kissed it with dramatic flair. "This moment, in fact."

Grandma chuckled. "Suzanne, eat your heart out!"

The two of them apparently needed some time alone. Scott and I shifted to one of the nearby tables, pretending to be interested in the silent auction items. Thankfully his parents joined us, along with Bryan and Julia. Everyone seemed to be in a happy, carefree mood. Nancy was full of questions about Acapulco. I avoided them, more than a little embarrassed that I'd seen the beach only from my window. And the airplane, of course.

"It was so good of you to come back in time for the fundraiser," Julia said. Her cheeks flushed pink. "I, um, I'm not sure I'd leave my honeymoon for a fund-raiser."

"We were happy to do it," I said. "Besides, the honeymoon isn't limited to a place."

"Speaking of places . . ." Charles gave us a curious look. "I'm assuming you'll both be living at Scott's place in Malibu?"

"Well, we're staying there tonight," I said. "Not sure about long-term. We're talking about that."

Several people from the cast and crew of the show entered the room, creating quite a stir with their loud chatter. As I heard the familiar voices, I turned and gave a little wave.

Athena drew close, giving me a "Well? How was it?" look.

I simply smiled. There would be plenty of time for girl talk later. Right now we had work to do.

Or not. Athena seemed stuck on the events of the past few days, not today's fund-raiser.

"You won't believe the calls that have come into the studio," she said. "All weekend long. And someone gave the paparazzi my home number. Can you believe it?"

"Probably Grandma." I laughed. "But I'm sure she doesn't remember doing it."

"Everyone wants to know what's happening with Jack and Angie next season," Athena said.

"I've been a little curious about that myself," I admitted. "Will they live happily ever after?"

Athena grunted. "Depends on how you look at it, I guess. There will be quarrels and struggles and all sorts of funny bits to add tension." I lost her at this point. She took to preaching. About writing, anyway. "Tension is what drives the story, Kat. Mountains and valleys, remember?" On and on she went, talking about that goofy plotline thing again.

"Of course," I said when she finally paused for breath. "But they can still live happily ever after." After a moment of introspection, I added my thoughts on the matter. "Someone very wise once told me that the real love story is the part that happens after the initial feelings have passed."

"Exactly. Mountains and valleys," she repeated. "So I guess it's safe to say that Jack and Angie *will* live happily ever after, as long as you factor in the humorous bits we're going to give them."

"Oh, give them lots," I said.

"Trust me." She waggled her thinly plucked eyebrows. "You have no idea what I'm going to put you and Scott through, since you left me out of your wedding."

Yikes. I could hardly imagine. Still, whatever it was, I'd

handle it. With Scott at my side, I could handle just about anything.

Soon we all kicked into gear. The silent auction was set to begin at 2:30, the entertainment portion of the fund-raiser at 3:00. Thankfully the room filled with people, and folks started placing their bids right and left. My eyes grew wide as I took in the prices they were scribbling down on the silent auction items. Julia's eyes were even wider.

"I didn't expect this sort of response, Kat," she said, her eyes filled with tears. "This is going to change the lives of those children."

"That's the idea," I said. "We want to give them hope—"

"And a future," Scott chimed in, appearing behind me. "And in case I haven't mentioned it, Kat and I are going to be making a private donation as well. Oh, and we plan to come to Ensenada in a few months to help with the actual building."

"R-really?" Julia shook her head. "I don't know how to thank you."

As I hugged her, I whispered, "Just keep doing what you do. God's hand is on you."

She nodded.

Scott looked at me with a smile. "We're going to be traveling a lot."

"Oh?"

"My parents want to know if we'll come to Alma soon. Dad wants my help designing the store. How do you feel about that?"

"Are you kidding? A trip to the spinach capital of the world? I can't think of anywhere I'd rather go."

"Be prepared to be inundated with fans," he said. "We're all the rage in Alma."

I had to laugh at that one. But speaking of being all the rage

. . . at a quarter to three, I heard several women in the room gasp. Many of them gathered around the stage, which made me even more curious. Coming closer, I saw Brock Benson, one of Hollywood's most popular actors. He stood front and center, talking to Rex. Scott gave him a little wave.

"Hey, Brock." Within seconds, the two were engaged in a conversation about today's event.

"Brock Benson?" Athena began to fan herself. She looked back and forth between Rex and Scott. "How . . . I mean, how did you do that?"

"He's a friend of Scott's." I shrugged. "And he loves helping kids. So Scott asked and he said yes."

"Amazing."

"Not really, Athena," I said. "Remember, Hollywood stars are really just people like you and me."

"They put their pants on one leg at a time," Scott's father said, sidling up next to us.

"Yes, they do," I agreed.

"Oh, but what lovely pants." Athena stared at Brock and sighed. Loudly.

Scott's dad slapped himself in the head, muttered, "Good grief," and headed off in a different direction. Me? I just laughed.

A few minutes later, Brock picked up a microphone and welcomed everyone. The crowd settled into their seats, ready to enjoy the festivities, and Brock opened in prayer. Those of us who were participating waited backstage in the wings. As Brock prayed, I thanked the Lord for so many things. Oh, how he had blessed me. And I had a feeling the adventure really was just beginning.

First up was Candy. Of course, she pulled out a Shirley Temple number. Those darling blond curls and that cute, frilly dress suddenly felt appropriate after all we'd been through together. I saw her now as an innocent child who'd been injured by the adults in her world. On so many levels, I could relate to her. And she knew it too.

She looked my way, her eyes wide as the music began.

"You can do it, Candy!" I gave her a thumbs-up and she nodded. Didn't take long, however, for me to see why her eyes were so wide. Off in the distance, her parents sat . . . together. Seeing them like that immediately brought a lump to my throat. Hopefully they'd laid down their all-too-adult battles long enough for this little darling to have a normal life. As normal as a child star could have, anyway.

Candy pulled off a delightful rendition of "On the Good Ship Lollipop," and we all cheered her on.

Next came Toby. I knew he had some sort of surprise up his sleeve but wasn't sure what until he put on a derby, grabbed a cane, and started into the theme song for *Hello, Dolly!*

I knew the kid was talented. I'd seen him act before, of course. And sing. And dance. But to do all three at one time? Not bad for a five-year-old. If we had any real talent scouts in the audience, they were probably scoping him out right now. Not that he would be going anywhere. No, I had it on good authority that all of the children would be back for the next season of *Stars Collide*. And speaking of children, I had to wonder if Athena and the other writers would add a baby to the mix. Or at least the news of a baby. I grinned just thinking about it. It did my heart good to see life moving on . . . both on and off the set.

As Toby sang, Grandma slipped into the spot next to me. *"Hello, Dolly!"* She released a happy sigh. "I always loved that movie."

"Me too."

"Can't tell you how happy I am that Barbra Streisand got the part and not me," Grandma added. "I'm not sure I could've done it justice the way she did."

"Big of you to admit," Rex said, slipping an arm over her shoulders. "But don't worry, Lenora. Your acting days aren't behind you. I have a feeling there are plenty of scenes in your future and you'll play them well." He waggled his bushy brows. "Now that you have a real-life partner, I mean."

"So true."

The audience roared with applause as Toby took his final bow.

Rex gave Grandma a quick hug. "Now, let's go out there and knock 'em dead, kid."

"Don't think we should carry it that far," she said. "But I'll give it my best. You do the same."

"Only my best for you," he whispered.

Grandma took the stage. She got a hearty cheer from the audience, and all the more as several of her old movie clips played in the background. I heard a couple of people gasp and even heard one lady say, "That's Lenora Worth! I own every one of her movies."

I hoped Grandma heard too.

Or not. Looked like she was a little busy setting up for her scene. We'd practiced together, so I knew just how it would go. Rex entered stage left, dressed like Dean Martin. I couldn't help but marvel at how much he looked like the real deal. And Grandma Lenora was in her element. As Rex entered, her face lit up. I could read the love in her eyes. No acting here. These two might be performing a love scene, but it was one borne of years of waiting.

Grandma delivered her opening line, the actual line from the Dean Martin special she'd been in all those years ago. Back and forth they went, one line leading to another. Talk about a sweet scene. And cute too. At the end, Rex—er, Dino—swept her into his arms and planted a kiss on her that she would surely never forget.

The crowd went crazy, especially the kids. Athena looked my way, her eyes wide and her mouth rounded into a perfect "O."

"Kat," she whispered. "Is there something I need to know?"

I just smiled. There would be plenty of time to share the news of their engagement later.

Or maybe right now would be a better option. With the whole room looking on, Rex eased himself down on one knee—not an easy task—and popped the question. For a moment the audience members took it as part of the act. Until he called my grandmother by her name and went into a soliloquy about her exquisite beauty.

When Grandma responded with a vibrant "Yes!" the crowd went crazy. Rex pulled out one dazzler of a ring and slipped it on her finger, then rose and gave her one last romantic smooch.

I glanced at Athena, who mouthed the words, "Mountains and valleys," then grinned.

This was definitely a mountaintop moment.

But talk about a hard act to follow! I was thrilled that Scott was up next. For whatever reason, he hadn't told me what he planned to do. I'd given it the old college try, guessing everything from juggling to card tricks. My heart jumped into my throat as he entered the stage with an acoustic guitar in hand.

I knew he sang a little. I'd figured that much out the first season of *Stars Collide*. But to accompany himself in front of such a large crowd? No way.

He looked directly at me, love pouring from his eyes, and then started strumming. I recognized the melody, of course:

"I Can't Help Falling in Love With You." Okay, so he didn't exactly sound like Elvis, but when I closed my eyes, I could almost believe he did. Almost. My honey had great pitch.

He continued on with that silky smooth voice, and I was captivated. Caught up. Transported. Carried away to a different place. *Calgon, take me away!* I listened to every word, realizing he was singing them just for me.

Athena must've been watching me as I listened. She jabbed me with her elbow. "I want what you have."

My eyes popped open. "What I have?"

She sighed. "Yeah. You've got the real deal, Kat. Sometimes I think it will never happen to me."

"Never say never." I gave her a hug. "Your day is coming."

Scott finished his song and the crowd went crazy, especially the ladies. I'd never heard so much whooping and hollering. Since the initial reaction to Brock Benson, anyway.

Brock took the stage again, announcing me. I entered the stage, my knees knocking. Something about a live performance nearly did me in. Talk about nerve-racking. I stared out at my audience, my heart working overtime. I knew they were all wondering what in the world I'd chosen to do. Would I sing? Act? Dance?

None of the above.

Instead I reached for a poem, one I'd found in my grandmother's trunk. The words were my mother's penned for me—her baby girl—just one week after I was born. Grandma Lenora had passed the poem on to me on my wedding day, and it was perfect. Perfect because it reflected the heart of God for his children. Perfect because the kids in attendance today needed to know just how much I cared about them. And perfect because it somehow reminded me that my mother had loved me more than life itself.

For a fleeting moment, I thought about my father . . . and

all he had missed. It was truly his loss. If he'd stuck around, he'd know that he had a strong, confident daughter ready to take on the world. With the Lord's help, of course. And with the love of a great husband.

I managed to get through the poem, my voice breaking as I read. My mother's words cut to my very soul, and I could almost envision her standing here, reading them herself. Apparently so could my grandmother. I heard her sniffles from the wings. Glancing her way, I offered a smile.

Somehow I finished without crumbling. And so did the other participants in the show. In the end, the audience members rose and gave us much more applause than we'd probably earned. Still, it was great fun.

When all was said and done, Brock made the announcement we'd all been waiting for. "Ladies and gentlemen, we have raised $86,750 for the orphanage."

"No way." Julia shook her head, clearly unable to comprehend such a thing. "Did I hear him right?"

I nodded. "You heard him right. And if I know Brock, he'll be first in line to help you build. Behind Scott and me, I mean."

"I . . . I don't know how to thank you all." She burst into tears, and I wrapped her in a warm embrace.

Grandma drew near, a worried look on her face. "Everything okay over here?"

Julia looked up and, through her tears, whispered, "I'm just . . . so . . . happy!"

"Oh, me too!" Grandma giggled. "What a glorious day . . . all the way around."

I laughed. "No kidding. Now that you've announced your engagement to the masses, I guess we'd better get busy planning a wedding."

Grandma shook her head. "No, sweetie. Just a private little

ceremony at the house will do for us. Oh, and speaking of the house, it's high time we talked about living arrangements."

Here it comes. The part where she says she wants Scott and me to move into Worth Manor. For all I knew, she was probably building on a west wing as we spoke.

"I've never had a honeymoon before. Never even been married. So I hope you don't mind that Rex and I will need a little privacy."

"W-what?"

Her cheeks turned pink. "I, um, I figured you and Scott would be moving into his place."

My honey drew near, slipping his arm around my waist. "Actually, I've been looking at a house in Beverly Hills just a few blocks from you, Lenora. I think it would be perfect for Kat and me."

"You . . . you have?"

He nodded. "Brock Benson's place. He showed it to me last week. He's downsizing to a condo so he can devote more time and effort to the kids in his after-school program."

"Wow."

"Mountains and valleys," Athena said, passing by.

I could only nod. Looked like the script of my life was really coming together nicely. Oh sure, I knew there would be tough days ahead. I was a realist, after all. We would somehow walk Grandma through this valley called Alzheimer's, and we would be stronger people because of it. But in the meantime, I would enjoy living on the mountain. I might even conquer the "God is my Father" issue, now that I had Rex Henderson in my life. Talk about the ideal father image. And when I thought of the godly father Scott would one day make, I could easily picture the Lord's heart for me.

Yes, things were definitely on the upswing.

Scott pulled me to the edge of the stage, holding tight

to my hand. "So, what do you think about the house idea? I knew you'd want to be close to your grandmother, so it seemed like the best option."

"Better than best," I said. "You've thought of everything." I slipped my arms around his neck and gave him a gentle kiss. "I love you, Mr. Murphy," I whispered.

"I love you, Mrs. Murphy," he echoed, brushing a loose hair out of my face.

We stood together in blissful silence for a moment as the crowd pressed in around us. Funny, with Brock Benson in the room, no one seemed to pay us much notice. Not that I minded. I rather enjoyed being off in our own little world.

"I've been thinking about this 'Kat with Nine Lives' thing," Scott said finally.

"Oh?"

"It does seem like the Lord keeps giving you new lives, doesn't it?" He shrugged. "Some scripted, others not so much."

"True. I'm Kat the granddaughter. Kat the actress. Kat the girlfriend—er, wife. Kat the woman who's been healed from the pain of her past. Kat the niece who found herself grafted into a large family." I giggled. "What else?"

"Oh, trust me. There are plenty of lives left to go. And I, for one, am glad we can't see into the future." He gave my nose a tweak. "Though I wouldn't mind seeing you become Kat the mommy. And Kat the PTA leader."

"Ooh." I smiled. "The first one sounds lovely. Not sure about the second."

"Well, you know what they say. 'Life is like a box of choco-lates. You never know what you're gonna get.'"

"Tell me you did *not* just say that." I punched him in the arm. "Haven't we had enough of that goofy guessing game?"

As he shrugged, a giggly voice rang out from the wings: "Tom Hanks. *Forrest Gump*. 1994."

"See what I mean?" he whispered. "You never know what you're gonna get."

He was right. And for once I was completely happy with that idea. Toss the script. This girl didn't want to see what was coming around the next bend.

No, I decided as I stared into Scott's gorgeous baby blues, this moment—the here and now—was all a girl like me would ever need.

SPECIAL FEATURE

STARS COLLIDE
SEASON FOUR, EPISODE ONE
"HONEYMOON IN PARADISE"
WRITTEN BY
Athena Pappas

The AMAZON RAIN FOREST at sunrise.
Crickets chirp. Early morning dew covers
foliage. Wide shot of rustic thatched
hut, exterior, with a Hummer parked out
front.

View dissolves to inside of hut, which
is beautifully decorated. Open laptop sits on IKEA-type table, displaying
Facebook page with *Stars Collide* logo on
top. Status update:

"ENJOYING OUR HONEYMOON IN PARADISE.
DON'T CALL US. WE'LL CALL YOU."

Tight shot on ANGIE, sleeping in a hammock surrounded by mosquito netting.
JACK sleeps in another hammock nearby.
The sound of a MONKEY calling to its
mate shatters the stillness of the dewy
morning. ANGIE stirs.

View dissolves to the exterior of the
hut, where the MONKEY examines the Hummer then moves to the hut, tapping at
the window frame. A blue and gold MACAW
joins him, perched on the windowsill.
Together they peer inside at the sleeping honeymooners.

                    ANGIE
            (stirring, eyes still
             closed)
        Jack?
            (stretching)
        Jack . . .

Tight shot on JACK's hammock. He stirs,
but does not fully awaken. He swats at a
mosquito.

                    ANGIE
            (coming awake, eyes still
             closed)
        Jack, I had the craziest dream.
        We were on our honeymoon in
        Acapulco. Then suddenly the dream
        shifted and we were in a canoe,
        floating down the Amazon. Huge
        snakes and all sorts of wild
        animals surrounded us on every
        side. Isn't that crazy?
            (yawns and stretches)

Wide shot on JACK's hammock, through
open window. We see the back of the
MACAW and MONKEY as they listen in on
the conversation. They are joined by a

large, red-eyed TREE FROG that hops onto
the windowsill, croaking loudly. Cricket
sounds fill the air. Other rain forest
animals begin to vocalize. A BOA CON-
STRICTOR slithers by in the grass.

                JACK
          (eyes still closed, half-
            asleep)
      Hmm? Wild animals?

"THE LION SLEEPS TONIGHT" begins to play
overhead. The MONKEY takes the opening melody, with the FROG croaking out
the rhythm section. The MACAW joins in,
adding just the right harmony. Crickets
do the choreography, joined by dancing
spiders. Angie's GRANDMA appears in the
doorway of the hut and begins to sing
the lyrics in an off-key, full voice.
Before long, all of the *Stars Collide*
KIDS pop up from various spots, both inside and outside the hut, adding their
voices to the chorus.

                ANGIE
          (sitting up in bed, looking
            through netting)
      Jack, wake up!

                JACK
          (falls out of hammock onto
            ground)
      Huh? What? Where am I?
          (looks around, rubbing
            eyes)

The MONKEY comes to JACK's rescue and
encourages him to join the dance.
GRANDMA takes ANGIE by the hand and
pulls her to the middle of the room.
Before long, everyone is in a circle,
singing and dancing with full abandon.
The MONKEY begins to show off, singing louder and dancing harder than anyone else. By the time the song ends, all
eyes are on him.
            (music ends)

                    JACK
            (looking at MONKEY, spoken
            to ANGIE)
You know, he's not half bad.
Maybe we should sign him.

                    ANGIE
            (slipping arms around
            JACK's neck)
Oh no you don't! We're on our
honeymoon. No business! We
promised.

                    JACK
            (eyeing MONKEY)
Yeah, but think of the
possibilities with Pixar and
Disney alone. This little guy's
really good!

MONKEY reverts to begging position, then
shows off his dancing skills.

ANGIE
(shooing him away)
Sorry, little guy, but not this
time.

View widens. ANGIE boots everyone out
of the hut, leaving the place empty and
quiet. She closes the window, casting
shadows of darkness over the room. Drawing near to JACK, she wraps him in an
embrace and begins to kiss him. TREE
FROG eases window open, sighing as he
sees them kissing. MACAW slips through
the crack in the window, flies to the
laptop.

Tight shot on MACAW, typing on laptop
with his beak. He is updating the status
report on Jack and Angie's Facebook page
to read:

"AND THEY ALL LIVED HAPPILY EVER AFTER."

FADE TO CIRCLE. MACAW PEEKS THROUGH CIR-
CLE. FADE TO BLACK.

Acknowledgments

I owe a huge debt of gratitude to each of the following:

Jennifer Leep, my amazing editor. Jennifer, it took some time to pound out this idea, but was it ever worth it! Thank you for giving me the opportunity to write Kat's story, and thank you for letting me add the deeper elements. Your trust in me means so much.

My wonderful team at Revell, particularly Jessica Miles, Michele Misiak, and Donna Hausler. Ladies, none of this would be possible without you. What did I ever do to deserve such an awesome group of worker bees?

My agent, Chip MacGregor. Thanks for believing in my stories. I know they are wackier than most. But you've helped me find my fit, and for that I'm eternally grateful.

My awesome critique partners, Martha Rogers, Janetta Messmer, and Kathleen Y'Barbo. Ladies, you were all so busy with your own projects, yet you took the time to give my story a Texas spit shine. I owe you.

My tribe of twelve. You know who you are. You are the wind beneath my wings. You give me the encouragement I need to keep going, even when this frail body begs to disagree.

My father. Oh, how I wish I could pick up the phone and call my dad to tell him I've finally written a story set in Hollywood. He would be so proud. It was his dream to produce movies, and though he's now writing his scripts in his mansion above, I am still here typing away. It might not be a movie, Dad . . . but it's close.

My heavenly Father. You are the ultimate Daddy. May you reveal your heart to all of your daughters, especially those like Kat, who cannot seem to comprehend a loving Father God.

Janice Thompson is a Christian freelance author and a native Texan. She has four grown daughters, four beautiful granddaughters, and two grandsons. She resides in the greater Houston area, where the heat and humidity tend to reign.

Janice started penning books at a young age and was blessed to have a screenplay produced in the early '80s, after living in the Los Angeles area for a time. From there she went on to write several large-scale musical comedies for a Houston school of the arts. Currently, she has published over fifty novels and nonfiction books for the Christian market, most of them lighthearted.

Working with quirky characters and story ideas suits this fun-loving author. She particularly enjoys contemporary, first-person romantic comedies. Janice loves sharing her faith with readers and hopes they will catch a glimpse of the real happily ever after in the pages of her books.

Come meet
JANICE THOMPSON
at www.JaniceAThompson.com

Read her blog, more interesting facts
about her books, and other fun trivia.

Follow Janice on Twitter

 booksbyJanice

A Romantic Comedy That Will Have You Laughing All Day

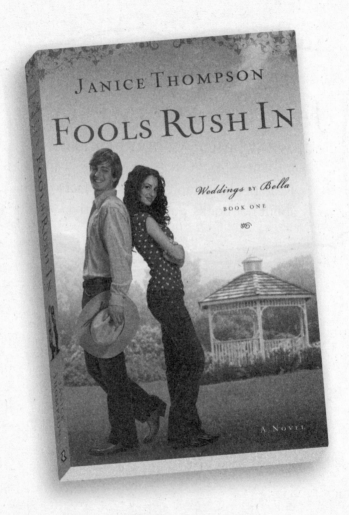

Don't miss book 1 in the Weddings by Bella series!

When *Hollywood's* most eligible
bachelor sweeps into town,
will he cause trouble for *Bella*?

Don't miss book 2 in the Weddings by Bella series!

Get ready for a double dose of wedding frenzy!

Don't miss book 3 in the Weddings by Bella series!

Can this hometown hero sweep his girl off her feet?

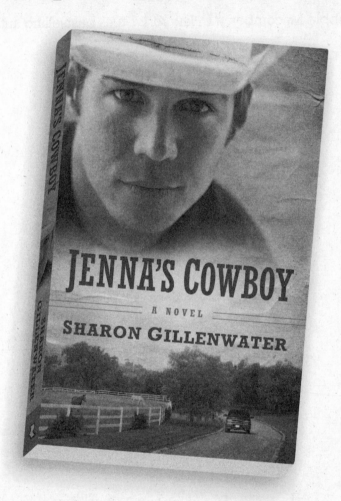

Jenna returns to her family's ranch to heal a broken heart. She never expected to see Nate Langley back in town—the first guy she was attracted to, the one her father sent away all those years ago. Can he heal her broken heart?

"Filled with Texas charm and the healing power of love."

—Debbie Macomber, #1 *New York Times* bestselling author

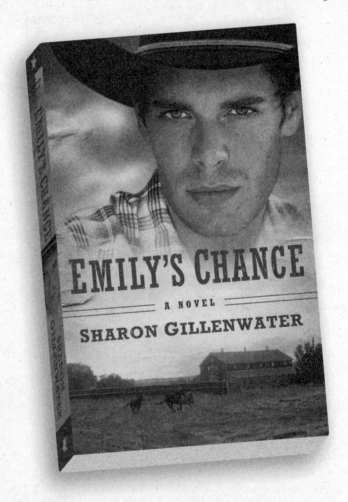

Emily's Chance is a heartwarming story of letting love take the lead that will have you wishing you lived in Callahan Crossing, Texas.

 Revell
a division of Baker Publishing Group
www.RevellBooks.com

Available at your local bookstore.

"This is one book you don't want to miss!"

—Crossings Book Club

Jay is new in town. He's young, successful, and single, and he's not afraid to plop down in a church pew to scope out the females. But in the murky waters of the South Carolina singles scene, Jay's whole world is in danger of being turned upside down.